OUT OF THE FRYING PAN

"You do not answer."

Again silence greeted the Yngling's question.

"Each tribe has a law against slander, and the council a law against lies in its meetings. Men are seldom charged under them unless the lie is harmful, and I will not charge you now. But . . ."

The Yngling's words were cut short by a keening noise from the other's throat, a keening that quickly grew to a howl of rage. Fumbling, wrenching, the chief tore off his sleeveless leather shirt, drew his sword, and charged the *lagman*.

The Yngling's sword was out too, and blind-eyed he met the man's berserk assault. The violent energy and quickness of Jäävklo's attack was shocking to Baver, who'd never before witnessed an attack to kill. But the *lagman* beat off the berserker's strokes, seemingly without any effort to strike back; either he was too hard pressed or he exercised an unexplainable restraint.

The Jäävklo's sword broke against the *lagman's*, almost at the hilt. With a howl, he flung the rest of it at his adversary, then turned and threw himself on the council fire.

Baen Books From John Dalmas

THE YNGLING AND THE CIRCLE OF POWER

JOHN DALMAS

BAEN BOOKS

This story is dedicated to

SPIDER and JEANNE ROBINSON

PROLOG

The Sanctuary was semi-dark, lit by a single, large oil lamp that set blurred shadows trembling and jumping. Seven men, robed in silk, sat in a circle on straw mats, legs folded beneath them. Another sat in the center. Their shaven heads were upright. Lamplight flickered on calm faces, glinting on eyes otherwise black, giving off an aroma too mild to conceal the fragrance of Korean pine from panels, timbers and floor. As dark as the room, was the sound that came from their throats—a deep and droning *"OM,"* protracted and near the limit of audibility, like the dying hum of some great bell.

They were questing. Vague images flicked behind unfocused eyes. Now and then something vaguely recognizable came to them, to be gone before it stopped shimmering. They didn't try to hold them. When—if—they found something significant, it would stay to be examined.

After a bit, they got one clearly, of conical tents—a campground—with a village of log huts not far behind it. Behind the image was a sense of context; this was some tribal gathering. The picture, still wavering, shifted,

1

then focused on a very large, physically powerful man. A man without eyes, they somehow knew, who nonetheless carried a sword. A man without eyes who walked briskly, meaningfully. Suddenly he stopped. And turned as if to look at the men who spied on him from their Circle of Power.

He *did* have eyes, strange eyes without pupils, that somehow seemed to lock with their collective gaze. Then the vision wavered and was gone, and they knew without discussion that they would not get it back.

The emperor, Songtsan Gampo, sat in his study before open, glass-paned doors. A light cool wind blew from the northwest across the Yan Mountains, played with the silver wind chimes on his balcony, and touched his face. Above his left shoulder an oil lamp, its flame shielded by a glass chimney, cast faintly yellow light on the manuscript he read. Remotely he heard a small gong—heard and registered, and ignored. A minute later there was stirring at his corridor door, and an exchange of muted words. Then his doorguard entered, a giant humanoid with short, rich-brown fur. It cleared its throat softly.

"Your Magnificence," it murmured.

Songtsan Gampo lowered the manuscript and turned without speaking.

"His Reverence, Tenzin Geshe, wishes to speak with Your Magnificence."

Dark eyes regarded the doorman. "Send him in."

The *geshe* could have communicated with him telepathically; given the Circle of Power, the distance from the *gomba*, the monastery, was no problem. But the emperor didn't allow mental intrusions except when he'd ordered them, or in true emergencies. One sent or carried messages, on paper or orally. Tenzin Geshe entered the room and bowed low. He would not speak until invited to.

"Yes?" the emperor asked.

"Your Magnificence," said the *geshe*, "your Circle of Power has been questing. And we have seen a man . . ."

He opened his mind to his emperor then, rerunning the experience.

When the *geshe* had completed his brief report, he was dismissed. The emperor sat with the manuscript ignored on his lap. The Circle had learned nothing explicit, except that the man existed and what he looked like. And that he'd been aware of them observing him, and had broken the connection. A man of unusual power then, obviously, but where he was, and of what people, there'd been no clue.

There had been a limited knowingness with the vision, however: the man was far away, and was important to him. There'd been no sign of what the importance might be. Logic suggested that the man would lead an army against his, when the time of conquest came, but that was only logic, not knowledge.

Songtsan Gampo sat with his mind clear of thoughts, waiting quietly for more, but no more came.

PART ONE

DEPARTURE

ONE

The council fire flickered ruddy-yellow, lighting the Neoviking chiefs who sat around it. It was a very large fire, by the standards of a people whose summer fires normally were small: fires for cooking, and smoke fires to drive the mosquitoes from their log houses.

Ted Baver squatted unobtrusively as part of the ring of chiefs, an honor granted him as a representative of the star folk. He had no role in their council, of course. He was there to watch, listen, record, and in the process learn. He held a small audio-video recorder before his face, as if aiming a pistol, and through and around its simple, fold-out viewing frame he watched the proceedings.

He'd grown used to squatting, this past year. Occasionally, absently, he squashed mosquitoes on his face with his left hand. The thump of an insect-hunting nighthawk braking overhead did not catch his attention. He was engrossed in the dispute before the council, aiming his recorder at whoever was speaking, capturing their words and image.

Jäävklo,* chief of the Glutton Clan, got to his feet. He was wide-framed, with remarkably muscular arms, his muscles more ropy than bulky. His face was creased, but at fifty feet by firelight, his black hair seemed ungrayed, and the skin on his arms, shoulders and neck was still tight. Baver guessed his age at between forty and forty-five.

Jäävklo spoke loudly, that the throng of northmen could hear, the hundreds who squatted unseen on the slope above the council fire. "Here is my answer to Ulf Varjsson of the Wolf Clan," he said. "In the Homeland, we of the Glutton** Clan had the poorest territory of all the Svear. It was poorest to start with, and as the world grew colder, it became impossible to feed ourselves adequately. Nor would the Reindeer Clan or the Salmon Clan adjust their boundaries with us. When we brought it up in council, Axel Stornäve refused to require it of them. There was bad blood between the two of us, Axel and me, and so he refused.

"Now the tribes have come to a new land, and possessed it, dividing it, each clan marking its own. The Glutton Clan has built cairns at their corners, and other cairns at needful places, according to the agreement among the tribes. Yet here at the ting, we find the Wolf people complaining that we encroach on them! We encroach on no one! We have done all things according to the agreement!"

He looked around the circle scowling, then squatted down again in the place that was his.

Nils Järnhann got up then, a huge, muscular young man only twenty-two years old, scarred on legs, face, and shoulder. His eyes were sky-blue glass, crafted by a machinist aboard the jump ship *Phaeacia*. They fitted properly but were conspicuously artificial, and around them the sockets were sunken. He turned his face to

---

*For those who are interested, a brief pronunciation guide for Neoviking names and words is included in the appendix.

**Also known as the wolverine.

Jäävklo as if the glass eyes saw. He was *lagman* of the People—reciter and interpreter of the Law and arbiter of disputes, who also presided when crimes were brought before the council.

"And the corners are on the tails of two ridges?" he asked. His voice seemed quieter than Jäävklo's, and mild, but it could be heard clearly by the tribesmen highest on the slope.

Jäävklo answered without rising. "They are."

"Can the tail of one ridge be seen from the other?"

"Distantly, yes."

The *lagman*'s wide mouth pursed briefly before he spoke. "The complaint of Ulf Varjsson, chief of the Wolves, has been heard, and also its denial by Jäävklo, chief of the Gluttons. The corners are not in dispute, but only the line on the plain. Here is how the dispute will be resolved: The Bull Clan of the Jötar and the Seal Clan of the Norskar will each provide four warriors to examine the disputed line. Tomorrow they will go to it, two days ride from here. There they will have a pyre built at each of the two corners. These pyres will be very large, so that in the dark, each fire can be clearly seen from the other. Freemen, as many as the eight warriors think necessary, will help them, providing the necessary wood and doing whatever else is needed. These freemen will be equally of the Glutton and Wolf Clans.

"At nightfall of the second day, four warriors will be at each pyre, two each from the Seals and the Bulls. They will light the pyres. The fires must be kept burning high till dawn. When the men at one fire can see the other, two of the warriors from each fire will ride toward the other, as straight as they can. It is important that they ride straight, because their trails must make a straight line between the fires, between the corner cairns.

"They will continue until they come to the stream, where they will set a tall stake in the bank on their side, tall enough to be seen plainly from fifty doubles [about eighty meters], tying a flag to the top.

"The other warriors, with freemen to help them, will follow the trail of the two through the grass. They will have oxen, and drag sleds with stones and long stakes on them. From time to time they will set a stake in the trail, with rocks set against it. Each stake must be visible from the two stakes nearest behind it. They will also put rocks around the stakes at the stream. Afterward the freemen, supervised by the eight, will drag more rocks to all those places, and build cairns as tall as a man. Each cairn must have a pole three spans tall sticking out the top, and the row of cairns must form a straight line. The Gluttons and Wolves must provide as many freemen for the task as the eight warriors require. The line will henceforth be as marked by the new cairns, and the old cairns will be torn down."

Nils Järnhann paused, turning his face from side to side around the council circle. *Ingenious!* thought Baver. *That not only takes care of the dispute, it establishes a procedure any clan can use on its own.*

But the *lagman* wasn't done yet. "This dispute," he went on, "creates a debt to the warriors who solve it, and to their clans. Therefore, their clans will each receive"—he paused, then repeated "—will *each* receive a payment of twenty heifer calves and twenty bull or ox calves, to be selected by the eight warriors. In addition, each of the eight warriors will be paid two saddle horses, which he can select from all the horses of the clan responsible. The clan which pays will be the clan that was in error on the line. Therefore, before the old cairns are torn down, the eight warriors will determine on which side of the new line the old cairns stand. If *all* the old cairns, all of them, stand within ten spans of the new line, or are on the Glutton's side, the Glutton Clan will be held blameless, and the Wolf Clan will pay. Otherwise the Glutton Clan will pay."

Baver's eyes found the two chieftains. Ulf Varjsson showed grim satisfaction. Jäävklo, on the other hand, had darkened with anger and chagrin. Meanwhile Nils Järnhann spoke on. "As to the request for feud rights growing out of the fight at the old stream cairns, they are refused both to clans and septs. Tomorrow at high noon, the two septs will each have ten warriors at the fighting ground, ready for a fight with hands and feet.

"And if any of those chosen enter the fight with a weapon, he will be declared outlaw and fair game, with only a single day of grace, regardless of whether he uses that weapon. Furthermore, his household will be held responsible for any blood payment incurred from the use of that weapon."

Baver could hear a soft murmuring from the hundreds of northmen listening unseen behind him.

"As to blood payment for men and horses from the fight at the stream," the young giant went on, "that will be the standard payment, made by the sept in error, the error to be determined by the new line. However, if all the old cairns are within ten spans of the new line, there will be no blood payment."

Again Nils Järnhann turned his face toward the two opposing clan chieftains. "There will be no appeal to these rulings, nor to the line laid out by the eight warriors of the Seal and Bull Clans."

He paused, then looked at Jäävklo. "Jäävklo, I have another matter to talk with you about, before the council, and before the People assembled here. You have told us that Axel Stornäve refused to require the Reindeer and Salmon Clans to give part of their territories to the Glutton Clan. Because, you said, there was bad blood between you and Axel. You have also said this before our present meeting, though never in council.

"What your words mean is that Axel Stornäve did not treat honestly with the Glutton Clan, that he withheld fairness because of an old grudge. I have talked with other chiefs about this. They told me the question of adjusting boundaries never came up in Council. When did you talk with Axel about it?"

"Just before the First Council of All Chiefs, held to discuss leaving the Homeland. He refused me then."

"Who else was there when you discussed it with him?"

"Arvid Smitsson, who now is dead, killed in battle with the horse barbarians."

"No other?"

Jäävklo shook his head.

"You shake your head; your answer then is no. Axel Stornäve called the First Council of All Chiefs to propose his plan to leave the Homeland, and to get the agreement of as many clans as possible. And he succeeded. Did this solve the land problem of the Gluttons?"

"Yes. But now we have another problem, and with Stornäve's own clan, the Wolves! Your clan! He has poisoned your minds against me!"

"We've solved that new dispute tonight. Now I'm looking at your complaint about Axel Stornäve and his honesty. So you told Axel of your problem on one day and he solved it that same day, is that right? Or the day after?"

A sullen nod.

"I am also told that you became chief only the winter previous. When had you had dealings with Axel Stornäve before that day?"

The Glutton chieftain didn't answer at once, and when he did, his voice was shrill. "You're trying to trick me! You're of the Wolf Clan too! You're trying to make me look like a troublemaker, you and Stornäve and Varjsson! You've talked with the chiefs of the Seal and Bull Clans, so they will give you warriors who will mark a new boundary that will steal our land from us!"

"I see. And you have witnesses to this?"

Jäävklo stood staring wildly at the *lagman*, who repeated his unanswered question. "When did you have dealings with Axel Stornäve before you first asked for a boundary adjustment?"

Jäävklo had no answer; to Ted Baver it seemed that the man's eyes bulged.

"You do not answer. Therefore unless corrected, I will assume that you'd never had dealings with him before. From what then did this bad blood develop?"

Again there was no answer.

"Each tribe has a law against slander, and the council a law against lies in its meetings. Men are seldom charged under them unless the lie is harmful, and I will not charge you now. But ..."

His words were cut short by a keening noise from Jäävklo's throat, a keening that quickly grew to a howl of rage. Fumbling, wrenching, the chief tore off his sleeveless leather shirt. The howl had broken into hoarse, grunting cries, wordless shouts, and when his torso was bare, he drew his sword and charged the *lagman*.

Nils Järnhann's sword was out too, and blind-eyed he met the man's berserk assault. The violent energy and quickness of Jäävklo's attack was shocking to Baver, who'd never before witnessed an attack to kill. But the *lagman* beat off the berserker's strokes, seemingly without any effort to strike back; either he was too hard pressed or he exercised an unexplainable restraint.

Then Jäävklo's sword broke against the *lagman's*, almost at the hilt. With a howl, he flung the rest of it at his adversary, *then turned and threw himself on the council fire*, where he lay roaring as if in rage, without trying to get up. Staring wide-eyed past his recorder, Baver shook, twitched, almost spouted sweat, and got half up as if to run and rescue the man. But didn't. Instead he continued to record. It seemed impossible that the Glutton chief had done what he had, and having done it, that pain did not drive him off.

And that no one pulled him off!

The raucous roaring stopped. Then Baver doubled over and emptied his stomach onto the ground. When he was done retching, he settled down onto his knees, staring as the *lagman*, who'd gone to the dead Jäävklo, grasped the corpse's feet and pulled it from the fire. Baver heard no one else be sick, though surely this horrible, this shocking event must have traumatized some of them, at least.

Then he remembered the departure of the Orcs[*] from the City of Kazi, and what the Northmen found there the next day. And wondered if after all they might handle this with similar dispassion, might treat it simply as an unfortunate display of aberration.

[*]Orcs—Name applied to the soldiers of Kazi the Undying, a Middle-Eastern emperor.

TWO

From—A video interview with Ilse in the botanical conservatory on the eve of the vernal equinox, Deep Harbor, New Home, A.C. 781. *By Lateefah Fourier*

LF: Intriguing, to have grown up that way. But before I go, our viewers will never forgive me if we don't talk about your husband, the Ingling. Did I say that correctly? The Ingling?

Ilse: Approximately. It's more precise, however, to say the *I* sound with the lips rounded. *Yngling*. The *Y* is like the umlauted *U* in German.

LF: Yngling. There! How did I do that time?

Ilse: Quite well.

LF: But "Yngling" is not his name, right? His name is Nils Järnhann.

Ilse: That's right. As a child he was known as Nils Hammarsson, because his father, an Ironsmith, is called Hammar. Which means hammer, as you might suspect. Järnhann is his warrior name, given him when he completed his sword apprenticeship. It means Ironhand. While still a sword apprentice, and not fully grown, he killed a man, a warrior, with a blow of his fist.

LF: The Northman culture certainly seems violent.

Ilse: It's a controlled violence. The warriors are violent, the rest of the culture not particularly so. The Northmen have a system of laws that contain most of the violence within the warrior class. The ordinary freeman is less subject to violence from within his culture than in my own country, Germany.

LF: And Ingling—Yngling—is a title, right?

Ilse: In a sense, yes. Long ago, "yngling" simply meant a youth in their language. Anciently, Anglic had a cognate, "youngling." All three Northman tribes share a legend of a young man who appeared in a time of danger perhaps two hundred years ago, when constant warring threatened to destroy them. They had no warrior class then; all men fought. The southern tribe, the Jötar, had gained the upper hand, and it seemed they would kill or enslave the Svear. And probably the Norskar as well.

Then an yngling appeared among the Svear, to become a great raid leader and war chief, and before long it seemed that they'd destroy the Jötar instead. Then an yngling came among the Jötar and saved them. After that he made himself known as the same yngling who had saved the Svear and Norskar. He said he belonged to no tribe or clan, but to all Northmen. And he had great power over them because of his wisdom and truth and justice, and gave them the Bans that set limits on warring and feuding, the Bans that let them live with relatively little fear and hatred.

LF: Can you tell us a little about those Bans?

Ilse: Of course. Warriors of the different clans still could fight one another, but they could no longer take one another's land. And the clan borders were reset to the earlier markers. Also, while they could still burn strawstacks, to burn haystacks or buildings was outside the Bans. They could steal livestock, but they could not kill it and leave it lie. They could still kill in vengeance, but only for specified wrongs and within approved feuds.

All the clans agreed to this. But there was a Jytska chief who hated him for it, who struck him with a poisoned knife he'd hidden in his shirt, so that he died. And instead of making a burial mound, they put the youth in a canoe and set it on the Jöta Älv, which floated it down to the sea.

Only then, the legend says, did they realize that none of them knew his name, so they called him simply "the Yngling." And the legend had it that in a time of great need he'd return, for the Northmen believe that after you die, you will be reborn.

Finally, as was certain to happen sooner or later, there came another time of great need. And when Nils appeared from exile—he'd been exiled for a killing—the things he did convinced them that he was the Yngling reborn to them. . . .

* * *

After what had happened, Ted Baver was surprised that the council didn't adjourn at once. He could smell charred flesh, and surely the Northmen did too; they saw, heard, and smelled more acutely than he did. But instead of moving that they adjourn, Nils Järnhann stood beside the corpse and recited what seemed to be a formula for the soul after suicide. Baver hadn't recovered sufficiently to follow it all in detail, although of course his recorder did.

When Nils had completed the formula, he announced he was resigning as *lagman*. And not only resigning as *lagman*; he was leaving the Northmen. There were questions then; the Northmen didn't want him to go. He replied that they were depending too much on him, abdicating too much authority to him, and that the function of the Yngling was not to preside.

The announcement startled Baver out of his mental shock. It seemed to him that the death of Jäävklo must be the real reason for the *lagman*'s decision. Or could it be depression because his wife Ilse had left Earth on the jumpship *Phaeacia*? The important thing was that his seniors on the mission, Matthew and Nikko Kumalo, considered Nils Järnhann one of their two prime resources. Ten days previously, they'd flown pinnace *Alpha* to Germany and the Dane land, to interview members of their other prime resource, the Psi Alliance. They'd intended to be back for the All Tribes Ting—the big annual assembly of the Northmen. But three nights ago they'd called from Neustadt am Weser, to tell him they wouldn't be back for at least another week.

Now Nils was planning to leave, and Baver had the impression that it would be soon. If it was before Matt and Nikko came back, they'd want to know where he was going, so they could maintain contact with him.

Meanwhile Isbjørn Hjeltessøn, the leader of the Council of All Chiefs, had solemnly asked the others for nominations for a new *lagman*. After half a dozen names had been called out, Hjeltessøn had dismissed the meeting and the chiefs, and the crowd on the slope had begun moving toward their camps. Or in the case of some of the Norskar, their cabins, for the Ice Bear Clan was host to the ting this year.

The crowd was leaving now, and Baver followed Nils. He'd had no personal contact with him before; had spent most of his time with the Salmon Clan of the Svear. Besides, the man was obviously very different from the rest of his people, and according to Nikko had a somewhat exterior viewpoint of them. To talk with him, at least at any length, Baver had told himself, might skew his data and prejudice his analyses.

Now, though, he needed to question him about where he was going, and when.

Baver caught up with him as the Northman approached his tent, a typical, conical affair about four meters tall and four in diameter, of hides sewn to fit, and laid over slender pine poles. Its door flap was open, and the leather walls glowed faintly; someone had started a fire in the fire pit. Which surprised Baver—the Northman was said to live alone.

"Nils!" Baver said to him, "may I ask you some questions?"

Nils slowed and looked at the ethnologist. He saw a man of ordinary height, soft by Neoviking standards but well proportioned. His skin was brown, his curly brown hair cap-like; he had it cut from time to time with clippers.

"Ask," Nils said.

"When are you going to leave?"

"Tomorrow."

Tomorrow! "Where will you go?"

"Eastward."

"Where eastward?"

Nils ducked in through the door, and Baver followed him. They were met by giggling, and the confused ethnologist looked around. There were two young women there, in their late teens he judged, perhaps local, and he realized what they were there for. Nils was as much a hero among the other clans, or most of them, as in his own. These girls were there to carry off with them some of the giant warrior's genes, with which to bless their family and clan. And no doubt to enjoy themselves and pleasure him.

Abruptly Baver stepped back into the doorway. "I— I've got more questions," he said. "I'll come back tomorrow before you leave." Then he ducked out, his face hot, and hurried off toward his own tent. *Those are damned good-looking girls*, he thought, *especially if you like them strong and unwashed*. He wished one of them had been waiting for him. When he got to his tent, he laid a fire, lit it with his fire-starter, and when it was burning well, put greenery on it to smoke out the mosquitoes.

He'd neglected to ask Nils when, tomorrow, he'd be leaving. He'd check with him in the morning, to make sure; 0800 would do it, he decided. Meanwhile—he took the radio from his shoulder bag and called Matt and Nikko; perhaps they'd fly back tonight if they knew.

But neither responded, nor did the pinnace itself. He was disappointed, but not surprised. If both were away from the *Alpha*, they'd leave the force shield on, and if the area wasn't safe, they'd leave the commast retracted to prevent vandalism; contact would be impossible.

He'd try them again tomorrow, as soon as he got up.

THREE

From—*The New School Encyclopedia*, copyright A.C. 920, Deep Harbor, New Home.

The Orc Wars, A.D. 2831–2832 (A.C. 779–780)—

Tribal chiefs and feudal lords had fought innumerable small wars since before records began to be kept again (about A.D. 2350). But in post-plague Europe there was no large-scale war until 2831. In that year the Orc Wars began.

It seemed predestined that there would be such wars, given the post-plague return to primitivism, with society organized variously under tribalism, feudalism, and despotism. What actually brought it about was the development of a new imperialism in the Middle East. Its outcome, however, was the result of a folk migration out of Scandinavia, in response to severe climatic cooling, the opening stage of the new, so-called Athabasca–Skanderna glaciation. . . .

. . . .On one side, two powerful military forces were allied, one the so-called Orcs, the other of assorted horse barbarians, united under the command of His Imperial Majesty, Kamal Timur Kazi, known as Kazi the Undying. These met and destroyed a series of European opponents: first the South Ukrainians; next the "North Ukrainians" (more properly Byelorussians); and later a mixed and ill-coordinated army of Poles, Magyars, Saxons, Neovikings, and finally migrating Finns, which combined was still much smaller than the imperial forces. The first encounter. . . .

. . . .Thus the Neoviking hero, Nils Järnhann, on the first occasion turned a situation of military overwhelm into the withdrawal of the conquering Orcs into the Balkans, and the dissolution of the horse barbarians into a still dangerous but unled mob of marauders. While on the later occasion, it is Järnhann who must also be credited with converting the terribly vulnerable Neoviking situation into the decimation and collapse of the Orcish army, and its withdrawal from Europe across the Bosporus into Anatolia. . . .

*   *   *

Baver had learned to cook Northman style, sort of. In the village, he lived in a bachelor house with two young, still unmarried warriors. An old widow came in twice a day, morning and evening, to cook for them, and he'd watched what she did. Watching, listening, and recording were his principal activities. En route to the ting, a six-day trek on horseback from the principal village of the Salmon Clan, he'd not only had his first experience in all-day riding on horseback, a genuine ordeal, but his first experience in cooking, and in eating what he'd cooked. It hadn't been so bad. By New Home standards, he'd never cared a whole lot what he ate, as long as he was decently nourished.

That night he dreamed of cooking. People kept appearing *in* his cook fire—which in the dream was much larger than ordinary—or over it in a big cauldron. The first time it wakened him, he'd been quite upset. After building up his fire a bit, and adding greenery to thicken the smoke, he'd gone out among the mosquitoes to one of the campground's straddle-trenches, to relieve himself. Before he fell asleep again, the thought had come to him that in his dreams, the persons being cooked had all seemed to be there at their own insistence. And when he slept again, though the dreams recurred, they didn't upset him as they had earlier.

It was the noise of boys playing that woke him to the day. When he got up, many of the adults had already eaten, and gone to the broad ting ground to talk or trade; wrestle or shoot or watch those who did; or watch the council. Baver relieved himself again; filled his waterskin at the stream; ate jerky, strong cheese, and hardtack; and tried once more to reach Matthew and Nikko, with no more success than the first time.

When he finished eating, his watch read 0806. He left his tent to go to Nils's and ask when, that day, the Northman planned to leave.

Nils's tent was gone, leaving the fire hole and a circle of pressed-down grass. While Baver stood staring, not knowing what to do, a boy came loping up, one he'd never seen before, tallish and gangling, with a narrow, hawk-like face and orange-red hair. He guessed his age at possibly fifteen years. On one shoulder the boy carried a bridle and light saddle; on his belt he wore a shortsword and knife. "Is he gone already then?!" the boy asked.

"It appears so."

"Do you know where?"

"No. I wish I did. Were you going with him?"

The boy nodded absently, staring at the trampled grass of the tent site.

"Can you track him?" Baver asked.

"If the horse guards tell me what direction he started in."

Abruptly the boy left, trotting briskly, and Baver followed him down grassy avenues separating clan camps, to the large rope corral of the Wolf Clan. It was guarded by a one-eyed old warrior with a rough scar bisecting his face, and by two boys about the age of Baver's guide but somewhat huskier. The youth questioned the old man, who pointed down the stream. The Yngling, he said, had left an hour earlier with his horses: a single saddle mount and a pack horse. The Northmen were not rich in horses.

An hour, Baver thought. *Not very explicit.* To the Neovikings, an hour was only a concept, carried down through the centuries from pre-plague days when they'd had clocks; now it referred to an interval somewhat shorter than half a day, but somewhat longer than "a little while."

The boy put down his saddle but kept his bridle. "What are you going to do?" Baver asked.

The question brought a stare before an answer. "Get my horse, of course." Then bridle in hand, the boy strode in among the horses. Baver stood feeling foolish for a moment, then turned to the one-eyed horse tender. "Do you think he can? Catch up with Nils Järnhann?"

The old man grunted. "Probably. He will be hurrying, and the Yngling probably won't be."

"Why does he want to go with him?"

"Hans is apprenticed to Algott Skalden, and has undertaken to complete the Järnhann Saga. He composed a number of the existing kantos, and people agree they are virtually as good as his master's. I suppose he feels he must follow Nils to know what happens with him. Though to follow the Yngling can easily mean he'll never live to recite it in the longhouse."

On this world, Baver realized, that was more than possible. "What's his name?" he asked.

"The boy's? He is Mager Hans Gunnarsson."

Skinny Hans. It fitted. "Thank you," Baver said, and waded in among the horses to where the poet's apprentice was bridling a wiry roan. "Hans," he said, "wait for me while I get some gear and my horse. I'll go with you."

The boy frowned at him. He didn't know this man, except that he was obviously one of the star folk. "For a little while," he said.

"Thank you. Thank you very much." Then, as if to seal a bargain, Baver thrust out a hand. After a moment's pause, the boy accepted it. The ethnologist was startled at the strength of the long fingers. Then he walked quickly out of the horse herd, and when he was outside the rope corral, speeded to a trot.

Baver didn't strike his tent; he intended to be back before midday. But on the chance that he might not be back before night, he stuffed his saddlebags with things, such as his radio, that caught his eye or thoughts. His recorder was already clipped in a pocket of his jumpsuit, and his pistol in its built-in pocket holster. Then he rolled his sleeping bag in his poncho and tied it. Finally, with his light saddle and everything else on his shoulders, he hurried toward the horse corral of the Salmon Clan. The Salmon Clan! The thought struck him that here, far from any salmon, the clan might consider choosing a new totem.

One of the horse boys helped him catch his horse, and he bridled and saddled it. Then he climbed aboard and trotted off toward the corral of the Wolf Clan.

Mager Hans had left without him, but the one-eyed wrangler pointed the way. "He is young," the old man said. Baver assumed he referred to Mager Hans's impatience, but the ethnologist remained irked with the boy. True, Hans had only agreed to wait "a little while," but he should have waited longer than he had. It seemed to Baver very important that he speak with Nils: learn where the Northman was going, so he could inform Matt and Nikko. And without help—Hans's or someone's—he had no hope of finding him.

The trail led down a creek bordered by aspen groves. The stream, mountain-born, here flowed through a lobe of prairie, flanked by dwindling, forest-clad ridges. Clans had passed that way en route to the ting, the Salmon

Clan for one. Thus the grass had been heavily trampled, and hadn't yet recovered. Baver wondered if it was possible to follow the trail of a solitary horse through this. A Northman could if anyone could, he supposed, but could anyone? Especially a teenaged poet!

The clan trails kept mostly to the prairie grass outside the aspens, but here and there were groves of pine as well, not restricted to the stream borders, and in places the trail wound between pine groves. After a brisk twenty-minute ride, he passed the last of them, and saw a slender, solitary rider, no doubt Mager Hans. The rider had crossed the stream and turned northward, where the ridges had shrunk to a pair of low, nearly treeless hills. He was climbing one of them. Baver shouted, and with his heels, nudged his horse carefully down the steep stream bank and started across, at the same time calling to the other to wait.

The other didn't, so Baver kicked his horse into a brisk trot till he caught up. Obviously Mager Hans had ridden to his tent before starting out; he'd added saddlebags, bedroll, quiver and bow to his gear. Now he rode with eyes fixed on the grass just ahead. Here there was no trampled trail, but Baver could see the signs that someone had ridden ahead of them.

"Nils's trail?" he asked.

The boy glanced briefly at him. "Ja Du."

"How can you be sure?"

"It was made this morning by two horses, one behind the other. A saddle mount then, and a pack horse. And who would leave the ting early, especially alone?"

Baver nodded. "I see." He adjusted his opinion of the skinny poet he rode with. From the top of the hill, he could look northeastward across kilometers of rolling, tall-grass prairie. Nowhere could he see a horseman ahead of them, but it seemed there had to be one; the trail was there. With Mager Hans's eyes more or less intent on the tracks ahead, Baver decided he'd keep his own attention in the distance. If he should spot Nils, Hans wouldn't have to watch the trail anymore, and they could speed up. Then he could question Nils and get back to his duties.

Baver wondered how a blind man could start out alone to travel—wherever it was Nils Järnhann was traveling to. And how he'd fought the warrior chief the night before: how he'd parried the chieftain's savage strokes and won. He hadn't allowed himself to wonder before. He'd been told of Nils's blinding by the Orcs, and that he still functioned. He'd visualized a warrior grown gaunt from trauma, gaunt and enfeebled, moving around slowly with a guide. At the ting he'd seen instead a man who walked briskly, as if with two real eyes, a man who might well be the strongest he'd ever seen.

And then there'd been the fight! Nikko Kumalo had said the man saw psychically, but Baver hadn't accepted that. Nikko was highly intelligent, and usually very professional, but she was a woman, he'd told himself, and therefore given to irrationalities.

He'd been thinking about these and other things when Mager Hans's horse quickened to a trot. Baver's head jerked up. Perhaps two kilometers ahead, he saw a horse and rider climbing a hill with pack horse trailing. They'd been concealed by the terrain till then, he told himself, but beneath the thought was the realization that his own attention had been poor. He thumped heels to his horse's ribs, and speeded after Hans.

As they drew nearer, Baver might have called out to Nils, but Mager Hans didn't, so the ethnologist kept quiet too. His primary task, after all, was to watch, listen, and record. The observer shouldn't inject himself more than necessary into the things he observed. As they drew near, Nils must have heard them—he was blind, not deaf—but he didn't slow. As they drew alongside the pack horse and slowed to a walk, the Northman spoke.

"Good morning, Hans Gunnarsson," he said. "Good morning, Ted Baver. Have you been listening to the larks?"

Baver stared, slack-jawed. The man hadn't even turned his head, yet spoke to them by name. "Ja visst," Mager

Hans answered. "They've been talking to the horses, those larks, telling them to be careful and not step on their nests. They have sharp tongues, those larks! Like my mother sometimes!"

The boy laughed, then sobered. "You left without me. That was not well done. How can I continue your saga if I don't know what happens?"

"I would tell you when I got back."

The Northman said it as soberly as a judge, Baver thought, yet there seemed to be playfulness beneath the words.

"You talked to me about the earlier things," Mager Hans countered. "But the best stuff I got from others: the Finn, Kuusta Suomalainen; and Sten Vannaren; and Leif Trollsverd; and Ilse; and the star man, Matts. But especially Ilse.

"But this time you've gone off alone, and who knows whether there'll be anyone else to talk with me about what happens. So now I've caught up with you," he finished defiantly, "and you cannot drive me away."

Nils laughed. "Well then, I guess I'll have to make the best of it." He turned his face to Baver. His gaze was not uncomfortable, unless one was troubled by his eyes. "And you, star man," Nils said. "Why are you here?"

"Nikko and Matt will want to know where you're going, and you didn't tell me last night."

"I did tell you. I am going east. North just now, because the Sea is in the way, but when I've gone north far enough, I expect to turn east."

"East! All of Asia is east of here! You need to be more explicit! They'll want to find you from time to time . . . contact you, you know."

Nils Järnhann's unnatural eyes were steady on him—how else could they be?—his expression mild and non-evaluative. Yet Baver squirmed beneath it, recognizing how arrogant his motive was. Basically he was complaining because the Northman was plotting his own course in life, following his own interests, not living according to the wishes and purposes of the expedition from New Home.

"East is all there is to tell you now," said Nils. "I not only don't know where I'm going; I don't know what places there are to go."

"Ah!" Baver grasped the opportunity. "There I can help! I can get maps for you! I should even be able to get them printed in your own language. The computer— The— An implement on the skyboat, can make them quickly for you." Baver's mind raced, and with it his words, in Anglic now, which the Yngling knew, though not every word. "I know something of the country off east. We studied it on my world, with the old library computer brought to New Home from Earth, eight hundred years ago. And I've seen something of it from the air, when we first got back here. There are great mountains—some of them eight kilometers above the sea— partly covered with glaciers, *jöklar*, that stretch for days. And there are vast scorching deserts; one of them, the *Dasht-e-Khavir*, is little more than a thick crust of salt on top of soft salty bogs. There are places where a horse can break through." *Well*, he amended mentally, *a loaded truck at least. Maybe a horse, in places.* "There are places where, if a traveler misses the crossing, the mountains crowd you southward to a vast sea, and to go between the mountains and the sea, you have to cross more deserts, or vast dangerous marshes. While the people . . ."

He became aware that the Northman was grinning at him—the look boyish despite the eyes—and Baver left his sentence unfinished.

"And how am I to get such maps," Nils said, "without turning back and waiting till someone brings them to me?" His face was serious now. "Shall I govern my life by a wish for gifts?"

Not only the Northman but the boy was staring curiously at Baver, and the ethnologist flushed. "Matt or Nikko can bring them to you. Possibly today. I have a radio." He patted his saddlebag. "I'll stay with you till I get in touch with them. Then one of them can"—he groped for a word—"can aim the skyboat at my radio and fly out with the maps." *At which time*, he added silently, *the responsibility becomes theirs, and I can get back to my own work.*

Nils nodded. "You're welcome to come along." He paused. "But now it's time to walk."

Baver knew what he meant. The Northmen, who mostly were too poor in horses to have remounts, made a practice of walking from time to time, or running, leading their horses to rest them. Nils swung from his primitive saddle, Hans following his example.

There was no question who was leader here. Baver too got down, then they started off through grass belly deep and deeper. And thick. It was not easy walking. They hiked for eighteen minutes by Baver's watch, then rode again. Shortly they intersected the broad trail of the clans which had come to the ting from the north, and the way became easier. They rode and walked by turns, the time in the saddle about twice as long as the time on foot. Just at sunset they rode down a mild slope to the bottomland above the Danube flood plain. It was sporadically wooded, here mostly with poplars. The woods were much browsed and rubbed by cattle, for this had been Orcish grazing land for years. The three men hobbled their horses and made camp.

There was a small axe in the gear on the pack horse, and by twilight a leather lean-to was set up, a fire burning before it. They were squatted down by it, laboriously chewing jerky, when Nils paused, and seemed to listen. Seeing this, Mager Hans listened too. After a minute the apprentice poet got smoothly to his feet and moved to his bow as if to string it.

Nils shook his head. "Let be," he said. "This regards me, not you."

Baver still had heard nothing. After a minute though, he heard a horse snort—a horse or something—some distance off. "What is it?" he whispered.

"The family of Jäävklo. They hold me to blame for his death, and intend to avenge it."

Baver stared into the darkness, feeling the hair bristle on his neck. If they killed the Yngling, surely they'd leave no witness. His hand slipped into a pocket and found his pistol. Despite Nils's comment, Mager Hans had finished stringing his bow, and had two arrows in the hand that held it. Nils still squatted, staring into the deep twilight.

Now Baver heard hooves, soft on soft earth, and at the same time saw horses and riders approaching in the near night. Slowly he knelt, and without lowering his eyes, took out his recorder. A moment later one of the intruders was within the firelight's edge. He stopped and dismounted, a burly man, perhaps 180 centimeters tall, Baver thought, and 100 kilos, with massive shoulders. He was dressed for serious fighting, with a semi-conical steel cap of Neoviking design, and short chain mail scavenged after fights with horse barbarians in the Orc War. Behind him, others dismounted too. For a moment no one spoke.

"So you've come," Nils said, "women, children, and all."

"We have no place," the man answered. "We can't leave my brothers' death unavenged. And when we've taken our vengeance, and it becomes known, we'll be outlawed."

Nils still squatted. "What is your name? You'll want me to know."

"I am Olof Three-Fingers, Olof's son." He held up his right hand; the little finger was gone.

"Ah." Nils bit another piece from a strip of jerky. For a long moment he chewed without speaking. The new-comer waited.

"What form is this vengeance to take?" Nils asked it as mildly and calmly as if talking about some stranger.

"A fight to the death. Your death. You know that, if you hear men's thoughts as they claim. We are not ambushers."

Nils grunted. "It's difficult to ambush someone who hears thoughts." He chewed for a few more seconds. "And I'm to fight just the three warriors. Well. Tell the others to let my companions be then. If you kill the star man, his friends will hunt you down with their skyboat and wipe you out, root and seed, women and children. And the young one with me is a poet's apprentice; he's protected by the law of every tribe. Take them with you, and let them go when you're well out of the country."

Baver tried to picture Matthew and Nikko hunting down the murderers. It would never happen.

"Am I to fight you one at a time?" Nils asked. "Or all at once?"

Olof Three-Fingers regarded Nils darkly. "All at once. We are here for vengeance, not glory. Now. Are you going to stand up? Or must I kill you squatting on your haunches?"

Nils bit off another bite. "You have with you fifteen women, am I right? Plus children, and seven freemen. Let me advise you. Instead of simply killing me, let me challenge you to a duel. Hans Gunnarsson here, and the star man, will witness that I challenged the three of you at once. It will make no difference to the outcome, but your family will not be outlaw, and it will save them the blood penalty."

One of the other warriors spoke then, angrily. "Do not agree to it!" he said. "He is trying to shame us!"

Olof Olofsson answered without turning to face the man. "Shut up. If he wishes to make that small amend before he dies, we will honor it."

Nils paused in his deliberate chewing, his weird glass eyes directed upward at the warrior who stood in the firelight. "Good. Then I will challenge you, all three. As soon as I've finished my supper."

"No!" said the one who'd complained before. "Finish his supper! Can't you see? He's stalling!"

Nils half laughed, half barked. "Stalling? To what effect? I am enjoying what may be my last meal. Have you eaten? Here! It will be your last, too."

He tossed a piece of jerky toward the man, who stepped forward angrily, drawing his sword. Olof Three-Fingers barked him to a standstill, hand raised as if to strike him. Then Nils spoke again, to Mager Hans this time. "And you, Hans Gunnarsson, unnock your arrow. I intend to keep the killing between warriors. A poet is not to be wasted."

Then a voice called from the rear of the family of Jäävklo. "Olof! Someone is coming! More than one!"

Looking back, the warrior swore. Nils got smoothly to his feet, his sword in his hand now. "Two of them," he said. "One is Leif Trollsverd. You know of him. The other is my kinsman, Sten Vannaren."

He is *telepathic then!* Baver told himself. *How else could he know?* Or had he staged the whole thing? Had he known or suspected that he'd be followed by these kinsmen of Jäävklo's, and arranged with his friends to follow? Leif Trollsverd would be an ideal choice for such a plan. Even Baver knew his reputation, a Norske warrior-hero famed as a swordsman, with his own saga from the Orc War. Even the warrior name given him, Trollsverd, implied someone dangerous, for *trolleri* meant magic, and in Neoviking tales, trolls were often savage as well as tricksters and magicians, with far more than human strength. By extension, a *trollsverd*—troll sword—would be terrible to face—powerful, magical, and savage.

It occurred to Baver that he should have his pistol, not his recorder, in his hands. For surely, with such a prospect, Olof and his kinsmen would attack Nils together now, cut him down and reduce the odds against them before Nils's friends arrived. Olof had said that vengeance was their motive, and Nils their target, and their prospects would be poor when the newcomers arrived.

But they waited, backed into the circle of light, facing the coming horsemen. Mager Hans threw more dry branchwood on the fire, as if to better light the fight to come. As if he wanted to see every detail for the Järnhann Saga he was preparing. Now Baver could hear the dull thudding of hoofbeats at an easy trot, surely more than two horses. They slowed, and Nils called out:

"Leif! Sten! Well come! Knut Jäävklo's kinsmen have come to visit, seeking vengeance!"

The newcomers rode into the edge of the firelight, or the first two did. Behind them were more. Two more, Baver thought, probably sword apprentices brought along for the camp chores and adventure, being forbidden by the Bans to take part in fighting among Northmen. Four men then, with pack horses. Leif Trollsverd and Sten Vannaren swung easily off their mounts, and as their feet touched down, their swords were in their hands, not flourished but ready. They too wore steel caps and hauberks.

The one who spoke first had a clipped reddish beard, and his accent came from Svealand. "We wondered," he said. "We were told they'd left the encampment and turned north, and decided to follow. As for vengeance— Knut Jäävklo wrote his fate with his actions in life, and the manner of death he chose was part of his penance. His clan still has the price of his dishonesty to pay, but that's just: It was they who made him chief."

"His kinsmen see it differently," Nils answered. "They blame me for his death."

Sten Vannaren nodded. "Has a challenge been made?"

"Not formally. Nothing has been said that cannot easily be passed over. Perhaps killing can be avoided."

Olof Three-Fingers shook his head. "We have decided. Perhaps it was ill done, in the heat of loss and anger, but we have told others what we intended; we cannot go back now."

"I understand."

Baver was surprised that Sten Vannaren was spokesman here, instead of one of the two heroes, and wondered if this was some obscure protocol in action.

"Well then," Sten went on, "challenge if you must."

Olof Three-Fingers gestured toward Nils. "He said he would challenge."

Nils shook his head. "That was to save your kin from outlawry or the blood price, and yourself the karma. Now it's no longer three on one, so you won't be labeled murderers, and if I challenge with equal numbers, I could be charged before the Council for an unsanctioned feud." He paused, looking intently at Olofsson. "Men before you have retracted words said in anger. And while some have looked ill at them for it, that passes, while others speak of them as grown in wisdom."

The Glutton warrior stared at Nils. "That may be," he said slowly, "but the cost of such wisdom is pride, and that is a price I will not pay. I challenge you, Nils Järnhann, Hammarsson, to pay with your blood for the death of my brother. Just you and I." He gestured at his two warrior kinsman. "These can challenge or not, as they please."

"I stand by my cousin!" said one of them, and the other, after a moment's lag, declared himself as well.

Leif Trollsverd spoke now in quick, clipped Norse. "I stand by my friend, the Yngling of the People," he declared. "It is not right that he fight alone against three."

"And I," said Sten Vannaren. "He is my kinsman and my friend." He paused. "It would be well if you spoke to your own kinsmen that you brought with you, who are not warriors, and told them what you want them to do when it is over. For it will be too late then."

The hotheaded of Jäävklo's cousins stepped forward with an oath, and once more Olof Three-Fingers restrained him. "I am headman here," he warned. "I say when we fight." He turned to Sten. "I will speak with those who are not warriors, and advise them. I will tell them to return to the clan, and that the feud ends here."

Baver stared as the three Glutton warriors went out to counsel their people. Surely at least three men would die here tonight, as he understood these matters. And even in a culture which believed in rebirth for the dead, how could they act so matter-of-factly? Surely such belief could be no more than a veneer, overlying the deep biological realization that dead was dead. And for the survivors, what of lost limbs?

He could hear them talking, but not what was said. It seemed that Olof Three-Fingers did almost all of it. After two or three minutes they came back into the circle of firelight, and Baver realized that Hans had moved back out of the way. Quickly he followed, and recorder in hand, stood to one side, staring through the viewing frame at the six warriors lining up in two facing rows of three, well spread out. There'd been a bit of jockeying between Olof and the hothead over who would face Nils Järnhann. Olof, with his seniority, prevailed, and sullenly the hothead faced off with Leif Trollsverd instead.

Baver realized with some dismay that his fascination substantially outweighed his disgust. Nils had donned his own steel cap and hauberk, and stood half a head taller than any of the others. But these men were all formidable looking, their hands large and thick with muscle on their sword hilts, their forearms bulging and corded. Leif Trollsverd was the smallest, an average-sized Northman who gave an impression of coiled-spring energy.

They raised their swords, each man with his dagger in the other hand. Then, with an oath, Olof Three-Fingers made his opening move, his blade rotating beneath Nils's, pushing it aside and thrusting toward the Yngling's belly. At once they were all in action, blades clashing, bodies and weapons in constant motion, feet in a balanced dance, forward and back, their breathing a cadence of grunted exhalations. Within seconds, Leif Trollsverd's sword cut a gaping wound in his opponent's thigh. Blood poured. The wounded man, the hothead, doubled his efforts then, in a frenzy, but the Norske fended him off seemingly without effort, and cut the man's sword arm so deeply that his sword dropped from nerveless fingers. With a shrill cry, the man lunged with his knife, and Trollsverd's sword struck his neck, cutting through the chain collette and driving him to earth, half beheaded.

Trollsverd stepped aside to watch the others, and Baver's attention went to Nils. The giant fought with an easy nonchalance that seemed almost slow but wasn't. Olof Three-Fingers, by contrast, fought furiously. Then Nils's blade cleft the man's helmet, and the Glutton warrior fell, eyes wide and bulging, mouth agape, brains oozing through the rent.

Of the three, only Sten Vannaren still fought, and it seemed to Baver that Sten's opponent might be the best of the three Gluttons. Blood flowed from cuts on arms and thighs, and each man had rents in his hauberk from strokes only partially fended. But neither seemed weakened yet. Baver waited in near agony for Nils or Leif to step in, but they seemed content or constrained to simply watch. For a moment the two swords seemed to lock overhead, and the Glutton warrior swept low with his knife. At that instant, Sten spun out of the sword lock, his blade sweeping down and across, driving through mail, shoulder, scapula, and into his opponent's chest, even as the knife sliced the side of his own leg.

For a moment the scene was still, without movement or sound. Then a burly freeman from Olofsson's retinue stepped into the firelight. Bending, he took Olof Three-Fingers' body under the arms, lifted, and began pulling it away. Almost at once, other men stepped up and dragged the others after him. Without a word that Baver could hear, the entire group of Gluttons began to leave, and within a minute or so he could see none of them.

Of the three victors, only Sten Vannaren had been wounded. He stripped off shirt and breeches, and the others bound his wounds with strips cut from them. Bound them tightly, that the scars might not be wide. On the left side, the Northman's chest was discolored and bloody; Baver wondered if any ribs had been cracked. The man must have a high pain threshold, he thought, or perhaps adrenaline made the difference. Surely he'd be sore in the morning.

Soon the three warriors rolled up in their sleeping robes and lay talking not far from the fire, their voices a murmur. No one had bedded in the lean-to, which had only room for one, or two lying close. Hans and the two sword apprentices lay somewhat apart from them on the other side, also murmuring. Baver, unwilling to intrude on the warriors but wanting the security of the fire, unrolled his sleeping bag near Hans. And found it wet! It had been tied behind the saddle, and must have gotten wet when he'd crossed the stream below the ting ground; being wrapped in his poncho hadn't protected it. His saddle bags were wet too.

Dismayed, he opened the sleeping bag and crawled in. It felt cold; cold and wretched. As usual the mosquitoes were numerous and hungry, and there was little smoke to drive them off; from time to time he mashed some of them bloody on his face. He eavesdropped on the boys' conversation to take his mind off his discomfort somewhat.

After a bit, their conversation died, and Baver spoke quietly. "Hans, what will the others, the Glutton clansmen, do with the bodies of their dead? They'll bloat and stink before they can get them home."

"Get them home? What good would there be in that? They will burn them. Tonight. Talk to their souls, then burn their bodies."

Talk to the killed? Baver thought. *Barbarians indeed! At least they'll get no argument from them.*

Getting an arm out of his sleeping bag, Baver felt through a wet saddlebag for his radio, and working one-handed, tried to contact Matthew. Perhaps they'd returned; perhaps they could still come out and rescue him from the mosquitoes tonight, and the wet sleeping bag.

But no one answered. Swearing silently, he returned the radio, drew his arm back in, and set his mind grimly to getting through the night. When he got back to New Home, he'd look up the fool who'd failed to provide waterproof bags with mosquito hoods.

FOUR

Mild though the night was, Baver had been cold and miserable, and as soon as it was light, he got up and spread his bag on some bushes to dry a bit.

When the sun was well up and they'd eaten, he rode out with Leif Trollsverd to see what Jäävklo's kin were doing. They didn't ride down to them, only as close as the top of the rise which overlooked their camp. The Gluttons were preparing to leave, moving sluggishly. They'd been up much of the night, he supposed, feeding the fire, ashing the bodies. And talking to burning corpses. Smoke still rose from what Baver assumed was the site of the funeral pyre.

I should have been there, he thought, *recording it. But I'd hardly have been accepted; they'd probably have killed me.*

The Northmen had consistently been at least neutral toward him, often friendly, but they *were* barbarians, and dangerous, and Jäävklo's family had been heavily stressed. Even though none of the survivors were warriors, any of the freemen could have been dangerous to him. None of the Northmen that he knew—men, women, or children—

seemed to fear injury much, or even death. And growing up as they did, in the strenuous life, they were invariably strong. Even Mager Hans was strong, for all his thinness.

Back at camp, Baver found Sten stripped to the waist, with Nils reexamining his wounds. His rib cage on the left side was dark with bruise, and scabbed. Sten twitched as Nils prodded, and Baver twitched with him. Undoubtedly some ribs were cracked, and if not for the man's mail, Baver told himself, the blow Sten had taken would surely have killed him. It was hard to understand how such a blow had failed to cut through the hauberk; perhaps the blade had been turned somewhat before it landed.

Afterward, moving stiffly, Sten pulled his loose leather shirt back on, while his sword apprentice packed his gear on his pack horse. Then he and Leif left with their apprentices and pack string, steering toward the other camp. To make sure, Baver guessed, that the members of Jäävklo's family had departed for the ting grounds or their clan territory. The two friends wouldn't leave their Yngling with the offended Gluttons still around; wearing warrior braids made no one proof against arrows, not even Nils Järnhann. And Neoviking hunter-herdsmen, Baver knew, shot very well indeed, perhaps as well as their warriors.

Meanwhile Hans had cut a large forked sapling and tied Baver's damp sleeping bag on it like some kind of fat and drooping banner. "Put the end in your stirrup," he said curtly, handing him the sapling, "and carry it upright. It will dry then."

Baver resented it more than he appreciated it; Hans treated him like a fool. But he took the advice.

With Leif and Sten on their way, Nils loaded his own pack horse, and mounting, led Hans and Baver down the bank of the Danube and into the broad river. They swam their mounts across, a long swim that tired the powerful Orc warhorses. Though smooth, the current was strong, and wet Baver to the buttock. It had wetted his saddlebags too, and red-faced he realized that Nils and Hans had slung theirs across their shoulders.

They continued north, on foot for a bit to rest the animals. After a few hours they turned east, parallel to the river, leaving the beaten trail for untracked territory. At the midday break, Baver opened his wet saddle bag and took out his radio. He was glad it was waterproof. Again he tried to reach Matthew and Nikko, and again to no avail. Anxiety touched his guts: Surely he should have caught them on board by now, or at least made contact with the *Alpha*, the pinnace itself.

He chided himself then. It was perfectly possible that the shield had been on and the commast retracted each time he'd called. He simply needed to be patient. It was one thing to tell himself that, though, and quite another to dispel the unease he felt.

Meanwhile Nils led on through kilometers of grass that ranged from crotch-deep atop some of the rises to higher than the horses' backs along some of the creeks they splashed through.

When they made camp that evening, Baver tried the radio once more, with no more success than before, and once again before he went to sleep. The failure kept him awake. If something had happened to Matt and Nikko, or to the *Alpha*, he was in serious trouble, on a hostile and dangerous world without a flying craft or modern weapons, aside from his pistol and a spare magazine. And there'd hardly be a second expedition from New Home within the year; perhaps not even next year.

After another two days they turned northeastward. To avoid the marshes, Nils said; these were extensive along the Danube after it turned north at the big bend. Meanwhile they'd seen no further tracks of horsemen, but now and then saw tracks and beds that Nils said were made by Orc cattle, abandoned when their owners withdrew by ship for Asia Minor.

Once, ahead of them, they saw carrion birds circling low, and rode to the spot to see what was there. They found the half-eaten remains of a calf. Nils said the wolves who'd killed it were close by, waiting for them to move on. Baver was horrified at the thought, and as they rode away, imagined wolves leaping on him from the tall grass, to pull him from his horse.

Periodically they crossed streams flowing eastward to join their waters with the Danube. Mostly these were bordered with sinuous bands of woodland. Away from the streams, an occasional thicket of dark scrubby oaks, or clump of poplars, had sprouted since fire had last swept the prairie. Less often, Baver saw single larger oaks, or groups of several, broad-crowned and fire-scarred, that had survived such fires.

He no longer got his gear wet when crossing the deeper streams.

Near evening, as they entered a fringe of poplars along a creek, they saw a band of cattle on the far bank, drinking. Murmuring brief instructions, Nils strung his saddle bow, then began to ease upstream while Hans moved down, to cross away from the cattle and flank them. Baver stayed behind as Nils had ordered. Shortly the cattle spooked, turned and galloped off, little more than their heads in sight above the high grass. The two Northmen galloped in pursuit, arrows nocked. Within a minute they were out of Baver's view, a wrinkle in the prairie intervening.

The band had separated, and a few minutes later a young bull came trotting back, surging brisket-deep across the stream. Seeing Baver it stopped, about forty meters off as it topped the bank. It eyed him, snorted, pawed the ground. The ethnologist took his pistol from its pocket holster. The animal would weigh, he thought, two-thirds of a ton—bone and muscle, gristle and horn; the gun seemed inadequate, trivial. The animal started toward him again. His horse jittered, shied, starting one way, then another, and he nearly lost his seat. In a moment of near panic, Baver realized that from its back, he'd have a hard time hitting the bull, let alone disabling it.

It charged. Baver pointed the weapon and fired. His horse bucked once, perhaps from the gunshot, and he felt himself leaving the saddle, arms flailing in an effort to land on his feet. He did, heavily, but couldn't keep them, staggering forward into a poplar trunk and falling. Hooves thudded past him two or three meters off. Then he was on his feet again, knees flexed, heart banging, ready to run or dodge. The bull slowed as it reached the prairie's edge, swinging wide as if to return to the stream at a little distance. Baver wondered if he'd hit it when he'd shot.

He watched it through the trees and the thin screen of undergrowth, heard it snorting as it trotted. After a minute it disappeared over the stream bank to reenter the water, and he neither saw nor heard it again.

Meanwhile his mount was gone, fled. He was alone: no horse, no saddlebag, no food. And no gun! He'd let go of it when the horse had thrown him! The realization nearly buckled his knees. Beneath the trees, the grass was thinner and shorter than in the open prairie, and on hands and knees he began to look for his weapon. While he searched, it occurred to him that his radio was in the saddlebag too, gone with the horse.

What if Nils and Mager Hans didn't come back? Surely they would?

But even after most of a year among them, he didn't really know the Northmen. He'd collected hundreds of hours of AV recordings of them, but to him they remained barbarians, another species, beyond prediction.

After ten despairing minutes that seemed like thirty, he found the gun and nearly kissed it. A fair breeze kept the mosquitoes down somewhat, and lying on his back, Baver closed his eyes, listening to the rustling of poplar leaves. And awoke to the sound of chopping. Nils and Mager Hans were back and making camp; his own horse stood near, grazing. Nils or Hans had taken the bit from its mouth, removed its saddle, and fastened hobbles on its forelegs. He felt mortified. The two Neovikings must think him a fool for falling asleep with his horse unhobbled. And an inconsiderate one for leaving the bit in its mouth. Meanwhile dusk was edging in, the breeze had died, and the mosquitoes were gathering.

He got up and helped Hans gather firewood, more of it than usual, while Nils built a lean-to. Then Nils built a rack of saplings, and hung bloody strips of veal on it to smoke and dry. Finally a fire was lit beneath the rack. Supper was calf liver, tongue, and flank, seared in the flames on sharpened sticks. And raw calf brain brought in the head, its natural receptable. Baver had grown used to Neoviking food, if seldom happy with it. He realized that eating the various organs was nutritionally important when so few vegetables were available; something the Northmen seemed well aware of. Nils apologized for not bringing him blood—a valued food—but he'd had nothing suitable to carry it in. It would foul a waterskin, he said; ordinarily one drank it at the site of the kill.

The cattle had run well, and their own horses had been tired. Thus they'd chased a calf for perhaps a *tusen,** Nils said, before they'd ridden it down and shot it. Afterward, riding back, they'd seen the tracks of other horses on the other side of the river, shod horses. Some refugee Orcs had passed there perhaps two days earlier.

Baver's hair crawled. Orcs! He recalled what Orcs had done to Chandra and Anne-Marie, when they'd held the two prisoner. "How many?" he asked.

"Nine, seven of them shod. Three orcs, three slaves, and three pack horses."

"You could tell all that from the tracks?"

"Not entirely from the tracks."

Baver sat chewing calf liver while he digested the information. The enigmatic "explanation" he let be. Suppose the Orcs had come along while he'd slept, and seen him. Would they have killed him? Tortured him? Or

---

*The *tusen* is a Neoviking measure of distance: a thousand doubles—double strides—roughly, 1,700 meters, about 5,600 feet in the old system.

simply ridden off with a fourth slave? Would Nils have tried to rescue him? He couldn't picture it. Even Nils Järnhann was unlikely to attack three Orcs to save a foreigner.

This was definitely not a place he wanted to be. Taking the radio from his saddle bag, he tried again to reach the pinnace and call in a pickup, but got nothing.

FIVE

The sun was low above the side ridge when Nikko and Matthew Kumalo, in pinnace *Alpha*, lowered gently toward the ground, toward the low cabin built for them beside a clump of birches. The children of the village, used to seeing the spacecraft, made little of its arrival. A few called to friends that it was coming.

The Wolf Clan, or that part of it which dwelt at the village of Varjby, had arrived back from the ting that day about midday. Then there'd been gear to unpack and put away. And though a small detail including dogs and cats, had been left to look after the village when the rest were away, there were nonetheless birds and small animals to evict from cabins, and new weeds to hoe or grub from the vegetable gardens.

Ulf Varjsson was at the smithy, getting rings made to repair a pack saddle, when he heard a child call that the skyboat was coming. He excused himself and left at a jog, his burly, forty-six-year-old body moving easily, even lightly. He arrived at the *Alpha* while the Kumalos were unloading their travel gear.

"Go' da'!" he greeted.

Both of them stopped what they were doing. The clan chieftain would not have come, surely not too soon, unless he had something important to tell them. "Hello to you," Matthew answered. He didn't ask what Ulf had come for. Courtesy required that they let him get to that in his own time.

"Was your trip a good one?" Ulf asked.

"Very good, thanks."

"You found the people you looked for?"

"Yes. And learned more from them than we'd expected. Ilse's brother was especially helpful."

"Good. Good. I have something to tell you about Nils Järnhann."

"Oh?"

"He has left to wander. He didn't say where; perhaps he didn't know."

He told them then about Knut Jäävklo's self-immolation—a strange business even among the Northmen—and Nils Järnhann's announcement afterward. It was Nikko whose special project Nils was, and it was she who asked if Ulf had any idea when the Yngling might come back.

"My feeling is, he planned to travel far. He rode down the creek and turned north."

North, Nikko thought. *From here, the first leg to almost anywhere is north, unless he planned to follow the Orcs. A thought struck her: Could he be going to the Neoviking homeland? That would be twenty-five hundred kilometers or more by any practical route.* Offhand she could think of nowhere else that might attract him. A few families had stayed behind, she'd heard, unwilling to leave, convinced that the worsening climate was an aberration, not a trend. If he was returning to see how they were, and tell them of the new land, would he follow the Danube west and north to Hungary, where he had friends? And thence through Germany and the Dane Land, finally to boat across the Kattegat to old Sweden? Or northeast, bypassing the mountains, then north through the Ukraine and west into Poland, to cross the Baltic?

"How many days has he been gone?" she asked.

The chieftain counted on his fingers. "Five," he answered. "And he is not alone. A boy, Hans Gunnarsson, is with him, and your own tribesman, the one that lives with the salmon people."

Startled, Nikko turned to her husband. As a woman, she should let him do most of the talking in such matters, or risk their reputations among these people.

"Ted went with him?" Matthew asked.

"That's what One-Eye Björnsson said. And Sten Vannaren saw them camped with Nils on the Danube." Then Ulf told about the fight there, with Olof Three-Fingers and his kinsmen. "It seems that Nils plans to ride east somewhere," the chief finished, "though where . . ." He shrugged.

"We need to find Sten," Matthew said. "There may be more he can tell us."

"He didn't come home with us," Ulf told him. "He's never been one to spend time in his home village; that's how he got his name. He planned to rest a few days with the people of the Ice Bear, and heal his wounds. They might be there yet, though I doubt it. Then he and Leif Trollsverd would go awandering, exploring."

"Thank you," Matthew answered. "We'll leave right away. Perhaps we'll catch them there."

They took off at once, Matthew at the controls, and as they lifted, Nikko tried to raise Baver on the radio. She got nothing. It took only minutes to reach Isbjørnaby. There they were told that the two warriors had left early that morning, not saying where they were going. Next they flew to Laxaby, the principal village of the Salmon Clan, in case Baver had returned there. He hadn't. The Salmon chief invited them to supper with his family, where they ate roast beef, and a pungent stew made with wild millet, wild peas, unidentified roots or tubers, and potent wild onions. Afterward, breath reeking, they got back in the *Alpha* and took off in the dusk. Instead of flying directly back to Varjby, they rode a gravitic vector straight upward to 280 kilometers, from where they could see the sunlit crescent of Europe to the west. To the east, across the Black Sea, lay 9,000 nightbound kilometers of the Eurasian continent, stretching to the Pacific.

"I'm surprised that Ted hasn't radioed us," Nikko said.

"There were times he couldn't have reached us," Matthew answered.

"But a lot more that he could have. Anytime the last couple of days. Do you think his radio could be malfunctioning?"

"Unlikely. It should last a decade or longer. The power tap too. Unless he's damaged it somehow."

Nikko examined the situation. "It's very unlike him to even have left."

Matt nodded. Ted Baver had been a surprise to them, a disappointment. Back on New Home, there'd been considerable competition to be part of the expedition to Earth. Baver had applied, passed the exams with high grades, impressed the interviewers, and been accepted. He'd opted for a post as junior ethnologist, studied hard, and come to Earth with them* as a second stringer. For the first weeks, given their involuntary involvement in the Orc War and its demands on the pinnaces, he'd had

---

*Their ancestors had migrated from Earth more than seven terran centuries earlier. When the colony was less than a decade old, ships stopped arriving, suddenly and inexplicably. The colonists had no jump ship of their own, and there were none at all on the landing grid when the possibility gradually dawned that they might have been abandoned.

They didn't know about the burning plague which reduced the population of Earth to about 10^{-4} of its pre-plague level. Fortunately it had never reached their world. They'd only known that ships had stopped coming.

They had little attention to give the mystery. The New Home colony was the first sent out from Earth after development of the Patel jump drive, but at the time of New Home's isolation, it was little more than the agrarian base for a planned, self-sufficient human world of the future. It took all the colonists' hard work and resourcefulness to establish a viable economy that included a significant, if shrunken, technological base.

no ground duties whatever. When the time came to choose a third person to stay behind and work with them, Baver had been one of the volunteers, and they'd chosen him.

He'd been great on exams, and enthusiastic when dealing with hypothetical situations. But on the ground, among the Northmen, he'd become a different person, fearful and wooden, unable to relate. By the time they realized this, the *Phaeacia* had left. So they'd given him a job he could do: recording, getting everything possible on cubes. They'd hoped he might adjust after awhile, loosen up. And he had, a bit, but still . . .

Yet now he'd left with Nils Järnhann, for where one could only guess.

"I'll record a message loop," Matthew said, "set the computer to signal when he calls, and sleep aboard *Alpha* tonight. We'll see what he has to say."

"What if he doesn't? Call, that is?"

Matthew Kumalo pursed his lips thoughtfully. "Then I supposed we'd better go out and see if we can find him." He shook his head. "It's the least we can do. And the most we can do. And if that doesn't work—" He shrugged. "We'll just have to hope he knows what he's doing, and that he'll get back okay. He *is* with Nils, after all."

SIX

It had gotten hillier. They'd been crossing a narrow valley, riding through grass higher than the saddle. Baver almost didn't see it, might not have if Nils's hadn't turned to watch. The pinnace was passing to the south, not too far off, visible just above a hill crest. At once Baver stood in his stirrups, waving and shouting.

The pinnace passed out of sight. Quickly, desperately he dug his radio out of his saddlebag and spoke into it. Shouted. And got no answer. It was then he noticed that the radio's power-on light wasn't lit. Had it been before when he'd tried to use it? He wasn't sure, hadn't noticed.

His face burned. How could he fail to notice something so basic?

Nils turned his horse and led them up the nearest slope into shorter grass, then on to the crest, where they sat awhile and waited. They'd be much easier to see there.

But the pinnace didn't return. Somehow Baver knew it wouldn't, not even if they waited there till nightfall. He also knew now that his radio was inoperable, and he had neither the tools nor the knowledge to fix it.

He knew little about technical matters. It was the sort of thing he'd relied on Matthew for; Matthew knew equipment.

After a while, Nils nudged his horse with callused heels and started northeastward again. Baver rode up beside him. *If he's actually telepathic*, Baver thought, *as people claim, and as he seems to be, he must know what I'm thinking*. But the big Northman barely glanced at him till he spoke.

"Nils, I want you to take me back."

"That would take six days or more. Then six to get here again."

"I—can make it worth your while." Even as he said it, Baver knew he couldn't. He had nothing the Northman wanted. Nils could have gone with the ship to New Home; Ram had even urged him to. Ilse, his wife had gone, the strange rawboned German woman who'd so impressed everyone. But Nils had refused.

"You can easily go back by yourself," Nils said. "You can follow our trail."

Baver shook his head. "I'd get lost. I don't know how to tell our trail from cattle trails."

The Northman raised a long muscular arm and pointed to the Carpathian Mountains lying dark with forest to the north. "Then ride with the mountains off your right shoulder. After a few days they will curve, and you must too, keeping them off your right shoulder. In time you will come to the Danube near where we crossed it. From there you'll have no trouble finding a village of the People. Someone will take you to the Salmon Clan."

Not the Salmon Clan, Baver thought. No. Once he got back, he'd insist on staying with Matt and Nikko, going with them when they traveled. He shook his head. "I'd get lost," he insisted. "I need you to take me."

The weird eyes rested calmly on him, their unconvincing blue glass without pupils or irises. "I will not take you," Nils said reasonably. "You can find your own way; there's no reason to get lost."

No reason to get lost! Baver turned to Mager Hans. "Hans, you take me. I can make it worth your while."

The boy shook his head."I have come to be with the Yngling and continue the saga of his life. It is my duty. You're a man. A man can easily make his way back from here alone."

Baver hadn't actually considered it before. Now he did, but only for a moment. He could get lost; he was sure it was possible. Even probable. His horse could throw him, or a wild bull could gore him. Or worse—

He turned to Nils. "Orcs could get me," he said.

"It's not likely. They're afraid now. Their hope lies in going unnoticed. And after what happened—since their defeat at the river, and the fall of the tower—they're afraid of the star folk. Besides, you have your gun."

Baver stared at Nils, then at the gangling boy poet. These people didn't care about danger. They didn't understand, and he was sure he couldn't make them understand.

Nils Järnhann looked away, to the northeast, and thumped his horse's flanks with his heels. It started, moving briskly, Hans following. After a moment, Baver followed too.

PART TWO

THE JOURNEY

SEVEN

From—"Frequency of Psionic Talents on Post-Plague Earth," by Ruta-Helena Chatawba. Pages 102–127, in *Advances in Philosophy Following the First Two Earth Expeditions*, Kathleen Murti, ed. University Press, A.C. 867.

Introduction

Wizardry and magic were widely practiced when mankind was young, and for a long time were not differentiated from the purely physical manipulation of material objects. "Nature" had not yet been differentiated in man's mind, nor had superstition been recognized as separate from knowledge.

In the 1st century A.D., alchemy arose out of this more or less undifferentiated mass of human activities. Alchemy strove primarily to produce eternal life and transmute "base metals" into gold. These goals made it particularly susceptible to fraud. At the same time, alchemy produced an incidental but increasing catalog of observed and measured qualitative data on the chemical properties of substances. Thus, out of alchemy grew the organized and rational science of chemistry, which may best be dated from the 18th century and the work of Priestley, Scheele, and Lavoisier. And with the rise of chemistry, the superstitious and groundless—or at least unattainable—facets of alchemy gradually died.

The "field" of wizardry and magic, which was more or less related to alchemy, took much longer to produce a science, psionics. Psionics as a term first appeared in the 20th century literary phenomenon called science fiction, in stories using the premise that some areas of magic and wizardry contained elements of reality.

As an actual science, psionics might be said to have its true early roots in mathematics, specifically in the area of complex numbers. By itself, however, this led only to interesting speculations that would bear no fruit until bridged to physical reality by developments in mathematical physics some decades later.

Meanwhile empirical research had been taking place, though it stretches the term to call it science. Sporadic early studies of telepathy began at Standford and Harvard Universities in the United States of America as early as A.D. 1915. These produced little, however, beyond statistical evidence that telepathy occurred and that it tended to be weak and unreliable. They did not establish mechanisms, or even establish conditions and limitations of occurence.

Mid-20th century psychological and psychiatric studies on the well-documented but unexplained performances of so-called "idiot savants" were not productive. A psychic photographer named Ted Serios was studied in the seventh decade of the 20th century, primarily by the Psychiatry Department of the University of Colorado School of Medicine. These studies established the phenomenon as genuine, and also tentatively established some operating rules. But the physical theory and instrumentation were lacking to explore them.

Except for the statistical studies of telepathy, information and evidence remained very largely anecdotal, however, until the 21st century. Even then, progress was seriously limited by a lack of adequate physical theory to accommodate and make scientific sense of observations. And by a lack of serious interest, at least by funding agencies, during a seventy-year period of social, economic, and geopolitical instabilities that indeed threatened civilization itself at times.

Most of the progress in psionics during that time was with telepathy, the psionic potential seemingly most frequent in the population and most amenable to cultivation using strictly empirical means and simple biofeedback equipment. But this hardly qualified as scientific research; the explanations remained speculative. What it did accomplish was to make limited telepathic skills sufficiently common and well recognized that psionics became accepted as a legitimate, if crude, science. A 2072 study at Oxford University, with cooperation from a number of other universities planetwide, showed a highly significant correlation ($P \leq 0.003$) between demonstrable telepathy and family. It did not, however, clearly establish that the correlation was based on genetic inheritance and not on other family influences.

In A.D. 2090, a Chair of Psionics was founded at the University of Damascus, with Dr. Timur Karim Kazi as chairman. In 2094, Kazi invented the psi tuner, and during the short period ending with the Great Death of 2105, interest burgeoned. But even the psi tuner was an intuitive invention whose principles were only loosely understood.

Beginning with the first reported case of the "Burning Plague," or "Great Death," on 18 July, 2105, within 15 to 20 days the human population of planet Earth was reduced from approximately

7.184 billion to an estimated 10 to 20 million, of which it is further thought that perhaps fewer than two million, worldwide, were still alive two years later.

The evidence is compelling that mortality was not uniform worldwide. Certain genetic stocks had substantially, or even much higher survival than others, though it is arguable that genetics was not the principal cause of that higher survival. On the other hand, evidence strongly suggests that persons with appreciable telepathic talent survived with much greater frequency than average, perhaps due to the linkage of a gene for plague resistance with one for telepathic sensitivity. More compelling, indeed almost indisputable, is evidence that functional telepaths—those who are routinely and reliably able to discern the thoughts of those around them—are far more frequent in existing terran populations than in populations before the plague. . . .

EIGHT

The emperor's greed, like his forefathers', was for power and domination, not grandeur. Thus his palace, including its associated buildings and grounds, was rather modest by antiquity's standards for emperor's palaces. Still, it was by far the most beautiful building, amidst the most impressive set of buildings and grounds, in the empire. Occupying the top of a broad hill, it overlooked the imperial city, still growing three generations after its founding.

On three sides were other hills, forested with a variety of broadleafed and coniferous tree species. And the emperor, Songtsan Gampo, was not insensitive to nature. When he wished to leave his desk, and the reports that tended to pile up on it, he'd step out on his office balcony to sit in the open air and contemplate the view.

It was not an ordinary balcony. Four meters deep and twelve wide, it was supported by inverted buttresses of stone, floored and furnished with elegant hardwoods, decorated in ivory and gold, and in summer green with plants.

Sometimes he received a visitor there, one not brought

to be intimidated, and for whom formality was no advantage. Mostly these were members of the ruling race, a people whose ancestors had migrated from their high harsh land some three thousand kilometers southeastward. On this day he received on his balcony the master of his Circle of Power, Tenzin Geshe.

He did not require that the *geshe* prostrate himself or even kneel; abasements were primarily for supplicants, the newly conquered, and those accused of something ill. It was enough that the *geshe* bow low from the waist.

"What is it you wished to see me about, *geshe*?"

"Your Magnificence may recall my telling you, some weeks past, of a man whom your Circle saw while questing."

The imperial gaze did not change. "I remember."

"We have felt a disturbance in the Tao, a possible portent of danger approaching from the west. It is distant yet, very distant, and hasn't the vibration of an army. It is a man, the man we saw."

The eyes reflected sharpened interest. "And you say he may be dangerous to us. You had no vision this time?"

"None, Your Magnificence."

"A barbarian from far away, without an army. But perhaps a threat." The high brown brows drew down in thought. "Send a demon to watch for this man and destroy him. If it cannot, then we will take further interest."

Tenzin Geshe walked back to the *gomba*, the imperial monastery known as the House of Power, thinking about what the emperor had said. He had not read his lord's thoughts; they'd been screened. But he had sensed a growing interest, or perhaps curiosity was the better word.

Send a demon? His Magnificence was sensitive to the field, but his experience was limited to reading men's thoughts. He didn't know demons, and beyond that was given to looseness in terminology and even concept. Demons were unreliable and capricious, and their power was primarily over the suggestible. Anyone aware enough to sense the Circle so calmly and at a distance, would likely ignore a demon or send it packing. Nor were demons suitable for scouting or spying. They were disinterested in activities with so little involvement.

No, he told himself, *I will gather an elemental. They are somewhat unintelligent, but it can probably hunt the barbarian down. And if it finds him, it will be powerful enough to do something about him.*

NINE

Naken stod han, svääd i handen,
önar lunn, å vass som pilar,
stood ä vjennte vad som hände.
Såg en rörelse i porten.
Uti dagjus kom en ojur,
kom en katt som kalls lejonen.
Stor som björn å mera våldsam,
kattkvick han, mä tänn som kniver,
inte född i fyra dagar.
Vänt mot Ynglingen å mörrde
skräckli mer än boms i vrede. . . .

[Naked stood he, sword held tightly,
calm eyes sharp and quick as arrows,
stood and waited what was coming.
Saw a movement in the portal.
Came a beast into the sunlight,
came a cat they call the lion.
Bear-big he, and much more savage,
cat-quick he, with teeth like daggers,
hunger gnawing, four days fasting.

Turned toward the youth and snarled then,
dreadful more than raging he-bear....]
From—*The Järnhann Saga,*
Kumalo translation

* * *

The day after they saw the pinnace, a cold rain fell without a break, blown at times by gusty winds. They sat it out in the woods along another stream. Nils had brought only a small piece of his leather tipi, enough for a lean-to that was too small for three. So they made a crude and leaky shelter of saplings, bundles of grass, and bark stripped from poplar trees. The leather shelter they used to protect their fire, and finished smoking the veal jerky to ensure it wouldn't spoil.

Baver was glad not to travel. Despite the injections they'd gotten on the *Phaeacia*, and the booster received on schedule from Matthew, he'd come down with diarrhea the night before, and a runny nose. (The diarrhea would recur occasionally for weeks, but not so intensely.) The worst thing about it was squatting repeatedly in the chill rain, his hands blue with cold and his jumpsuit round his ankles.

More memorable, a bear came that day. They heard him snuff, and came out into the rain to stand him off. Big and hump-shouldered, attracted by the smell of meat, he was only twenty meters off, and reared up tall on his hind feet to see more clearly. Baver held his pistol in a frozen grip. Hans's long fingers gripped two arrows with his bow hand, and had another nocked.

Nils didn't even draw his sword. Instead he spoke to the bear, calmly, reassuringly, and after a long minute or so it dropped to all fours, turned and ambled off.

The next morning the three of them went on, and over the next week traveled north and east over hundreds of kilometers of not-quite sameness, mostly riding, but walking periodically to rest the horses. Twice they encountered the remains of ancient towns, recognizable by the change in vegetation. Patches of woods occupied the long-since broken pavements. Brush and scrub trees had overgrown the mounds of broken concrete that were ancient buildings, mounds some of which had been mined for the reinforcing rods, and more or less buried by windblown dirt. Clearly, during some recent century, there'd been a prolonged drought period with dust storms.

Once, at a river, they saw the remains of old bridge footings. Another time they encountered an ancient raised railroad bed, crossing a broad wetland like some improbably straight esker. A nearly continuous stringer of woods grew along it. The rails of course were gone, no doubt salvaged long before the plague.

During the four years of preparing for the expedition, the courses Baver had liked best were those on terran ecology, and he thought he saw the why of the woods on the roadbed. The dense stand of reeds and tall grass, so hostile to tree seedlings, would have been interrupted by the roadbed of crushed rock, even after dust storms had added soil to it. While tree seedlings had obviously been able to establish along its edges, probably migrating along it from the Carpathian foothills visible to the west. And the marsh would rarely be swept by fire—rarely enough that the young trees had time, between fires, to mature and grow thick protective bark.

His mental reconstruction of the process pleased him, and he began to pay closer attention to the country they passed through.

It had been swept and depopulated by the Orcs, and only once did they see people, five poorly dressed men on horseback following a river upstream. They'd seemed cautiously friendly, but the little Anglic they knew was a pidgin too strange for Baver's understanding. He caught "Orcs" and "travel" and "good place." Nils said they were fishermen from the Danube delta, looking for new land to colonize, drier land, now that the Orcs were gone. Their horses were Orc horses, left when Northman patrols had tracked down and killed Orc refugees who'd been terrorizing the fisherfolk.

It seemed to Baver that they'd said too little too brokenly to impart all that, and at any rate he doubted that Nils had understood their pidgin much better than he had. Perhaps he was as telepathic as Nikko said, as telepathic as the Northmen believed. Or perhaps he'd put the picture together logically from what he already knew and what he'd observed. Surely the fishermen's horses were fine animals, Orc animals, not the nags you might expect delta fishermen to have, if they had horses at all.

They crossed the largest river they'd seen since the Danube, then turned eastward away from the Carpathians, and late that day camped in the woods along another wide river. Over the next week they left behind the last of the occasional oak groves. The grass remained luxuriant but less so, and the only trees were along the streams. The large rivers flowed more or less southward now.

As they rode, Baver, at Nils's request, gave Hans lessons in Anglic. The boy showed impressive recall of new words and phrases. Baver suspected it was from training as a poet, in a culture which memorized far more than it wrote.

They began to see people again—hamlets near streams, with garden plots, small grain fields, and herds of cattle tended by men on horseback. They must be east of the country the Orcs had swept, Baver decided. But even there, there seemed to be few young male adults. They'd gone to the Orc War, he supposed, and been slaughtered. The people weren't actively hostile, but the herdsmen—adolescents and old men—strung their bows and watched the three of them closely until they'd passed by.

Baver was tired of grassland and marshes, the saddle and mosquitoes. He began to daydream that the *Phaeacia* had returned, and that three pinnaces were hunting for him, to take him back with them to New Home.

The country grew drier yet, and except in marshes and wet meadows, the grass notably shorter and less thick. Finally they came to the ruins of a great city by a broad river, with some massive buildings and large monuments still standing. Baver asked that they stay there a day, and Nils agreed.

The greatest monuments were on a hill, heroic structures with heroic sculptures, and they rode up there. The statues and wall reliefs all were huge, but one was far larger than the rest, standing sixty or seventy meters tall, Baver judged, including an upraised arm. It was of a robed woman, the hilt of a broken sword clenched in one monumental hand. The figures were mostly of soldiers though, of heroism and death, and to Baver the place felt haunted. It gave him actual chills. Clearly a terrible war had been fought there—a terrible battle at any rate—far more terrible than the Orc War.

He recorded what he saw, and wished he could read the inscriptions; though weathered, they looked legible, but even the alphabet was unfamiliar to him. If he visualized the geography correctly, he told himself, this had been Russia long ago. The language would be in the *Alpha*'s onboard computer, with a translation program.

Crossing the river at the city, they hit a broad grassy trail. Baver recognized it as an ancient highway, its pavement long since fragmented by frost and roots, the fragments covered by blowing soil. It was recognizable from its cuts and fills, its mild and even grades attracting what few travelers there were.

As they rode eastward on it, the country became increasingly dry. Within two hundred kilometers, the grass was mostly less than knee high, the stands thin. Encounters with other travelers were days apart, and uneasy. The strangers would see the giant Northman, and Baver's jump suit, and pass in suspicious silence. The herds here were widely scattered, wild and usually untended, as if the local people found it easier to hunt their meat than herd it.

The travelers ate mostly marmots now, numerous and fat, victims of Hans's seldom-erring arrows, or occasionally of Nils's. It took only a minute or two to gut and skin one, and one was supper enough for the three of them, with some left over for breakfast. They'd dry and smoke a second for saddle rations the next day. Early on, Nils had taught Baver to gut and skin. The ethnologist had been squeamish at first, but soon was taking his turns at it like the others.

Nils pushed for as much speed as they could make without wearing down the horses. Nonetheless, they sometimes camped as early as midafternoon, where there was water. Then, while the horses grazed, Hans would withdraw to a distance and recite aloud to himself, composing and polishing verses for "The Järnhann Saga." Now and then he'd try one on Nils, who'd sometimes correct or elaborate the story told. Baver was impressed with the boy's skill. In the evenings, Hans got lessons in swordsmanship from Nils, though he hadn't been chosen by his clan to be a sword apprentice.

Early one evening they camped a dozen meters off the road, on the lower slope of a hill. A spring flowed from a sandstone outcrop there, to form a rivulet that disappeared into the ground at the foot of the hill. Someone had dug the spring out and lined the hole with rocks, to make it more easily used. Baver was checking his wristwatch for the Earth date, when a thought occurred to him. Digging through his saddlebag, he took out a sheet of folded plastic.

On it, the previous winter he'd drawn the Neoviking calendar,* as used in their old homeland by the northern clans. It was a lunar calendar, and he'd charted it against the ancient solar calendar, the Gregorian.

Getting to his feet, he took it to the big Northman. "Nils," he said, "I've wondered about something." He showed him the chart. "You measure time by moons. Here's the Moon of Iron Cold, supposedly beginning right after the shortest day, when they start getting longer. But the year measured that way is about five days

---

*For a Neoviking calendar, see the appendix.

longer than the solar year, the year by the sun. After twenty years the Moon of Iron Cold would come in spring. How do you get around that?"

Nils grinned. "Simply. Each clan has a post in an open place, or did in the homeland, and a stake to mark the longest noon shadow. The Moon of Iron Cold begins with the next quarter after the shadow is longest, whether that quarter is the full moon or the night of no moon, or the half moon with its back to the . . ."

"Nils!" It was Mager Hans. He stood on his horse's back some fifty meters uphill, pointing toward the lowering sun. "Someone is coming! A man with three horses!"

Nils stood as if peering westward with his strange glass eyes, Baver beside him. A man approached on horseback, followed by a packhorse and a remount. He didn't slow as he came near; the road would take him well clear of them. On an impulse, Baver took out his recorder and began to record.

When the man was about eighty meters away, Nils raised his right hand in a sort of salute. The rider returned it, riding on to the rivulet, where he and his horses drank. When they'd done drinking, the man walked to the little camp, leading his horses, his right hand raised again.

"Friend!" he said. In Anglic, as if taking them for Europeans.

"Friend," Nils answered.

Baver said nothing, simply looked, thumbing off the video switch on his recorder, letting it hang from his neck like a large amulet, to function unobtrusively on audio only. The man frightened him, looked tough and lethal, and the ethnologist didn't want to offend him. About Baver's height—175 cm—he was barrel-chested and thick shouldered, his legs short for his height, and notably bowed. His head was large, and his face broad and flat. A raised scar crossed one side, while on the other an ear was partly missing. His wide-set eyes were lustrous black, and peered through slits that slanted up and out. The skin on face and hands looked thick and leathery. Baver guessed his weight at near a hard hundred kilos.

The horse barbarian looked only briefly at Baver, despite the jump suit. His primary attention was on Nils, whom he examined for long seconds. When at last he spoke, his Anglic was accented like an Orcs. "I've seen you before," he said, "but not close up. Have your eyes always been like that?"

Nils smiled. "That was two summers ago. My eyes were different then."

Baver giggled, an act that surprised and dismayed him, and he covered it awkwardly with a cough. He'd had the briefest vision of Nils taking his glass eyes from his head and presenting them to their visitor. The man scowled at him for a moment, then spoke to Nils again.

"I give you power over me: my name is Achikh, son of Korchi, of Bilgä's clan, of the Black Stallions. My people are the Buriat."

"I give back the power, with more. I am Nils, called Ironhand, Hammar's son, of the Wolf Clan. My tribe is the Svear, my people the Northmen. I hope you make camp with us."

"And I," said Hans, "am Hans the Slim, Gunnar's son, of the Wolf Clan of the Svear."

Their eyes turned to Baver then, and with a start he realized he was expected to follow suit. "I'm, umm, Ted, uh, the ethnologist, son of Carlos, of, uh, the Starship *Phaeacia*, of the planet New Home."

Achikh, son of Korchi, stared at Baver, who realized he couldn't read the man's face at all. It turned away then, releasing him, paused at Hans and stopped at Nils. "I thank you," he said, then turned and led his animals a short distance off. Within a few minutes he'd set up a sizeable shelter tent, large enough for the man, his gear, and a small cooking fire. He worked swiftly, pegging and lashing things securely. When he'd finished, he came over to Nils and his party.

"Will you sleep in the open?" he asked.

Nils nodded, a slight smile on his lips. "It will not rain tonight."

Achikh gestured toward the east. "There will be a moon later."

"The moon does not affect our peoples."

The man shrugged. Meanwhile Hans had cut some low, brittle shrubs and started a fire. "Where are you traveling to?" Nils asked.

"Home."

"Is that far?"

"It is unlikely I can get there before winter. Where are you going?"

"Toward the rising sun."

The scarred face grinned, surprising Baver. "How will you know you've arrived?"

Nils laughed. "When I find something interesting enough to stop for."

They talked for hours. Achikh had left home nine summers earlier, one of a band of nearly sixty youths driven by a hunger for sights and adventures. They'd wandered mostly westward, fighting occasionally, finally allying themselves with a vagrant band of Turks—Kazakhs, actually—youths adventuring as they were, and learned something of their language. The Kazakhs had heard of a great ruler called Kazi the Undying, who hired horsemen like themselves. Deciding to look into it, they'd continued west together to find him.

In the army of Kazi was a band of warriors mostly of the Kalmul people, whose language and customs were close to Achikh's. The orcs joined the two bands into a short century.

Achikh had a knack for language—he'd learned more Turkic than any other man in his band—and rapidly grew conversant in Anglic, the language of the Orcs and command. For that reason he became "the speaker"—the interpreter and liaison for his century, which was part of a cohort of horse barbarians, the rest of which were Turkic.

He'd been in the crowd in the arena when the captive

Nils had been sent in to fight first a lion, and then, unarmed, an Orc swordsman.

"I still don't understand what happened," Achikh said. "You killed the Orc, and the next thing I knew, I woke up with a headache. All around me, men lay unconscious or stunned, or like myself, newly wakened and confused. And you were gone."

He paused as if giving Nils a chance to explain, but the Northman only nodded. Achikh continued. Then, he said, Kazi had sent his army to conquer Europe. In a northern country with forest, marsh, and prairie inter-mixed, they'd met the Neovikings. His centurion had been killed, and he himself had taken command. Then the Orcs had turned back; the rumor was that Kazi was no longer the Undying, that he'd been killed.

"Killed by you," Achikh added, his eyes fixed on Nils. "That's what was said."

Though the Orcs withdrew then, the horse barbarians didn't. Most of them rampaged westward into a country of forests, cultivated land, walled towns and stone castles, a country where the people spoke an unfamiliar tongue, though most could speak Anglic, more or less.

Baver listened, enthralled. The man was a marvelous storyteller, the better for his accent. His cohort had left that country behind, entering one with a different-sounding tongue, and been part of a great and terrible battle by a river. When it was over, the horse barbarians had been defeated, scattered.

He'd led his own century, what was left of it, still westward, no longer an army but a plague of raiders, living off the land, living for the fights they found and the women they captured. At length, in a country of low mountains and heavy forests, his century, numbering less than thirty warriors by then, had been ambushed on a forest road by a force of knights and bowmen. They'd been backed against a mountain river, and Achikh had jumped in, to strip off harness and hauberk while the current had swept him along the bottom. When at last he'd surfaced, gasping, a score of arrows had flown at him. Quickly he'd dived, still desperate for air, and every time he'd surfaced to gulp a breath, there'd been arrows. It was, he said, the most difficult thing he'd ever done, diving back under three times, four, while his lungs shrieked for air. He still dreamed of it now and then. Finally, half blacked out, he'd reached swifter water and been carried away out of sight.

That was as far as Achikh told it, that night, for he realized the moon was rising. For a moment he looked at it, sitting yellow on the rim of a rise to eastward. "I will sleep now," he said, and trotted off to his tent.

Baver didn't often initiate a conversation with Nils anymore, while to Hans he spoke mainly in the context of Anglic lessons. He rarely had anything to say once he crawled into his sleeping bag. Often, as he waited for sleep, he'd lie staring at the stars or moon, scarcely thinking, until he drifted off. Or at the dying coals, if it was cloudy. And on those nights, it seemed he slept the best, commonly with dreams that, while usually unremembered, left an impression of having been pleasant or at least innocuous. Since he'd become aware of this, he'd made a practice of watching the stars or coals. Occasionally, though, he'd fantasize rescue or women till sleep came.

Sometimes he listened in on short conversations between Nils and Hans, invariably started by Hans. Some of these, now, were partly in Anglic, as Hans learned more of it.

On the evening of Achikh's arrival though, after the newcomer had gone to his tent, and Nils and Hans had lain down in their sleeping robes, Baver turned his face toward Nils.

"Why did Achikh say that about the moon?" he asked.

The Northman, who lay on his back, face up, didn't turn.

"His people believe that moonlight will give evil spirits power over them. They avoid it when they can; especially they avoid sleeping in it."

"What utter nonsense!" The words were out before Baver could stop them. They were a major professional malfeasance: he was not to correct or disagree, or evaluate aloud in any way. He was only to collect, record. *Well*, he thought, *it's too late now. And anyway it's the Northmen I'm studying, not Achikh's people.* But still he was uncomfortable over having said it. "Do—" he began tentatively, "do your people believe in evil spirits?"

"No. My people do not."

Baver felt relief; he had not offended. "How do you suppose such beliefs get started?"

"Because evil spirits do sometimes trouble people's thoughts and dreams," Nils replied. Then after a moment he added: "But my people aren't aware of this. To them, dreams are dreams, though some may be prophetic."

Baver stared at him in the darkness. Nils went on: "Evil spirits don't have power of their own, as his people think. They have only the power that people give them. My people, not knowing of evil spirits, give them none. Achikh's people, knowing of them and believing them dangerous, sometimes find they are.

"In the war, Achikh rode beneath the moon more than once, and sometimes slept beneath it. Nothing bad having happened, his belief has weakened, but he prefers not to take the risk."

Remarkable, Baver thought, and wondered how Nils came to believe in evil spirits when his people didn't. "Before Achikh gave you his name, he said he was giving you power over him. What did he mean by that?"

"His people believe that if a shaman, or someone with the powers of a shaman, knows your name, especially your full name, they can work spells on you. So they're careful about giving their name to strangers."

"And can they? Work spells?"

"They can cast a spell. So far as I know, it's the victim though, not the shaman, that makes the spell work."

"You said you gave him back the power with more. What did that mean?"

"I gave him my cognomen, Ironhand. The cognomen

is thought to contain something of the person's soul; holding it is supposed to give the shaman particular power over you."

Baver lay a long minute examining what Nils had said. "Have you been around Achikh's people much before?" he asked. "You know so much about them."

"Only this evening, with Achikh. When he speaks, it opens his mind to me, or those parts of it which lie beneath his words."

The answer sent a wave of chills over Baver. *Telepathy again!* He still doubted, but suddenly he was uncomfortable being there with Nils.

In the morning, Achikh squatted down with them, to breakfast on marmot and talk with Nils. When they'd finished, an agreement had been made. They'd travel together until such time as one or the other chose to separate.

TEN

Actually, invisible attributes, Achikh was no more dangerous-seeming than a Neoviking warrior; less than the giant Nils Järnhann. But it took more than a week for Baver to feel reasonably comfortable around him. It was partly the thick dark leathery skin, and partly the prominent facial scar. And partly the rolling, bowlegged walk, when he was out of the saddle. But perhaps more than all of those and subsuming them, Achikh was *different*.

When they first traveled together, Baver had hopes that Achikh would leave them. Having a remount, the horse barbarian rode almost continuously; surely he could travel faster on his own. But he stayed with them, seemingly glad of Nils's company.

The thin short grass of the country they were in now was easier for the horses to walk through. Thus Baver, without asking, had skipped some of the running breaks for a week before Achikh had joined them. He was worried about wearing out his boots. Nils had accepted this without reaction, as if he didn't notice. Hans, on the other hand, continued to run when Nils did, though his weight was much less a burden for his horse.

Nils at once undertook to learn Achikh's language, and within a week was speaking quite a lot of it. Hans too made rapid progress: It was as if his tongue was designed for wrapping around foreign sounds. And then there was the boy's memory, and the oral tradition of the Neovikings; he'd been conditioned from childhood to store and collate spoken words—poems—and recite them accurately.

Meanwhile, lessons in Anglic had ended; where they were going, it would likely be unknown.

After a few days, Baver too undertook to learn Achikh's language. It gave him something to do in the hours on horseback. He had no particular talent for languages. He'd learned the Neoviking tongue aboard the *Phaeacia*, with the language tutor strapped to his head, absorbing and drilling the vocabulary and grammar inputs that Nikko had provided. To learn a language in this stupid way was slow and exasperating for him.

But he learned, refusing to seem stupid to the others. Besides, as they learned more, they used it more. In time, it seemed to him, all they'd be speaking was Mongol, and he'd be left out if he failed to learn it.

Marmot and an occasional small bird, poorly cooked over an open fire, continued to pall on him. Achikh's packhorse was a lactating mare, so at first they had a bit of mare's milk to supplement the marmot. Both sour and very rich, it didn't sit well on Baver's stomach. The mare soon dried up though.

Now and again they met travelers, or saw someone tending cattle. Achikh's modest Turkic was a different dialect, but it served to dicker for a bag of *airag*—fermented mare's milk—or curds. His exchange was silver coins, split as necessary for change, the last of his European loot. Baver wondered if they ate vegetables or fruit at all in this dry and treeless land.

Once they stopped at a cluster of large round tents made of what seemed to be compacted hair, and whitewashed to reflect the heat. Achikh called them *ger*; Baver had no idea what the occupants called them. Achikh's pack mare was a powerful animal much larger than the local ponies, and ready to be bred. He traded it for a lactating mare, which gave them their own source of *airag*, and her foal, which they could trade elsewhere. Afterward they were invited to eat, and ate all they could hold; it seemed they were expected to. Baver drank more than he could handle, vomiting till he thought his eyes would fall out. The next day was beastly for him.

Another time they encountered a band of armed and mounted men—everyone was armed and mounted in this country—who demanded their horses. Achikh was prepared to fight, but Nils, open hands spread before his shoulders, rode up to their leader till they were thigh to thigh, then grabbed him suddenly by the right arm with one large hand. The man was not too dark to pale, nor too tough to grimace with pain. At the same moment, Nils drew the man's sword with his other hand and held it to the owner's belly.

Achikh spoke sternly and at length to them—told them the giant was a great shaman sent by God. Then Nils let go the leader, and reaching to his own face, removed his eyes, holding them out to the man. The brigand stared, first at the emptied sockets that seemed to look at him, then at the glass eyes, and backed off with a cry as if they were scorpions. Quickly he wheeled his horse, yammering loud, high-pitched commands, and the whole band galloped off.

Nils still held the man's sword. Smiling, he reseated his eyes, dismounted, and stuck the sword in the ground. Achikh, staring, hadn't yet moved. He had nothing to say for quite awhile, but when at last he spoke, it was as if nothing had happened.

Baver suspected the story would survive forever among the local tribesmen.

ELEVEN

The weather, already hot and parched, grew hotter. Some waterholes were dry, and water became a problem. When they went afoot to rest the horses, they walked instead of running, that they wouldn't sweat as much, and this slowed them. Achikh suggested they steal some horses so that everyone would have a remount, but Nils declined. They were making decent progress, and if they stole horses, they could easily pay with their lives.

For several days they saw not even a cloud. Then one morning they did see clouds, a few, and the air felt less dry then it had. Ahead of them a rain cloud began to form and build with remarkable speed. After a little they stopped on a hilltop, sitting their horses almost knee to knee to watch it. In the eerie speed of its development, it reminded Baver of time-lapse photography he'd seen in college, of the birth and growth of a thunderhead. His scalp crawled watching it.

Before long it was complete, with an anvil top beginning to form in the stratospheric wind. It was closer now, and black rain curtains joined it to the ground.

"A spirit cloud," Achikh muttered in his own language. "We'd better get off this hill."

Baver caught all of what he said, word and meaning; he was doing better. They rode down into a broad basin, each of them keeping an eye on the approaching storm. At the bottom they hobbled their horses, then Achikh picketed his as well, warning the others to do the same. *He must expect the storm to frighten them*, Baver thought. Even a hobbled horse, he'd discovered, can make itself hard to catch.

They staked them well apart, so a single lightning strike wouldn't kill more than one. Then the horses secured, they stood watching the storm approach. Lightning darted from its skirts; more was no doubt hidden by the rain curtain. Baver glanced at Achikh. The horse barbarian had donned his long leather raincape, his face looking conspicuously unhappy. The others donned theirs too, and Baver put his poncho on. The storm was near enough now that they heard its thunders muttering. Then, as it moved toward them, its top cut off the sun, and the muttering became rumbling, then a constant rolling boom that grew louder. Achikh threw himself on the ground and covered his head with his cape. A wall of rain raced toward them. Cold wind struck. Dust blew, and sand. Random raindrops spattered, large and cold, and bangs punctuated the booming.

BLAM! BLAM! BLAM!!! Baver too pulled his head inside his poncho, and flattened himself. He'd been in thunderstorms before, but somehow this felt different. The raindrops quickened, thickened, splatting the poncho he hid beneath. A thunderclap slammed so near, his heart nearly stopped. Then, through the booming and banging, he heard a sound like all the horses in the universe stampeding, and peeked out in alarm from beneath his poncho.

Hans was also on the ground; Baver found that somehow reassuring. Nils sat on his heels watching, and that was reassuring too. Then he looked where Nils looked, saw what made the noise, and his reassurance fled. Crossing the steppe was a wall of hail, less than a kilometer away and rushing toward them, preceded by bouncing white hailstones that, to be individually visible at that distance, had to be bigger than the Northman's fists. They were the million hooves! Now the sound changed to a loud and swelling growl. Baver's poncho threatened to whip free of his hands. He gripped it more tightly and hid his face again.

The growl became a grinding deafening roar that seemed to overwhelm even the thunder. The wind became a gale, and the rain a furious beating. Baver saw no way they could survive the bombardment that charged down on them, but held tight to his poncho nonetheless. The grinding roar went on, and on . . . and after a long minute he peered out again.

The hail was passing them to one side. Struck dumb, he watched it, the edge no more than sixty meters off. Nils still squatted; if he was watching in his uncanny, eyeless way, he did not trouble facing it. After more long minutes the hail was past, its roar changing back to a growl, the growl diminishing. The wind still swirled, the rain still slashed. Icy water soaked Baver's exposed legs; though they were on a mild slope, he lay in an unending shallow flow of it, for the ground couldn't soak it up fast enough.

Soon the downpour slacked too, became merely a hard rain that continued. At length Baver sat up, and Hans. They could get no wetter. Only Achikh still lay prostrate; he stayed on the ground till the rain was only sprinkles and the thunder distant rumbling.

In front of them lay a belt of white that might have been a kilometer wide, extending over the rise two or three kilometers ahead. Four hundred meters in front of them it bent, curving northward just enough to miss them. As Baver stared, the sunlight broke through onto the opposite slope and swept their way, bathing them with light. The broad river of hailstones gleamed in the brightness and began to steam.

Baver walked to it. Ice lay more than knee deep, though less at the edge, the irregular stones indeed as big as Nils's fists, but some were frozen together into lumpy masses three times as large. He stopped several paces off, feeling the cold from the mass of ice before him.

And turned away, chilled by more than hailstones.

Six of the seven horses had pulled their picket pins. The seventh and the foal lay killed by lightning. Three of the six had disappeared. All that Baver could think was that they'd panicked and fled, running with their slow, awkward, hobbled gate into the path of the storm; they'd be somewhere under the ice, hammered to death. *Trampled* to death.

He stared at Nils. The Northman had done it, he had no doubt, had somehow diverted the overwhelming assault of hailstones, and saved their lives.

A drying fire was out of the question; all potential fuel was soaked. But the sun was intense, though the air was cool, and by the time they'd gathered the surviving horses, the clothes were drying on their backs. Of the three horses left to them, two were the packhorses. Achikh's they left as a packhorse; Nils's would have to be ridden, bareback. Nils abandoned his helmet and heavy hauberk, and they transferred the rest of its burden to Achikh's horse.

They set off then, Hans and Nils afoot, leading off at an easy lope. They headed more or less eastward, bypassing the wide swath of ice, and atop the next rise stopped again. There they took advantage of some low shrubs to spread their cloaks and sleeping robes, and Baver's light bag. Then, while these steamed in the sun, the travelers ate strips from one of yesterday's marmots, dried the night before above the fire.

"What did you do back there?" Baver asked. "To make the hailstorm turn." And felt foolish before he'd finished. When put into words, the question seemed absurd.

Nils's glass eyes seemed to fix the ethnologist. "There was a being in the storm, as Achikh said. I could feel it there. It had been formed from—" He groped. "From spirit stuff, the spirit stuff of storms, and commanded to find us. To hunt us down and kill us."

Baver stared alarmed that Nils had said such a patently foolish thing. He missed entirely that it was no more outrageous than his question.

Nils went on. "But such a being, if it has enough intelligence to hunt and find, need not do as commanded. Thus I met him within the cloud. We mingled in the spirit, and he swerved, sparing us."

"You told the hail to miss us and it did?" Baver couldn't keep the disbelief from his voice.

"I told it nothing. To mingle in the spirit creates a— together-feeling that is stronger than commands. If it had refused, or if it hadn't been strong-willed enough to reject the command its shaper had given it . . . But we were fortunate; we live."

Nils turned his face away then, and bit off another mouthful of dried marmot.

When they'd eaten, they sat around on their haunches, letting their things dry further. Meanwhile Nils's statement stayed on Baver's mind. That and his own question; he could hardly believe he'd asked it.

Storms, he rationalized, *are unpredictable. It could have changed course for probably several reasons. Being in shock, I couldn't think clearly: I asked what I did only by default. But Nils . . . He made claims!*

If he believes what he said, he's not entirely sane. I've never heard any of his people mention spirits or "spirit stuff"—the spirit stuff of storms!—so the belief can't be cultural. It's idiosyncratic with him. Or was he lying to me, seeing if I'd believe?

He didn't know which possibility was the most unsettling.

They'd made good progress since the storm, considering they'd taken time to spread things to dry at every break. They'd traveled till after sundown.

Hans lay on his back, staring at the stars. At an intellectual level he knew that the star man, Baver, had come from one of them, but at an emotional level it was hard to accept. Star Folk should be—wonderful: wise, handsome, fearless, in all ways impressive. Baver couldn't even start a fire, not even with dry weeds, and hadn't tried to learn. He let others do for him.

Actually none of the star folk had impressed him. The things they *had* impressed him, but not the people. But the others, Matts and Nikko, were at least not foolish and bumbling. He supposed they were able enough at Star Folk things.

His sharp young ears listened now for breathing. Only Nils was near enough, less than an armspan away.

"Nils!" he whispered.

"Ja-ha?"

Hans spoke in their own language. "You said the storm-being was formed from spirit stuff. And commanded. Who formed and commanded it?"

Nils's chuckle was hardly a breath. "I met them once, at the end of spring. They were looking at me through a— The spirit world is beside ours but separate. These others are in our world, far east of here. That much I am sure of. They know how to look through the spirit world to see places where they are not. Though perhaps not clearly, and seemingly without knowing where they look. That's as much as I know of them. It is they I go to find."

Hans shivered in his robe. "Sending the storm as they did, they are not friendly."

"True."

"Do they know where we are right now?" Hans was thinking that something else might come upon them while they slept.

"It seems improbable. The storm-being had been searching for days."

"Why do you go to find them?"

"I'll know when I get there."

"Will you fight them?"

"Perhaps."

"Then I will fight them with you!"

"I'll be glad to have you with me."

"Do you suppose Achikh will fight too? He does well

at drill. I can think of warriors who'd be hard pressed to beat him."

"I agree. And if he is still with us, he might."

Hans said nothing more for a minute or longer. Then: "What do you think about before you fall asleep?"

"Often I fall asleep at once. Other times I lie still and leave."

"Leave?" Hans felt alarm at that.

"My body is still here, but I leave. I cease to be in this world. I enter another."

There was another minute's lapse. "What is it like?"

"It is very peaceful. Now, though, I am simply going to sleep. You may wish to also."

Baver lay listening, but the two Neovikings said no more. *Leave! Enter another world!* And they were going to find the one—the someones—whom Nils imagined sent the storm! Nils was crazy!

But despite himself, Baver half believed, and was afraid. For his sanity if nothing else.

TWELVE

"My dear Songtsan, intriguing and conspiring to rule the Mongols is a waste of time. I have the procedure for you: Allow me to take a hundred thousand soldiers to the frontier, sixty thousand of them cavalry, and invade. Crush all resistance, then *conscript* as many as you want of the survivors."

The general who spoke was as tall as the emperor, who himself was tall. He was also thirty kilos heavier. His silk robe, which nearly reached his knees, was indigo, the color reserved for the royal family, and heavily brocaded with the figures of men fighting. A scarlet sash gathered it about his thick waist, and held a curved sword with a blade nearly a meter long. Beneath the robe's hem, yellow silk pantaloons were bloused into knee-length boots, their toes upcurved strongly, their glossy, golden brown leather inset with lacquered images of wildlife: pheasants, deer, a tiger . . . His horned helmet was hammered steel concealed beneath gold plate; its rim coiled silk, scarlet and indigo. Its sky-blue silk skirt, which protected his bull neck from the sun, was embroidered with tiny eagles and falcons; vines and flowers added color.

Emperor Songtsan Gampo would have had any other man executed for telling him that one of his projects was a waste of time. But this was his favorite younger brother and best general, so he merely shook his head and answered drily. "There is a time to cultivate a people and a time to break them, a time for allies and a time for slaves." He shifted slightly in his seat. "We have a whole world to conquer; fighting enough even for you. And the Mongols are attainable as allies; valuable allies. They will be the razor-sharp head of my spear, to gut resistance. Men who grew up in the saddle, with the bow, make better cavalry than men who did not. Men who spend their lives on the move, who live on horseback, often on what they can kill, and on milk from their mares—such men do not tire and do not frighten."

He changed direction then, his voice comfortable, smooth as silk. "The Koreans are excellent fighting men, yes? How many of them volunteered to serve with us, after you'd broken their army?"

The answer was sullen but honest. "None. Oh, a hundred, maybe two, but not good men."

"And how many soldiers did you find it necessary to post there to control the country?"

"Sixty thousand."

"And mostly cavalry."

"It was necessary! Otherwise we'd have needed four times as many garrisons—at least twice as many men— and even those could not control the roads as we do now."

The emperor eyes gleamed like black marbles beneath hooding lids. "So we have a conquest which bleeds us," he said.

Drukpa sounded aggrieved now. "But Korea and Mongolia are not the same! Korea's mountains are thick with forests perfect for rebels and bandits! And it was necessary to be harsh in victory, to break their will!"

"It didn't work. It didn't break their will."

His general said nothing to that.

"Well. You are my brother. You conquered Korea on

my orders, and did what seemed necessary at the time. And you are right; Korea and Mongolia are very different. Mongolia is mostly open to the sun, and to our eyes. And their people are indeed different. The Koreans are stiff-necked, unyielding, and they were united, more or less, behind their king. The Mongols, on the other hand, are more practical and relatively reasonable. And they are fragmented into various tribes that sometimes fight against each other and seldom agree on anything of consequence.

"Had you been less harsh, the Koreans might well have been no less intransigent than they are, and even more difficult. But the Mongols are susceptible to manipulation, and I want at least fifty thousand of them in my army when I send it westward to conquer the world. That will be far better than leaving sixty thousand of my own cavalry, or a hundred thousand, as a garrison in their country. I have chosen one of their chiefs to be supreme, and I will guide him to domination. Then I will honor him, perhaps marry his favorite daughter, and bring his sons here as 'my proteges'—my hostages. And . . ."

He stopped, for in the corridor outside his door, a silver gong had been lightly tapped. "Enter!" he said.

A runner entered and bowed. "Your Magnificence, Tenzin Geshe is waiting, with information for you."

"I will—see him now. Send him in."

The emperor turned to his brother. "I don't expect this to take long. Our meetings seldom do."

A moment later the *geshe* entered the chamber and bowed deeply. "Your Magnificence."

"What do you have for me, *geshe*?"

"It has to do with the barbarian the Circle detected in the west, the man who subsequently began to travel eastward in our direction."

"And?"

Tenzin Geshe opened his mind to Songtsan Gampo. The emperor's lips thinned.

"You failed."

"Indeed, Your Magnificence. At least the ones I sent

have failed. I did not send a demon; they are too limited and unreliable, and I have no leverage over them. Instead I gathered, created, three storm elementals, and sent one to cover each of the travel routes, to watch for the man and kill him. One of them is lost, it disassembled; one is still where I sent him; and the other has returned.

Songtsan Gampo frowned impatiently. "So? What went wrong?"

The *geshe*'s mind replayed in detail the encounter of the storm elemental with the travelers on the steppe, as he'd read it from the elemental's time track.

The emperor pursed his lips, scowling. "And it could not resist the man? Then how is an elemental superior to a demon for our purpose?"

The *geshe* bowed more deeply still. "Your Magnificence, much that is told of demons is untrue. A demon has no power except over the victim's mind. True that is enough, in some cases, to wreak havoc, but not with this man. An elemental, on the other hand, has power over physical substances—storm, earthquake, volcano. And storms can move about, strike almost anywhere, while an earthquake or volcano is restricted. But this man has greater calm, greater strength of serenity, than we had realized; than we could have imagined. He sat facing violence and death, and ... We have seen what happened."

The emperor frowned thoughtfully. He was almost invariably intolerant of failure, and even more of "reasons" for failure, but he knew from his own limited dabblings that wizardry could be most difficult to work. And this *geshe* was not only exceptionally gifted; the man was a continuous education to him. "How does an elemental have power over substance while a demon does not?" he asked. "Enlighten me."

"Your Magnificence, a demon was once a man, who visited such evils on other men that he cannot confront returning in another incarnation to balance the kharmic equation. The enormity of his debt overwhelms him, rendering him more or less demented! He dwells in the lowest level of the astral plane, a level of guilt and continuous distress, and cannot éscape to a higher level until he has willingly reincarnated and balanced his equation."

In his single-mindedness, the emperor missed the lesson implicit in the *geshe's* explanation. Instead he took over the explanation at that point. "And the wizard gives him form," he said, "that he may move abroad within the material plane."

"The wizard helps him give himself form, Your Magnificence, from spirit stuff. Provides guidance, and a certain necessary focus that he cannot provide himself. Once he has it, he may or may not be grateful, and loyal to a point. And usually he cannot long retain that substance he has taken, which alone keeps him in the material plane."

"Umm. And elementals?"

"The air, the earth, the sea—all have energies of their own. Great energies, including a diffuse, low-grade intelligence of a sort. And they are already in the material plane. I, with the energy of the Circle, gather—gather and *mold*—a quantity of that energy; a large quantity. The result is a powerful entity with its own limited intelligence, an entity which perceives, and which directs itself according to its maker's command. And unlike a demon, when it disperses, it no longer exists, except as the diffuse energy from which it was formed."

"Um. And subject to its maker's command, you say. But not this time, it seems. It met a new commander."

"Not exactly, Your Magnificence. The man did not command it. He simply established an affinity with it. After which it could not bring itself to destroy him."

"The difference has no practical significance."

Another bow, very deep this time.

"And this is what you came to tell me?"

"In part, Your Magnificence. In addition, since that encounter, the Circle has not been able to locate the man at all, even to sense his continued existence."

"And you are concerned by this?"

"Indeed, Your Magnificence. I have little doubt he still plans to come here."

Smiling, the emperor turned to his brother. "How many of your soldiers, Drukpa, would it require to kill one barbarian wizard?"

The general snorted. "One. Oh, perhaps as many as four or five ordinary soldiers, if the wizard happened also to be a great fighting man." Raising an arm, he caused its sleeve to slide to the elbow, and flexed a remarkably large and powerful forearm. "A warrior like myself could handle any wizard," he added. "I am not susceptible to their tricks and illusions."

The emperor turned back to the *geshe*. "There! You see? And imagine what one of my yeti guards would do to him! We will not worry further about this shaman you speak of. But I am interested in him now; I would like to study him." He cocked an eyebrow. "I have heard of a spirit, a demon if you will, being called up and caused to clothe itself within an animal, a bird or other creature. What do you say to that?"

Tenzin answered carefully. "I have heard of it, Your Magnificence, but from no one who knows how."

The emperor's face tightened. "Find out!" he snapped. As if at the end of his patience with this difficult *geshe*. "Find out how to do it, and see it done! Put one into an eagle and send it forth to find this man and follow him. And keep me informed as to the man's location and activities."

A final deep bow. "As Your Magnificence orders."

Tenzin Geshe maintained the obeisance until the emperor dismissed him, which, given the emperor's frame of mind, took a long half minute. Then he turned and left.

"Does the *geshe* have cause to worry about this wizard?" Drukpa asked.

"It's very doubtful. My good *geshe* is perhaps the most potent adept in the empire, aside from Jampa Lodro, who is old and very holy. But Tenzin is one-sided. He overlooks the physical factor."

"What was he thinking when he left?"

"He wasn't. He was carefully avoiding thought."

"And yet you trust him?"

"I will know at once if he ceases to be loyal. I do not need to read his thoughts to know that. Only his aura."

"But he withholds his mind from you!"

The elder brother's gaze, suddenly cool, found the younger's, and Drukpa lowered his to his knees. "There is a level," the emperor answered, "at which you must allow a man that, or you destroy his usefulness. Remember that, brother. And I know of no one else who can do for me what Tenzin does." *Except,* he added to himself, *old Jampa, who refused, and is too holy to punish. And perhaps*—the thought took him by surprise—*perhaps the man he seeks for me. Might I be able to attach the barbarian's loyalty? . . . Could that be why he comes here? To serve me?* The notion sparked a cautious excitement in Songtsan Gampo.

Tenzin kept his mind essentially still until he'd distanced himself enough that he could think behind a screen without being obvious, should the emperor return his attention to him. He strode out of the Inner Garden almost without noticing the great ogre, the "yeti," guarding the gate in the privacy wall. The ogre stood 225 centimeters tall and weighed 200 kilos. Watchful but incurious, its red eyes followed the *geshe* across the palace's outer grounds, which were almost as much a garden as the Inner Garden was.

Tenzin had a problem. For a demon, he had little doubt, could not be effectively housed within an actual, material animal. He knew of several attempts by powerful wizards; all had failed. With focus by someone sufficiently adept, a demon could form for itself an animal *likeness* from spirit stuff, but it was neither very stable nor reliably controllable. Certainly it would not fool the wizard they watched for.

Arriving at the *gomba,* he sat on a bench beneath the thujas, briefly brooding. Then a possible solution occurred to him, one that quickened his pulse, though there might be difficulties in carrying it through. For each species of plant and animal there was a pool of species beingness, of a higher order than the beingness of storms. A mind/spirit beingness far more difficult to manipulate, but with more potential. *With the Circle to work with, it may be possible to gather an elemental from the pool of some species—some species which forms packs or flocks . . . And if I could then implant that concentrated beingness into one physical individual . . .* It would be an animal elemental incarnate, more intelligent than a storm could possibly be.

It should probably be a bird, he decided, for the mobility needed, but an eagle wouldn't do. They were too solitary; their largest association was the mated pair. They gathered at carrion, on occasion, but such behavior was opportunistic and accidental, not social; they seemed to do nothing in concert except tend their nest. Then there was the question of how much intelligence one bird could house without burning out. It seemed to him it should be something fairly large, with considerable individual intelligence. Wolves were supposedly intelligent, and great wanderers, he'd heard. Might they be suitable? Perhaps the wizard and his companions would shoot a wolf out of hand though.

He would sleep on the matter tonight. Tomorrow he and the Circle could begin exploratory work on it.

THIRTEEN

For more than three weeks, Nils, Hans, Baver, and Achikh continued with only two mounts and a packhorse. Thus on the trail, at least two of them were on foot at any given time. Achikh never walked except to rest his horse, which meant that the other three shared one, only one of them riding at a time. And because it too needed rest, every fourth turn the horses were led; then all of them walked. Baver wore a wristwatch, and when he explained it to the others, and volunteered to time the shifts, they accepted. He gave each shift twenty minutes, and was scrupulous about not shorting his own turns at walking.

Nils and Hans trotted when it was their turn to be afoot together, and for the first week after the storm, Baver trotted the shifts when he was afoot with Nils. He was in far the best condition of his life, and pleased at it. But his boots were showing serious wear, and fearful of being barefoot for thousands of kilometers, he ceased to trot, to reduce the stress on them.

Hans had been barefoot the whole trip without ill effects. Nils had begun with the moccasin-like boots the

Northmen sometimes wore, a well-worn pair, and when they'd come apart, he too had gone barefoot with no ill effects. But Baver was convinced that if *he* went barefoot, he'd end up crippled.

Achikh occasionally felt some discomfort at riding while his trail companions walked or ran, but he couldn't bring himself to give up his own mount. He was a Buriat, and this meant always to ride. Except in dire need, to walk demeaned him in his own eyes; he was unhappy simply to have no remount, which necessitated walking every fourth shift to rest his horse. On the other hand, the others were not truly horsemen. They were foot-goers who rode when chance provided.

Thus he explained it to himself, and thus Nils explained it in Scandinavian to the resentful Baver.

Meanwhile their lessons in Mongol suffered, for when two ran or walked and the other two rode, instruction was difficult. They worked at it mainly between the evening meal and lying down to sleep, an interval that was sometimes brief. Though when Nils rode, it was almost invariably beside Achikh, practicing.

Almost daily, Achikh suggested or even urged that they steal horses, enough for a mount and remount for each of them, partly because of his discomfort at riding while they walked, and partly because their progress was slower now than he liked. Each time, Nils refused: they didn't need a band of angry herdsmen tracking them, their quivers full of arrows.

Actually, when Nils and Hans were afoot together, they kept up nicely with the trotting horses, which impressed the burly Buriat greatly. But Baver's walking pace, though typically close to six kilometers per hour, slowed them somewhat. And beyond that, the horses were finally showing signs of wear.

This too worried Baver. In fact he had two main fears. One, he feared that Achikh would get frustrated and leave them, leave them with the one horse that wasn't his. And two, he feared that all three of the others would abandon him, simply cease to accommodate his own slow pace, leaving him to keep up or be left behind. Thus after a week without trotting, he tried it again for a few turns, but the condition of his boots alarmed him too much to keep it up.

The road stayed north of the more arid southern steppes, but it was late summer now, and creeks and waterholes were commonly hours apart. Not infrequently they kept going till dusk or even night brought them to water. Or to a dry camp, where they made do overnight with what remained in their waterbags. On one such day, with the setting sun throwing their shadows far ahead of them, they passed at a distance a camp of some four dozen large round tents, and a greater number of small tents equivalent to sheds. According to Achikh, the people around there were Kazakhs, or some people whose Turkic dialect was like Kazakh. Not much farther on, they came to a creek upstream of the Kazakh camp, and stopped to make camp themselves.

While Baver prepared to roast their daily marmot catch (he started fires skillfully now), Nils drilled Hans with the sword, a routine they skipped only occasionally, though sometimes shorted. Meanwhile Achikh rode off to the Kazakh camp, not much more than a kilometer away. He would, he said, try to trade their worn-out horses for fresh, perhaps with an extra thrown in because the Orc horses were much taller and more handsome than the local stock, and fleeter when in good condition.

By twilight he was back. The Kazakhs had refused his offer, he said, refused it rudely. The camp was in the charge of the chief's mother, an ill-tempered, bad-mouthed woman. Most of the Kazakh men were away; only old men and young boys remained there with the women and children. According to the chief's mother, the warriors had left that morning early, to catch and punish a band of thieves who'd stolen a calf. They were expected back the next day.

Achikh didn't believe her. He'd noticed that the horse herd was small for so many *gert*, as if the men had left on some longer, more distant trip with lots of remounts, a trip that might take hard riding. A war or raid, he thought; it was too early in the season for major hunting. Actually, he'd decided, she was wary of possible robbers, and wanted him to think the camp's protectors were close at hand.

He looked hard at Nils. "This is the best chance we'll have to steal horses, and I will get some whether you approve or not. When we are mounted, we can ride by night; by daybreak we'll be far away, and with remounts we won't need to rest the horses longer than it takes them to drink and eat."

Nils regarded him calmly. "The moon will rise not long after midnight," he pointed out.

"I will ride in the moonlight. It doesn't frighten me."

Baver sat tense; this was the point of decision, crucial decision. If Achikh insisted and Nils refused, they'd part. And if they parted, the three of them would be left with just a single horse. The Kazakhs might even take out their anger on them for lack of having Achikh in their grasp!

If Nils agreed, on the other hand, they'd have to ride hard, without sleep, and he didn't know whether he could do that or not. And the Kazakhs might catch them anyway. He couldn't even plead innocent then, mounted on one of the stolen horses.

"What will they do to us if they catch us?" he asked.

Achikh turned and stared, not used to having Baver speak to him except in the context of language lessons, and answered in Anglic. "They are barbarians; they would probably impale us if they caught us. But they won't catch us."

Baver's guts clenched at the word "impale," as if the stake had already entered him. And if *Achikh* considered them barbarians— His head snapped around to look at the northman. "Nils," he began . . .

But the Northman replied to Achikh even as the word left Baver's lips. "You will do what you must, and we will see what happens. If you do not come riding back with a band of horses, I'll see what can be done to rescue you."

At this answer, Achikh stared for a moment, bemused. "Good. Let us eat. Afterward I'll try my luck." He grinned then, the grin startling Baver. "I have always enjoyed horse raids," he said. "They are so dangerous."

It had been dark for more than an hour when Achikh left. Baver watched him disappear into the moonless night. The Buriat had argued that it would go much better, much more surely, if he had help. Hans would liked to have gone, Baver thought, but the boy had said nothing, waiting for Nils's response, and Nils again declined. Baver didn't know whether to be relieved or not.

"What do you think?" he asked when Achikh was out of sight. "Will he get them?"

"I doubt it. I think he'll be caught. I think they expect him to do this, and they'll be ready."

"Why do you think so?"

The northman shrugged. "That's simply how it feels to me. I have no evidence to point at."

"Will they attack us then?"

"Perhaps a few of the older boys may come," Nils replied. "We'll see."

We'll see! Baver collapsed in on himself. The northman had said it as if discussing the possibility of showers. He could imagine a dozen boys, twelve and thirteen years old, coming out on horses with bows and arrows, to surround and skewer them.

He lay down on top of his sleeping bag and closed his eyes. He'd grown used to sleeping among mosquitoes, which at any rate were far fewer here on the dry steppe, and mostly he slept readily when they camped. Tonight, though, he was sure that sleep would be impossible. Still, perhaps if he lay on his back with his eyes open, and focused on a star . . .

He was asleep in minutes.

*   *   *

Achikh had already noted the layout of the Kazakh camp and the location of the horse herd. Earlier it had been more dispersed than he'd cared for, especially for working by himself. Now, by starlight, it seemed more concentrated. It was also closer to camp than he liked. As if wolves had worked here recently: horses will crowd camp at night when wolves are around, for the security it offers.

As he neared, he let his horse move pretty much at its own pace, muttering to it occasionally, tapping its barrel with a hard heel from time to time. Alone he could not simply startle the band and drive them to his own camp; they might go anywhere. He'd have to cut out half a dozen, rope them together and lead them, which meant a relaxed and quiet approach.

In the darkness, he didn't see the Kazakhs who were waiting, lying low on the backs of their horses, till after one of them raised his catching pole and dropped a noose over Achikh's head from behind. Then he yanked it tight around the Buriat's neck and they were on him, two adolescent boys with quick wiry strength, and two older men, no longer quick but strongly muscled. Others had moved up too, arrows nocked, in case Achikh wasn't alone.

Normally he would have fought till dead or unconscious. But Nils had said he'd see what might be done to rescue him, and he remembered what a powerful wizard the giant Northman was. Thus, after his first violent resistance, Achikh went slack and let them tie him.

The halfmoon was well up when Nils shook Baver awake. "Come. Put on your boots. Something has happened to Achikh. We will go to the Kazakh camp and see if we can help him."

Baver struggled out of a dream of captivity, sat up and looked around. *We will go to the Kazakh camp!* Repeating it mentally brought him fully awake. Achikh wasn't with them; his shelter tent hadn't even been set up. And there was more than just moonlight to see by now, he realized. The eastern sky was silvering; in another hour or so the sun would rise. Somehow even a little daylight made the Kazakhs seem less dangerous, less deadly. Though deadly enough.

They remained just long enough to eat some of a marmot that had half dried, half smoked on a rack over last evening's fire. Then they each drank a few swallows of mare's milk, bought a few days earlier, thickening and souring in a sack made of horse gut. Baver washed his down with tepid creek water, and they left on foot, leaving their hobbled horses behind, not even packing their gear.

After walking the better part of a kilometer, they topped a small rise. From it they could see the tents, dismal-looking humps on the steppe, lined up in rows in the half-light. Each, Baver knew, was made of felt mats tied over a bowl-shaped frame of slender poles, like the other semi-permanent camps they'd visited. There was no sign of activity, surely not outdoors, and no smoke visible from the smokeholes in the roofs. Even to Baver that meant the camp slept. *Now*, he thought, *Nils will decide which tent Achikh is held in. We'll go to it, and Nils and Hans will slip inside to free him, maybe kill the Kazakhs there. I'll stand by the door with my pistol, in case anyone comes.* He felt grimly pleased with his analysis, and at the same time surprised at it.

But Nils didn't change to a stealth mode. He led with long strides toward the largest of the tents, then at about thirty meters stopped, and bellowed in Mongol that he wanted to speak with the chief there. Baver was dismayed that the Northman had thrown away their surprise advantage, especially since there was no reason to think that any of the Kazakhs understood Mongol.

Understandable or not, it drew a response, albeit delayed. In less than half a minute, people began emerging from tents, some calling out when they saw the situation. Most wore robes they apparently slept in. Some had belted on weapons. Others carried bows, and a handful or quiverful of arrows. Several came from the largest tent. When fifty or sixty had assembled, Nils strode toward them, Hans beside him and a step back. Willy-nilly, Baver followed. He saw bows half bent in the hands of several women and adolescent boys. The older men held swords, as did a heavy-set woman who stood before the door of the main tent, and toward whom Nils strode. He didn't stop until he stood within four meters of her. Then he spoke again in Mongol: "You have our friend."

Baver's guts had frozen in his belly. There seemed to be nothing but hard hostility among all the Kazakhs he could see there. They were staring at Nils, whom they'd no doubt kill first. The Northman had come shirtless, probably to strengthen the impression he'd hoped to make. The amount of running the giant Neoviking had done lately had refined his powerful musculature to an extreme degree; his muscles were like thick steel cables with the individual wires visible through his skin. Even in the dawnlight he was awesome.

The woman with the sword examined him narrowly, then snapped something in sharp but fluid Turkic, a language Baver found aesthetic in more ordinary circumstances. Several people went into her tent. The rest continued to watch Nils Järnhann, most of them glowering. The Northman stood calm and impassive. If he really could read minds, Baver thought, he'd still have no way of understanding thoughts in Turkic.

In less than a minute, two of the older men came back out, dragging Achikh, who was wearing a wooden yoke perhaps eighty centimeters long, his wrists tied to it with thongs. His ankles were tied too, with cord that might have allowed him little steps of thirty centimeters or so, had the Kazakhs not been dragging him.

The woman snapped angry Turkic at Achikh; he answered in the same language, though haltingly and without anger. Their exchange took the better part of a minute, then Achikh turned his face to Nils and spoke in Anglic.

"She wants to know who you are, and what you want."

"Tell her I am a shaman of the Northmen, and the

man who slew Kazi the Undying. Also tell her I want them to free you, and trade horses with us.

"These people set little store by shamans, and I doubt she knows of Kazi. They are likelier to kill us all than to free me."

"Tell her, and we'll see what happens."

There was another exchange in Turkic, her own growing louder as she talked. Hands tightened on sword hilts. Bows were half raised. Achikh spoke to Nils again.

"She pretends to be unimpressed, but she has heard of Kazi. She will not talk with you unless you all give up your weapons, both swords and knives."

Nils looked mildly at her without touching his weapons. "Ask her if she knows where her fighting men are," he said.

Achikh stared at him for a brief instant, then turned his face to the woman and spoke. Her reply was imperious. "She says they have ridden out to catch and put to death some thieves who stole cattle here."

"Tell her her men are camped beside a stream that flows from some mountains two long days' ride north from here. The mountains are not very high, but high enough that there is forest on their backs. They are there to hunt wolves, and do not expect to return for some days. The chief, Shakir, leads them, her eldest living son. He will want her to trade with us."

He said it in two installments, Achikh interpreting by halves. When he was done, the woman peered long at the Northman without speaking, taking in his size, his obvious great strength, his strange eyes. Finally she spoke briefly, perhaps a dozen words.

"She asks how you can see what you claim to see."

Nils said nothing, simply reached up a hand to his eyes and removed them. He stepped toward her, the glass semi-orbs on one callused and very large palm. She looked at them, then at his face, and her breath hissed out as she backed away. There was scurrying, but no one shot. Over a subdued hubbub of voices, she barked extended orders in Turkic.

"She told them not to harm you," Achikh said. "She told them you are not an ordinary shaman, but a shaman from Allah, which is the name they give to *Tengri*, that is, God."

She spoke again, this time to Achikh, not looking at Nils now. "She asks you to please put your eyes back in your face," Achikh interpreted.

Nils did, and the whole crowd seemed to relax. Once more the woman spoke, looking intently at Nils, no longer hostile.

"She says she will trade horses with us, two of theirs for each of ours. She asks how many we have to trade."

"Tell her we do not wish to take advantage of her generosity, that our people are great runners, and use horses for trade. Tell her it is running that makes us stronger than other people. Nonetheless we will take seven, and leave them the three we came with." While Achikh translated for her, Nils turned to Hans and Baver. "Hans, run to camp and bring the horses. Ted, go and help him."

They turned and loped off. As he reached the top of the rise, Baver glanced back at the Kazakh camp, awed at what had happened. Seemingly Nils had been right about the Kazakh warriors. And about her son's name. How had he known?

The only answer he could think of was that Nils had read it in her mind despite the language difference.

FOURTEEN

They spent the entire day at the Kazakh camp while women tailored boots for each of them, well and closely stitched, handsome and comfortable! The chief's mother was no longer hostile or even suspicious, only displeased that they wouldn't stay long enough for the boots to be properly decorated.

The next morning they left. Now Achikh had a remount again, and the others each a horse. The seventh horse was an additional pack horse which carried gifts, including a *maikhan*—a sizeable leather tent for traveling—and large bags of fermented mare's milk, the now familiar *airag*, which the Kazakhs called *kumyz*. Each of the travelers had also received a heavy, short-handled axe about sixty centimeters long. Baver wondered what use these would be on the steppe, unless— Perhaps they were weapons.

As they rode, Baver asked Nils how he had known what he had about the Kazakh warriors. Nils explained that when asked if she knew where the warriors were, the truth rose to her near-consciousness. Where he perceived it, with pictures and related concepts, although her spoken answer was a lie.

This time Baver believed what he was told.

*   *   *

On the sixth day, while they rested at noon, eight horsemen caught up with them, fierce-looking Kazakhs closing at a gallop, trailing a dust cloud. They were armed of course, with some thirty remounts trailing.

Baver stood watching with serious concern and a hand in his holster pocket as they pulled up in a big cloud of dust. While the dust settled, the leader sat his saddle perhaps four meters away, looking quietly at Nils as if evaluating what he saw. "It is you again," he said at last in groping Anglic. "I thought that, but hard to believe."

"And you. I am glad to see you again, Shakir."

Nils said it slowly, that the Kazakh might more easily understand. The man looked surprised for just a moment, then swung down from his saddle. "You learned my name from my mother," he said.

Nils grinned and nodded.

"You know what I am called. What are you called?"

"I am Nils, Hammar's son."

"Nils." Shakir repeated the name as if to himself. "After you killed the lion, we called your name 'Golden Giant.'" He paused, pursing his lips. "You are different now. Look different." Shakir tapped one of his own eyebrows. "Eyes," he added. "My mother said you took out eyes, held them in hand." He peered into them intently, and found no life there. "What became? They not like that before."

"I was in an Orc prison. An Orc pierced them with his knife tip." He tapped a glass eye with a finger, without flinching. "These were given me in their place. By friends," he added, then indicated Baver. "Some of his people."

It was clear that Shakir wanted to say something to that, but couldn't find Anglic words for it. He turned to Achikh, and in Turkic said, "My mother told me you speak our language. Will you interpret for me? My Anglic is too limited."

Achikh nodded. "I do not always speak your tongue correctly, but maybe well enough."

"Tell the big one, Nils, that I never loved the Orcs. They offered us fighting and looting, and all we wanted to eat, if we joined them. After we joined them, we saw much we thought ill of, but it was not possible to leave then. And there remained the prospect of battles and pillage."

Achikh passed the message on.

"Also tell him that, as for debts, I believe we are even, he and I, since we met in the forest that second time.

When Achikh had repeated this in Anglic, the Kazakh asked, "How old are you, Northman?"

"I am in my twenty-third summer now," Nils said, and signed with his fingers.

"Twenty-three summers! If you say so, I can only believe you. But your soul is old, Northman, old, and purified by fire."

Then he bowed deeply to Nils Järnhann.

The Kazakhs squatted, and ate their noon meal with the travelers. As they ate, Shakir spoke to Nils from time to time, sometimes in Turkic through Achikh, and sometimes in halting Anglic. Gesturing at Baver and speaking in Turkic again, he asked: "Of what people is he who wears trousers that come to his throat? Those who can give eyes to the blind are surely wizards."

When Achikh had translated, Baver blushed.

"He is a star man," Nils answered. "His ancestors were ancients who flew to the stars to live, very long ago."

The Kazakh frowned. "Flew to the stars to live?"

Nils nodded. "They were mighty makers in those days. They made boats that fly endlessly high. They flew out and found a star that is much like the world we live in. They made their home there, and now they have come back to visit. They are peaceful. They do not like to fight, though the Orcs learned that when they must fight, they are dangerous."

The Kazakhs looked carefully at Baver, then Shakir turned back to Nils. "That is a very strange story. It is hard to believe."

Nils nodded. "It is uncanny. But I have been on the

sky ship they came on. I have seen the world many *tusen*
below me. At a glance I have seen from one sea to the
next, and all the lands between. And many others of my
people have seen the star folk come and go in the small
sky boats they use to fly from the ground to their high-
soaring ship."

The Kazakhs sat digesting that for a long minute.
When Shakir spoke again, he changed the subject. "And
the boy," he said, "is he your slave?"

"We Northmen no longer have slaves. He is a poet's
apprentice." (Here Nils had to explain for Achikh, before
the Buriat could interpret.)

"Ah! A poet! Tell the boy I apologize!" Shakir said.
"Boy! Will you speak poetry to me?"

Hans, who'd darkened and scowled at being thought
a slave, lost most of his scowl now, and standing, recited
in his tonal dialect, almost singing the words, his young
baritone rich and firm:

> *"Gryma Kassi, hären brötte,*
> *strävan sönder, dröd i dammen,*
> *stred emot den unga hjälte.*
> *Han vill dråp den som har gjort d'.*
> *Över gräsbevuxne slätten,*
> *halsen vrålande i vreden,*
> *svääden höll i jätte hänner,*
> *anföll han den vjenntne Yngling. . . .*

When the poet's apprentice had finished, all the Kazakhs clapped their hands politely. Hans blushed. Then

---

*Nikko Kumalo's translation runs:
Cruel Kazi, vast host shattered,
dream of conquest broken, trampled,
strode toward the youthful hero.
Killing him his one intention.
Over grassy, flower-grown meadow,
raging, roaring, howling hatred,
great sword gripped in fists so fearsome
charged toward the waiting Youngling. . . .

Shakir spoke again, soberly. "Tell him that while I do not understand the words, I know his poem is excellent from the very sound of it. What is his name?"

"He is Senig Hans, Gunnar's Son," Nils said, and followed that with clan and tribal affiliations. Baver caught the change of cognomen from "Skinny" to "Sinewy," and realized how apt it was. Despite all the running and walking, the tiresome diet and frequent sword drill, Hans had gained considerable weight since they'd left the ting. But none of it was fat; he was whipcord-lean.

Shakir nodded acknowledgement. "Tell him I am Shakir, Son of Rashid, of the Súbhi Band of the Kazakhs." He gave orders to two of his men then, and they led a string of four horses to where the travelers' horses were picketed.

"Tell Nils these horses are my gift to him," he said to Achikh. "In case our debts were not quite even." He cocked an eye at the Buriat. "Tell him the Kazakhs are not a stingy people like the Kalmuls."

Achikh's face tightened with anger, and he got to his feet, hand on his sword hilt. Nils rose with him, and laid a hand on Achikh's shoulder, his gaze on Achikh's eyes. "Good friends," he said, slowly for Shakir's sake, "please do not fight." He looked then at the Kazakh, who had also gotten to his feet. "Achikh is my good friend, who has traveled far with me. He shared his horses' milk with us, before a great storm killed most of them. We have become like *andat*, sworn brothers."

He turned back to Achikh. "You told of watching me in the arena, in the City of Kazi. But you did not mention that I broke my sword in killing the lion. Do you remember it?"

Achikh nodded glowering.

"And then I dueled the Orc officer, and killed him. Do you remember where I got the sword to do that?"

"Someone threw one to you from the stands."

"The one who did that was Shakir. Though I was a stranger, he would not see me toyed with by an Orc, mutilated and slowly killed before the crowd."

Achikh relaxed somewhat. "He intended to insult me," he answered slowly, "thinking me a Kalmul because we speak the same tongue, or very nearly, and because I've learned his own. I am not a Kalmul, I am a Buriat, but I took the thought for the act." He shrugged big shoulders. "Nonetheless—"

Then Shakir spoke, facing Achikh:

"Tell Nils that if Achikh is like a sworn brother to him, then I withdraw my offense against Achikh, if Achikh is willing."

Achikh translated.

"I hope you are willing," Nils said to the Buriat.

It was hard for him, but Achikh nodded. "What he did for you was a very good thing," he said. "Very brave. And it defied Kazi. Few would have dared it. Besides, the Kalmuls are a difficult people. I cannot blame him for disliking them."

He turned and thrust out a hand toward Shakir. For a brief moment Baver feared the Kazakh would refuse it. Then Shakir reached, and met it with his own. For a moment their handshake threatened to turn into a grip-down contest. Finally Achikh grinned. Shakir laughed. Then both men laughed together, embracing and slapping each other on the back. Baver stared astonished.

Shakir turned to Hans. "And you, poet: Your work will be famous beyond your people. I know it." While Achikh forwarded this added praise in Anglic, Shakir unfastened his belt and removed from it a curved knife in a sheath of intricately carved horn. "This I give you in admiration."

He held it out. The poet's apprentice stared, hesitant, then took it and drew the blade. It was slender, razor-sharp, engraved in some hair-thin script.

"It reads," said Shakir, " 'long life to the holder. May his honor always shine.' "

He turned to Nils again. "As Achikh is not a Kalmul, I have advice for you. Do not follow the road over the pass between the great lakes. The Kalmul have been lying in wait there this summer for travelers. They kill them out of hand and take their possessions. It would be wiser, though longer and much more strenuous, to swing north and cross the mountains above Belukha. That way you are likely to get through alive."

Ten minutes later the Kazakhs were on their horses again, riding back westward. Watching them go, it seemed to Baver that he knew of no one among his own people, or any people, as courtly as Shakir, a sweat-stained barbarian. It also occurred to him that Shakir and his men had ridden hard for several days to catch up with them, apparently just so he could see Nils again and gift him with horses.

And what had he said? *Your soul is old, Northman, old, and purified by fire.* Something like that. A strange thing to say, but ... It seemed to Baver that it defined something he'd sensed himself and had failed to put his finger on. Though Nils could seem quite boyish, there was a sense about him of being old, old and wise.

For the first time now, the ethnologist looked at something he'd long accepted but had refused to really examine: That this giant, this boy-man Nils Järnhann who had no eyes, could see. What kind of man was he?

As they rode on, Nils and Achikh talked it over and decided to follow Shakir's advice. Years before, Achikh himself had crossed the great Altai range via the Pass Between the Lakes. Without incident or threat. It was by far the lowest and best crossing. But now and then some Kalmul clan would set up camp there for a season or a year, or longer. There they'd graze their sheep and cattle, and reap the occasional band of travelers; he'd heard that from the Kalmuls he'd served with in Kazi's army.

Meanwhile, best they travel as hard as their horses allowed. The other Altai crossings were said to be much higher, and impossible once the snow came, which would be early there.

That day they rode long before they found water again. At last, in thickening twilight, they came to a sizeable stream, twelve meters across and crotch-deep despite the season. Its banks were low but steep. After drinking, it took only a little time to hobble the horses and make camp. Then, while stars thickened in the sky and three fat marmots roasted, the travelers went back to the water, where naked they bathed and washed their clothes. To bathe in running water, or wash clothes in it, was taboo among Achikh's people, the Buriat told them. But he'd been long away, where customs were different, and they were not yet among his people.

Baver straightened, and standing thigh-deep, looked upward at the sky, feeling an unaccustomed relaxation and sense of contentment. "Nils," he said curiously, "how do you see, with no eyes?" And surprised himself by asking, for he hadn't been thinking about it when the words popped out.

"I see in the spirit," the Northman said.

The answer meant little to Baver, but having asked, he decided to get it clarified. "Did you see in the spirit when you had eyes?"

"No. Then I saw mainly as others see."

"Mainly?"

"I also saw other people's pictures—what they saw— through their minds. When I gave attention to it. This I still do."

"Well— When you give attention to what other people see, or think, can you see in the spirit at the same time? Or can you only do one at a time?"

"I can do both at once, but I had to learn. It took practice. It also took practice, a little, to see in the spirit from the body's viewpoint. At first my viewpoint would wander a little, and my body would stumble sometimes, or run into things."

As he wrung the river water from his jumpsuit for the third and final time, Baver tried to imagine what it must have been like at first, but gave up quickly. Splashing to the bank, he climbed it and spread the jumpsuit on a large shrub, next to his underclothes. And shivered; he was wet, and the air cool. Though the day had been hot, they were in the last moon of summer; his watch said September 5. The lengthening nights were no longer as warm as they had been. The shallow water felt warmer than the air now, and he waded back into it, squatting chest-deep near Nils, who was sitting cross-legged, soaking, and looking at the sky.

"What are you thinking about?" Baver asked.

"I am wondering which star Ilse is on now," Nils said. "Which star you came from." He turned to look at Baver. "Can you show me?"

The star man shook his head. "I'm afraid not. It's in the constellation Lupus. We can't see it from here; we'd need to be farther south." Baver remembered the girls in Nils's tent that evening at the ting, whom presumably the Northman had later copulated with. "Do you miss Ilse sometimes?"

Nils's answers, usually prompt, were slow this evening, coming after intervals of silence. "Sometimes," he said. "And the baby, Alfhild. It will be her nameday soon."

Baver wasn't a father, but he thought he knew how Nils might feel. Nils went on: "Ilse is the only person I know who is as I am. It was good for both of us that we found each other."

Baver recalled hearing a kanto of *The Järnhann Saga* that dealt with Ilse. She sounded quite heroic in it. And the Northmen referred to her as "den döjtsa häxen," the German witch; supposedly then she had powers like Nils's. More meaningful to him were comments he'd heard about Ilse from Nikko and Celia, aboard ship, though privately he'd rejected them at the time; they'd been impressed. Physically, on the other hand, the rangy, raw-boned Ilse had looked to him less exciting than either of the two girls in Nils's tent at the ting. She might be called handsome, but not pretty.

"Does it bother you that Ilse went to New Home with the *Phaeacia*?" he asked.

Again the answer lagged, but without any sense of pondering or hesitation. Rather, it was as if mentally the Northman was operating in slow motion this evening.

"No," he said. "It does not bother me. Each person has things they must do. Hers included going to your world. As mine includes going east this summer."

Baver looked at another question, and wondered if it would trouble Nils unduly. But if Nils could perceive the thoughts of others around him, perhaps he'd already perceived it.

As if in response, the Northman said, "It's possible that I'll be killed or die before they come back. Dying is the other side of living. But if one rejects his weird, he grows little. You could be in your own world now, but you chose to come here, and stay here a time, to do things and see things you would not have seen otherwise. Someday, dead or alive, you will know the reason. Someday, perhaps sooner, I will know more fully why I travel east now."

Nils stood up then, water streaming from his naked body. "I'm going to stand by the fire and dry before I crawl into my sleeping robes."

Baver followed him. *Someday, dead or alive, you will know why!* Examining Nils's words, the chill Baver felt as he padded toward the fire had nothing to do with the evening air. Yet it wasn't a matter of fear; Baver didn't know what it was.

Achikh had seen them coming and laid more brushwood on the fire. Baver stood beside Nils with his back to it, hot behind, cold in front. The strange Northman had never seemed quite human to him until tonight, he realized. But now, having talked of personal things, he did. He still seemed very different than other men, but definitely human nonetheless.

FIFTEEN

They left the "road," which had been angling south-east, and held eastward, pressing now at Achikh's urging. One never knew, he said, how early the first heavy snow would come to the high mountains. Or if it came particularly early, whether it would melt or stay. Each day they broke camp at dawn and rode till dusk or dark. They walked infrequently, making good use of their remounts, and avoided herdsmen's camps as much as they could without major sacrifice of time. So far the Kazakhs hadn't been hostile, but the danger was there.

They made no morning or noon fire, eating leftover marmot for breakfast as they rode, with curds and semi-liquid *airag* at their midday break. Most mornings were cold now. Sometimes there was frost on the grass, and one morning slivers of ice on the edge of the waterhole they'd camped by.

But except for a three-day span of showers that were not especially cold, the days were bright and warm, and virtually cloudless. The diet no longer bothered Baver, and the occasional diarrhea he'd been troubled with, early in their trek, was long past. He found himself enjoying this part of the journey, despite getting up and breaking camp in the morning chill.

From time to time he wondered about Nikko and Matthew, but now without frustration. He'd become somewhat fatalistic; he'd get back to them when Nils did, if Nils did. Meanwhile there were further lessons in Achikh's language and in wildland ecology. It seemed that Nils and Hans understood the steppes nearly as well as they did their forests, as if the same principles operated in both. The landforms, the orientation of streams, had more meaning for Baver now. Actually he'd known much about them before. His problem had been in relating the information to the reality around him.

Now it seemed to him that if he found himself alone here, he might well make his way back to the country of the Northmen by himself, though he'd have to beg his food.

The country had been unusually flat for a time, and they made excellent progress. Now it became rolling, and judging from the direction of stream flow, they were gradually climbing. One day as they topped a hill, he glimpsed distant mountains, a faint bluish line peeking over the horizon of tawny, early autumn grass. The next day he watched them grow, slowly but clearly. That afternoon, crossing a small ravine, the travelers found scrubby pines on the northeast-facing slope, the first pines they'd seen since leaving the Balkans. By sundown the mountains, though still far off, were near enough to show snowfields near the crest.

The next day Achikh changed direction, angling more to the north, putting the mountains somewhat off his right shoulder. Still they grew gradually nearer. Occasional other ravines had pines now. A couple of days later, the mountains, the Altai, lined the eastern distance as far as one could see to north and south.

Far to the north, they could just see a high snowpeak that Achikh judged was three days ride ahead. This peak, he said, must be Belukha, the great mountain that Shakir had told them of. They'd cross the Altai to the north of it.

*   *   *

The next day they topped a rise to see a broad basin in front of them. Near its center, perhaps four kilometers away, lay an extensive camp of round felt tents, several times as many as in Shakir's camp. Bands of cattle grazed the basin's bottom and slopes, tended by men on horseback. Achikh swore, and gestured the others back, joining them behind the hillcrest a minute later.

"They are Kalmuls," he said. "Their tents are laid out in the Mongol way. I didn't think they'd be so far this side of the mountains."

They turned southeast then, keeping the crest between themselves and the basin. "Why should we fear the Kalmuls more than we do the Kazakhs?" Baver asked.

"The Kalmuls are thieves," Achikh said. "Not just in time of need, but always. It is their way. It is also their way to kill those they rob. And always they encroach, if they see the chance. If some Kazakh band was grazing this area this year, the Kalmul scouts would have told their chief, and they would have stayed away. Next year they will probably leave, expecting the Kazakhs to learn of them by then."

Baver shivered. "And if they knew we were here, they'd kill us?"

Achikh grunted a yes. "And with a camp this large, we're likely to find more of them. Side-camps at least. We'll go straight toward the mountains, ride till dark, and ride again when the moon rises. When we get to the foothills, we'll turn north through the forest. It will slow us, but . . ." He shrugged.

"What will we do if they see us?" Baver asked.

"Keep riding. If there are only a few, they may not attack us. And they may decide we are not worth a day's ride, or half a day's, to get help."

Achikh pulled ahead of them then, pausing near the top of every hill to dismount, crawl to the crest, and see what lay on the other side. When they were well past the basin, they swung due east toward the mountains. It was necessary then to cross the narrow valley that, northwestward, opened into it. Achikh lay longer than usual, observing, before remounting and leading them on. There were patches of pinewoods on the slope they rode down, and they avoided talking; Kalmul warriors might be within hearing, unseen among trees.

The mountains were conspicuously nearer by sunset. Forests clothed their foothills and lower slopes, dark blue-gray with distance. Their higher shoulders were lighter gray—alpine tundra—while the farther, higher ridges and peaks showed dark gray stone, with crescents and patches and stringers of last winter's snow. Belukha reared to the north, head and shoulders above the others.

They rode till twilight, then camped beside a brook in the cover of trees. They made no fire, pitched no tent.

The moon, a sickle, rose somewhat after midnight, and they rose with it. Before they left, Achikh had them take their axes from the packhorses and lash them to saddle rings. "Why?" Baver asked.

"We may be chased."

"But—the axes add weight! They'll slow our horses!"

"If we're chased closely, we'll lose our packhorses. And to be in the forest in winter without axes . . . We'd be better off caught."

It seemed to Baver they'd be better off to carry their bedrolls then, but he said no more about it. They left, breakfasting on *airag*, passing the bag around as they rode. By sunup the foothills were noticeably nearer. By afternoon the hills they rode over were steeper and more broken, their east slopes more forest than not. After a short while they came to a valley with a small stream that ran southwest among groves of poplars, pine, and aspen. Achikh turned them upstream, riding the hillcrest.

They'd continued a few kilometers when Achikh saw the leather tents of a travel camp, hidden from them till then by trees. He hissed a warning, and motioned them back from the crest.

"Do you think they saw you?" Baver murmured.

The big shoulders shrugged. "If I was, then there's no

one there except a slave or two keeping camp. Otherwise we would have heard them. I saw four tents, but there may be more."

"Four tents? How many people would that mean?"

"More than twelve; perhaps as many as twenty. It's usual to sleep four or five in each, as we do."

They rode on then, seldom stopping but never hurrying, the Buriat and the two Northmen watching and listening constantly. Baver too was mostly alert, woolgathering only occasionally.

Near sunset, as they approached the crest of a hill, a band of Kalmuls crossed it the better part of a kilometer to their right. Both parties saw each other at the same time, and the Kalmuls started toward them at once, galloping, whooping warcries. Achikh thumped his heels against his horse's ribs and sent it running over the crest, the others following, angling down the other side.

As they'd crossed the crest, Achikh, Nils and Hans had looked back. More than a dozen Kalmuls were in noisy pursuit. Several others, slaves, had stayed behind with the Kalmuls' pack animals, which were loaded with wild game; it was a hunting party. They'd glimpsed antlers of elk and moose, then saw no more of them, for there was open forest on this side of the ridge, and they had entered among the trees.

In the openings, the humps and holes of pocket gophers were numerous. Rocks stuck up from the ground, and there were fallen trees to jump over. It seemed to Baver that his horse, at a full gallop, was in imminent danger of going down, pitching him headlong.

It was impossible now to see their pursuers, to know whether or not they were gaining, but Baver had no doubt they were. On him at least. For he was falling behind the others, even behind Nils, whose weight must surely slow his horse. He knew the others would be kicking and urging their horses to as much speed as they could get from them. He, on the other hand, was holding on desperately, not urging at all, doing his best not to fall off. He'd ridden thousands of kilometers since he'd left the ting ground, but none of it at a full gallop. His horse left the ground, clearing a fallen pine, and landed with a jar that nearly unloaded him.

Soon he passed the two pack horses, and saw the re-mount string veer off downslope. Perhaps, he thought, the Kalmuls would see them, and stop to capture them, but he put no faith in it. Then even Nils was out of sight ahead, and Baver, in desperation, put his heels to his horse after all.

After a kilometer more, his mind began to function. He was impressed at how his mount kept galloping. They'd been angling downslope continuously. Now he was leveling off, pounding along near the bottom as he entered a glade. The ravine had narrowed, and ahead narrowed more, its sides steep, the near side almost precipitous. At the far edge of the glade, he saw Nils and his horse disappear into denser forest, dense enough that it seemed suicidal to enter it at a gallop.

Seemingly Baver's horse agreed; it slowed perceptibly as it drove toward the thick growth of trees. As it plunged into them on the game trail they'd been following, they passed Nils standing behind a high-jutting rock, sword in both hands. Baver slowed his horse sharply, managing not to lose his seat, and drew to one side behind a dense growth of young pines. It was dim there; the hour was sunset, and they were among trees, deep in the bottom of the ravine. His hand found his pistol, drew it and released the safety. Then he simply sat his horse, peering through a gap in the trunks, back along the trail.

Sooner than he'd expected, the first of the Kalmuls thundered in amongst the trees. Nils had drawn himself back out of sight, and to Baver's dismay let the first two horsemen thunder past. He found his pistol pointing, and as the first of the Kalmuls raised his sword, shot him from the saddle, the horse galloping by so near, Baver's mount shied. The next Kalmul, not prepared to face an attack by miniature thunderclap, drew up, the horse rearing, and Baver shot again. This bullet hit the animal under the jaw and drove up into its brain. It went over backward onto its rider, who screamed. Baver's pistol banged again, and the scream cut off abruptly. Another horse had charged up riderless, leaped the fallen horse, and ran on.

Baver wasn't sure how many rounds he'd fired, how many he had left. He looked toward Nils. A horse was down there too. Nils had cut the forelegs from under it and was in the process of dispatching its rider. Another Kalmul lay nearly cut in two beside the trail. Baver could hear shouted Mongol, back in the opening, but the string of charging warriors seemed to have paused. Then, sword sheathed, Nils surged through the thicket of young pines and began clambering up the steep near-precipice behind him, half hidden by its trees. Without stopping, he glanced back at Baver and shouted one word: *"Ride!"*

Baver took time to holster his gun—he needed both hands to ride at a gallop—then turned his horse and rode.

He'd gone less than a hundred meters when he saw Hans coming back. "Go!" Baver shouted. "Nils said ride!" Then he was past the young Northman, who hesitated a moment, then turned and followed, catching up and staying close behind. Behind the thudding of their own horses' hooves, Baver could hear others following now, and suddenly Hans's horse screamed. The sound added speed to Baver's, and there was Achikh, sitting his horse behind a great boulder, bow in hand and arrow nocked as Baver galloped past.

Without thinking, Baver drew back his reins. His horse stopped more quickly than he'd expected, and he ended up on its neck, clutching. Dropping to the ground, he knelt behind a thick-boled pine. There was a shout, then another, as Kalmuls poured into sight not forty meters off. One plunged from the saddle, an arrow in his chest. The others reined in their horses and drew their swords. With both hands Baver leveled his pistol, the way he'd done on the range in training, but more quickly. And fired. The round banged loudly, and one of the Kalmuls half fell, losing his sword, clutching at shoulder or neck.

Changing targets, Baver shot at another, and with the sound, this man fell backward, sliding off his horse's rump, one foot hanging for a moment in a stirrup. The others hesitated for just a moment, then Achikh sent an arrow into another, and he too went down.

The other two turned their horses and charged back the way they'd come.

Baver stood watching after them, immobilized by the realization that he had killed—at least wounded—four human beings. And felt no shock or guilt at it! He wasn't quite sure how to take this latter fact.

Two high soaring ravens had watched the chase with interest. Beneath their individual awareness, ravens have something of a hive intelligence. Thus they knew, from the experience of others, that men pursuing men often means death to men and horses, and food for ravens. They are scavengers who find their food by sight, not scent, and have superb vision. They are also very curious, noticing the incidental as well as the important. They were aware, for instance, that one of the humans was exceptionally large and had unusual hair, with long, straw-colored braids.

Even their sharp eyes couldn't make out what went on beneath the thicker growth of pines, but they heard an unusual booming sound that repeated, heard a horse scream, and another. Men and horses drew up in the opening, then two turned back to where their horses could begin picking their way up the steep slope. After a minute's hesitation, the other horses charged on into the forest growth.

The great black birds began to circle downward to investigate more closely, croaking loudly in their deep harsh voices. Finally they perched in the top of a pine, peering down between the branches. There were bodies on the ground, of men and horses. Another human stood on the trail with arrow nocked and ready, watching the big, yellow-haired man climb the slope above. He shot just one arrow; it rattled and fell among the dense young pines on the slope. Then the bowman settled back to watch and wait.

There were more booms farther along the ravine.

The watching ravens continued to call. Another, near the edge of hearing, passed the report on, both the simple cry and the mental imagery beneath it. Except for the fallen men and horses though, it meant little to the birds.

A few minutes later, the Kalmul riders who'd ridden on, came back to where they'd first been ambushed. By now dusk was definitely settling, and the refugee on the slope was lost to their sight among rocks and trees. They counseled briefly, then called to those who'd climbed their horses to the ridgetop to cut off the refugee's escape. There was a moment's exchange of shouts, then they all started back the way they'd come, back to their cohorts who'd been told off to collect the pack horses and remounts. They'd lost nine men and three horses— Choban would be enraged by that—but at least they wouldn't return to camp empty-handed.

And obviously the people they'd chased were not entirely human. The one, the giant, had yellow hair! And equally obvious, they had a very strong *kam* with them, a powerful shaman who made small thunders to kill with. And anyone with any sense at all feared thunder. With luck, then, Choban would settle for the horses, and not send them out to track these people down.

SIXTEEN

Achikh, Hans, and Baver backtracked, hoping to find Nils alive, riding warily most of the way, then finishing on foot. They found his horse first, grazing in a glade, with a Mongol pony which Hans made his. The Kalmuls were gone. By then dusk had thickened enough that they didn't see Nils till he'd climbed most of the way down the slope.

Briefly they consulted. Achikh's guess was that the Kalmuls would return to the big encampment, and that in the morning the Kalmul chief would send a force to hunt them down.

They continued on in growing darkness until a grassy slope gave them a climbable route to the ridgetop. There they rode on till there was only starlight to see by—a somewhat risky situation, given their lack of remounts. Then they lay down on the ground and slept, each, including Baver, telling himself to wake up when the moon rose.

When at last it did, it was little more than a fingernail paring in the sky. They were stiff with cold, and left at once, traveling northward, leading their horses at first, at a brisk walk, to warm their own bodies. Before long, dawn seeped up the sky. Through the day, Belukha grew nearer, her crown white with glacier, her shoulders with snowfields.

On the next day a great raven spiraled down, and landed on a young pine not far ahead of them, clinging precariously to a branch almost too small to bear it.

Hans stared. "It's as large as an eagle!" he said, "or nearly. Surely as large as an osprey."

Achikh gazed intently through his slitted eyes. "I have never seen one so large," he said. "Ravens are wise birds, and some have wizard powers; all the Buriat know that. But this—this is no ordinary raven. It is a spirit raven."

Baver eyed it. His experience with ravens was neither close nor extensive, but it was a big bird. It spread its wings as they passed, as if to steady its balance, and he guessed its span at a meter and a half. Its head was massive, its black eyes beady, intent, and intelligent.

Nils stretched out an arm as if pointing to it, and to Baver's amazement the bird lifted from the pine and flew to the Northman. For just a moment its black feet gripped his wrist, while the horse shied nervously, then the bird rose again to spiral up and up, so high that except for its grace in flight, it might have been a distant crow.

"We have no pursuers," Nils said. "Not within his sight." He gestured at the circling bird.

Achikh peered at Nils narrowly, but not in skepticism. His only question was: "Can you trust him?"

"It is difficult to lie to me," Nils answered.

They dismounted then, and minutes later the raven came back to them. They let the horses graze awhile before going on.

The next morning they came to the end of the steppe. Forest spread in front of them, seemingly endless and unbroken. They also came to the end of Old Wives' Summer, or a break in it at least. For the day had broken gray and damp, with a chill wind pushing dark rags of cloud along beneath a heavy overcast.

"It will snow," said Achikh, gesturing at the mountains. "We are too late to cross this year."

Nils nodded. "Let's go on until we find a large stream, and build a hut there, then find game. Otherwise spring will uncover our bones, and our friend raven will use us for food instead of fellowship."

Before the day was done, it did begin to snow, thickly. By the time it began to stick, they'd come to a stream some forty meters wide, and hurriedly built a shelter near it, of saplings and the bark of large birch snags. It was a cold and miserable camp without the bedrolls they'd lost with their packhorses. The smoke from their fire hung low around them in the wet air, reeking. By the end of a largely sleepless night, the snow lay more than thirty centimeters deep.

Then, with the axes Shakir's mother had given them, Achikh and Hans felled and limbed numerous pines of minimum taper and twenty to thirty centimeters thick. Baver, driving one of the horses, dragged the slim logs to the site Nils had chosen. There the Northman, his deft axe perpetual motion, slabbed them flat on two sides and carved the corners to fit. After a bit, Hans came to help him.

By midday the sun came out, and the snow began to settle and melt, water dripping from the trees. By evening the walls of a hut stood chest high on Baver, with crude openings on two sides as windows, and a longer one for a door. The ethnologist's job had expanded: Now he was not only skidder, but moss bringer and chink stuffer, filling the cracks between the logs to keep the wind out.

The snow was largely gone already, and Baver asked if they might not make it over the mountains after all. Achikh shook his head. "In high mountains the snow falls much deeper, and melts much more slowly. I doubt we could push through, surely not without knowing the way. We would die." He shook his head, clearly not happy with the situation. "We must winter here."

SEVENTEEN

From—"*Yunnan Ogres*," by Guillaume W. Das. Pages 84–95, In *The Occupation of Post-Plague Terran Habitats by Large Predators*, Maureen Boileau and Jauna C. Costas, eds. University Press, A.C. 876.

The Sino-Tibetan imperial court is not what one ordinarily thinks of as a habitat for large predators—except of course predatory humans. However, at one time the emperor had a guard unit consisting of large furry predators referred to by the court as "yetis." These are not the reputedly shy indigenous animals once believed to reside in the upper forests of the Himalayas. They are an extraterrestrial species brought to Earth during the exploration decades of the 21st century, and housed in secure special habitats where they could be observed by students and public without being aware of it.

Because of their size and predatory, quasi-human appearance, in vernacular Anglic they were dubbed "ogres." We will so refer to them here, to distinguish them from the indigenous yeti, real or mythical.

The sole extant source of scientific information on ogres is a cube published by the Interstellar Zoological society in A.D. 2078, and brought to New Home in the library of the colonist ship *Vicente Hidalgo*.

Physical Description

In appearance, an ogre is a large erect humanoid with short brown to occasionally rufous fur over the entire body including the face—everywhere but the soles and palms. A slight crest of fur extends along the midline of the skull above the forehead, down to the end of the spinal column.

Ogres have five-digit hands and feet, including opposable thumbs on the hands. The legs are quite humanoid and the feet quite long. They run on the balls of the feet, and when sprinting lean well forward, taking long strides. They jump remarkably well, considering their weight.

The torso is very powerful, most notably the high and rather narrow but otherwise human-like shoulders. The arms are long, compared to human arms, with the forearms and hands especially long. The upper arms are very thick and muscular, their grasp ferocious. They can pull close and crush, or hold their victim for biting or choking.

The claws on their feet are useful for traction. The claws on their hands however, are vestigial, being little more than thick fingernails. In hunting, the lack of effective claws on the hands is largely made up for by an extremely powerful grip.

Their jaws are elongated into a short, blunt muzzle, and their dangerous teeth are similar to those of gorillas. As in the gorilla, the skull of the ogre has a well-developed sagittal crest to which are anchored the thick jaw muscles that provide their crushing bite.

Ogre Behavior on Their Home World

On their home world, ogres were, and presumably still are pack hunters, preying mostly on large herd animals. There, adult male ogres average more than two meters tall and typically mass about 200 kilos. Females average somewhat smaller—150–180 kilos. Ogres sprint much faster than humans, and even over middle distances are considerably faster than human athletes. But they are not as fleet as their prey animals. Their success derives from intelligent teamwork in the hunt, and endurance over long distances. They are more agile than might be expected, and extremely strong—considerably stronger, pound for pound, than a competitive human weight lifter.

While ogres use their innate speed and strength to bring down prey, in defense of their "nursery grounds" against other predators, they use crude but effective stone weapons.

Ogres are not scent hunters. Their sense of smell seems little or no better than a healthy, alert, primitive human hunter's must have been in the Paleolithic. They have superior night vision, and on the steppes and savannahs of their home world they often hunt by night. However, night is intensely dark in their wild terran environment, the forests of Upper Yunnan, and there they are said to hunt almost solely by day.

Post-Plague Natural History of Ogres on Earth

Most of their post-plague natural history on Earth is conjectural, of course. The following reconstruction, based in part on interviews with humans in the Sino-Tibetan Empire, seems quite convincing, however. The IZS cube tells us that small ogre packs were installed in several zoological parks. These included the Kunming Zoological Park at Kunming, China, where the subtropical montane climate was thought to be reasonably well suited to them. Their park habitats were all, of course, quite secure against breakouts. However, during the chaos and insanity that accompanied the Great Death, someone at the park apparently opened their habitat entry, releasing them. Otherwise the ogres would have starved to death.

Initially on their release, they no doubt dwelt in and around the city of Kunming, preying on domestic animals and the infrequent human survivors of the plague. They probably increased rapidly at first. The females begin to produce offspring between ages 9 and 11, biennial twins being the mode where conditions are sufficiently favorable. Very soon they must have had to leave the city to find sufficient food. For a time they probably did well preying on livestock, but over the first few decades, forests would have encroached more and more on the cleared land, while livestock would have decreased. The ogres must have transferred their attention increasingly to deer, wild pigs, etc, which must have flourished in the young pioneer forests. Thus the ogres no doubt continued to find reasonably good hunting until the dense young forests had closed their canopies and darkened. Then the supply of large game animals must have decreased markedly, and the ogre population would have leveled off or even decreased.

There were additional reasons that ogres were not to prosper for long in the Upper Yunnan region. Adapted to a much drier climate and open, mostly sunny savannahs and steppes, the very humid forest climate of the Yunnan Plateau proved unhealthy for them. Apparently they had done well enough in the zoological park; it was open to the sun, they had a heated refuge from the rain, and presumably there was apparatus which dusted them occasionally with fungicides. And of course they were well fed, with their food medicated as necessary.

But in the dark, damp, Yunnan forests, ogres are subject to chronic and sometimes acute fungal diseases of the skin, especially of the genitals and toes. In the wild populations of today, despite centuries of natural selection for resistant genes, such fungi are particularly damaging to infants, who contract them from the mother's pudenda during birth. Such infants frequently become blind. Too, jungle rot of the feet rather often hobbles adolescent and adult hunters to a greater or lesser extent, enough to hamper hunting and make them dangerously surly toward other ogres.

Further, ogres had evolved in much more open country. They were intelligent enough to modify their hunting methods to heavy forest, but they could not modify their physical equipment. Genetically, they were what they were. And in heavy forest, there was not a lot of big game to eat, while monkeys and wildfowl were seldom within reach. Furthermore, tigers and leopards began to wander in and establish themselves, providing serious competition. No doubt they sometimes even preyed on the ogres, though mostly they must have learned not to.

Meanwhile the scattered human survivors had been multiplying too, and learning to live effectively as hunter-gatherers and gardeners. When ogres came into conflict with established humans, no doubt the humans at first must have died and been eaten, or moved out of the district, carrying reports of the ogres with them. In time, however, the humans responded with spears, arrows, axes, and swords.

Squads of well-armed and truculent humans patrolled the marches of their settlements, and when ogres ravaged a hamlet, a force of humans was likely to track them. Such punitive expeditions often ended in the death of the ogre predators.

Presumably the ogres learned to fear humans. Certainly the humans feared ogres. Stories of ogre savagery, told before fireplaces, became a rich part of the folklore of southwestern China.

From rather early in the post-plague era, humans

skirmished with humans from time to time, and not all the ravaging of Yunnan farm settlements was by ogres or rogue tigers. Thus in time there came to be organization and chiefs, and eventually kings and armies. And between local wars, the early local "kings" sent patrols out to hunt and kill ogres. Thus the ogres were forced back into the rougher, more remote country, where wild populations persist today in scattered small bands. A party of would-be heroes can still make a name for themselves by going hunting in the wild Hengduan Mountains and bringing back the scalps or hands of one or more ogres. And more than a few would-be heroes have been killed or even eaten in the attempt.

Domestication of the Ogre

In earlier times, when ogres existed in nearer proximity to human settlements, ogre infants were sometimes captured and reared through childhood. Thus not only their intelligence but their trainability became known. It also became known that with puberty, at about age nine or ten, these one-time winsome and interesting baby ogres became surly and dangerous. They were almost invariably killed then for safety reasons.

Ogres have a voice box and mobile lips, and as cubs are taught to talk by older pack members. They are not articulate by human standards, but wild ogres do have language of their own, and in the Sino-Tibetan empire, juvenile domesticated ogres are taught to speak functional Tibetan, being intelligent enough to grasp and learn a foreign grammar. The structure of their ice apparatus, particularly the elongate mouth, prevents the pronunciation of the velar sounds. Thus they pronounce *k* and *t* as *g* as *d*. The loose, mobile lips permit easy pronunciation of the bi-labials, but the large canine teeth make mastery of the voiceless labio-dental *f* difficult, and it is usually pronounced as *th*.

Imperial Domestication & Training

While still a young man, King Songtsan I extended the boundaries of his family's rule from the Gulf of Tonkin north to the Yellow River, and eastward to its confluence with the Siang, creating the first large Sino-Tibetan state of the post-plague era. His eldest son, who would later become Songstan II and take the title of emperor, knew of baby "yetis" being trained like children. There were telepaths in the royal service, and it seemed to the crown prince that ogres reared in proper circumstances, with telepaths to monitor their minds and whatever might be troubling them, could be trained to drill, stand guard, and fight. And surely no other ruler in the world would have such a guard force. How much he thought to depend on ogres for security is not known, but certainly they'd make a impressive looking royal guard unit.

Training did not go well at first, but well enough that the project was continued. Actually the ogres proved more intelligent than expected, but more intractable as well, from puberty on. Handlers were killed and maimed, but royalty could always conscript and train new handlers. Emperor Songtsan III was the first to have an actual guard force of armed and drilled ogres. By that time the ogres being worked with were the third generation born in captivity. Their recent ancestors had been brought up under the careful direction of telepaths, and given a ready-made and partly factual "tradition." The surliness and dangerous rages characteristic of unconditioned adult ogres was reduced in the guard to occasional moodiness, and during the rut, to truculence. In the rutting season, they were therefore taken off duty and sent to stud.

Ogres were healthier in the relatively dry climate at Miyun than in Yunnan, despite the cold winters, against which they were warmly dressed and housed.

The emperor Songtsan IV had an ogre guard force numbering eighty. Its eight squad leaders had been bonded to him personally as cubs, and beyond that, all eighty had been hypnotically implanted in cubhood with a command of loyalty to the emperor. . . .

EIGHTEEN

The first storm of autumn had darkened the palace at Miyun. Rain snarled against walls, and rattled like flung gravel against windows and shutters. Gusty winds swatted and whuffed. The wind chimes had been taken in to prevent their blowing away, and servants had lit censers to placate the house gods they persisted in believing in. The emperor, who preferred a free flow of fresh air through the palace, weather permitting, tolerated the censers and the beliefs they reflected. Their fragrance was preferable to unperfumed domestic odors.

Tenzin Geshe hardly noticed. His *gomba*, his monastery, smelled always of pine and faintly fragrant lamp oil. After holding his bow for an appropriate time, he straightened. "Your Magnificence," he said, "the Circle and I have just visited the mind of the raven elemental we created. Ravens have found the barbarian you are interested in. The elemental has gone to him, and the three men with him, and shown them to us clearly. The man is a giant, as I'd sensed before, with eyes that are dead and do not see. He sees without them, using wizard powers."

"Indeed! And where are these men now?"

"In the steppe on the other side of the Altai, traveling northward toward the taiga."

"Northward? With winter coming? Why?"

"The raven did not have that knowledge, Your Magnificence."

"Hmh! How was that? You told me it would be able to read the barbarian's mind."

"I had not counted on the barbarian's powers being as strong as they are, Your Magnificence. He seems to protect himself and those with him from being read. But we know where they are now, and as long as the raven retains contact, we'll continue to know."

"Ah! Well . . . I am extremely interested in this giant barbarian; he has caught my curiosity strongly. Be sure your bird does retain contact with him."

The emperor pursed his lips, and his voice became more commanding, losing its mildly interrogative tone. "Now that you've succeeded in creating a raven elemental, I have another job for you. I want you to create a yeti elemental to serve as my personal bodyguard. It must be more intelligent and perceptive than any other yeti, and altogether superior in energy and strength."

Again Tenzin bowed. "Your Magnificence, my experience in creating elementals of animals is limited to—a bird."

The emperor brushed the comment aside. "This yeti elemental must be dominant over all other yetis and completely devoted to me." He raised one eyebrow meaningfully. "I would not have it equivocate as some of my human servants do."

Tenzin Geshe bowed low and held it. "Of course, Your Magnificence."

"Then do it. Wait here while I call the captain of my yeti guard. I will instruct him to review the entire guard with you, and also the young yetis in training. You may pick whichever one you wish as the receptacle. Keeping its purpose in mind of course."

He struck a small gong, and almost at once a runner

entered. The emperor instructed him, and the runner backed out.

Tenzin carefully avoided thought; screening in the emperor's presence would be a dangerous affront. But later, in the *gomba,* he allowed himself to think that things were seldom as simple as His Magnificence seemed to imagine. Manipulating the mental energies of large, intelligent, and sometimes truculent predators was not the same as manipulating those of peaceful birds. Birds which, if more intelligent than other birds, fell well short of yetis.

Still, if he could, he would. It was never a good idea to disappoint the emperor.

NINETEEN

After the first snowstorm, the travelers had a sixteen-day return to mild weather. The nights were cold though; a chill wind flowed down off the snow-covered mountains every evening after sunset, freezing the ground by morning.

They worked incessantly from dawn till after dark. At the end of the seventh day, the rude hut had a low roof of poles, and bark held down by more poles. There was no chimneyed fireplace; the local mud was unsuitable for making one. Instead they had a fire circle in the middle of the floor, and at each end of the hut beneath the ridgepole, an opening beneath the roof. Through these openings the wind would blow, when there was wind, carrying out the worst of the smoke.

After the seventh day, while Hans and Baver cut and dragged firewood, Nils and Achikh hunted. Achikh said he'd never seen a luckier hunter than Nils. The raven helped; it found a moose for them, and then another.

Baver learned to scrape hides till the last bits of flesh and fat were gone, then to rub them with tallow and pound it in with the sides of his fists, to make them pliant for clothing and winter boots.

There was a meadow along the stream, where the horses grazed the coarse dead grass and sedge. Achikh feared they wouldn't live through the winter without hay, so the men harvested grass, great armfuls of it. They'd use it as bedding till the horses' situation became desperate, then as a supplement to whatever the horses found to eat.

From the beginning, the Buriat and the two Northmen set snares and deadfalls in the taiga, and began to harvest snowshoe hares, which were numerous, and lynx; even sable. One night wolves howled, and in the morning the horses were close outside the hut. Meanwhile a wolf had triggered a deadfall, and contributed his pelt.

While hunting, Nils found where a bear had raked up duff from the forest floor, stuffing it in the opening beneath the sprung root disk of a fir that had blown partly over. It would be his winter den. They'd wait till after winter came, Nils said, and the bear had holed up. Then they'd visit the den and kill him for his fur and flesh.

Achikh said he'd never seen such good hunting ground. Game was so plentiful and easy to approach, it appeared that no one had hunted there before.

With the roof on they moved into the cabin, and worked by firelight when darkness came. Baver learned more skills. He sewed pelts into clothing, using sinew and a bone needle; helped scrape the fat off a third moosehide; made window coverings of sewn moose gut. Made mittens of the wolf skin, fur-side in. Nils made a door for their low doorway, splitting and shaving boards from a pine log, cutting tiny notches for fastening them together, then hanging it with leather straps. It was not a tight door, but lacking awl and hinges and proper doorposts, it would have to do. Nils also made a trough from a poplar log, to melt snow in and hold their water supply.

The trough did double duty. Nils and Hans split thin staves from birch, soaked them in the trough in boiling water, bent them around blocks and tied them, continuing the soaking and increasing the curvature till the bend was sufficient and permanent. Before long they would all have skis.

Achikh tended their snares and hunted, cut firewood, and made various things from leather.

In the evenings while they worked around the fire, Achikh continued their lessons in the Buriat dialect of Mongol. He also told stories in it that gave them insights into his people. This story telling would continue throughout the winter, and Baver set out the recorder to get them on audio while he worked. Occasionally when the press of his more immediate tasks allowed, he got video as well.

He came to understand almost anything Achikh said in Mongol, and learned to speak it easily himself.

Achikh also told them his people's beliefs and taboos, that they might not offend when they reached them, perhaps to be punished.

After sixteen days, true winter came. One morning they awoke to find the hut cold, and twenty centimeters of dry fluffy snow on the ground. Baver thought it must be at least minus fifteen or twenty degrees Celsius outside. His watch made it October 24.

They harvested their bear, a large male. A fourth moose gave his life, his hide, and his flesh to their survival. Already, it seemed to Baver, they had meat enough to feed them through two winters. The raven stayed with them and was fed by them, living in the thick treetops. Hans named it Svartvinge. Nils was its chosen; the others it accepted. The nights grew colder, while the sun, its course ever lower, its stay ever briefer, seemed scarcely to warm the air at all by day. This was not the Arctic, Baver knew, but visualizing maps he'd seen, it was probably Siberia, albeit southern Siberia. And what he'd learned of Siberian winters, in his studies on New Home, was not reassuring.

It was a long winter, and colder than anything Baver had ever imagined. Nils said it was considerably colder than his original homeland. Achikh said it was colder than his, too, but here the forest protected from the sweeping winds. The snowfall was much greater here, he said, and blamed it on the adjacent mountains. The hut was never as warm as a proper cabin, by quite a bit, but wearing furs it was tolerable.

The meadow grass was buried and flattened by the snow, and the horses tramped trails through the deep snow to browse the goatsbeard lichens from the tree trunks.

Svartvinge got so he would come into the hut in the evening, to sit on a boot-drying peg and commune silently with Nils, or so it seemed. But half an hour of the smoky air was invariably enough for it. Then it would fly to one of the smokeholes, perch there for a moment, and launch itself out.

Hans had continued to grow and fill out. Despite the hard life, he must have gained fifteen or twenty kilos since they'd left the ting, Baver thought. And surely he himself must look different now. He wished he had a mirror, preferably full length.

When the cold was not extreme, they often hunted or explored. If nothing else, it got them out of the smoke reek and let them breath clean air. Nils and Hans skied almost as easily as they walked. Baver and Achikh also became reasonably adept, although their skis fitted more loosely than skis on New Home, with their sophisticated bindings. Baver learned a great deal about the animals they saw and sometimes killed.

Achikh made him a laminated bow, short but stiff. He learned to make and fletch his own practice arrows, and practiced until he was pleased with himself, though clearly Achikh thought him hopeless as an archer. He'd shoot at a target tree outside the cabin, a rotten birch stub that didn't damage the unpointed practice arrows when they struck it. He could usually hit it at twenty doubles—forty steps—though his accuracy wouldn't suffice to consistently kill marmots as the others had the previous summer. He was pleased with himself nonetheless. They'd teethed on bows and arrows, he told himself, while he was new to them.

After a time, the days became noticeably longer, but the nights were as cold as ever and the snow continued to deepen. All winter long they'd hear wolves occasionally; the horses, increasingly gaunt, would gather by the door on those occasions. One night, on what Baver's watch told him was February 16, the horses whinnied with fear. The Buriat and the Northmen went out with arrows nocked and bows half drawn, Baver with them carrying two torches. A number of wolves crouched down in the torchlight, eyes gleaming, and in a moment, three had been shot. Two of the three who'd been pierced with shafts, tried to flee. Nils pursued them and killed them with his sword. It was hurtful to a man's soul, Achikh commented, to let a wounded wolf crawl away and die slowly. They used the furs, of course.

Afterward they still heard the pack howl from time to time, as it passed through the area in its hunting, but the pack members stayed well away from the hut.

One evening Achikh, who'd been exploring new territory along the foothills, found where an ancient highway had been. It was overgrown now with forest, but recognizable by the cuts and fills. He'd taken time to explore it, and it did indeed go up into the mountains as if to cross them. It seemed that when spring came, they wouldn't need to find a route across the Altai; the ancients had made one for them.

At length the days were as long as the nights, more or less, and the surface of the snow sometimes grew wet where the sun shone on it. Not long afterward—a couple of phases of the moon—they'd find a hard crust on the snow in the morning, sometimes lasting all day. Sometimes one could walk on it without skis. Now the horses truly suffered, for they broke through the crust at every step and could hardly lift their hooves back out. Nor could they paw the snow away to get at last summer's

meadow grass. The small stock of bedding hay was doled
out, and when it was gone, the men collected lichen for
the horses to eat, and branches of Siberian fir, which
they'd seen them browse.

The days continued to lengthen. The birds of summer
began to appear. The snow settled in earnest, and sometimes no crust froze on it overnight; when it did, it
melted by midmorning. Hans wondered that Svartvinge
didn't leave them; ravens nested when there was still
snow, he explained to Baver, and surely he must have a
mate somewhere. Achikh said a spirit raven might not
nest, might have no mate. Nils grinned and said nothing
at all about it.

Noisy meltwater ran down the stream over the thick
ice, and they traveled little. The days grew long, the snow
soggy and much shrunken. Achikh said the steppes would
be bare now, and the first spring flowers showing. Baver
asked how long it might be before they tried crossing
the mountains. Achikh said the snow in the high country
would still be deeper than a man's height.

The ice went out and the stream rose further, but not
enough to cover all the meadow. Fortunately, because
the snow had melted on it, and the scarecrow horses
were eating last summer's dead grass and sedge there.
None had died, but another month of winter would
surely have killed them all.

At Achikh's suggestion, Nils felled another large birch
and split wide thin planks from it. Then they each began
to carve a wooden shovel. In the high passes, Achikh
believed, they'd have to dig paths for the horses in the
worse places, or wait halfway through the summer.

Baver accepted the thought without a shudder.

PART III

THE BURIAT GREAT COUNCIL

TWENTY

It was high summer. A slave was tending a band of cattle grazing between two rolling hills near the Tola River. The sun was hot, and he sweated. Just now he watched four men riding eastward toward and past him, along the ancient road. Such traffic was not unusual, but even at some distance, his sharp herdsman's eyes found more than a little unusual about these four. None were dressed in Mongol garb. One was a giant who rode naked to the waist, as did one of the others; foreigners, obviously. Also, though clearly they seemed to be travelers, they had neither pack animals nor remounts.

A great dark bird rode the withers of the giant's horse, perhaps an eagle trained to falconry. He'd heard of such.

A long hour would take them to the great encampment at Urga, a buried city site long mined for its steel and copper. There, just now, the four Buriat tribes were gathered in congress, to council, trade, and drink. And perhaps elect a Great Khan who would lead the entire Buriat people.

It seemed to the slave, who was also a Mongol, that his master should be told of these foreigners. Turning his horse, he cantered off over a hill to the freeman who supervised him, and reported what he'd seen. The freeman, in turn, sent a messenger to Urga.

From Urga, a marshal was dispatched with an *arban* of men—more than enough to deal with four foreigners—and they cantered off westward down the ancient, grassgrown road. Shortly the four came into sight over a rise a kilometer ahead, and two of them did appear shirtless. Foreigners certainly!

The marshal barked an order. His ten men kicked their horses into a gallop, then drew bows from their saddle boots and fitted arrows to them.

Baver felt instant alarm as the group of Mongols charged toward them. Svartvinge raised his broad wings and sprang lightly from the withers of Nils's horse, wing-strokes making hard whooshing sounds as he rose. Baver turned his attention to Achikh, who led them; seen from behind, the husky Buriat showed no reaction. Nor did Nils seem perturbed, and surely he would know if the oncomers intended to skewer them.

A second later Achikh spoke, and the four stopped to wait. Baver's guts clenched as the Mongols came on. At some twenty meters the *arban* drew up before them in a cloud of dust, arrows still nocked but the short, thick bows unbent.

"Who are you, and what are you doing here?" the marshall barked.

"I am Achikh, son of Kokchü. And you are my old friend, Elbek. I have come to see my eldest brother, Kaidu."

For just a moment the man's mouth was a round O. Then, "Achikh!" he shouted, and grinning rode his horse up beside Achikh's, where the two men embraced, both talking at once. The *arban*'s ferocity and tension were gone; most of them were grinning too. When their leader had completed his greeting, two of the others also rode up and embraced Achikh as an old friend.

Then Elbek assembled his duty face. "And those with you," he said. "Who are they?"

Achikh had them identify themselves, which they did in Mongol, at once a strong point in their favor. "We are friends," Achikh went on, "who have traveled together for a year now. They were out adventuring when we met. I had already known Nils Hammarsson as a famous fighting man, the most famous in the west."

Elbek looked at Nils in open appraisal, his glance pausing only briefly on the Northman's eyes. "I can believe that," he said. He gestured upward then, at Svartvinge circling and croaking. "That is a strange bird to use in falconry," he said chuckling, then returned his attention to Achikh. "And now you will see your brother. Well."

Elbek glanced about and gave an order, then with the four, started down the road eastward, he and Achikh leading off. The *arban* let them pass, and brought up the rear.

"As I remember it, Kaidu had already been chosen chief before you left," Elbek said. "He is chief still. Old people say surely the best since Kutula—better even then Kokchü. Old Toghrul says there is something about chiefs whose names begin with *K*. Your brother does not rage, but sees widely and judges fairly, as he did among us when we were children and he an older boy. Now a great congress of the tribes is being held, and when it is over, it is possible that the Buriat will have a Great Khan again! If they do, I think it will be Kaidu. He is meeting with the clan chiefs and the heads of the great families today, in the Council Grove. It may be he cannot see you till supper. We will find out."

"Let us not distract him in council," Achikh said. "We will tend our horses first, and eat and drink. Then perhaps we will sit in the rear of the listeners."

They were near enough to the great encampment that now there were numerous bands of horses grazing about, along with small bands of cattle and sheep brought to feed the multitude, the thousands who were at the congress. Occasionally men or children would ride near enough to examine the strange-looking foreigners from a little distance. Then they crossed one last rise, and before them, by a river, spread the encampment. Here was no array of leather travel tents. Several thousand greased felt *gert*, large and not large, lay spread in ordered groups. Most had been whitewashed. The broad, flat carts they'd been transported on were drawn up in neat ranks.

Elbek took them to the chief marshal, who was an older cousin of Achikh's, and he in turn had some lesser members of Kaidu's retinue turned out of their *ger* to provide proper lodging for the newcomers. A woman was assigned to cook for them, a meal consisting of beef boiled and beef roasted, of curds, of *airag* flavored with beets, and of honey-sweetened tea, which seemed to be regarded as a special delicacy. Achikh explained that honey and tea were produced far to the south; and gotten in trade from the Chinese.

Then Mongol clothing was brought for them—silk for Achikh as the chief's brother, and woolen for his guests. Clearly they'd been worn by others earlier, and not washed, but Baver was much less fastidious these days. They had nothing that fitted Nils; he would wear what he'd come in, dirt and all. Before they changed, water was brought to them, and bowls, though no soap, and they all stripped and washed. The nearby river invited, but they remembered Achikh's lessons on taboos and lesser injunctions.

When the council adjourned in midafternoon, the four newcomers were taken to the great *ger* of Kaidu, the chief, where guards took their weapons before they went in.

They entered bent low, especially Nils; the doorway required it. Svartvinge rode through on Nils's forearm. Kaidu sat waiting on an actual chair, carved from a single great block of wood. At each side of him, others sat on thick felt cushions, while before him, nearly twenty sat crosslegged on the floor mats.

"Kaidu Long Nose" was the chief's complete appellation, Achikh had told them. On that basis, Baver had expected someone with a long nose, but on New Home or among the Northmen, Kaidu's nose would have been considered quite modest. Only by Mongol standards was it long.

He'd been told of their arrival, and had prepared for them. A cushion immediately next to him was vacant, and there was room for more to sit on the floor in front of him. Baver kept an eye on both Achikh and Nils, for clues on what to do. Kaidu stood up when they entered. The rest turned to look. For a long moment it seemed to Baver that everyone's attention was stuck on Nils, his size, physique, and eyes, and perhaps on Svartvinge, whom he'd transferred to his shoulder.

Kaidu beckoned them to the front, where he embraced Achikh, then stepped back to arm's length, beaming at him. "Little brother!" he said. "You've grown. You've become a powerful warrior, and I see scars where there were none before." After they'd embraced again, he looked once more at his brother's companions. "Who are these others?" he asked.

Achikh introduced them, speaking formally, giving them their appropriate surnames, titles, and group affinities. Kaidu gazed long at each of them, but especially at the giant Northman with the uncanny eyes. Then he in turn introduced the men who sat on cushions. One was Fong Jung Hing, ambassador from the Emperor of China, a calm-seeming, quiet man whose aristocratic, fine-featured face seemed as foreign among the Buriat as Nils's Scandinavian features. Another was Teb-Tengri, whom he introduced as the principal shaman of Kaidu's tribe, the Black Stallion Tribe. Baver recognized the name Teb-Tengri as meaning something like "Most Heavenly." The shaman was a rather tall man of perhaps twenty-five or thirty years, and gaunt for a Buriat, with an arrogant face and bearing. Baver wondered if he was unwell, or if his gauntness was due to fasting; Achikh had once said that shamans sometimes fasted to sharpen their powers.

The introductions over, Kaidu seated his new guests, Achikh on his right, and the three foreigners in the back row among those on the floor. The chief moved his gaze first to Nils, then to Svartvinge, and finally to his shaman, to whom he spoke now. "Tell me, Teb-Tengri, what you see in this great raven and its master."

The shaman stared long at Svartvinge, then more briefly at Nils. Finally he spoke. Declaimed. "The bird is a great devil, Kaidu son of Kokchü, and the yellow-haired foreigner another. They have come here to do you great ill."

The *ger* became silent for a long moment. Baver felt his heart thudding, and realized he'd stopped breathing. The chief, however, had lost none of his poise.

"Indeed?" He looked at Achikh beside him. "And what would you reply, brother?"

Achikh had gotten to his feet by then, hand on sword-hilt, voice tight with anger. "Your shaman is alive this moment only because of the *yassa* against killing inside a dwelling."

Kaidu's eyebrows jumped. "Ah? And you, Teb-Tengri—what would you recommend be done with these whom you say are devils?"

Teb-Tengri's voice was as implacable as before. "Kill the bird first, then its servant, using methods to prevent their souls from escaping their bodies."

Kaidu still had shown no emotion deeper than very mild surprise. Looking at Nils he said: "And you—" He paused, groping for the foreign name, then gave up on it. "What do you say to this serious accusation?"

Nils bowed slightly without rising, and his voice, when he spoke, was mild. "Most men have something they don't want others to know of." He turned his strange gaze toward Teb-Tengri. "Your shaman, for example." He paused, glass eyes fixed on the gaunt face, seeming to look into and through it. "He fears I will tell what it is."

The shaman's face seemed to freeze.

"Actually," Nils went on, "there is another man in this room, besides himself and me, who knows his secret. Another with wizard powers. As Teb-Tengri already suspects."

"Um." Kaidu looked curiously at Teb-Tengri. "I am interested, but perhaps it's best to pursue this no further. Shaman, if you agree to forget this business of executing the foreigner, I will not ask him what your secret is. For secret or not, your powers are useful to our people and to me.

"As for the foreigner's bird, it is an owned bird, and not to be harmed."

Teb-Tengri opened his mouth as if to protest, then clamped it shut. Baver's thuttering heart slowed a bit.

Kaidu turned to Nils. "Among us, an owned bird has protection, and he who kills one is subject to suffocation. This *yassa* is intended to protect falcons and other hunting birds, but it states simply birds." He turned his face to Teb-Tengri again. "Heed me, shaman."

Once more he stood up. "This audience is now over. Everyone will leave except my brother and—" Again he groped unsuccessfully for Nils's name. "You," he said, pointing. "The Northman."

When the others had left, all of them but Kaidu's two bodyguards, the chief sat again and spoke to Nils. "You said that someone else in this room was a wizard. I must know who this person is."

"It is the emperor's ambassador, Fong Jung Hing."

Kaidu's lips pursed, and he nodded thoughtfully. "I believe you in this. I had wondered." He looked up at his bodyguards, who were also his cousins. "You will say nothing of this to anyone," he told them, stressing what was already his policy for private meetings. Then he looked at Nils again. "Now you must tell me how you know."

As he had done before, at critical times, Nils reached to his face, removed his eyes, and held them out in his

TWENTY-ONE

h told Kaidu some of his experiences and obser-
in the West, including Nils's fights in the arena,
h the lion, then with the Orc. When he was done,
evening, and soon time for supper.

u had already arranged to have the council as his
guests, and Achikh begged to be excused. He
to see his mother before he slept. Kaidu agreed.
ew too well the ugly relationship between Achikh's
er, Khada'an, and his own mother, Dokuz. And he
rred that it not color his friendship with his
ger brother, whom he saw as potentially a power-
upporter.

ctually Achikh was a half-brother, but the distinction
generally ignored in the Mongol culture. And while
du didn't mention it, of course, most of the tribe
sidered Dokuz's mistreatment of Khada'an as more
less disgraceful. Mothers-in-law were often harsh to
ughters-in-law, but not usually with such rancor, espe-
lly when earlier they'd both been wives of the same
an. And to a degree, the public disapproval reflected on
mself. Thus Kaidu was careful always to treat Khada'an
espectfully, and speak well of her.

hand to Kaidu, who stared in shock, first at the empty sockets, then at the pieces of colored glass in the callused palm. An oath breathed from his lips, and he turned to Achikh.

"Brother," he husked, "did you know of this?"

Achikh nodded. "He is a very great wizard. Also a man who speaks carefully and keeps his word."

"May I advise the great chief?" Nils asked quietly.

Kaidu nodded, his nerves taut with the shock of what he'd seen.

"Do not judge Teb-Tengri by his secret," Nils said. "That lies in the past, before he was a grown man, and what he did then, he wishes he had not. Judge him by his character now, the good and the bad, and his shaman skills. Also, can he be trusted? How far? And with what?

"As for those skills— He distrusted me. With eyes like mine, it's not surprising that someone might take me for demon-possessed. But one who has great shaman powers should see more deeply than that. Teb-Tengri is clever, but his wizard powers are minor."

While Nils spoke, Kaidu relaxed considerably. Quietly the Mongol chief put one of the glass eyes on the cushion to his left, where Teb-Tengri had sat, and covered it with a kerchief. The other he put in an empty drinking bowl on a stool to his right.

"Part of Teb-Tengri's usefulness to you," Nils was saying, "is that your people believe in him. Also he is a Buriat. Beyond his own self-interest, which may or may not rule him in a given instance, he has in mind the interest of his people and his tribe. That is not true of foreigners, however able, however powerful. Fong is a much more powerful wizard, but his loyalties are to his emperor."

"And your loyalties?"

"My loyalty is to the Tao."

"Hmm. I have heard of the Tao, but do not know what it is. It is a very old belief that is lost to us. Do the people of the west have it?"

"A few do. I learned of it from my first teacher, Raad-

giver, counselor to chiefs
him through many genera
it as an idea. Since then i
real to me."

Kaidu had watched Nils
Now he contemplated the N
eyes fixed on the sunken sock
kled lids. Finally he said, "Te
see without your eyes?"

"Easily." Nils put Svartvin
stepped forward, taking the on
kerchief, the other from the dri

When he'd returned them to
subject. "Your brother has had
and adventures in the west," he
would find them interesting and e

As for Nils and the others, they would be fed in their own *ger* by the woman assigned.

Word was sent to Khada'an that her son had returned and would visit her for supper. Her *ger* was not large, but it was large enough for herself and her household, and to entertain a few friends. Its furnishings were excellent. All in all it was appropriate to her unusual status—a younger widow of a chief who was not wife to the inheriting son. For normally, the inheriting son inherited his father's wives, except for his own mother. Typically his own mother would rule the women of the household—his wives and inherited wives—as the mother-in-law. Such rule could be pleasant or unpleasant.

Dokuz, Kaidu's mother, was Kokchü's first and eldest wife, a famous beauty with a face flatter than an owl's. She was the favorite daughter of the rich and powerful Mengetu family. Khada'an, Achikh's mother, was his fourth and final wife, neither beautiful nor ugly, and Achikh was Khada'an's only surviving son, the sixth son of eight, by various wives, who'd survived their father. Khada'an's family, the Tokurs, was neither rich nor powerful, though respected for their integrity and the quality of their horses.

According to Dokuz, her dislike of the younger woman grew out of Khada'an's inanities when the women would sit in the *ger* and do the many tasks that women do there. Besides, Khada'an did not look the part of a chief's wife, for the wives of any prominent man were expected to get fat, preferably very fat, and Khada'an, while filling out moderately, would measure only half of Dokuz's girth.

The gossip, though, was that her hatred had other roots: that Kokchü preferred to take Khada'an to his bed, though she gave him only one living son and two daughters.

Fortunately for Khada'an, Kokchü's mother was alive till almost the day of Kokchü's death. And under the old lady's even-handed management, Dokuz could abuse

Khada'an only with her sarcasm, while even in that her mother-in-law enforced restraint.

When Kokchü died, Kaidu inherited his wives, and Dokuz became the mother-in-law. Now she not only tongue-lashed Khada'an cruelly, but gave her demeaning and exhausting tasks in the household, as if she were one of the slaves. And indeed the slaves were better off, for the matron spoke to them far less harshly.

All of this Achikh already knew. It was the decisive reason why the seventeen-year-old youth, who had adventurous tendencies anyway, left home as the leader of a reckless teenaged band.

Now, on his first evening back, Achikh ate supper with his mother. A supper of beef and kidneys and brain and curds and *airag*. When he finished, he listened to a bitter recitation of his mother's resentments. After he'd gone traveling westward, she said, she no longer felt tied to the chief's household, and begged Kaidu to let her return to her family. Twice he'd withheld his permission. Not that he took his inherited wives to his bed, unless they requested it. He'd refused her simply because of his mother, who wished to retain her for her own cruel purposes. At her third request he'd relented, sending her back destitute to her father, whose charity fed and clothed her. She'd had to beg from her brothers to get the furnishings she had around her.

She also told him that as her son, he should publicly reject Kaidu as his brother

Achikh told Nils all of this late that night atop their sleeping robes, while Hans and Baver listened. They spoke in Anglic so far as possible, in case others were eavesdropping. "Then I went to my Uncle Jelme, my mother's eldest brother, wondering what I should do. Should I reject my elder brother Kaidu, who had taught me much as a child and had always treated me well? Most would say he was kind to release my mother; many would not have done it. But to send her away with nothing . . .

"Jelme told me that that was untrue. Kaidu had sent her off with cattle, sheep, horses, three slave girls, and household furnishings. Not that she'd come home rich, but she'd been far from poor."

Achikh sighed, hands behind his head, gazing at the dull glow of the coals reflected from the *ger*'s roof. "You need to have known my mother when I was young," he said. "She was always loving, more than most mothers. And she really loved my father, who was good to her. When he died, though, Dokuz was terrible to her, and it changed her, made her deeply bitter. I could not stand to live in the same *ger*, certainly not in winter, when one is inside so much.

"It was typical of Kaidu to let her go. Perhaps he did refuse her twice, but if he did, I am sure it was because his mother insisted. To release my mother was like letting her slap Dokuz's face, and I'm sure that Dokuz didn't accept it without being unpleasant to Kaidu too. She'd know her other daughters-in-law and her maids would talk about it behind her back.

"So Kaidu was generous, and I cannot reject him. But it grieves me that I must refuse my mother her request. I am her only son."

They all lay silent then awhile. Baver thought how cruel people could sometimes be, but in a culture like this one, so bound by tradition . . .

"Achikh, my *anda*," Nils said, "it is sad indeed that your mother was so changed. But you have done well to decide as you did. To reject Kaidu would be unjust, as you said, and it would feed your mother's hatred without satisfying it. For she has clearly lost her sanity, and would hate as much afterward as before. Also, what she asked would hurt you and Kaidu, while you know as I do that it would not hurt Dokuz. Dokuz would use it to justify what she'd done."

My anda. Baver was impressed. The word was equivalent to "soul brother," and the impression he'd gotten was that, beyond adolescence, it was used very selectively. Once before Nils had said they'd become *"like andat,"* but this time he'd said "my *anda."*

After Nils had validated Achikh in his decision, the Buriat warrior told them other things he'd learned from his Uncle Jelme.

The congress here was centered around a council, which consisted of the chiefs of all four tribes and the twelve principal clans. So far the council had dealt with routine matters: feuds between clans of different tribes, disputes over grazing and water—that sort of thing. They would also, perhaps tomorrow, discuss matters related to who, if anyone, should be Great Khan of all the Buriat. Only two chiefs contended for the position, Burhan Rides-the-Bear, who was chief of the Red Spear Tribe, and Kaidu Long Nose. Burhan did not seem avid for it, but he did not want Kaidu elected. And Kaidu almost surely would be, if unopposed, for just now among the Buriat there was a ferment to unite under a strong khan. They were concerned about the Chinese, actually the Sino-Tibetans, to the south, who had conquered the Uighurs and more recently the Koreans. And it seemed to most that only united under a Great Khan could the Buriat long survive.

Kaidu had earned much attention, a year earlier, by proposing that the tribes unite to make war on the Yakut-Russ, to the north, and take from them the wild and rugged forest region below the great lake called Baikal. There were grazing lands intermixed there, and much wild game. The Buriat had hunted in that country for as long as men knew, though the Yakut-Russ sometimes harassed and attacked the hunters. Possessing that land, the Buriat would have a place of retreat, should a great Sino-Tibetan army come to the steppes to enslave them, as they'd enslaved other peoples. And from the shelter of the endless forest, they could strike and harass any Chinese conqueror.

This Kaidu had proposed. Others had been quick to say that it was easier proposed than done; the Yakut-Russ were thinly scattered, but they were formidable fighters. Others had suggested how they might beat the Yakut-Russ and hold the land, while others yet had found fault with their reasoning. Still others had said that the realm of the Yakut-Russ was immense, and the region below Baikal a very small part of it. That mostly the Yakut-Russ were reindeer herders, and since the region below Baikal was not well-suited to reindeer, it was not important to them.

Thus had gone the debate, with no consensus growing out of it. Then Kaidu had withdrawn his proposal, knowing that the people would continue to talk about it, arguing among themselves, while his friends among them spoke for it. In another year or two, the tribes and clans might be ready to agree, and elect him their leader.

That had been a year ago.

This much Achikh had learned from talking with Jelme, his uncle, and he shared it with Nils in the presence of Hans and Baver. What he didn't know, hadn't the perspective to know, was that the Buriat were the most political of the three Mongol peoples, and the most inclined to assign power and loyalty beyond their clans to their tribes and chiefs. During the preceding two centuries, they had twice elected Great Khans to lead all the Buriat. These arrangements, however, had not taken root. The organization of khan rule, what organization there'd been, had been superficial, and in the absence of continuing strong incentives had come apart.

Each time, however, it had served its purpose: it had broken an invasion out of China.

Achikh wasn't the only person in the Buriat camp to make a report that evening. Fong Jung Hing had made one earlier, long distance.

The procedure could be somewhat cumbersome, but it was far quicker and easier than a courier riding 1,200 kilometers. Also it provided two-way communication—the exchange of information, and particularly of questions and answers—in a matter of minutes.

With Fong on mission, the Circle of Power had at least three adepts linked from suppertime till midnight—enough to detect any thought that Fong might "cast toward them." When a call was detected, other members of the Circle were sent for if necessary; five was adequate, even four in a pinch. And a runner rushed to the palace to inform the emperor.

With Tenzin as a guide, the Circle created a conduit, with the emperor the receiver. He would come at once, even if asleep when sent for, and sit in the middle of the Circle in what a twenty-first-century psychologist might have called a trance state, but in fact was a state of heightened, focused sensitivity.

Meanwhile Fong waited. Those who worked closely with the emperor had their patience well-developed. When he felt the emperor's psychic touch, Fong began their mental dialog: "Your Reverence, the barbarian you are interested in has arrived here at Urga. With the raven.

"The man's appearance is as Tenzin read it from the bird—very large, very powerful, and seemingly a great warrior. Certainly a superior telepath.

"His talents go much beyond that, however. He has great force of personality, and he is clever." Then he reran mentally the man's conversation with Kaidu, up to the time when the chief had cleared the *ger* of its other guests. "At that point," Fong said, "it was required that I leave. And as I am accompanied at all times by guards who both protect and constrain me, I could not loiter near the chief's *ger* and listen through the mind. The raven was there, however. Tenzin can learn for you what happened in my absence."

The emperor nudged his envoy's mind with a question.

"Where he will go from here," Fong answered, "he did not say, any more than he did in the hearing of the raven. Perhaps he spoke the truth to his companions last winter, when he said he didn't know, beyond accompanying the Mongol to his people. Perhaps he is someone who simply desires to see new places.

"But Your Reverence, there is something about him that makes him—unusually interesting and perhaps even dangerous. *He seems not to think to himself. I discern no internal monolog.*

... "No, Your Reverence, it is not a matter of screening. I would know if he screened. He simply does not carry on an internal monolog, and beneath his words, his mind seems still. It's as if he were in deep meditation constantly, even while talking and moving, seemingly alert. Obviously alert. The raven was not able to tell us that, of course. It could only show us his movements, let us listen to his words."

There was little more to the psychic conversation; then the emperor discontinued it. He next took a brief report from Tenzin Geshe on what the raven had seen. As he returned to his apartment, Songtsan Gampo felt a thrill run through him. This barbarian was indeed interesting. More than interesting: exciting! Tenzin had sensed the man as a threat, but Tenzin was always cautious. And opportunities often entailed danger. The barbarian held some special significance, it seemed to Songtsan, some special promise. Perhaps from him he'd learn something new and powerful, a key that would open the world to his grasp.

For just a moment, as if standing on an exhilarating height, he felt possibilities he couldn't quite perceive. Marvelous possibilities that went well beyond conquest!

Then the height sagged, and he lost his certainty.

But Songtsan Gampo was a man of spiritual strength as well as vast material power. And of great patience, when it suited him. He would wait, see, react, and take the initiative when the time came.

TWENTY-TWO

From—*Modern China*, by Giulio Matsuda. University Press, A.C. 832.

. . . . No written records have been found of the post-plague Tibetan migration into those parts of China previously peopled by "Chinese," that is, by people ethnically Chinese. Certain assumptions and conclusions can safely be made, however. Considering the physical appearance of the ethnic Tibetans in modern China, they presumably came from the eastern Tibet-Qinghai Plateau and adjacent mountain districts.

One might ask how there came to be so many. According to the Terran census of A.D. 2100, the last available, the total population of ethnic Tibetans within Tibet itself, and in the adjacent Chinese states of Xinjiang, Sichuan, Qinghai, and upper Yunnan was fewer than seven million. According to planet-wide estimates of plague and short-term post-plague mortality, the expected number of Tibetan survivors should have been somewhere between five hundred and five thousand. In the instance of a people many of whom lived a relatively self-sufficient life, not vitally dependent on the technological infrastructure, five thousand seems not unreasonable.

An additional peculiarity lies in the genetic strain of Tibetans to which modern Sino-Tibetans seem to belong: the Goloks. Judging by the degree of their population recovery, Asian nomads in general seem to have been less severely decimated by the plague, or more probably by post-plague privation and disease, than were other genetic stocks. But seemingly the Goloks were the least affected of all; one might hazard a guess that something like five percent survived, possibly ten or fifteen percent, instead of a small fraction of one percent.

Apparently becoming aware of the depopulation of China, with its much kinder climate, significant numbers of Goloks began moving down the river valleys into Guizhou, Qinling, lower Yunnan, and lower Sichuan within a generation or two. Numbers capable of dominating the scattered Chinese survivors they found in those areas. . . .

*   *   *

The next morning Baver opened his eyes to Hans's voice, not loud, but intense and worried. "Nils!" the boy was saying. "I cannot find Svartvinge! He is not on the roof, and I cannot see him flying!"

The doorflap was open and bright morning entered, to lose itself in the *ger*'s interior. Their sleeping robes were on beds of new hay near the wall. Nils rolled to his feet with no apparent disorientation. *He must already have been awake*. Baver thought sleepily. For a moment the Northman simply stood there as if listening, not to Hans, or *to* anything, but for something. Or so it seemed to Baver.

"The shaman has killed him!" Hans was saying. "Or had him killed! I know it!"

"Maybe he flew off to investigate something," Baver suggested, and got a dirty look from Hans.

Nils shook his head. "I don't think so, either one."

I don't think so. It occurred to Baver that such a statement was unusual from Nils. Usually he was sure of things.

"What, then?" Hans demanded.

"If he was near, within a few *tusen*, I would sense him and know where—in what direction. And if he'd been killed, I'd sense some residue of the act . . ."

He stiffened then, scanned the dim *ger* for a moment, and moved quickly to where his gear lay—battle harness, axe, bow and quiver, saddle . . . and dropped to his haunches. When he stood again, it was with the body of Svartvinge in his hands, like a large bundle of black feathers. The Northman said nothing, simply peered at the bird.

Baver found himself getting to his feet. From Hans, two words hissed: *Han förgiftas!* "He is poisoned!"

Baver stared.

"No," said Nils. With one hand he pinched lightly the latch of the dead bird's jaws, opening them more widely, and with the other took something from the beak or mouth. Squatting again, he lay Svartvinge on the floor, then without rising, examined the object the body had given up to him. Baver and Hans both came to see.

"What is it?" Hans asked.

To Baver it looked like a smooth pebble, rounded and slightly flattened.

The Northman sighed audibly. "A message."

"A message?" Hans and Baver said it together, then glanced at each other before they turned back to Nils, who stood up now.

The Northman nodded, and went to the fireplace in the center of the *ger*. Someone had replenished the fire, perhaps Achikh, who was gone, or Hans. There was a pile of firewood near it; Nils picked some of it up. "Bring fire," he said, and turned to the door. Achikh came in just then and stood aside, letting Nils go out, and peering after him. There was a small iron shovel by the hearth, its handle wrapped with leather. Hans shoved it into the fire, picked up a small, glowing mound of coals, and followed Nils, careful not to spill any.

"What is it?" asked the Buriat.

Baver pointed at the bird on the floor. "Svartvinge is dead," he said, and left after Hans into the early morning chill, Achikh behind him, saying nothing. Three meters in front of the door, Hans put the hot coals on the trampled ground where Nils pointed. Nils laid the wood on it, piece by piece, building it high.

It flamed up quickly. Hans had already gone back for more wood. Shortly they had a strong fire crackling, and for a minute watched it burn, hot enough to stand back from. Then, without a word, Nils went back in and brought out Svartvinge and the iron poker. The blond hair on his forearms crisping and curling, he laid the bird gently on the fire, then backed away and squatted at arm's length to watch. The breeze was light and variable. The smoke eddied a bit, and the smell of burning feathers assaulted Baver's nose.

It seemed to him that someone should say something, but he had no idea what. As if he'd heard Baver's thought, Achikh began a ritual chant, something about Tengri—God, not Teb-Tengri—calling to paradise the spirit of the deceased. Baver saw Hans's lips moving too, though he heard nothing from them. He wondered if the youth might be composing a verse, and that later, when he was satisfied with it, they might hear it.

Some tribesmen and women had come near, attracted by the odd activity. Several, when they realized what was going on, sheared off. When Achikh began his chant, two or three had joined in; clearly it was traditional. Those who didn't join in were perhaps put off by the species of the deceased. Among the watchers was the woman assigned to cook for them. She watched only briefly, then went into the *ger* to begin preparing breakfast for the four.

The body burned up quickly; even so large a raven,

more than seventy centimeters long, weighed only a few kilos. Nils squatted without speaking, his only movements to poke the fire up. The others stayed too, unwilling to leave until Nils left. When finally the fire had burned down to coals, Nils stood, looked around at the others and nodded soberly. Then they went in to breakfast.

As they ate, Baver recalled his mother's bird, a beech warbler. It would sing when they uncovered its cage in the morning—a lot nicer sound than Svartvinge ever made. But Svartvinge had character. He remembered the winter evenings in the forest hut, when Nils and Svartvinge would sit in silent contemplation of each other.

And Svartvinge had left a message. He wondered what it was.

After a quiet breakfast, the four walked to the floodplain of the Tola, and the open grove of old, thick-boled poplars in whose shade councils met. There was a loose flow of Buriat men walking there now, mostly in clusters. Here and there people would greet each other, perhaps stop to talk. Already within the grove's edge, numerous people squatted waiting, talking primarily about what they expected to hear discussed.

As the four approached the listening area, a tall, strongly built young warrior accosted Achikh.

"Achikh Runs-Away!" he said with false geniality. "I heard you'd come back. I am Barak, son of Jaghatai. You wouldn't recognize me; I was still a boy when you left." He looked for a moment at Nils and Hans and Baver, then back to Achikh. "I heard you'd taken up with foreigners, but found it hard to believe.'

Achikh said nothing, simply looked at the youth with hard eyes.

"What brought you so low," Barak went on, "that you so abandoned your pride?"

Achikh replied, using a formal style of speaking. "You were right when you said I would not remember you. You are not someone whom a warrior of pride and family would remember. Your father I remember. Your family

I remember. Your father and your family are worth remembering, but who are *you*, and what have you done? You are not simply young; you are callow. You have no wisdom. You speak freely but think little. The Mengetu Family must be embarrassed over you. If I cared to speak with one of the Mengetu family, it would be your father or one of your uncles, not a foolish boy."

Barak, son of Jaghatai, had been blushing before Achikh was half done, but he'd made no move, because fighting was forbidden at the council grove. Now he began to challenge Achikh to go elsewhere and fight him, but a heavy hand gripped his arm from behind and spun him around.

"Boy! Shut your mouth! Go to the *ger*; I will speak to you later!"

Barak froze. "Yes, father," he said, though to have his challenge cut short had almost broken his heart, after the provocation Achikh had given him. He hurried away, in his upset stumbling once over his own feet.

Jaghatai stared hard at Achikh, then gestured at Nils, Baver, and Hans. "A great council will be held here. On whose authority do you bring these foreigners? Even the emperor's ambassador is not allowed."

Achikh met the man's hard glare coldly, and answered, still in formal mode. "Kaidu the chief invited them. Out of respect my brother the chief invited them. They are free men, not the creatures of some emperor. They were not sent by some foreign ruler to do his bidding. The big one is Nils of the Iron Hand, a great wizard and great warrior. You see his scars, or some of them. My brother the chief invited him, and with him his friends. With his own sword, Nils of the Iron Hand killed the emperor of the west in single combat. Cut off his head with a single stroke, though the emperor was a giant, far larger and stronger even than he. This fight was witnessed by many on both sides.

"But before that, as a naked captive, he was cast into an arena, a broad pit, to fight a lion, a large fierce beast. Naked and given only a borrowed sword with a weak blade, he fought the lion, which is a tiger without stripes. He fought and killed the lion, breaking his sword in its skull. This was before a great crowd, of which I was one.

"Then the emperor sent down his champion to kill Nils of the Iron Hand, sent his champion in armor to butcher him. Still naked, and with another borrowed sword, Nils of the Iron Hand killed the emperor's champion. Again before a great crowd. I saw this too.

"Also, in private, he has proven his wizard skills to my brother, the chief. He has shown his wizardry to my brother the chief, and it was greater than any wizardry seen by him before. Thus my brother the chief invited Nils of the Iron Hand, and his close companions, to the council, as his guests."

Jaghatai's mouth had clamped shut early in this recitation, but when Achikh was done, he looked at the three and spoke. "Be welcome then," he gritted, and turning, stalked away.

Along with Achikh, the three sat not in the front and center—which would be arrogant and offensive of foreigners—but not far from the front, either, nor too far to the side. Wherever they'd walked, eyes had been drawn to Nils because of his size and obvious strength. He wore his leather shirt now, but it had no sleeves.

The listening area filled quickly, and as it did, the council came and took their seats on cushions brought by slaves. Finally Kaidu Long Nose stood up—he was the council's leader—and called for silence. When he had it, he spoke again in a strong voice. His mode of speech was formal but not repetitive; the council had much to discuss and hopefully settle in the three days left to them.

"Yesterday," Kaidu said, "we listened to complaints between tribes, and settled them justly. Today we shall speak of others matters, matters of broader scope." He paused, looking the crowd over. "Including a matter of which we have not spoken before."

That got their attention; they expected him to bring up an invasion of the Yakut-Russ.

"A year ago we also held a great congress here. At that time I proposed that we unite to seize the forest region below Baikal. Since then I have come to see matters differently." He gestured toward the front row of listeners, where for the first time Fong Jung Hing sat among bodyguards and keepers. "The emperor's ambassador has been here for almost a year—since a single moon after our last congress. He has made an offer which we all need to consider. Also I have had four ambassadors in China, traveling widely. Their reports have confirmed and enlarged on what my spies had learned for me earlier."

Baver could feel a tension in the crowd, a restlessness, an uncertainty.

"I will tell you what my ambassadors have seen," Kaidu went on, "before I tell you what the emperor proposes, and what I believe we should do. We have always known that China has a vast multitude of people. The emperor's ambassador says thirty million, which is a thousand thousands, and then thirty times that. More than all the Mongol people—the Buriat and Khalkhaz and Kalmuls—and also their horses and cattle and sheep.

"Of that multitude of Chinese, more than six million are Goloks—a thousand thousands, six times. The Goloks are good soldiers; many of them are warriors. They rule the empire, and the emperors have been Goloks from the beginning.

China has many towns, each with its garrison, each garrison with its troop of Golok cavalry. And every town, every district, has young men who, at the emperor's call, will put aside their work and muster with their swords and bows, their halberds and spears. Also, the country is full of people growing food and making all manner of things, including weapons and clothing and armor for the soldiers."

Kaidu looked his audience over. "Much of this I told you before, but it is worse than I knew then. Couriers on swift horses ride daily throughout the empire, and in many places there are signal towers within sight of each other, with men who know how to speak with a flag on a long pole. Also on these towers are men with far-seers, made with the hollow stems of certain saplings, with wizard glass set in the ends, which make distant things look near. Thus soldiers and other armed men can be gathered quickly from whatever towns and districts the emperor wishes, into armies small or large.

"Beyond all this, the emperor has large and dangerous ogres who fight for him. We had heard of them before, and doubted. They sounded like stories told to naughty children, to frighten them, but they are real. My ambassadors have seen them. They are far taller than men, stronger than the bear, more savage than the tiger. And they wield their great swords with the skill of masters.

"I would not wish to fight the empire. Our forefathers fought and drove away the armies of earlier kings and emperors, and we are not lesser men than our forefathers. But the army of this emperor is far more dangerous than earlier armies. Even in the depths of the Yakut-Russ forest, I would not wish to fight the emperor's army."

A voice rose from the crowd then, a voice impatient and angry. "What *do* you wish to do then? What do you propose?"

Kaidu took the gauntlet without a pause. "In the empire are great districts covered with leafy forest; land where the summers are long, with much rain, and the winters short and soft. Land well suited to growing the food the emperor's people eat. Every year his people clear more of those forests, and it grows abundant food. The emperor does not care to possess our land, where the soil is often bitter, and even in the memory of young men the winters have grown longer.

"He has conquered northward only to protect his outlands from raiders. The lands he wishes to possess are westward and southward. What he wants of us—" Kaidu stopped a long five seconds, making the people reach for what he had to say, then repeated slowly. "What he wants is that we be his allies. The lands he would conquer are mostly open lands, without fixed towns, without forts of stone. They are lands much like our own, but without the iron winters, and they go on forever, to the ends of the Earth."

Up till then, Kaidu had not raised his strong voice, which traveled far without shouting. Now though he spoke more loudly. "What the emperor wants is that we be his allies. That we make war westward. That we spread consternation and confusion through the western lands, while his own armies, vast and powerful, conquer and subjugate. Then, in the conquered world, the Mongols, especially the Buriat, will have first choice of the horses and cattle and slave girls. And the Mongol women, especially Buriat women, will wear silk and silver.

"I say 'Mongols' because he would have the Buriat raise all the Mongols to our banner. He would have the Buriat raise and lead all the Mongols. To the west, the Kalmuls are lurkers and skulkers by preference, and seldom follow any leader, though everyone knows they are dangerous fighters, swift and tireless horsemen. And more than any people, they are ravenous for the animals and goods of others. If the Buriat, powerful in union, were to press the Kalmuls, if a united and powerful Buriat people pressed them, they would join us for the looting they can have as the emperor's allies.

"While to the east, the Khalkhaz have fat herds and fat wives, and their leaders had rather watch their cattle graze and their colts race in the deep grass, than go to war outside their own pastures. Though they will fight like the bear to protect their possessions. And more than any Mongol people, the Khalkhaz worry about the emperor coming, for theirs are the richest pastures, their grass the tallest. They even raise grain and beets for their slaves to harvest!

"But their young men chafe at the lack of fighting. If the Buriat people were united, and proposed to the young men of the Khalkhaz that we go conquering westward together, most of their young men would shout 'yes!' And if this meant that the emperor's armies would go west instead of north, then their elders would not gainsay them."

Achikh had sat quietly, deeply disturbed at what he heard. And more deeply disturbed at what he saw around him, for many men's cheeks had darkened with excitement, and their eyes had taken the glint of a knife blade.

Then discussion began within the council, and there were questions from the crowd. Some, like Achikh, distrusted the emperor. Some did not want to leave their own steppes and mountains and herds. Especially the chiefs of the Red Spear clans resisted the proposal. The faces around Kaidu became more thoughtful, most of them, weighing, evaluating. And it seemed to Achikh that his brother might not get his way after all, though the voices raised for conquest, from whatever clan, still spoke strongly.

As the four sat on the floor eating supper, Achikh asked Nils, in Anglic, what he'd thought of the council meeting. Nils answered that it was not unlike council meetings of the Northmen. "What did you think of it?" he countered.

Achikh didn't answer at once. Baver wondered about Nils's question. If he knew the thoughts of the people around him, why would he ask? Perhaps to get Achikh to formulate his thoughts? Or simply to see what he'd say?

"I think," Achikh said at last, "that Kaidu spoke very skillfully. The things he said excited the people, many of them, made them want to do it in spite of doubts." He paused. "I am glad that Burhan Rides-the-Bear spoke so skillfully against it. For to trust the emperor, I think, is to trust the tiger, trust the lightning. I have seen one emperor, and fought for him. I think this one would be no better. One who becomes emperor, and remains emperor, must be ambitious beyond reason and ruthless beyond feeling."

*   *   *

After eating, Nils and Hans went to the paddock of the chief, where their own horses were kept, those they'd arrived on, and horses that Kaidu had gifted them with. Then they rode out of camp a short distance to drill with swords, an activity Hans didn't like to miss.

They did their forms for awhile, taking turns, Hans watching Nils and asking questions, Nils watching Hans and making comments. Soon they were sweating, though the sun had set and the cooling begun. When they had finished, they swung into their saddles and rode to the top of the rise beside them, to look out over the great encampment and drink water from a skin.

When he'd wiped his chin with his wrist, the apprentice poet spoke. In Swedish, which he preferred but had not used much lately. "If Achikh's people go to war for the emperor," he said, "will you join them?"

Nils shook his head. "I did not come here to fight for any emperor."

"Why *did* we come here?"

The Northman chuckled. "I only know that my weird sent me. You said you came so you would write my saga. And Baver—Baver believes he left the ting with you so he could let his friends know where I was. Later, he believed, he followed along because he couldn't find his way back alone. And both were true for him. But mainly he came because his weird drove him to it; the rest were simply reasons to believe in and give. The star folk do not believe in weirds, so often they must strive to imagine explanations, and then convince themselves that what they imagine is true."

Again they sat quiet, watching the dusk thicken while their horses grazed the feather grass and fescue. The details of the encampment blurred, and lost themselves in twilight. After a bit, Hans spoke again. "I do not understand the star folk," he said. "And Baver! He is so helpless!"

"Oh? He was at the start, but he does many things now. He's learned much. He had never lived in the forest before, or on the steppes. He had seen little of anything except towns, and nature was a stranger whom he'd heard about but didn't know.

Hans scowled, not wishing to alter his position. "And he has no interest in training with the sword!"

"True. It is not something his people do. They are people of peace. And their ancestors abandoned blades long ago, for more serious weapons."

Hans contemplated Nils's answer. He hadn't been along on the campaign against the Orcs, though he'd been one of the adolescents who'd hunted their survivors. The campaign itself had been only for the warriors. But he remembered what the warriors had said about the star folk's weapons. They'd been more than effective, if killing was the goal, but there seemed little honor to be won with them.

Nils nudged his horse's flank with a callused heel, and they started down the mild slope toward camp, the star folk still on Hans's mind. He tried to imagine flying between worlds. As they approached the first row of *gert*, he said, again in their own language, "I would like to ride in a skyboat sometime."

"Perhaps you will, Hans," the Yngling answered. "Perhaps you will."

TWENTY-THREE

. . . . stod å titte sej på liken,
släkting till han, Olof Snabbhann,
å på den som dråpte gubben.
Titte på å log föraktfullt.
"Ju men Du ä modi kjämpe!
att Du dråpt' d' gråa gubbe,
mä din knivslag i sin järta.
Kansje vi kan möta när jag
kjämpeflätor ha i åren,
om Du stanna ikke hemma."

Rytte då den rasne kjämpen,
slog på pojken mä sin näve.
Men den yngres näv var snabbre,
slog i käken som en hammar,
brytte halsen, läggde kjämpen
låg i dyen, död som fiske.
Så fick han sin kjämpenamne,
Järnhann för sin mäkti näve.

[. . . . looked upon the lifeless body

of his kinsman, Olof Quickhand,
and at he who'd killed the old man.
Looked at him and sneered disdainfully.
"No real warrior shows his valor
in the murder of a graybeard,
in the knifing of an old man.
In a year, my hair in warrior braids,
we can meet in single combat—
That is if you're not too cowardly."

Roared with rage the red-faced warrior,
Swung his heavy fist to strike him.
But the Youngling's fist was quicker,
struck the warrior like a hammer,
broke his neck and sent him crashing
to the mud, his dead eyes staring.
It was thus he earned his warrior name,
Ironhand was what they called him.

From—*The Järhann Saga,*
Kumalo translation

*   *   *

The Buriat great council met again in mid-morning, and arguments continued. After a time, a clan chief stood and declared that whatever the final decision might be on alliance with the emperor or invasion of the Yakut-Russ, and whoever might end up as Great Khan, there was one matter about which they had only a single choice: union! They must unite! The only alternative was to remain as they were and be overwhelmed by the empire.

The only real questions before them, he went on, were whether to invade northward, or to ally themselves with the emperor. And with that settled, who would lead the united Buriat tribes: Kaidu Long Nose or Burhan Rides-the-Bear.

This gave rise to more than an hour of speeches, some terse, some florid. Finally, at noon, Kaidu stood and proposed that the great council adjourn for the day. Let the clan councils meet and discuss the matter of alliance or invasion. The great council could meet again tomorrow or the next day.

The council agreed, and the meeting adjourned.

With Hans and Baver following, Achikh and Nils walked through the dispersing crowd, speaking Anglic for privacy. "If you had a voice in it," Achikh asked, "which would you vote for? Alliance or invasion?"

"Invasion northward," Nils said. "I would not see your people leading another imperial army westward to attack my own."

The answer dissatisfied Achikh. He'd wanted Nils to speak from the Buriat, not the Neoviking viewpoint. "And who would you vote for, for khan?"

"Burhan. Kaidu would make the best chief, for he is both wise and clever. But he has been spelled by Fong, or by the emperor through Fong, and on matters important to them, they will control his decisions."

"*Spelled!?*"

"There is a means of controlling someone's mind. It is not easily done, nor does it work on everyone. But it can be done. Given time, it can be done to almost anyone by certain wizards who can enter the mind undetected. Like Fong."

Achikh looked worriedly at the big Northman. "And this has been done to my brother Kaidu? Are you sure?"

"To your brother and two others on the great council." Nils named them, translating their surnames into Anglic so the people whom they walked among wouldn't know who was being spoken of. Each was an influential clan chief within the Black Stallion tribe. "Fong is a powerful wizard; in the West he'd be called a psi. The emperor seems to be another. And between the two—the emperor and Fong—is a greater power I do not understand yet."

By this time the crowd had thinned somewhat. Baver was wondering if Nils could do that sort of thing: enter a person's mind and control it. And if the Northman had ever controlled him. As they walked, a bellowing voice called to Achikh by name. They stopped.

A huge, burly Buriat strode up to them, his eyes on Nils rather than Achikh. Four cronies were with the man, all hard-looking. "Foreigner!" he said arrogantly, and looked the Northman up and down. He was five or six centimeters shorter than Nils Järnhann, but outweighed him by twenty kilos, Baver judged.

The man nodded, as if he approved what he saw. "You speak Mongol, I am told."

Nils nodded.

"Good! Good!" The Buriat grinned then, an unpleasant grin. "I have never, even as a boy, found anyone who could give me a real match in wrestling. Perhaps you can. I challenge you! You understand?"

Achikh broke in then, in Anglic. "This man is Kuduka. He has been famous as a wrestler since his childhood. Before he was grown, before hair grew on his face and only a little on his belly, he was famous for wrestling grown men. He has a hold with which he breaks their backs, he is so strong, and he is retained by the Mengetu family. I do not doubt he was sent by them. You can refuse to wrestle him; almost everyone does."

The Northman pursed his lips. "Where is your horse?" Nils asked the big Mongol. "As large as you are, you must have a very large, strong horse."

The Buriat frowned, puzzled. "Horse? What has my horse to do with our fighting?"

"Take me to it," Nils said, "and I'll show you."

The man stood indecisive for just a moment, then wheeled. "Come," he said, and strode off toward one of the paddocks, Nils and his companions following, Kuduka's friends bringing up the rear. Baver's right hand was in the holster pocket of his worn jumpsuit, gripping his pistol. In the paddock, Kuduka led them toward a large horse, which came to him. It was a stallion about sixteen hands tall, enormous for a Mongol horse, and powerfully built.

"This is my favorite. It is he I ride for hunting."

Nils nodded. "Before I answer your challenge, you must let me strike him with my fist."

Kuduka stared uncomprehendingly. "Strike him?" He frowned, then nodded. "Strike!" he said.

Nils struck the horse on the nose, and it fell like a rock. Instantly Kuduka was on his knees beside it, lifted an eyelid, then seemed to sniff, to smell, as if for the horse's breath. Finally he got to his feet, face writhing. "He is dead!" he said.

"That's why I'm called Ironhand," Nils replied calmly, then made his point. "Among my people, the man who is challenged has the right to name the form or weapons of the fight. If I accept your challenge, then the fight must be with fists. No grappling permitted."

Kuduka paled, and shook his head. "I challenged you to wrestle. Wrestling it must be!"

Nils shrugged. "Fists or nothing!" he said. For a long moment Kuduka stood confounded, then Nils turned his back and began to walk away. Several voices called out in warning, Hans's first. Nils, instead of turning to look, dove low to his left, hit the ground rolling and came up onto his feet with sword in hand, somehow not getting tangled up with his scabbard as he did so. It was a move Baver had seen him drill repeatedly with Hans, and made none to soon, for Kuduka's sword stroke was close. The big Mongol adjusted quickly, sword hacking, clanging against Nils's. Baver's attention left Nils then. Gun in fist, he watched Kuduka's henchmen. Achikh and Hans too had drawn weapons, but Kuduka's companions, though with swords in hand, seemed content for the moment to watch the two giants fight.

Kuduka was remarkably fast for his size, and skilled, and just now had the energy and savage commitment of a berserker. Yet despite the ferocity of his attack, technique was there to, too thoroughly drilled to be lost in the heat of his bloodlust. Nils, on the other hand, seemed fully occupied with avoiding or fending the blows that rained on him, though he did it most skillfully. Meanwhile men came running to watch, and quickly the fighters were ringed by a small but growing crowd.

At the first brief pause, each man had drawn his knife with his left hand, but first blood was let by Nils's sword, which partially fended, hacked Kuduka's left deltoid deeply. Yet the Mongol did not falter. Instead his frenzy increased. His face was contorted, his eyes wide and red, and he snapped and foamed at the mouth like a raging boar. Once he stumbled, yet recovered so quickly, so nimbly, that he took only a modest cut on the back, a gash by the sword tip. Someone was bellowing at him in Mongol to stop. The one shouting was Jaghatai, who did not, however, move to interfere.

Nils's defense had awed Baver; despite the onslaught he'd endured, the Northman seemed to have only a single cut, though it was long, a knife slash across his belly. Blood welled from it. Now he altered his tactics, took the offensive and drove Kuduka back. The Mongol began to tire, his breath hoarse gasps. He was bleeding profusely from a thigh cut that it seemed to Baver should have put him down. Suddenly he sprang backward and *threw* his sword spinning at Nils. As the Northman dodged, the hilt struck his face, then the weapon wheeled on into the ring of men behind, scattering them.

Nils didn't pause. He pounced, plunging his blade into Kuduka's body just below the breastbone, and the Mongol fell backward, blood spraying. For just a moment Baver stared at the fallen man, then his eyes moved to Nils. The Northman's body streamed sweat, and his chest heaved. The skin on his left cheek had been split by the hilt of Kuduka's thrown sword, and blood streamed from it. The cut in his belly seemed not deep; otherwise surely his guts would be bulging out through it.

The Northman looked around him and turned in the direction of the *ger*. It was also the direction of Kuduka's four henchmen, and he glared them out of his way with a look unlike any that Baver had ever seen on Nils before. Achikh and Hans had fallen in behind him, and Baver hurried to catch up.

At the *ger*, Nils's equanimity had returned, so totally it troubled Baver. Achikh examined the belly gash while Hans and Baver stood by. It was more than a centimeter deep, ugly but not critical. Tonus made it gape, but nowhere had it gone through the abdominal wall. Achikh bandaged it as well as he could. Scant minutes later an old woman arrived from Kaidu's household, a woman known for her skill with wounds. Removing Achikh's bandage, she ordered Nils to pinch the wound shut. From a skin she carried, she took long, strongly curved thorns, and with them fastened the gash closed, then put on a new bandage she'd brought. That done, she left, muttering to herself about men and sharp weapons. She'd ignored the injury to Nils's cheek. No doubt there was nothing to be done about it. It was swelling badly, and the entire left side of his face had turned the color of port wine. Baver suspected the cheekbone was broken.

Yet anyone who'd seen the fight would say the Northman had come out marvelously whole.

Nils did not lie down, but sat upright with his legs folded under him in a way Baver had seen him sit before, a way seemingly impossible for such muscular legs. He ignored the others, and seemed to enter a trance. Some kind of healing trance, Baver suspected.

Twenty minutes later Kaidu arrived, and Nils aroused at once. The chief looked the Northman over. "Old Yesüi tells me it isn't deadly," he said. "If it was, someone besides you would die for it." He turned to Achikh. "Tell me how it happened."

Achikh's recital of events was substantially as Baver recalled them. Kaidu nodded. "That agrees with what I've already been told." He looked at Nils again. "Iron Hand, you have rid the tribe of a great nuisance, and before witnesses who say it was no fault of yours. I will have some people questioned, in case someone put Kuduka up to this."

Then Kaidu left.

Achikh's lips pressed tightly. In Anglic he said, "Of course someone put Kuduka up to it. Barak. I'd bet a horse on it."

Nils's chuckle was brief and humorless. "Bet Kuduka's horse then," he said. "For I do not think it was Barak."

"Who then?"

"I'm not sure. But not Barak I think. Perhaps—perhaps Fong, acting for the emperor."

"The emperor? Why would the emperor want you dead? How would he even know you exist?"

"It may have been a test, more than an attempt to kill me." Earlier I said there is a power of some kind acting between Fong and the emperor. I was touched by that power two days before leaving the ting. Later I sensed it at times in Svartvinge. It is the power that created Svartvinge from the spirit of all ravens."

Hans stared. "Svartvinge was the thing of some evil power?"

"Svartvinge was a raven as the hailstorm was a hailstorm: he was the great raven. But he was sent, as the hailstorm was sent. I knew that when we first communed."

No one said anything to that for a moment. Then Achikh spoke. "When you communed, did he tell you about this power?"

"He knew nothing except that he was to find me. That was the purpose given him when he was created. He was unable to question it or even wonder about it. But I could see more deeply into him than he could."

It was Baver who spoke next. "What—what did you commune about, those nights in the cabin?"

"We simply communed. Experienced each other. Now his beingness has dispersed back among his people, and through him, all of the raven folk know mankind more deeply than before. While I—I know ravens now as few ever have. I know what it is to circle high, and to feel afar the beingness of other ravens. While he learned to screen his mind from whatever, or whoever, created him.

Thus it, or they, could only observe what he saw and the sounds he heard, not what he sensed inwardly.

"When I first met Fong, I felt the same power behind him. I know no more about it."

He fell silent then, but Hans had more questions. "Is Fong like Svartvinge? Created and sent by that power?"

"Fong was sent by the emperor, but he is a natural man, not created by the power. More I cannot say. I do not know."

He spoke no more to them after that, but returned to his trance. Achikh discovered that guards had been set around the place; they told him that Kaidu had ordered them there. They were to let no one enter the *ger*, or approach it closely. Yes, they said, if any of the occupants left, they would be free to reenter, and their cook would be allowed in, and Kaidu himself of course, if he chose, but no others.

After a bit, Achikh and Baver left together, got their horses and rode off northward, downstream along the Tola. Achikh had never previously spoken to Baver as a personal friend. Now he pointed out places he'd known as a boy and youth, when Kokchü's clan had camped nearby. With Achikh's agreement, Baver recorded it all. The cubes in the grip of his recorder would last for years, as would the power tap.

They were back at the *ger* in time for supper. Hans told them that Nils hadn't moved. The swelling in his face had gone down. The discoloration had turned to purple-black, and thence to a shading of greens, yellows, and purple. It seemed to Baver that that was an unusually rapid progression, but he wasn't sure. His personal experience with bruises had been limited, and restricted largely to childhood.

After supper, Achikh and Hans went out together to drill with swords, leaving Baver behind. Nils, who'd eaten nothing, said nothing, nor showed any sign of awareness of his surroundings. He simply sat there, legs folded, back straight. Baver fell asleep before the others returned.

It was Hans who woke first in the morning, with half-light showing dimly beneath the door and through the smoke hole. Enough that he could see Nils was gone.

Hans needed to go to the latrine, and assumed that that was where Nils had gone. But outside he saw no sign of him. It was raining, an unusual rain. Not the typical summer shower, this was more like an autumn rain that can fall for hours, or even from one day to the next. He ducked back in, leaving the door wide for added light. Nils's things were gone!—saddle, sleeping robe, weapons . . .

"Wake up!" he called. "Nils has disappeared!"

At the urgency in his voice, the others rolled out of their robes and got up. "He is at the latrine," Achikh grunted. "That's all."

"No! He's not! I looked! And see?" He pointed to where Nils's gear had been.

Achikh went frowning to the door and peered out. Nearby, guards were still on post, squatting glumly in the rain. No, they said, they hadn't seen the giant. They thought he was still inside.

Trotting, Achikh hurried to Kaidu's *ger*, where the chief's doorguard, after a brief conversation, let him in. Kaidu, alarmed and angry at what Achikh told him, sent for the commander of the *arban* assigned to guard the Northman. While they waited, Kaidu told Achikh what the healing woman had said: that the Northman's wound had gone nearly through the belly wall. That it might burst open and the guts bulge through if he did anything strenuous.

It turned out that the evening watch had seen the giant leave with his sleeping robe draped over him. He was carrying things under it, but what was impossible to see. Yes, it had seemed strange, but he was a foreigner. Who could tell why foreigners did the things they did?

Besides, it hadn't started raining yet. And wounded as he was, they assumed he'd be back.

No, they hadn't thought to follow him; they'd been posted to keep anyone from entering the *ger*, not to keep him from going anywhere. Besides, he was a foreigner; you couldn't guess what he was doing. Half an hour later they'd been relieved, and hadn't mentioned it to their replacements—it hadn't seemed necessary, and besides, it was raining then.

Nils's horses were gone from the paddock, the one that Shakir had given him, and the two that Kaidu had gifted him with. The horse guards on duty, who were slaves, knew nothing about it. Kaidu, angry now, had the horse guards of the earlier watch brought to him. Yes, the giant had come and gotten his horses well before midnight. They thought it was all right. They were his horses.

What way had he gone? They hadn't noticed; it had been very dark. It hadn't started to rain yet, but the overcast had been heavy, and one could see only a few paces.

Kaidu's anger died. "He is a wizard," the chief said thoughtfully. "Who can understand the comings and goings of a wizard? A foreign wizard, especially. And if, in the afternoon, his wound was dangerous, what might his wizardry have accomplished with it since? I'd hoped to recruit him as the shaman of my house. He is wiser and more honest than Teb-Tengri, and more able. But . . ." He shrugged.

Achikh jogged back to the *ger* where his companions waited. Hans and Baver had already bundled their things; Hans would follow Nils, and Baver intended to go with him. "Hurry," Hans said to Achikh. "We will wait while you get ready."

Achikh shook his head. "No," he said, "I'll let him go. It is not my place to tell him to come back, or to follow him when he refuses. And I believe my brother needs me. But if you'll wait a little, I'll see that you have a pack horse and supplies, that you need not slow down to hunt along the way. You'll be slowed enough by tracking."

It galled Hans to delay, but he was a Northman, and trailwise beyond his years. Besides, the cook had just arrived. So they waited, he and Baver, and ate.

Meanwhile Kaidu sent horsemen spiralling out from the encampment, under orders to continue till they found tracks that they thought were the Northman's. They were not to follow them, but to mark the place and bring back word. Hans and Baver should stay till then.

It was afternoon before the two left. By then a cool wind was breaking up the clouds. Briefly, Baver thought Achikh was going to change his mind and go with them, but he didn't. They left alone, with supplies and a small banner of Kaidu's house that had a safe-conduct rolled up in it.

TWENTY-FOUR

Hans and Baver had set out riding briskly, for Nils's tracks had been headed southeastward on the ancient highway, and tracking didn't seem necessary. It should, they thought, be enough simply to follow the road. They'd hoped to catch sight of him before dark. He had his wound, after all, and he'd started before midnight. Surely he'd had to stop and rest. Probably he'd holed up in his shelter tent when it began to rain, to sleep at least until it quit.

But the days were growing shorter, and dusk arrived before they caught up with him. "Shall we go on?" Baver asked. "He has to be weak after losing blood the way he did."

Hans had seen more wounds than Baver, and paid closer attention to them. Nils had bled freely enough, but the loss had not been great, especially for someone his size. What troubled Hans most was that Nils had chosen to leave without him. He must have had a reason, but nonetheless— Hans nodded; someone following the road as Nils was would surely not leave it far to camp— not far enough to miss, even in the night. If they stayed with it, making good use of their remounts, they'd catch him before daylight.

They stopped briefly to let their horses graze. For their own supper, they made do with curds and *airag*, then pushed on. By midnight Baver was having trouble staying awake in the saddle. Hans, on the other hand, wasn't sleepy. He had something to occupy him—watching for sign that Nils might have left the road, farther than he'd expected. When the halfmoon set, about midnight, he thought of camping. Instead he took a chance and pushed on. Twice he stopped at arroyos. One had a tiny creek, and the other might have water a little upstream or down. At each he dismounted and knelt, examining as best he could, with eyes and fingers, the grass and ground along the old roadbed for sign of someone having left the road. And found none. Nor did the dry arroyo have tracks in the bottom. Hans mounted again and pushed on.

Baver awoke in the saddle from a dream of pursuit. Mounted Orcs had been thundering after them, and he and Hans were riding donkeys that refused to run, insisting instead on trying to lie down. Dawn was lightening the sky, and he had no clear recollection of anything other than dozing, waking, and restless dreams since the moon had set. Vaguely he recalled changing horses a few times.

Hans had stopped, and Baver's mount had followed suit. "We've passed him," Hans was saying. "There are no fresh tracks here." He sounded chagrined, angry with himself.

"Maybe we should stop and wait for him," Baver suggested. "Let him catch us." He was aware of hunger now. His sleepiness had passed for the moment.

Hans shook his head. "You can wait. I'm going back and find him. He could be hurt. If he left the road, his horse might have stepped in a marmot hole and fallen with him. His belly could have burst open."

They did stop long enough to hobble the horses and let them graze and rest, while they had something to eat themselves. Then they turned back, riding the way they'd come, both of them watching the roadsides. After a bit the sun rose. Some time afterward they came to Nil's tracks, or at least tracks they assumed were his, leaving the road. They followed them. There was no creekbed there, no sign of water. The tracks left at right angles to the road, and for awhile their spacing indicated a brisk trot. So Hans said. To Baver, the combined tracks of mount, remount, and pack horse were a confusion. About two kilometers away, or a little more, they turned and roughly paralleled the highway. The trot continued, though it had eased a bit.

Here it had rained little or not at all, and the tracks were mostly scuffs and nicks in the hard ground. The bunch grass was too sparse to show his passage, but there was enough of it to conceal his tracks, except from close up, which slowed their pursuit. The two pressed on, slowed by the need to stay on Nils's trail.

It seemed to Baver that Nils had done this deliberately, to keep from being caught up with. If he was truly telepathic, and it seemed he must be, then he might even have sensed them coming and left the highway only a little ahead of their passing. But the star man never seriously thought of suggesting they turn back. Hans would never agree anyway. And he wasn't about to go it alone; his newly-acquired survival know-how felt seriously inadequate in a world of Kalmuls, Kazakhs, and other unpredictables.

About midday they came to the broad trail of sheep being herded crosscountry. Nils's tracks were lost in the profusion of hoofprints—sheep and the herdsmen's horses. Hans found no indication of prints crossing the others directly. For several hours Nils had roughly paralleled the highway, deviating only to keep some terrain in between. The herd had been driven diagonally toward it. Nils could have followed it to the road or beyond, or followed it a short way and then continued as before.

Hans had been picking his way along the far edge of

the herd trail, watching for sign that Nils had left it. As they approached the road, it seemed to Baver they'd surely find his tracks there again, but they didn't. *So much for intuition,* he told himself.

Hans reined up in exasperation, and looked at Baver. "If I follow the herd trail, can you go back and see if he went the other way on it? Look for tracks going the other way than these, then keep to the edge and see if he left it. Surely you can do that!"

Baver felt there was nothing sure about it at all. "Where will we meet?" he asked.

"Here. On the road."

"The last time you said you'd wait for me, you didn't."

"I will this time."

Baver nodded. "All right," he said. He untied his remount from Hans's, leaving the packhorse, and backtracked along the west edge, first at a trot, then at a slow walk. To his great pleasure, he found where he and Hans had hit it; he could find tracks! But after another hour he'd found none he recognized as going counter to the herd, nor any leaving the herd trail. Turning, he trotted his horse back toward the highway.

Crossing a little rise, he could see no sign of Hans waiting there. When he reached it, he dismounted, hobbled both horses, and let them rest and graze. He himself lay down on the lumpy ground with an arm shielding his eyes, and went to sleep at once. It seemed to him that Hans, despite his promise, might have abandoned him, but he wasn't going to worry about it.

It wasn't much later that Hans woke him; he hadn't slept long enough to feel gummy-eyed and confused— maybe twenty minutes.

"Did you find anything?" Hans asked.

Baver got up and shook his head. "Our tracks, that's all."

Hans looked grim. "We'll ride the road then. He followed it far, and when he left it he rode in the same direction. He must be going where the road goes. Maybe he'll come back to it."

He didn't sound optimistic, only determined.

Near sundown they came to a live stream with poplars growing along it. By that time both of them were nearly falling out of the saddle. Hans had killed a marmot. Now he dismounted, Baver following suit. They hobbled their horses, gathered deadwood, built a fire, and skewered the marmot, setting it to roast. Then they pitched the tent, refilled their waterbags, ate the marmot half raw, and crawling into the tent, fell quickly asleep. They wouldn't wake till dawn.

PART IV

DISPERSAL

TWENTY-FIVE

At the time of the Great Death, the Yan Mountains had had little natural forest. Most of it was of trees that stood bare in winter: oak and chestnut, maple and ash. Planted forests had been more extensive, mainly Korean pine, with lesser areas of other conifers. Then the Death came, and suddenly there was no more logging, no more cultivation. Feral dogs multiplied, decimating what livestock there was. Before long the smaller feral dogs had disappeared: They lacked a suitable ecological niche, and in hard winters were preyed upon by the larger, which in turn were eaten by wolves that drifted in. More and more old fields and pastures were conquered by forest, and with ecological succession, the hardwoods tended to crowd the conifers out. At length the climate began to cool, and the conifers increased, including species that migrated in from the Changbai and Da Hinggan Mountains to the east and north.

The few human survivors and their descendants had mostly moved southward, where the climate was softer. Bears had drifted in, and considerably later Siberian tigers.

The town of Miyun had crumbled. Centuries later it would be mined for steel and cement by returning humans. The new Miyun, the empire's capital, was kilometers away and higher, between the old Miyun and long-dead Chengde. The site had been chosen by the young Songtsan II for its beauty. Also the Great Wall passed nearby, providing abundant building stone.

The imperial palace occupied much of a high hill. It's surrounding wall enclosed more than sixty hectares of land—parade ground, gardens, and various buildings—all enclosed by a high wall of stone blocks. It was referred to as "the Dzong," which in Tibetan means fortress.

It didn't resemble at all the ancient fortresses of Tibet. They'd been built to withstand sieges and assaults by armies which, though pre-technological, were much more sophisticated than anything existing in the post-plague world. Large habitable areas of the Earth still were occupied thinly or even not at all by humans. Thus large wars for territory were just beginning to occur again, and long-lost techniques for the siege and assault of strongholds had not been reinvented.

But the Dzong, though designed more for privacy and beauty than defense, was as much a fortress as any in the empire.

A runner had notified Songtsan Gampo that Lord Fong was waiting to report, and with one particularly large yeti guard, the emperor had stridden across the parade ground, then wound downslope through shaded, pool-dotted gardens to the modest *gomba* of his Circle of Power. It had been built thirty years earlier beside a quiet shadowing grove of ancient, thick-boled *thujas*—arbor vitaes dark and shaggy, long escaped from cultivation.

The sleeping rooms of the monks were on the second story, and the library on the third. The Sanctuary of the Circle was on the first, along with the kitchen, the eating room, the latrine, and several other rooms.

The Circle sat in a sort of semi-trance, waiting, holding

the channel open between itself and Fong, more than twelve hundred kilometers away. The emperor stepped into the middle and assumed the lotus posture.

Telepath that he was, and with the Circle providing a carrier wave, the emperor's connection with Fong was immediate when he opened himself to it. Words whispered in his mind, overlying the concepts, and supported at times by images. Overall, their exchange was approximately as follows:

"Your Magnificence, the elemental raven provided by your Circle of Power is dead. The circumstances are not clear, but I have the distinct feeling that it deliberately disassembled. The Northman was observed burning the body outside his tent in the Buriat encampment early this morning."

Songtsan Gampo acknowledged the information silently. Tenzin had told him earlier that the elemental had disassembled, and the shock had killed the body.

"Since then," Fong went on, "the Northman has fought with one of the Buriat, a huge man, larger even than himself, renowned as both a wrestler and swordsman. A remarkable fight; the entire camp is abuzz with it. He killed the Buriat with his sword—after first killing the Buriat's horse with his fist! But he himself took a great cut on the abdomen, though it did not disembowel him. Reports of its seriousness differ, and I cannot verify any of them; all large cuts look ghastly to me. I watched the fight through the mind of a tribesman."

Visually he replayed it for the emperor. When he was done, the emperor asked thoughtfully: "Is he likely to be executed for this?"

"It is highly unlikely. For several reasons: The Buriat seems to have started the fight, and the crowd seems content or even pleased with the result; the Buriat was a notorious bully, and widely disliked. Most importantly, Kaidu has taken the Northman's part in it. Also, the Northman has left the camp. Alone. And no one seems to know where to or why. The rumor in camp is that someone was trying to have him killed, and that he believed he could not long survive there.

"Even his companions did not know in which direction he'd gone. I was able to approach them closely enough to read them on that. I also have very interesting information from the boy who is a clansman of the barbarian. It is not entirely clear—I was unable to probe the boy— but seemingly the barbarian is more than two hundred years old."

Songtsan Gampo's mind jerked at that. "Two hundred years? That's impossible!"

The reaction told Fong that his emperor very much wanted to believe. "Your Magnificence," he said, "my information was from substrate, not a thought flow, and somewhat unclear. But it seems the barbarian has twice saved his people: once two hundred years ago, and once recently. The boy is concerned for him."

Songtsan Gampo sat without further reaction for long seconds. Meanwhile Fong kept still; he sensed that the emperor would have a reply. Finally he did. "Surely someone there has at least an idea of where he's going."

"Not where he's going, but his tracks have been found. On the road between Urga and the ancient capital. His ex-companions are following him now. It seems he left before midnight, wounds and all, and wasn't missed till after daybreak.

"It's as if he were coming to you."

The emperor sat mentally quiet, contemplating this. After a long minute, Fong cast another thought. "Another thing, Your Magnificence."

"Yes?"

"One of his companions, called Ted, seems to be an ancient."

"An ancient? You mean he too is old?"

"Your Magnificence, you've heard the legend that some of the ancients had flown to the stars before the Great Death."

"Of course."

"Judging from this Ted's thoughts and those of the

barbarian boy, not only is the legend true, but a ship of ancients has returned across the sky. This Baver seems to be one of them—one of the ancients, or more probably one of their offspring. The barbarian boy thinks of them as 'Star Folk.'"

Songtsan Gampo had no further questions, and when it was clear that his envoy had nothing more to volunteer, he ended the communication. Then he looked at Tenzin Geshe and spoke aloud: "You have heard all this. Create another elemental raven and have the barbarian found. Also his two friends. If they are traveling on or along the highway, it shouldn't be difficult. I do not want them lost again. I will have them captured alive, especially the barbarian and the—star man."

With that the emperor got up, and with his yeti bodyguard left the sanctuary. That the barbarian might be two hundred years old felt more real to him than the idea of "star folk," but best to take them both alive and question them. After all, Fong seemed to credit the stories, and the Chinese had demonstrated repeatedly not only his powers but his acuity.

The emperor's bodyguard had always been exceptionally large and strong for his age. His short-napped fur was a rich auburn red, and he'd been named *Maamo* from its color. Then Tenzin and the Circle had installed an ogre elemental in him. Maamo didn't know what had happened; he only knew he'd changed, suddenly, in strength and dominance, personality and intelligence. He had the same memories as before, but he felt like a different being.

He didn't wonder about these changes, he simply accepted them. Yunnan ogres are not often introspective.

Meanwhile he followed Songtsan Gampo two paces to the rear. If anyone had tried to attack the emperor, the attacker would have died quickly and violently.

TWENTY-SIX

Tenzin and the Circle waited till morning to gather a raven elemental. When it was done, and they had given it its purpose, through it they called a great raven to them, the largest in the Yan Mountains, and the bird came and was possessed by it, becoming the quintessential raven, dominant over all the rest. Tenzin considered it superior to Svartvinge: It was more closely instructed, and proof against any affinity with the barbarian. When it found him, it would read him from a little distance, and the Circle would know all that the great bird saw and read.

At once it flew forth, and before long, every raven as far north as Gil'ui and Baikal, and as far west as the Altai received its request, relayed through the field of raven beingness. They were to watch for three men. Also from the elemental, each received an image of the three, accessed from the collective raven experience.

Surely the three would be found, for ravens cruise almost constantly by day, looking for anything dead, small or large, and in the process see the living.

*   *   *

Tenzin Geshe was not concerned when, for several days, he'd heard nothing from them. Miyun was very far from Urga, 1,200 kilometers, most of it open, steppe or desert, while ravens are birds of the forests and mountains. But after ten days he began to be anxious, for he felt sure that the Northman had intended to come to Miyun. And over the centuries since the Great Death, forests had spread westward, especially during the climatic cooling of the last hundred years. Some 400 kilometers west, the Northman would enter a rough land with numerous groves and woods on slopes that faced north and east, a land where ravens hunted. The Northman should have reached there by now, and been reported.

Was my premonition wrong? Tenzin wondered. It had been strong enough. The Northman could have changed his mind later, but then where to? Surely not into the Gobi. To cross it westward would be a journey of death in any season but spring. While if he'd turned northward—By now that should have taken him into woodlands too, where the ravens would have discovered him.

Or—if the Northman made it far enough east, he'd reach forest where large areas had few openings. There, conceivably, the ravens might miss him for days, if he kept carefully to cover. But . . .

Could he be traveling by night? Ravens roosted by night! And it was the sort of thing he might do!

He'd overlooked the possibility! And he had the emperor's strict injunction!

Abruptly he left his shady balcony and went into the Sanctuary, where he sat aside from the Circle to contemplate the problem.

Tenzin contemplated a problem not by pondering. Rather, he dispelled all other thoughts, defined his problem clearly, then entered a trance to let happen what would.

As a novice, long years earlier, the procedure would have been impossible to him. To sit quietly to meditate had meant opening the door to every anxiety, every aggravation and idle thought, every grudge and grief. And if his mind began to quiet, sleep was likely to slip in and claim him. But over the years he'd looked at them all: anxieties, aggravations . . . the roots of all his most intrusive thoughts. Old grudges had died, old griefs had lost their force, and confidence grown from experience quieted what was left. Seldom now did anything disturb the stillness of his meditation, and drowsiness rarely intervened.

This day he sat in deep trance for nearly three hours, and came back aware of things he'd never before noticed.

The Sigma Field had been somewhat known eight hundred years earlier, though imperfectly and incompletely. It had been defined and described mathematically with equations that enabled a technology to grow out of it. Equations that gave rise first to the sublight-speed warp drive, which actually was a drive, and later to the hyperdrive, which was no drive at all, but could transfer a ship to a remote point with a lapsed time differing from zero (very substantially from zero) only because of the limitations of matter, especially life forms.

Tenzin's knowledge of the Sigma Field was far less precise, but it was broader, more comprehensive. He couldn't have begun to design a warp drive with what he knew, let alone a hyperdrive, but he saw possibilities that Hampton and Mazour and their graduate students, some eight hundred years earlier, had not. To him the Sigma Field was not a complex of esoteric equations. It was like a mesh, a kind of net that clothed reality, and a template that gave it form. In a way it was alive, like a river is alive, flowing over and through and around. And like a stream, it was aware only at a very primitive level.

He thought of it as "the fabric of Tao," which it is not.

It also seemed to him that like a net, the strands might be separated somewhat, not by hands but by his focused intent, powered by the Circle. And into the mesh something inserted which was highly aware. An elemental.

Besides Tenzin there were twelve members of the Circle now, Songtsan Gampo having dipped deeper into the list of adepts compiled for him some years earlier. This permitted seating no fewer than four at any time, while still allowing adequate rest.

But seven, plus Tenzin as the director and manipulator, was the optimum number, called upon for special needs. And it was seven that the *geshe* seated now.

Ravens would not do for his newly recognized need. They were not assertive enough, not aggressive enough, probably not intelligent enough. What he needed was an elemental with a sufficient innate sense of the mesh that individuals of the species communed with one another psychically. Like ravens, but something more intelligent. He decided to gather a wolf elemental. Once in the mesh, it seemed to him it might "permeate" an area of it and become aware of all life over a considerable region. And after learning to function in the mesh, hopefully it could identify whatever it found.

Thus a wolf elemental was gathered: aware, intelligent, vibrant with fear, and for awhile he calmed it. When it seemed to Tenzin sufficiently calm, he held it as with a hand, and with the other opened the mesh. Then he urged the elemental to enter. It touched the field and resisted. He pushed, and the resistance increased; clearly an obedience command had its limits. Carefully he opened the mesh wider, but the resistance remained. And wider . . .

TWENTY-SEVEN

The cult, led by its master and his three sevens of acolytes, had encircled the village and attacked at dawn, when most of the villagers still slept. The cult members knew exactly what they were to do, while the villagers, though more numerous, were confused and terrified.

The attack was intended to kill the young men and anyone who resisted. It succeeded, except that a small handful escaped into the surrounding jungle. During the attack, women, children, and old men were struck down, some of them unconscious, a few dead, most simply cowed. When the young men were dead, the women, children, and old men were herded into a few lodges and held under guard until the cult had tallied its own injured, which were few.

Then the master examined the prisoners, questioning the old men, alternately scowling and nodding at the women and girls. Those he selected were taken under guard to a large hut. He gave his men leave to use the others as they would, but took only one for himself. When he had finished with her, he went out into the little plaza, where the chickens and pigs had calmed down after the fighting, and were foraging. He stood gazing thoughtfully at the Great God who loomed above the village, smoke curling upward from it in the near-windless morning, as it had for weeks now. Crying, screaming, and coarse laughter sounded from the lodges, but the Great God gave no sign of hearing.

He did not doubt though. *It is waiting,* he thought. *It is ready.*

Since the moderate eruption seven years earlier, he'd been preparing. Six years ago he'd begun proselytizing and recruiting throughout the region, speaking always moderately and quietly in the villages, but playing on old fears of the mountain, and reminding the people of beliefs that were older than *cristianismo,* which had been forced upon the people by foreigners long ago.

When he had followers enough, they'd withdrawn, forming a village of their own, their numbers increasing gradually with new recruits. There they'd prepared for three years. Then, a month earlier, the Great God had belched, and smoke had been rising quietly from its top ever since. And one night, while praying in a mushroom trance, the master had felt the Great God's eagerness vibrate through his bones, telling him he had seven nights to prepare.

He had made as ready as he could. He and his three sevens had sweated in their steam huts, fasting, eating only the sacred ants and certain special mushrooms, and in the spirit had communed with the Great God. Then, with the others of the cult, they had smoked the holy seed heads. After which, full of the Great God's spirit, the men had danced while their women chanted the special prayer-song.

The attack had gone almost perfectly. Clearly the Great God had heard and watched, had found their actions good.

The cult master began to move again. After scanning the plaza, he drove a stake near its center, tied a long cord to it, and paced a semicircle at the cord's end, jabbing the ground at every fifth stride with his steel-headed spear. Some of his men—those who were being punished for some misdemeanor—had been standing unhappily, waiting for orders. They sprang into action now. Some began to dig holes where he'd marked. Poles were set, and the ground tamped firm around them, then firewood and broken furniture were dumped near each. A table of heavy split planks, planed and smoothed and stained nearly black, was lugged from the small adobe church by eight sweating men and set down in the middle of the semicircle of posts, at the place he'd staked. Then, when the master had assured its proper orientation to the Great God, they evened the ground till the table stood level and steady.

It all took somewhat less than an hour. By that time the crying and screaming had long stopped; the only villagers left alive were those sequestered in a hut. These were herded out, nine girls and three older men, all naked except for their crucifixes. The men had been beaten and castrated. Eight of the girls and the three men were tied to stakes. The eight were not molested sexually; they were the bridesmaids. One of the older men, *el sacerdote*, was invited to renounce *el cristo*, and when he refused, the master cut his belly open so that his guts spilled to the ground. He screamed, then prayed so loudly to his Lord, the cult master feared it would anger the Great God, and had his mouth tied shut. By the time it was done, his state of shock was so profound, he was beyond speech anyway. Wood was piled around them all on their stakes. Next all of the cultists filled their pipes with sacred seed heads, lit them, and smoked. When they were high, they lit the fires.

Amidst the screaming, the ninth girl swooned and was carried to the table. There, with a single smooth stroke, the cult master cut her throat with a razor-sharp knife of obsidian.

The ground shook, jumped, set the branches bobbing on the trees. A sound greater than thunder stunned the cultists, drove them to their knees. Their master looked upward at the Great God and saw a turbidity flow, a dense, furnace-hot cloud of incandescent ash and fumes rolling down the mountain toward them with astounding speed. He cried out, partly in exultation, partly in terror . . .

TWENTY-EIGHT

Something inserted into the Sigma Field with a shock that jarred Tenzin Geshe out of the group trance. Briefly he sat stunned, then looked around. One of the Circle lay unconscious, another was on his knees, retching. The rest appeared shaken, as he was himself.

He didn't need to enter a trance again to know that what had entered the fabric of the Tao was not the wolf elemental. It was something far more powerful. Something depraved. And his immediate fear was that they could not get it out.

Tentatively he felt for it, and psychically touched it. Just now it seemed inert, as if it too had been shocked by what had happened. *A demon,* he thought. *The emperor has asked for demons. Now it seems we have one. Though how it had happened . . .*

However it had happened, they had a demon in a position of power, or potential power, beyond any that anyone, man or demon, had even approached before, it seemed to Tenzin. A position that he had given it.

He would not tell the emperor until he'd had time to probe the situation and learn more about it. He felt a deep foreboding. It seemed to him that he had brought about a terrible misfortune, a calamity for more than himself, for more than the emperor. A calamity for mankind.

How long, he wondered, might it take to work off the karma he'd earned this night?

TWENTY-NINE

For several days after he'd lost Hans and Baver, Nils traveled in the same direction the road had been going, but at some distance away. His wound gave him no trouble. The trance he'd sat in, in the *ger* at Urga, had been a healing trance taught him by his wife, Ilse, whom the Neovikings called the German witch. Healing had progressed considerably in the hours before he'd left.

He might have returned to the road to ride by night, but the days were too hot for sleeping on the ground, in either shelter tent or sun.

After several days, the country became desert, and both Nils and his horses suffered from dehydration. So presuming there'd be water there for travelers and their animals, he returned to the road. But when evening came, he left the road to sleep, and let his hobbled horses nibble on what little growth of grass and shrubs there was. He didn't picket them; they'd have starved there, constrained to a rope's length.

Meanwhile marmots had become nonexistent, and the big Northman ate only the occasional small lizard he could catch. His only option was to tap a vein on one of the horses and drink the blood, but he needed their strength more than he did his own. His belly complained, but he ignored it.

Beside the road there were dug wells, one or more a day, marked by the low trees that grew near them, their roots tapping ground water. Each well had a windlass, a large leather pail with a weighted rim to raise the water, and a horse trough to pour it in. It was obvious that someone maintained them.

On this third day back on the road, he saw a low streamer of dust well ahead: travelers. He left the road to watch them pass from a distance. There were perhaps two score horsemen, and a long train of strange, tall, ungainly animals piled high with packs. They were the first travelers Nils had seen, or sensed, since he'd left the road to avoid his friends.

Finally there were hills again. The grass thickened and stood taller, though still there were no springs along the road. The wells continued. There were marmots again, too, and Nils filled his belly.

A day later, in late afternoon, he came to the first shallow draws where the Mongolian Plateau began to break toward the Chinese lowlands. With a barbarian's sense of nature, he knew that ahead would be low mountains, probably rugged, whose crests would be lower, or mostly lower, than the plateau he'd been crossing.

The highway began to drop, entering a broad rounded lobe, offshoot of a canyon. Now and then he saw a pine sapling, or several, with their tops above the grass. As he rode down it, he saw to his left, about a kilometer away, a small stand of well-grown pines in a side draw of the lobe. Immediately below the stand, near the mouth of the draw, stood a grove of leafy trees suggesting water there.

Nils turned his mount off the road, his remount and packhorse trailing behind, and rode to the trees. The leafy grove had a seep at its upper end, and Nils scooped a shallow basin, using the mud and stones to form a small birm on the downslope side. He filled his waterbag there, then let his horses drink, and after removing saddles and packs, and the bits from their mouths, hobbled them to let them graze.

Finally he built a small fire and set a marmot to roast. After eating, he bedded down beneath the pines and slept till sunup. It seemed like a good day to lay up and let his horses rest and graze. Meanwhile he loafed, napped, and meditated. Later he hiked out into the grassland to find and shoot another marmot.

That afternoon he heard a distant raven croak, the first he'd heard for weeks. Remembering Svartvinge as both friend and spy, he reached out and melded with the bird, gently enough that it wouldn't realize. It had seen his horses and was coming to investigate. *Also, something had imprinted it to watch for him.*

Smoothly he withdrew his mind, and grabbing his weapons, crept beneath a thick bank of prostrate juniper, where he lay still.

An occasional harsh *gr-r-rawk* told him the bird had arrived overhead and was circling, surveying. Not only were there the horses to be seen, but the shelter tent. After a bit he heard it call again, once, twice, seemingly from a nearby tree, because the call was from the same place. Two years earlier, Nils had freely left his body and moved about, to spy on places which he couldn't get to physically. He'd have done it now, too, but the ability was gone. Had been for most of that time—since Ilse had left. And knowing that the bird's attention was on finding him, he did not meld with it again to see through its eyes; that would risk detection.

Instead he melded with one of the horses, and nudged it to look toward the woods. Seemingly the raven was hidden by treetops; at least he couldn't see it. So he waited, holding the horse's attention on the lower end of the woods. After two or three minutes he saw the bird rise above the trees, climbing easily into the afternoon sky to fly away southeastward. Horses and tent had attracted its suspicion, but it seemed to Nils that having failed to spot him, the raven had concluded that no human was there. Svartvinge would have concluded differently, but this bird was no elemental.

Nils napped some more then, under the junipers, and that evening set out by dusk for the road. After that he rode only by night, to avoid the ravens, and hid by day. Woods became increasingly frequent, and cover was no problem.

He saw as well by night as by day, for light played no part in his vision. Thus one night about midnight, he saw a great defensive wall in the distance ahead. It seemed to him it wasn't manned, but nonetheless, at the next point where the terrain was reasonable, he turned aside and rode northeastward, crosscountry. He didn't think about it and decide, he simply did it, as he did most things.

Riding crosscountry slowed him. There were steep pitches and rough terrain. The country was more forest than open and unlike their rider, the horses couldn't see well in the night. But he didn't second guess himself.

THIRTY

Fong felt more secure in his relationship to Kaidu than ever before, because Teb-Tengri was out of favor: The arrogant shaman had offended once too often. Nonetheless there was still a hostile factor that had influence with Kaidu: Achikh. After Nils had left, Fong had no difficulty reading Achikh telepathically. Thus he knew what Nils had told the warrior: that he, Fong, had put a spell on Kaidu, and manipulated his mind.

Achikh would surely tell his brother that, and while Kaidu might not believe it—in fact, Fong had seeded just that disbelief—others might readily be convinced. For there were more than a few who distrusted the emperor's envoy, or were jealous of his obvious influence. And these men had their own influence with Kaidu. While Fong, in turn, had to leave Kaidu largely independent, self-determined, or the man would lose his force, his charisma and credibility.

Thus what Fong whispered in Kaidu's mind—for the Chinese psi master had hypnoconditioned the chief to receive his silent suggestions—what Fong whispered was that Achikh might covet the chieftaincy. Why else had he returned? And that he might well be conspiring to gain it.

He put it no more strongly than suggestions. For the connection between Kaidu and his younger brother clearly grew from more than brotherhood. Fong suspected they'd been comrades in arms in earlier lives, fighting beside each other, perhaps dying together. Ties from such lives were strong. And Kaidu was a strong-willed man, and Fong's power over him less than absolute. Thus his suggestions had to seem reasonable, the sort of notions that might occur to Kaidu independently, were it not for past-life ties.

The suggestions had taken root, and Kaidu became curt with Achikh, regarding him with distrust. Achikh felt this, as indeed others did, and he thus avoided Kaidu, spending most of his time training for war. In this he became popular, for he had learned techniques from Orc drill masters that were new and interesting to the tribesmen.

The Buriats had voted Kaidu to be their Great Khan, and the clans had dispersed to their own territories. Kaidu and his household and herds remained near Urga, however, it being the traditional location of Buriat Great Khans when there were such. A considerable number of young men swore themselves *nöküt* to Kaidu, a bond even stronger than family, and each great clan left a *mingan* of warriors with him, a thousand fighting men, while lesser clans left two *jegut* or more, two hundred. Whose households also stayed, with herds to support them. These covered a great territory on the south flanks of the Hentiyn Nuruu and the valley of the Tola, where the grass was better than in most of their land.

They equalled in all 10,000 warriors, a *tümen*, and began training together, commanded by Kaidu's older cousin Arpa. A much larger army could be gathered if the need arose. But the 10,000 was a mobilized force far more powerful than any other among the three Mongol nations. Kaidu then sent messages to the tribal chiefs among the Khalkhaz and the Kalmuls, describing for them his analysis of the empire's power and the emperor's offer. He invited them to join the Buriat leaders in a meeting to discuss a possible alliance. He said nothing of the force he'd already gathered. Word of that would reach their nations as quickly as his messengers, and for him to mention it might be taken as a veiled threat.

Achikh had not sworn himself *nökür*, and this, along with Fong's subliminal suggestions, troubled Kaidu, although his brother was serving as *beki* over a hundred warriors.

Kaidu fidgeted, waiting for word, though he knew that the tribes of other nations would take time to discuss the matter before sending even a noncommittal reply. Which was the kind he expected at this point. But in his restlessness, his attention went more and more to Achikh, and he called him to him. They met in the evening in Kaidu's *ger*, both men still sweaty after their day of training.

Kaidu had ordered Fong to be there too. The Chinese felt cautiously pleased. He knew the chief's mind, and expected a break between the brothers. Which would destroy any influence Achikh might still have, and perhaps lead to his exile, or worse.

Achikh's weapons were not taken from him when he entered the khan's *ger*. They were brothers, and there had been no break between them or any hint of one, and Kaidu kept guards by him these days. When Achikh entered, Kaidu stood up and greeted him.

"I am glad to see my brother Achikh," he said. "I am told you have done outstanding work with your *jegun*. People have told me, 'Achikh brought back knowledge of much value from his travels.' " He paused, then: "Why haven't you sworn yourself *nökür* to me?"

The sudden question—accusation actually and with a note of bitterness—surprised both men. Achikh held his brother's eyes as he answered. "I have wanted to swear *nökür* to you, but I have not been able to. I believe it's not good that you have allied the Buriat with the emperor. I believe that this foreigner"—with a scornful head toss he indicated Fong—"has spelled you, and caused you to decide as you have. He is a wizard. We both know that. I believe he is a wizard who knows how to spell people secretly."

Kaidu's face first paled, then darkened with blood, and his brows knotted, but Achikh plunged on. "I believe your earlier plan, to invade the Yakut-Russ, was far better. For then the Buriat would stay a free people, not commanded by any Tibetan. The emperor has promised us honor and wealth and vast lands, but when we have been separated from our families and our herds, and great Chinese armies lie between, what . . ."

"SILENCE!!!"

Kaidu was trembling with anger now. With more than anger. Fong's hypnoconditioning had caused him to do what he would not otherwise do, given the circumstances, his heritage, and the information he had. And his brother's words had forced these incompatibilities into contact in Kaidu's mind. Nor had he any way to rationalize them; the only responses available were irrational, and he sensed this but could do nothing about it. Further, he had committed his honor, his chieftaincy, *his people* to this plan, *and Achikh's words shot doubt into his mind.* Fong knew it, but dared not intervene now.

Achikh knew it too, but the cannon shot of Kaidu's enraged command paralyzed his tongue. It seemed to him that he was a dead man, or would be before nightfall. So he did what seemed to him the most honorable thing. His sword hissed from its scabbard, and Kaidu's guards, as shocked as Achikh by their chief's explosion, reacted slowly. The younger brother took one stride forward, and although the Chinese tried to avoid it, his blade sliced through Fong's fending hand and took him in the side of the neck, cutting through muscle, severing the spine. Blood fountained as the emperor's envoy toppled sideways, his head flopping on one shoulder, more than half cut off.

Then Kaidu sprang upon Achikh insanely, hands at his throat, and Achikh let fall his sword, unwilling to spill his brother's life. They fell to the bloody floor mat, Kaidu on top, panting, his hands choking.

THIRTY-ONE

After riding for several days, Hans and Baver had entered a stretch of the driest land they'd seen, a true desert. There they met a party of Mongols, who threatened them. Kaidu's safe conduct stood them in good stead then. That and their seeming lack of valuables, beyond their weapons and their few horses. The Mongols were Khalkhaz traders and their retainers and slaves, who'd been to the imperial capital. In appearance the merchants didn't match Baver's preconceptions, for they carried swords, bows, and well-filled quivers, and looked fully competent with them. Their short robes, though, were of silk instead of the customary wool, and they had a caravan of camels trailing behind, laden with goods from the empire.

Neither Baver nor Hans had seen a camel before, though Baver knew them from history courses on New Home. The camel's padded hooves did not much mark the road, but the many horses did, and after the caravan, there seemed little hope of finding Nils's tracks. In fact, though neither said it, there seemed little hope of finding Nils. But they'd keep on. What else could they do?

Several days later they passed what Baver thought must be a courier—a small wiry man on horseback, riding hard, with a small string of remounts cantering behind. The man scarcely glanced at them as he passed trailing a train of dust.

The Mongolian Plateau began to break into ridges and mostly rounded canyons, with here and there groves of pine or birch or other trees on sheltered north and east-facing slopes. One day they heard the deep croaking of a raven, and looked up. Both remembered Svartvinge, and regretted his loss.

The next morning, ahead and to their right, they saw a great defensive wall crossing a ridge crest, and this too Baver knew from courses he'd taken. It had stood far longer than pre-plague cities, which had been mostly of knock-down construction, their buildings built to be replaced.

Farther on, the wall crossed the road, or had. It had been breached there centuries earlier, in building the highway. There were no soldiers manning it.

Two days later they saw what Baver took to be a high imperial official, a horseman richly dressed, escorted by a troop of heavy cavalry. The troopers looked formidable in chain mail, helmets and breastplates. They were some two hundred meters away when they rode into sight. Baver felt instant unease, and told Hans they'd best get off the road. Hans didn't argue. They pushed their horses up a slope and into the forest, where they watched from among the trees as the party passed a hundred meters below.

They spent that night among the poplars beside a brawling mountain stream. When Hans awakened Baver, it was still dark.

"Get up," he said, speaking loudly to be heard above the water. "I had a dream. I want to leave this place."

They saddled and bridled their animals, loaded the packhorse and left, eating breakfast as they rode. The last of their *airag* was gone—it was all they'd had, crossing the desert—and they were back to a diet of marmot again.

The sky began to pale shortly after they set out. "What was your dream?" Baver asked.

Hans didn't answer at once. Finally he said, "It was more real than any other dream I've had. It seemed I'd wakened, and it was daylight. So I walked in the forest, up the slope, to see what I could shoot. I had shot a grouse, and was pulling the skin off it, when I heard men at our camp, shouting. I went back down and saw them riding away. They had our horses, and you were their captive.

"Then I woke up. You don't know how relieved I was to find it still night, and you still there."

They rode on a few score meters before he spoke again. "The next side ravine that comes down to the stream, we'll leave the road and turn up it. And lie in wait. We'll see if armed men come."

They rode on in silence for a few minutes. "What kind of men were they?" Baver asked at last.

"They were warriors, or at least they were armed. Though not armored like those we saw yesterday. And their clothes were all alike, red and yellow."

Soldiers, Baver thought, probably light cavalry, if they'd worn no armor. Hans's dream felt suddenly more real. It was unlikely that Hans had seen uniforms before, except armor, and presumably he had no concept of them.

Daylight grew. The road took them downhill now, through heavy forest. Near the foot of the slope, they rode into the open. A dozen meters below them, the road crossed a small side stream and turned, and—

Riding out of the forest on the other side of the stream was a troop of horsemen, light cavalry uniformed in red and yellow. Their commander saw the two travelers, and shouted an order. The troop spurred their mounts to a gallop.

Hans said nothing. He kicked his own horse into a dead run and left the road, galloping down the last brief slope and up the side ravine, the spares and packhorse pounding behind. They splashed through shallows and into the woods, Baver following. The first three cleared a windfall, then Baver's jumped, caught a hoof on a branch and landed falling. Baver catapulted from the saddle, crashed into a tree and lay stunned. Before he could regain his wits, soldiers had ridden up and were dismounting. One of them jumped on him.

Baver struggled. The soldier was small but tough. Baver, on the other hand, was considerably larger, and tougher than he realized. He rolled the man off him and had him down, striking at his face to free himself from the man's tenacious grip. Then others jumped in, and he was buried beneath them.

THIRTY-TWO

Tenzin Geshe sat in a lotus posture, his open eyes unseeing. What he saw, he saw psychically, in his trance realm.

Meanwhile, around him the Circle of Power knew nothing, directly, of what he sensed or what he did. He'd briefed them beforehand, but in their power trance they wouldn't remember that. With a little effort, they could review the session later, but just now their sole function was to blindly channel power through their leader, and stabilize his psyche against possible assault.

He was cautiously probing the demon they'd admitted into the fabric of the Tao the night before.

Tenzin's trance was not a power trance, nor was it the trance of meditation. It was simply a means of gaining access, and began with a directive, an intention. Nor did it still the mind. It began with stillness, but once submerged in that stillness, he perceived, analyzed, and made decisions. Thinly, he even felt emotions.

The demon was still somewhat numbed. It had no real notion of what had happened to it nor where it was. Like a week-old infant, it experienced its new environment vaguely and with only a beginning of understanding. But there was that beginning.

Like a week-old infant. It had been "born" less than twenty-four hours earlier, in a trauma more severe than childbirth, and into a situation for which it had not evolved. Yet it felt to Tenzin that it might develop its potential rather rapidly.

He probed its nature, looking for weaknesses that he could exploit. He'd sensed almost at once that it was or had been human. A demon then, by his definition. He'd examined demons before, while exploring the lower astral realm. They'd been crafty but mostly weak, working their petty or occasionally ugly evils on humans of weakness.

This one had power. Power he and the Circle had given it by opening to it the fabric of the Tao.

Gradually he unraveled its nature by probing its memories of what had brought or sent it there. Actually they proved to be the memories of many individuals—memories consistent, memories primitive, memories brutal and degenerate. He was dealing with a compound demon!— a number of human psyches that had merged in a moment of jubilation and terror and death. Death to all at once, in a unifying moment of ritual evil. A death that seemed to them stupendous and enormously meaningful. And—

They didn't realize they'd died! To them it seemed a transformation without death!

That explained much of what he felt in contact with them: they thought they'd been taken up and transformed by their god. A concept of god which was not the Tao, but some phenomenon of nature, deified in their minds. At the moment they'd been terrified, but now it seemed like victory to them. Like success. Because they could sense the power they'd been given, even if they didn't know how to use it yet.

He continued to probe. Their unity was the result of one psyche, who as a man had been powerfully charismatic, dominating the rest absolutely. Then, trapped in the fabric of the Tao, it had been he who'd begun to function mentally. He who'd decided they'd been transformed by their god. And he who sensed their potential power. The rest, merged with him, had simply accepted.

And it would be he who learned, bit by bit, how to use that power; that much the *geshe* was sure of.

It seemed to Tenzin that what had been born was like a new organism. And its leader had become its sole functional mind.

He withdrew from his trance and from contact; the demon had sensed him dimly, sensed his probing. It was necessary now to plan, to find a means of removing it from the fabric of the Tao and send it as individual souls to the astral realm where they belonged. Until they could confront the physical realm again, and the karma they'd created, and be reborn to begin paying it off.

He also needed to inform the emperor. Something like this could not be hidden from Songtsan Gampo; he was too good a telepath. Better to tell him than have him discover it himself. But he would be angry.

Tenzin ate a supper of barley and vegetables, then went to report. He found Songtsan Gampo in an expansive mood. A member of the Korean royal family had agreed to take the throne there as the emperor's tributary. Even now his three sons were on their way to Miyun as the emperor's wards—his proteges and hostages. While just that day, a courier had ridden in with the news that district headmen had begun to arrive in Seoul to pledge the new king fealty.

Also, a few days earlier, ravens had found the "star man" and the barbarian youth, though not the barbarian wizard. Now a courier had arrived from the troop he'd sent to capture them. They'd captured the star man basically uninjured, and were bringing him to Miyun. The barbarian youth had escaped, but he was of little importance.

It seemed to Tenzin that the emperor was as pleased by this as by the major news from Korea. "Wonderful,

Your Magnificence," he said. "The star man should prove a wellspring of information."

"Indeed." The emperor raised a knowing eyebrow. "Meanwhile you are worried, and come to tell me of some calamity you've created. It can't be as bad as you think, dear *geshe*."

The comment brought the situation to the surface of the *geshe*'s mind. Songtsan raised both eyebrows, then laughed. "Tenzin, Tenzin! You are a remarkable wizard, but—" He shook his head. "Evict your demon from the fabric of the Tao? Nonsense, Tenzin! You've done wonderfully; far better than you realize. What you must now learn to do is rule it, not evict it!"

Songtsan Gampo habitually thought behind a screen when other telepaths were with him, though he denied them the privilege. An emperor had his prerogatives. Thus Tenzin Geshe didn't know what his emperor failed to say: That Songtsan Gampo intended to bond the demon to himself, once Tenzin and the Circle had established control of it. He would bond the demon to himself, and tell it he was its god.

THIRTY-THREE

Baver regained a groggy consciousness while being tied across the back of a horse, and tried to raise his head. A soldier cursed—at least it sounded like a curse—and cuffed him. Whereupon the commander rode up to the soldier, and bending struck him hard on the head with the flat of his sword. The man fell to the ground, partly from the blow and partly in self defense, while an angry string of words rattled from the commander's mouth.

The language was one Baver felt sure he'd never heard before. Chinese? he wondered. He'd heard Chinese several times on a cube, ancient Chinese, on New Home. Alex Malaluan had been hypno-learning it. It had sounded more tonal than this. But then, languages change, some more, some less.

With quick fingers, a different soldier untied him. Two others helped him off the horse, onto his feet, where his hands were retied in front of him, leaving twenty centimeters of twisted thong between them to give him some freedom of hand movement. This done, he was boosted into the saddle.

He was aware that virtually all the soldiers were staring

at him. He supposed they'd never seen anything like a jumpsuit before, with its pockets at chest, hips, and thighs.

It occurred to him then that Hans wasn't there. Perhaps he'd gotten away. Or was dead. There was no way to ask. But these people didn't seem to be in a killing mood. Did they have orders to bring in prisoners alive and well?

And what had there been about himself and Hans that inspired the chase? Perhaps it was simply that Hans had bolted. Or no, Hans hadn't bolted till after the soldiers had kicked their own horses to a gallop. And there had been Han's dream!—prophetic in a way. Perhaps accurately prophetic if they'd stayed where they'd camped.

He wondered what they'd do with him. And why the commander had struck the trooper for actually rather modest abuse. Baver had seen and heard enough, on this primitive world, to know that here, merely cuffing a prisoner was benign behavior.

There was more to this, he decided, than appeared on the surface.

During two long days of riding with his hands tied, Baver was treated with consistent brusque decency, and learned a few words of the soldiers' language, notably *chu* and *kyöra sagiyö: water* or *drink,* and *eat* or *food.*

The third morning brought them to the ruins of a large city. An old city, some of it dating to well before the days of knock-down-and-replace buildings. Probably a major capital, because some of the individual buildings were so large, or had been. A lot of them were more or less intact, implying that they predated the technological era with its widespread use of steel beams and reinforcment bars.

The capital of ancient China, Baver decided. He groped for the name: Beijing, that was it. Now an army was barracked there, in scores or maybe hundreds of long, single-story stone buildings. Nearby were farms, their mud-brick buildings clustered in hamlets. There was wheeled transport, both wagons and carts, and the road was rutted from the last wet weather, but dusty now from drought.

From Beijing the troop turned north, the midday sun at their backs, and after a while they were in forested hills again—the Yan Mountains, though Baver didn't know their name. Late the next day they came to a town of perhaps twenty thousand, in a valley of farms; an unwalled town. A large hill rose above it, with large buildings surrounded by a defensive wall. Atop the hill was what Baver thought must be the imperial palace. From a distance its size impressed him, and as they came closer, its beauty. They rode into the town on a road paved with stone blocks, till they came to a great gate that swallowed the road.

It was at the gate that Baver saw his first Yunnan ogres. He'd never heard of them before, and they both awed and astonised him. Each was well over two meters tall, looked enormously strong, and wore an indigo uniform with buttons and trim of copper. Their helmets were steel, though he didn't know it, for the steel was plated with polished bronze. Each held a great sword at shoulder arms, while on his other shoulder was slung an enormous bow. Baver doubted he could do more than lift the sword, and was sure he couldn't begin to bend the bow. The creatures looked intelligent and alert, their eyes on the coming cavalrymen and particularly on himself, an obvious prisoner.

At the last minute, one of them stepped in front of the troop's commander. And spoke! Its speech sounded to Baver not unlike that of the soldiers he'd been traveling with, though the voice had a different timbre, with a sort of "hard-napped fuzz" to it unlike any human voice he'd ever heard.

Then the column waited calmly. No one dismounted or spoke. Almost the only sounds were the occasional clop of a shod hoof on stone, a slight snort, the buzz of horse flies and swish of tails.

One of the ogres had planted himself in the gateway,

sword loosely ready in one long hand. The blade was
one-and-a-half-edged, Baver noticed, one edge sharp the
whole length, the other only half. The long hand had an
opposable thumb, and thick nails that might be thought
of as blunt claws. The feet were bare, and their claws
curved strongly enough for traction.

From inside the gate came the sound of shod feet
marching in step. Then a squad of human guards came
out. Like the ogres, they wore uniforms of indigo and
copper. With them came what was clearly an officer, by
both uniform and bearing. He seemed to be senior to
the cavalry commander. Haughtily he rattled off several
sentences, then two of his men strode to Baver and lifted
him down. These were large men, larger than most of
the troopers, and with hands beneath Baver's arms, they
walked him through the great gate and into the palace
grounds.

Baver had visited the national garden on New Home.
The palace grounds were at least as beautiful, and exotic
to boot. He realized this even as he was hustled along a
graveled path to a building, lovely on the outside, which
inside proved to be a prison. At least the cellar was. They
took him down a corridor and pushed him into a cell,
where one of them untied his hands.

They left him standing there and slammed the barred
door behind them. A key or keys seated massive bolts.
The only light was that from the corridor, and from an
airshaft with a barred opening.

Baver stood bemused, not willing to sit, as if sitting
would make the situation more final, more irrevocable.
Well, he told himself after a long couple of minutes, *they
didn't go to all that trouble just to lock me up. Something's bound to happen before long.*

With that he did sit, and wondered where Hans was,
and Nils. He didn't even think of Matthew and Nikko
and pinnace *Alpha* just then. They belonged to another
world, an earlier life.

                    *   *   *

Songtsan Gampo could sense the prisoner's mind as he was led up the great marble stairway and along the broad hall with its panelling of tropical hardwoods from Guangxi, inlaid with carved ivory. It was a worried but not inordinately fearful mind, able to notice its surroundings and even to appreciate them. Images stirred in it, and comparisons with other halls and rooms.

Two guards marched Baver to the door of the audience chamber and inside. One was a Mongol, a mercenary. Their strong hands halted the prisoner three steps inside, Baver's eyes taking in as much of the room as possible without obviously gawking. This was clearly the imperial audience chamber. There was a throne on a raised dais, and on it a strong-faced man wearing beautiful robes; surely the emperor. Ogre guards stood behind the throne on either side, while to his right stood an ogre notably larger than the others.

The emperor's visitors were required to offer an obeisance, the degree varying with the person and circumstance. Even the emperor's brother Drukpa bowed when he entered. Baver unwittingly had done nothing. The emperor spoke quietly to the Mongol, Corporal Nogai, who then spoke to Baver in fluent Buriat Mongol. "You are expected to bow to the emperor," he said mildly, and demonstrated.

Baver bowed from the waist, not deeply. The emperor monitored him telepathically and found no sense of defiance or disrespect, only embarrassment that he'd had to be told.

A star man indeed, the emperor thought, *just as Tenzin had said.* He smiled slightly to put the man somewhat at ease, and spoke to him, Corporal Nogai translating into Mongol a sentence behind.

"We welcome you to our empire and our palace. Even though you entered our territory without permission, in our imperial wisdom we believe you intended no harm. Therefore we do not now plan to punish you. It is enough that you be restrained from wandering and spying."

Baver wondered if he was expected to reply. Unsure, he decided not to, beyond a perfunctory acknowledgment. "Thank you," he said.

The slanted oval eyes were on his, emotionless; the emperor and his translator went on. "You are a foreigner. Your clothing is of interesting design, and the material seems unfamiliar to us, though as dirty as it is, it is not possible to be sure. Where did you get it?"

"In my homeland, far to the west." The lie seemed to Baver the lesser of undesirable alternatives. Telling the truth might get him in trouble as a liar, or perhaps for disrespect to the imperial throne. Or it might get him branded a lunatic. And actually the only untruth in what he'd said was *the west*.

"Indeed. When you have been returned to your quarters, clean clothes will be provided. These will be washed and returned to you.

"Now, your homeland: What is it called? Perhaps I have heard of it."

"I think not, Your Highness." He turned to Corporal Nogai. "Is that the right term to use? Your Highness?"

The interpreter passed the question on, commenting that the Mongol language was not fully adequate for court etiquette, and that while the prisoner's knowledge of Mongol seemed quite functional, he was not fully articulate in it. The emperor didn't tell the interpreter that he wasn't much interested in Baver's verbal answers. His interest was in the concepts and images that his questions brought to or near the surface.

"The term 'Your Highness' is adequate," the emperor answered. "And what is your function in your homeland?"

"I am—" Baver groped. He knew no Mongol words for ethnologist or student. "I am one who learns. From teachers and from watching people. I am one who lives among foreigners and watches them, in order to learn how they live and think." He felt uncomfortable with his answer—it might well sound unbelievable here, even incomprehensible—so he added, "It is respected work in my homeland." *So respected that hundreds applied for the ethnologist positions on the expedition,* he remembered. *If it hadn't been for my doctorate in ancient Earth history, I wouldn't have had a chance.*

"They will be interested when I return and tell what I have learned here," he added. "They will probably send people here to trade with you, if you'd like to trade." It seemed like the sort of comment that might help get him out of there alive. And it was probably true, as far as that was concerned, though there'd hardly be any camel caravans carrying goods between them.

"Indeed. And what do your people make or grow that we might want, here in the empire?"

"I didn't bring samples, Your Highness. But we make machines which cut trees much faster and more easily than an ax, and others which can cut an entire tree trunk into—" Again he groped, then moved to touch the table near the emperor, to demonstrate boards. A human guard's hard hand gripped his shoulder, while the throne ogres' swords hissed from their scabbards. The emperor's voice in Tibetan cut through the situation, and the hand withdrew, though the ogres' swords remained free.

"Show me what you planned to show," the emperor said, and Baver did.

"But you have none of these marvels with you? You seem to have many pockets. What do you have in them? Perhaps there is something you've overlooked."

It struck Baver like a hammer then. Nils had said that Fong was a telepath who served as a spy as well as an envoy, *and who somehow communicated what he learned to the emperor, perhaps a thousand kilometers away. So the emperor too would be a telepath!*

As soon as he thought it, Baver knew it was so. The emperor's expression hadn't changed, but the eyes had. It was as if he'd looked into them. In Tibetan, the emperor snapped an order, and both guards gripped Baver's arms. He gave another. Corporal Nogai took both pistol and radio from Baver's pockets and handed them to the emperor.

"What is this?" the emperor asked, holding up the pistol.

"A weapon. Be careful with it. See the hole in the end? When the right button is pushed and the right lever squeezed, a deadly piece of metal flies out, swifter than the speed of sound. It can kill from a little distance or close up."

The emperor's eyes studied it, then turned to Baver. "Why didn't you use it when my soldiers pursued you?"

Baver hadn't even thought of it. "It would not have driven them off," he said, "and they would have killed me then. Besides, that's my last mag ..." He groped for an appropriate Mongol word and didn't find what he needed. "It is mostly used up," he finished.

Songtsan Gampo pursed his lips and nodded, then held up the radio. "And this?"

"It is used to speak with others at a distance. Even a long distance. But it's broken. Otherwise I wouldn't be here. My friends would have come for me long before I got to your country."

The emperor's eyes seemed to Baver near to drawing his brains out of his eye sockets. "There is something else," the man said.

Baver shook his head. "There was. I just thought of it. My—" He frowned. "It's a small machine that stores things that happen, pictures and sounds of things, when it's pointed at them. For example, if I had it here and pointed it at you while you talked, it would store the event to be looked at again later. Looked at and listened to. I have many things stored, in little cubes like square jewels."

The emperor's eyes hadn't left Baver while he'd spoken. "And you could show them to me?"

"Barely big enough to see. To enjoy them, you need a—a thing to look with. My people have them on our world and on our ship."

The eyes had left Baver. The emperor frowned, his lips pursed. "And this—thing. It is in your saddlebags?"

The thought struck Baver then that the soldiers might

have brought his saddlebags. Surely would have. Somehow he'd assumed they were still back with whatever was left of his horse.

The emperor smiled slightly and shook his head, then turned the radio over in his hands, frowning. "A weapon which is almost used up, and a thing which is broken. They do not seem like much." He handed the radio to the interpreter with a few words in their language, and the man returned it to Baver. "We will look into the matter of the box which stores the past in it," he said. Then asked, "Just how far away is this homeland of yours?"

For a moment Baver thought to think of other things, sing songs in his mind perhaps, because he didn't want to tell. What ambitions might it arouse in this emperor? But he knew he wouldn't leave this room before they'd wrung the information from him, and it might well be impossible to withhold from a telepath anyway. "Our homeland is a whole world," he said, "so far away that the light from our sun takes more than seventeen years to get here."

The emperor stared long and hard at Baver, inwardly sorting images and impressions. The strange foreigner thought what he said was true; there was no doubt of that.

He spoke to the guards who'd brought Baver. "Take him back to his cell," he said. "Let him go without further food today, to worry him a little, but give him a soldier's breakfast tomorrow."

He would meditate on what he'd learned from this man, he decided.

THIRTY-FOUR

Nils had pressed hard since he'd left the road. He'd swing into the saddle soon after sundown and continue till half light in the morning, following game trails. The horses, he'd found, saw little or no better at night than most humans, and where it was necessary to travel over windfall-littered or otherwise treacherous ground, he'd dismount and lead them.

At times he found himself near the Great Wall, which was buried in forest and somewhat meandering. It was unmanned. Once he explored a length of it, found a gateway with its gate long gone, and passed through.

He still didn't know where he was going, but traveled on intuition. It would have been impossible for most men.

Mostly it was wild country, without sign of man except for the wall. He heard wolves one night, saw bear tracks along a stream, and again at a spring. Once on a mud bank he found tracks that made him think of the lion in the arena of Kazi the Undying. Seemingly they'd been made by some giant cat, for there were no marks of claws. Were there lions in this country? He knew no reason to doubt it.

One dawn as the sky paled, he was following the crest of a forest ridge, watching the slopes on both sides for suitable cover to spend the daylight hours. The righthand slope was too steep to be promising. He paused on a rocky overlook to gaze southward, and some five or six kilometers off saw a hill with large buildings on its upper slopes and crown.

He turned downslope there, and picketed his horses beneath a thickness of old maples, leaving them to browse the abundant maple seedlings. Then he hiked back upslope to the overlook, where he lay on his belly. He tried to project his spirit to the distant structure, but nothing happened. Perhaps if he knew someone there, and knew he knew ... It seemed to him he was looking at the imperial palace; at any rate it attracted him strongly, and at the same time repelled him. It also seemed the place he was to go, but ... Not yet.

He continued to stare. Usually—continuously these last weeks—he moved decisively, whether or not he had a rationale for it. But just now there was no impulse to follow.

The sun was scarce degrees below the horizon, four or five, and the sky approached daybright. His concentration was broken by a *gr-r-rawp!* in the sky above him, and without raising head or eyes he looked up. An early raven soared effortlessly, a very large raven. In that moment his viewpoint entered its mind, and he was looking down at himself. Like Svartvinge, it was a raven elemental. But unlike Svartvinge, this elemental had been imprinted to resist him; in a moment it had cast out his mind, violently, and Nils found his viewpoint back with his body again, about his head.

His intrusion, brief but intimate and deep, had shaken the bird, shaken it powerfully because of the injunction it lived with, and turning, it fled toward the palace.

Now Nils knew his next move, though not the one beyond it. He trotted downhill to his horses, untied them and mounted one, then rode away, although it was daytime. The raven's master would soon know of his presence here, and Nils was not ready yet to meet him or the soldiers he might send.

He rode northward through the morning and into the afternoon, keeping mostly to heavy forest, putting distance between himself and the place where he'd been seen. For a while he waded his animals in a creek, leaving it when a blowdown blocked the way.

Finally he stopped in a stand of aspens, and hobbled his horses to the grass and wild pea vines that grew in their light shade. Then he trotted to a nearby group of young maples, in whose cover he lay down and quickly slept.

He awoke to the scream of a horse, and grabbing his sword, scrambled to his feet. There were other sounds, sounds he recognized at once: a bear roared hoarsely, and there was brief thrashing, as if a horse was down, struggling. Nils ran toward it. His packhorse passed him, hopping faster than one might think possible, given its hobbles. Its pack saddle was broken and hanging. A moment later he saw the bear, standing on a fallen saddle horse. He could not see the other.

The bear's weak eyes spotted the moving man, and it reared to see better. Nils stopped. It was a large animal, a big boar-bear, and it made no sense to dispute a dead horse with it. Nils drew back and turned aside, circling. The bear never took its eyes off him. Twice it made short rushes, and each time Nils backed off. Then he saw the other saddle horse. It was down too; a fallen tree had hidden it before. Its neck and head lay loosely.

Nils turned away, leaving the bear to its kills, picked up his bow and quiver where he'd slept, and trotted off on the trail of his packhorse.

He caught up with it some three hundred meters off. It had stopped, but its eyes were wide and wild, its head tossing. Touching its mind with his, he stood calming it, then approached it slowly, talking to it.

The bear had smashed the pack saddle, and the horse,

snorting, flinched with pain when Nils touched its barrel. Ribs seemed broken. He soothed it further, stroking its mind and nose. Then he cut the packs off, cut the straps and removed the pack saddle, took off bridle and hobbles, and left the animal. It couldn't be ridden as it was, and with luck it might survive. Meanwhile a Northman afoot was not greatly hampered.

He'd jogged and walked for perhaps three hours when he came to an oblong opening in the forest, a clearing of perhaps a dozen hectares. It held grain stubble, a hay meadow, and a sizeable patch of what appeared from a distance to be potatoes; the upper end was blue with flax in bloom. Two children stood bent among the potato plants, perhaps picking off beetles. On the far side stood a hut, sheds, and a small barn, all made of poles fitted at the corners and roofed with thatch. A woman was working in the yard, at what he couldn't tell. He slipped back out of sight among the trees, and circled the little field to the side with the buildings, at one point splashing through a brook. There was a dog he hadn't noticed—it had been sleeping—and spotting Nils, it began to bark. Abandoning stealth, Nils strode openly toward the hut, though staying beneath the trees. He left his sword sheathed despite the dog, which charged raging at him, to pull up two meters off, barking with fangs bared.

The woman peered around the corner of the hut, saw Nils coming, and disappeared. Nils touched the dog's mind, and while it continued barking, it no longer sounded savage.

A well-grown boy ran from the barn and disappeared into the hut. Nils watched telepathically through the boy's eyes, saw hands reach and take a bow from the wall, string it, and grasp three arrows. Then the boy raced outside again.

He appeared to be about sixteen, lean and wiry, work-toughened. Nocking an arrow, he drew it partly back, and shouted something in a language Nils had never heard. The thought behind it was clear though—*stop or I'll kill you!* Followed by shock and fear when the youth saw the blank, pupil-less eyes.

Smiling, Nils stopped, spread his long thick arms, palms forward, then slowly reached and unbuckled the harness that held his sword and quiver, and lowered it to the ground. His bow still rode on one shoulder, but unstrung.

The boy shouted something more, and there was an exchange with a younger child. Then a girl of about ten or eleven years ran fleetingly into sight around a corner of the hut, thin legs flying, and disappeared into the forest to fetch their father.

Nils tapped his chest and spoke in Mongol, to indicate he didn't speak the local language. Then he held his hands in front of him and pretended to ride a horse. The boy watched scowling. Nils raised his hands high, made a sound like a bear roaring, and pretended to strike with one of them. Next he whinnied, and fell to the ground.

The boy's scowl dissolved in laughter. Nils, grinning, got to his feet, and the boy's gaze sharpened again.

"I am lost," Nils said, first in Mongol, then in Anglic, and finally in Swedish. The boy shook his head at each. Nils wasn't surprised; he'd only done it to pass time till the father came, and to establish a willingness and desire to communicate. Next he pulled his belly in, and with a pained look pressed a big hand against it, then pantomined eating. He wasn't acutely hungry—he'd killed and eaten a grouse a few hours earlier—but again he established communication, and a sense of this huge foreigner as a human being who was less dangerous than he looked.

Without taking his eyes off Nils, the boy shouted that the stranger was hungry. A woman's voice answered, and a minute later another child, a boy of five or six, peered around the corner. He drew back out of sight and wailed that he was afraid. His big brother shouted back sharply that he should come out "right now." Nils grinned. The

he couldn't afford to let pass. As for
leave that to Chen. The blacksmith ha
rous youth, had seen much and known th
of men.

woman's voice spoke firmly through a window, but the
child did not reappear. After another minute the mother
came around the corner with a thick heel of bread and
a small chunk of cheese on a wooden plate.

She paused, staring, and spoke in rapid Chinese: she'd
never seen so large and terrible a man. Her eldest son
answered. The content of it was that the foreigner
seemed friendly, and that something was wrong with
his eyes. He kept his bow half drawn though, and his
own eyes on the Northman. The woman approached
Nils by circling around to one side, her eyes on his.
She put the plate on the ground three meters away,
and backed off.

Nils could sense the father coming now. Bowing, he
thanked her, then went to the plate, squatted down on
his haunches and began to eat. The little boy's curiosity
had overcome his fear, and he was watching around the
corner. "That's not enough for someone that big!" he
shouted. "That's only enough for me!"

The father strode from the woods, an axe in one hand.
After pausing to size up the situation, he approached to
within half a dozen meters of the Northman. Nils was
aware that his strange glass eyes were troubling the
farmer. "Who are you?!" the man asked. "What do you
want?!"

Nils didn't answer, only looked at him. He couldn't
have said what he wanted in any language; he didn't
know. Then a distant raven croaked. It couldn't see them
from where it was, but Nils spoke urgently in Mongol
and pointed toward the sky, backwards toward where the
raven had called from. And mimicked the raven's call,
though quietly. He flapped big arms, then with his fingers signed the raven looking down at him, and shook
his head vehemently. With that, disregarding the boy and
his bow, he strode to the hut and went inside. An old
man was there, in a chair made of withes. He looked at
the Northman in alarm, and began to yammer.

Nils grinned at him and knelt down beside the door
as the others followed him in, the farmer bringing his

harness with its sword and quiver; things of value were *not* left lying about outside, to be rained on and get rusty or moldy. The eldest son had relaxed his bow, though he carried it still with an arrow nocked.

Nils spoke to the farmer in Mongol: "The emperor has a shaman who has spelled the ravens to watch for me."

The farmer frowned and shook his head, but in his mind was the beginning of a thought. For even with Nils's accent, which wasn't heavy, he thought he recognized the language. "He sounds like old Chen at the festivals," the farmer said.

His wife nodded, worried to have this giant barbarian in her house.

"I'll take him to Chen and see what I can learn about him. I think he said *emperor*. He may be a wanted man."

The wife at once looked frightened; she was very afraid of the authorities, Nils realized. But she answered on another tack. "Take him to old Chen? That will cost time! There is too much work to do!"

The farmer scowled at her. "I will take him."

"But Wu! He is dangerous!"

"He does not seem hostile. And there may be a reward. Jik will come with us. He will walk behind us with his bow, and shoot the foreigner if he does something wrong."

She felt uncertain that an arrow would kill so large and powerful a man. "When will you go?" she asked.

"Pack food for us. We will go right away."

Thwarted but still upset, Mrs. Wu wrapped several round, pancake-like pieces of flatbread around two slices from the end of a cheese like a large salami, and put them in a linen sack. Nils grinned inwardly; she'd packed nothing for him. She would not waste more of her family's sustenance on this dangerous-looking foreigner.

Farmer Wu looked down at the squatting Northman and spoke to Jik, who half bent his bow in response. Then Wu beckoned Nils to stand. Nils did, and Wu handed him his harness and gear, which Nils buckled on.

Next the farmer gestu... and made walking mot... gestured toward the doo... sound, and gestured dow... his eyes. He then pointed... some sixty centimeters in d... cape that hung on the wall,... putting them on.

"He's afraid the raven will... said. "Perhaps it's a magical rav...

The father snorted. "The cap... shoulders. Take the cover from y... him."

The woman was stricken. Blank... one was lost, they'd have to pay to... in the forest they kept no sheep. Sh... stupid, enticing bears and wolves a... tiger.

Nils draped the blanket over his big... it at the throat, then adjusted his gear s... covered and his quiver did not lump cons... done, he tied the wide straw hat on his b... grinned widely, partly in amusement but a... the role he was acting. Then, in response to... gesture, he went out the door, the man a... following.

It wasn't a reward Wu was interested in; he... tioned that only to quiet his wife. He was loo... survival. Nor did he feel strong misgivings as the... although this whole action was drastically foreign t... don't-do-it-till-you've-worked-it-all-out style characte... of peasants. A style grown out of the slim margin... error within which they survived.

Because Lo Pu-Pang had been narrowing that margin, and too many had lost their land and daughters when they couldn't meet the bailiff's demands.

And it seemed to Wu that this giant barbarian was an opportunity of some kind, a possible solution to their

THIRTY-FIVE

Stor tidragen han t' flikkor,
ofta kjikt i ham på sölstig,
blikkor fölte ham om middag,
nog dröd när en mö i sjymning,
viskte bjääli t' vä ellen.

[Fascinating he to women,
often glanced at him by morning,
followed him their eyes at midday,
lingered near sometimes at twilight,
whispered to him in the firelight.]
From—*The Järnhann Saga,*
Kumalo translation

*   *   *

The Wu farm was at the end of a valley, at the end
of a cart track nine kilometers from Lü-Gu, the district's
principal village. More than a kilometer up the road was
the next clearing, where several farms centered around
a hamlet of ten or a dozen farm homes. From there to
Lü-Gu, the valley land was mostly cleared and cultivated,

the farmers living in a series of tiny hamlets. Their houses, like Wu's, were log huts.

It was unlikely that Wu would ever have close neighbors. Above the last hamlet, the valley narrowed to little more than a ravine, at its end widening into the small bowl where Wu had built; there was only land for one farm there.

In country at the edge of a wilderness, Wu's choosing to farm where he did, out by himself, verified for Nils what reading the man's aura and mind had already indicated: that he was independent, self-reliant, and not much given to pampering his fears. Seemingly Jik was growing up to be the same.

The brook meandered, and to avoid repeated fords, the cart road followed along one edge of the valley bottom, where forest overhung it. Nils and the two Chinese met no one on the road, nor overtook anyone. Late and early were the times for that, not afternoon. The people in the fields paid little or no attention to them. Their attention was on their work, which would either feed them through the winter or fail to.

The road skirted one final wooded hill, low and flinty, a point that intruded somewhat into the valley. When they'd rounded it, Nils could see the village a kilometer and a half ahead. It might have held five hundred people.

He stopped and shook his head emphatically. "I cannot go there," he said in Mongol.

Wu frowned; the barbarian's meaning was plain. Actually he'd already thought of stopping where they were. Beyond this point the road left the shelter of the forest's eaves; it was the last best place to hide the barbarian. And to be seen in the village with him would be risky. But would Chen come so far to talk with him?

"Chen here!" Nils said, and pointed to the ground where they stood. "Chen! Chen here!" he repeated.

"He is saying Chen, father!"

"I heard! I heard! I'm not deaf!" Wu pursed his lips. "But what is the rest of it?"

"I think he wants us to bring Chen here. I think he doesn't want to go into town."

"Huh!" And the giant barbarian had already said something about the emperor, or had seemed to. He must indeed be a fugitive, Wu decided, and afraid of being recognized.

Nils pointed at himself, and then at the woods beside the road. He walked his fingers in that direction, then squatted down for a moment.

"He wants to go in the woods and wait for us! He wants us to bring Chen here! He must know him!"

Wu nodded. If the barbarian knew anyone here at all, it would be Chen. Fugitives were rumored to come to the old blacksmith for the things they needed: an ax, arrowheads, even swords.

Chen's beautiful but headstrong daughter had married the bailiff, Lo Pu-Pang. People said she'd agreed not because she was afraid of Lo, but because he was the only man in the district who could buy her the nice things she wanted. And her aging father being so willful and unruly—increasingly so with age—it was no doubt her influence that had kept him from prison or worse.

Wu didn't intend to involve himself in such matters. He'd leave things to Chen. Chen had been a smith with the army on the frontier when he was young. Had hobnobbed with Mongol mercenaries, learned their language, and even now would sometimes speak it at one and all when he'd been drinking. Sounding much like the big barbarian. And it seemed to him . . .

He nodded. "Stay with him. I will go into the village and talk to Chen."

The smith didn't see Wu come in, but he was aware when the farmer's body blocked the light through the door, which was open for the breeze. He quenched the sickle blade he'd been hammering, making the water hiss, then wiped sweat with a forearm, and turned.

"Ah! Wu! It is you! I was afraid it was that worthless son-in-law of mine!"

Chen had only one daughter, and therefore only one son-in-law. Wu told himself that to call the bailiff worthless, even privately, was foolish. Someday, unless events intervened, Chen would offend the official one time too many. One day a squad of the bailiff's hoodlums would come in with their cudgels and swords and beat him, put chains on him and take him away. The smith's well-known strength would avail him nothing; they'd cut off his head if he fought them. And the common people needed him, for who else would make cane knives with thick, strong, sword-like backs—swords shaped like cane knives really—or broad-axes suitable for fighting when the time came? Many farmers had one of those, with a long handle he could fit to it.

Wu stepped close to the smith and spoke in an undertone. "A barbarian has wandered onto my farm. Speaking what sounds like the Mongol tongue. He is wary of being seen by people. I left him in the woods outside of town, at the Pine Point."

Chen also spoke quietly. "What is your interest in this barbarian?"

"He is a giant." The farmer gestured, indicating height and shoulders. "Very big and strong, and wears scars. He must be good for something beyond more ordinary men." Wu's eyebrows suggested the rest of it. The district was not far short of armed revolt. Meanwhile he said nothing about the barbarian's eyes. "But I cannot understand what he says," he added, "nor he I. Perhaps I can bring him in tonight and . . ." He shrugged.

"Hmm!" Chen examined Wu as if looking for something that wasn't plain to see. "Well." He thought for a moment. "You can't bring him here. My son-in-law distrusts me. Lately he has someone watching my shop when I'm here, and my home when I'm there." He paused. "A big Mongol who is a fugitive, you say. Is he armed?"

"With the biggest sword I ever saw. He is the biggest man I ever saw."

Chen pursed scarred lips. "Such a one might indeed

be useful." He stepped to a corner, and from a shelf took a jar, removed the lid and drank a long swig of whatever it held. He was thinking. The bailiff's most important duty was to collect the emperor's taxes, and the taxes continually grew. There was nothing to be done about that. But the bailiff's collection fee also grew. Now it added one-third to the taxes. His wealth was said to exceed that of everyone else's in the village—everyone's combined.

Even as a boy, grandson of the old bailiff, Lo Pu-Pang had been greedy, and boastful of his possessions, displaying them. They had to be the best, and everyone must know it—the best kite, the finest pony . . . And at last the most beautiful wife.

Lo knew he was deeply hated, and kept an ever increasing company of mercenaries to protect him and enforce his demands. These armed men had become a law onto themselves, doing whatever pleased them. They abused both villagers and farmers, and the cost of their pay and maintenance—"district defense cost"—was added to the taxes and his fee. Another story—and this from Kwong the grain merchant, who did much business in the capital—was that Lo recruited his mercenaries from the prison at Miyun. It was easy to believe.

But if there was an armed revolt, a successful one, the army would be sent. Heads would roll then, no doubt including his. Though it might be worth it, depending on what kind of man the new bailiff was.

He also remembered how daring and reckless some young Mongols could be, and what fighters! Surely one that had gotten this far from home, and had so offended the authorities that they might follow him into the hills, must be reckless indeed. If he could somehow get him inside the bailiff's fortress, perhaps into the same room with him . . .

With an abruptness born of decision, Chen stepped to a pile of scrap iron and selected three pieces. Then he pumped his bellows till the fire in the forge was white hot. With the tongs he thrust in one of the pieces, after a long moment withdrew it, and began to hammer. Heat, hammer, and quench! Heat, hammer, and quench! The hisses were explosive, and the place smelled of steam and hot metal. He kept it up till he held a finished grappling hook in his tongs, with a ring to take a rope, then took a file to its three hooks till they were pointed. Finally he wrapped it in a cotton towel that hung by the quenching tank, to conceal what it was and eventually to muffle the sound it might make. This done, he laid it aside, grinned at Wu and bowed slighty. The farmer thought he knew what the smith had in mind.

The smith took another swig from the crock. "I will talk to this Mongol," he said softly, "and see what he is like. At the Pine Point, you say. And your son is there with him?"

"I will take you," said Wu.

"No," Chen replied. "You stay here. You will help ensure that the man who is watching, the man of my son-in-law, stays, and doesn't follow me."

"I?"

The smith wasn't listening. He hung up his leather apron, his thick, muscular forearms flecked with scars from hot flakes of metal sent flying by his hammer. Then strode to the door, stepped outside, and called back for anyone to hear. "I'm expecting a farmer to come. If I'm not here when he arrives, tell him I'll be back when Doctor Liang is done sticking needles in me. You don't know what it's like to stand all day at my age. My knees are killing me."

Pretending to limp, he walked to his home then, fifty meters away, in the front and out the back, to the shed where he kept his horse. There he took down a ten-meter coil of rope and tied on the grappling hook. Then he saddled the animal, rode it along behind a mulberry hedge to an alley, followed the alley to another street, and headed south out of town.

As he rode, he thought about his daughter, the bailiff's wife. It ground him to think that at first he'd been pleased with the marriage. But she'd been a difficult girl, passionate, willful, dissatisfied. With an eye for young men; he and his wife had had to watch her like a hawk! Marriage, they thought, would calm her. And it had, but . . . Sometimes, when he saw her, he could tell she'd been crying. And three years with no pregnancy! He wondered if Lo was impotent, or preferred unnatural acts.

Jik recognized the blacksmith and came out of the woods to meet him. "Honorable smith! Where is my father?" he asked.

The smith rode the horse into the edge of the trees before answering. "He is watching my shop. Where is the Mongol?"

Mongol? The boy felt uneasy at that; the giant was no Mongol, though who knew what he was. "He is back where no one can see him from the road. Come! I will take you to him."

Nils had not climbed the slope, but simply hiked back along its foot, to settle behind a sapling thicket. As the smith rode toward him through the trees, he stood up and stepped out, Mrs. Wu's hat in hand, blanket over an arm, exposing his blond hair, long braids, and sword.

"What?!" began the smith, for clearly this was no Mongol. Then Nils spoke.

"You are Chen, who speaks Mongol?" He put it as a question, though he knew.

"I am. But you . . ."

"I am a Northman from far to the west, who has been among the Mongols. My name is Nils."

"Ah!" Chen stared, taking in not only Nils's size and musculature, but now his eyes. "You are blind!"

"I am not blind. I have wizard eyes, and see by night as well as day."

Breath hissed out of the old smith, like air from a bladder. "A wizard!"

Nils nodded, grinning.

A wizard, Chen repeated to himself. *One who can see*

in the dark. His plan took new reality for him, and with sudden energy he began describing it.

Chen sent Wu home at an hour when he'd be seen alone on the road headed south.

Chen himself was a widower and alone, who sometimes took his supper in the tavern. This night he would eat there and spend the evening drinking with old friends, to deflect possible suspicion. Drinking more than usual, and pretending to be more affected by it than he actually was. Happily Dr. Liang came in. They were friends, and Chen drank with him. Doctor Liang, who with his wife and youngest daughter was also the village candle-maker and seller, was considered a conservative and proper man whose primary eccentricity was his friendship and occasional drinking with the smith. As such he provided a particularly suitable alibi.

Chen remained sober enough to worry. Not for himself; it seemed to him he'd taken care of that. But he didn't want the barbarian to get killed; that, it seemed to him, would add to his own karma. Of course, any karma earned should the bailiff be killed, or any of his guards, he would happily accept, because someone needed to do something about Lo Pu-Pang.

It was a slow evening in the tavern, and after awhile, Chen and Liang were almost the only customers there. Finally the tavern keeper announced that no more drinks would be served. Liang asked Chen to come home with him and spend the night. Actually the doctor wanted the muscular smith's protection between the tavern and his own door; otherwise some ruffian might ambush and rob him. And his wife wouldn't scold him if the smith was there.

Chen readily agreed. Apparently the deed had not yet been done; he'd heard no uproar from the bailiff's compound, or report of one. And agreeing with Liang's request would extend his alibi through the whole night. Meanwhile he was a little edgy that something had gone wrong, and that the plan would come to naught.

It was so dark out that Liang went back into the tavern and borrowed an oil lamp from the tavern keeper, to help him find the key holes in his gate and door.

Jik and the giant barbarian had napped off and on through the day, waiting till well after dark, as Chen had directed. Hopefully they'd meet no one on the road. Nils had left shirt and boots behind, as well as bow and quiver, wearing only breeches and harness, carrying only sword and knife, and the coiled rope with its grapple. He'd be climbing, and unnecessary gear would be nuisances.

It was more than night-dark; it was like being in a sack of charcoal. The moon had not risen yet, and a thick overcast cut off even the starlight. Jik's problem in leading Nils to the village was to keep from blundering into the ditch. Or so he thought. He didn't realize that Nils saw as well in the dark as by day. Thus it took them considerably longer to reach Lü-Gu than Jik had expected, Nils keeping cheerfully to the Chinese youth's pace.

Jik intended to avoid village lanes, where they might encounter villagers. Instead he followed the mud-and-straw brick walls of householders' back vegetable gardens, walls which formed a mostly continuous outer skirt around the village. Indeed, most village yards were surrounded by such walls, commonly higher than a man. As Jik groped his way along, dogs barked, but in Lü-Gu, dogs barked off and on every night.

The youth was not intimately familiar with the village. They should have stayed outside the skirt of garden walls, circling till they came to the much higher, stronger wall of the bailiff's compound. When they encountered a ditch filled with irrigation water, he became confused. Thus they slipped through a gap between two garden walls and he felt his way through an orchard to a village lane.

Jik was truly worried now. He had little idea where they were, and this was taking longer than intended.

He looked about helplessly. Then around a corner, a light appeared. Two men turned into the lane, one of them carrying a lamp, and Jik saw both an opportunity and a danger. "Stay here!" he hissed. "Don't let them see you." Remembering that his companion spoke no Chinese, he pushed him into a niche they'd just passed, a corner where two neighboring walls failed to align. A tree grew there; it would help conceal the man. Then swallowing his fear, the youth hurried to meet the two men with the lamp.

One of them was Chen! "Excuse me, honored grandfathers," Jik said. "I am lost. Can you tell me where I can find the temple?" The temple, he knew, was very near the bailiff's.

Liang peered at the boy. "Who are you?" he asked.

Chen interrupted; it wouldn't do to have young Wu identify himself. "You are young Tung, are you not?"

Jik swallowed. "Yes, sir."

"Why do you want to go to the temple?" Liang asked. "It's not open at this hour."

Again Chen answered for him, or seemed to. "It's the darkness; he's gotten lost." He pointed. "The temple is just up the lane, boy. Not more than eighty meters."

Jik bobbed. "Thank you, honored grandfathers." *Only eighty meters! And not far past it was the bailiff's wall!* Alone he hurried past the two old men in the direction Chen had pointed. He could hardly stay and wait till they'd gone on; Liang would ask more questions. He'd go, then hurry back for the barbarian when the way was clear. He could tell from their breath, and indeed by the physician's speech, that the two men had been drinking. Hopefully they'd fail to notice the barbarian standing in the niche.

He stopped in a gateway and watched the two amble past the barbarian's hiding place. Not much farther on they stopped at a gate, and after a moment went through it, taking their lamp with them.

Jik went back to find the barbarian and take him to the bailiff's. The barbarian wasn't there.

The boy's stomach sank. Where could he have gone? Then an answer struck him: *The barbarian might have gone back the way they came. He might have lost his nerve.* The boy shook it off and waited a few minutes, hoping that Nils would pop up after all—that he'd simply found a better hiding place—but the barbarian didn't show. Finally Jik left. Being alone, and knowing now where he was, he made his way through the village to the main road, and turning right, followed it south out of town.

He'd go to the Pine Point, where the blanket was hidden, and his mother's hat, and the barbarian's bow and quiver. The road turned almost sharply there; he should be able to find that, at least. And the things were just within the edge of the woods, eighty-three steps from the road; he'd counted. He hardly dared go home without the blanket. If the barbarian's quiver and bow were still there, he'd wait for him. Otherwise he'd go straight home, as his father had ordered.

As soon as Nils heard, telepathically, Chen's answer to Jik, he slipped back through the darkness to a cross lane, and waited there. After a minute the two older men entered Liang's yard, but still Nils stayed where he was. He didn't want the boy with him at the bailiff's wall. He'd serve no purpose there, and if something went wrong, Jik might be unwilling to run away soon enough, and be caught.

He watched until the youth left, then moved swiftly past the temple to the compound. There he padded around the wall, scanning telepathically for the locations of any guards.

Four were posted atop the wall and one at the front gate. The men on top had probably been assigned one to a corner, but those for the southwest and northwest corners had met on the middle of the west wall, where they were smoking hemp together, chuckling, and talking in murmurs. Chen had told him there should be no dogs; his daughter had mentioned that her husband despised barking. Nor scanning could Nils sense one, watchdog or lapdog, though there could be one asleep in the house.

The compound's wall was about six meters high, the compound perhaps sixty wide and eighty long. Nils decided to go over the back wall some meters from the deserted northwest corner. When he reached there, he took the rope from his shoulder and laid the coils on the ground. Then he swung the grapple and tossed it onto the top. Wrapped as it was, it landed with only a dull clunk, not loud, but certainly audible in the night.

Nils stood motionless, scanning. With so few minds awake nearby, his psi reach was sufficient that he could sense even the guard at the front gate. In the quiet of night, three had heard the sound: the two hemp smokers, and the man at the northeast corner. But they weren't alarmed. The latter told himself it was the guard at the northwest corner; that was the most convenient supposition. The hemp smokers listened hard for perhaps twenty seconds, then dismissed the sound. It was too dark, they were enjoying their conversation, and anyway it was nothing.

Nils waited several slow minutes, then pulled cautiously. The hook moved a few handspans, then grabbed. He pulled harder; it seemed firmly set. Leaning back, he began to climb.

He reached the top without difficulty. The wall was about two meters wide between embrasured parapets. While he coiled his rope, he looked around. Open stairs led down into the courtyard from each back corner. The bailiff's manor was a tee-shaped building, itself a minor fortress. The stem of the tee was single-storied and had a number of slot-like windows. A scan of the sleeping minds inside identified it as the barracks. the two-storied crossbar was the manor itself. Its windows were larger, its roof a balustraded garden.

To human eyes, none of it would have been visible from the wall on so dense and dark night.

Cat-quiet, he went to the vacated northwest corner, down the stairs and into the courtyard. It too was largely garden, with fruit trees and flowerbeds. Swift and silent, he crossed it to a door at the base of the tee, and up the several steps to stand outside it. Carefully he raised the latch, but the door didn't give to his pressure.

Without hesitating, he slipped quietly to the ground again and around the west side of the house to the front. He sensed a guard inside, seated and sleeping beside the door. Carefully carefully he raised the heavy latch. Carefully he pulled, then pushed; the door remained firm, as if barred inside.

Lips compressed, Nils frowned, then continued around the house. On the east side there was a second-floor balcony with a low balustrade, and double doors ajar. Inside was a faint light, as if a candle burned there, or a small lamp. Also inside, he sensed, was the man he sought, asleep beside the smith's daughter, and no apparent way to reach him except with the grapple. He didn't hesitate. Uncoiling the rope, he swung and then tossed it.

In itself it made little noise, but the sleeping cat it struck and knocked from the balustrade squalled once indignantly, and raced inside, through the open doors and under the mosquito curtain.

Nils froze, his short hairs rigid at the sound. Upstairs the bailiff stirred, grunted in his sleep and rolled over. His young wife sat stiffly upright beside him, then got up. She listened hard, Nils listening with her. He felt her relax and lie back down, but wide awake now, wondering what could have frightened her cat so. An owl perhaps? As a girl she'd had a cat, and an owl had killed it in the night, killed and skinned and eaten it beneath the plum tree.

Gently Nils drew on the rope. The grapple moved scarce inches before it caught, but the young wife's senses had been sharpened by the cat's alarming squall. Thus she heard the slight scraping, and stiffened again in her bed, scalp tight, nerves tingling.

It occurred to Nils that he might better have thrown his grapple onto the roof, almost anywhere along the building. He'd have avoided the disturbance, and had the wall to brace his feet against for climbing. It would have been simple to let himself down to the balcony from there. As it was, he had a wakened woman at the top, and a free hang to climb up. But with his grapple engaged, he was committed.

Meanwhile the darkness was changing, just a little. The half moon, he realized, must be edging above the bordering mountain ridge, casting its first rays across the heavy overcast. Within minutes, visibility for human eyes would improve enough to endanger him. He'd be exposed then to the guard at the southeast corner.

He waited only seconds while the bailiff's wife began to relax. Then he reached up and began to climb. Even for his muscles it wasn't easy. Lean as he'd become, he still weighed 114 kilos, and the rope was slender—a centimeter and a half thick—offering little to grip on. It took him a grim half minute to reach the top and hoist his upper body onto the railing. Where he found himself looking into candle flame, and the eyes of the bailiff's wife, peering at him through the mosquito curtain! In his efforting, he hadn't sensed her getting out of bed, coming to the doorway to investigate the faint sound she'd heard—his effortful breathing.

She stared, her almond eyes wide, almost round.

"Sh-h-h!" he hissed, then pulled himself over the rail and stood. She moved only a short step back, still staring, not at his strange eyes now, but at all of him, huge, bull-muscled, half naked, and utterly foreign. She decided this was all a dream, strange and unreal.

He put a finger to his lips, and parted the curtains. Heart thudding, she stepped aside to let him pass. Lo Pu-Pang still slept; Nils felt the young wife's unbelieving eyes as he leaned over the bailiff. He reached—clutched! His grip was inhumanly strong. His thumbs crushed the trachea and compressed the carotid as the fingers dug deeply into the man's poorly toned neck muscles. The bailiff's eyes bulged open, and for just a moment his body strained upward before collapsing back.

Nils held his grip long enough to ensure the man's death, then straightened and breathed a long sigh. He'd been holding his breath. He'd killed many men in fights, and some fighting men by stealth, but this was his first murder. The wife was beside him now with her candle, staring at the corpse's gaping face. Then she set the candle on the bedside table, threw her arms around the Northman's waist, pressed her face against him and wept silently.

There was no grief in it, only an upwelling of relief, an unburdening of repression, and she clung to Nils thus for a long minute, her tears wetting his chest. When she stopped, she looked up at him, and he could sense her arousal. She stood on tiptoes, and he bent till they kissed, long and passionately, her fingers pressing his lean flesh. Then she led him to a couch beside a wall.

Afterward she fell asleep, and he left as she'd expected. She'd already decided: When she awoke, if her husband . . . If this had been real, and no dream, she'd scream, then say she'd wakened to find him dead. No one could accuse her of such a murder; she hadn't nearly the strength for it.

Nils didn't go down the rope. He left it where it hung, and silent as smoke, slipped down the inside stairs. In the entry hall, a single oil lamp burned on a bracket. The guard had been changed while Nils had been with Chen's daughter, but the new guard already dozed in a chair by the door. Nils killed him with a knife thrust through the eye socket, deep into the brain, avoiding the slippery blood that followed slitting throats.

It seemed to him there'd be a direct connection between the bailiff's residence and the guard barracks. There was—a set of double doors. Before trying them though, he unlatched the front entrance, a possible retreat lane. Then, with sweat starting again, he opened the doors to the barracks wing, just a crack, and looked through.

On the other side, a hall led to another set of double

doors, and on each side of the hall were two separate doors. He slipped inside, and very carefully opened one. A candle guttered in the small room, and a man lay sleeping, presumably an officer. A young woman, actually a girl, slept beside him. The man's breastplate, greaves, and plumed helmet hung on pegs, and his sword belt on another. Without waking the girl, Nils killed him as he'd killed the entry guard, then left, closing the door behind him.

On the other side, a man lay in bed alone. He died the same death. In the third, two men lay sleeping together, legs tangled. Very carefully he killed one, but something, some psychic thread, caused the other to stir, to mutter. The man's lids fluttered, and the knife slashed deeply across his throat. Blood gushed, then slacked off, and Nils wiped his hands and knife on the bedding. The fourth room was empty. Its occupant was either on duty or had died across the hall.

Next Nils went to the double doors at the hall's end, and opened one of them. Here as in the entry hall, a single oil lamp flickered, this one by the door. This was the barracks proper, with two rows of long grass-filled mattresses on the floor, about forty in all. He could smell the grass through the odor of lampflame and unwashed bodies. Some of the mattresses were unoccupied. At the head of each was a wicker chest, and on the wall, pegs with gear hanging. Between the rows was abundant room to muster and stand inspection.

Nils snuffed the flame and the room went dark. The only light was faint, cloud-thinned moonlight through small windows in the east wall. He went to the nearest man, then moved crouching down the west row, killing each in turn—

Until, when he'd almost reached the end, he heard a bellow of alarm and rage from the hall outside. The dead guard had been found in the entry hall. Men were springing from their beds at the noise, confused in the blackness, staring toward the sound. Several groped for their weapons on the wall. Nils moved like a giant beweaponed dervish then, slashing, slaying. There were shrieks and shouts. The double doors burst open, and a man stepped in with a lamp. More men were turning toward the uproar; swords were being drawn. Nils's great blade swept and hewed, and men fell, until only eight or ten still stood, desperate. Seeing death upon them, they rallied.

Nils gave way then, backing quickly toward the far end of the barracks, and the guardsmen, encouraged, pressed him. The foremost he slew, and the second; the rest hung back. One called to bring halberds, another called for a bow. Nils reached the door, slipped the bar, threw it open and ran into the courtyard.

Instantly they were after him, though not too closely.

He raced to a stairway and up the wall. The guard at the corner waited for him, and struck down at him with his sword. Nils fended it as others reached the stairs behind him. His huge left hand shot out, grabbed the guardsman's ankle, shoved upward, twisted, jerked. The man's arms flailed to keep his balance, and Nils's sword thrust up into him. Then the Northman pounced to the top of the wall, spun, and struck down his leading pursuer. The rest hung back again; there were only a handful left. He turned his back to them, hopped onto the parapet, and sword in hand jumped off.

He lit crouching, not falling, and loped off into the night. He was outside the skirt of garden walls, and no one was willing to pursue him.

PART V

CLOSURE

THIRTY-SIX

Baver sat on the sleeping shelf in his cell. It was night, and the only light was the faint glow from an oil lamp down the corridor. He was grateful for that much. Charles DuBois had told him about the dungeon in the City of Kazi, and like the rest of the crew he'd gotten a mini-briefing on what had happened to Chan and Anne there. Then there was the canto in the Järnhann Saga, about the dungeon Nils had been in in Hungary.

This is probably one of the most civilized prison cells on the planet, he told himself. *No leg irons, I've got my own latrine bucket, my own water pail—and the sleeping shelf has a straw mat on it! It's not even really filthy!*

He half grunted, half chuckled. *Semi-barbaric accommodations for a semi-barbaric prisoner.* He *had* become semi-barbaric, at least outwardly. But semi-barbaric hadn't been enough. The true, hundred percent barbarians had escaped.

Or was Nils actually a barbarian? In antiquity, barbarians had evolved into civilized men—men whose society was ruled from towns, by governments. Could barbarians evolve into something besides civilized man? Maybe Nils was that something else; maybe he only seemed to be a barbarian because he lived in a barbarian milieu. Or was he simply a new and fuller flowering of barbarianism?

Flowering of barbarianism! This time Baver's chuckle was genuine.

What, he asked himself, *would Nils do if he were here?*. The answer seemed obvious: Nils would sleep. He wouldn't fret, and he wouldn't try anything heroic. Not unless there was a good prospect that it would work, or some prospect anyway.

Or—If there was no prospect at all that it would work, no prospect at all of freedom, probably Nils would do something to go out on his own terms. To create an effect, probably dramatic, instead of going down silently.

Or would he? Baver shook his head. When it came to Nils Järnhann, guesses were suspect. Good guesses required understanding, he told himself, and he certainly didn't understand Nils. Admired him, liked him, was intrigued by him—yes. But he didn't understand him.

He stood up, stretched, bent and touched his feet. And told himself he should try exercising to exhaustion; maybe that would help him sleep. But somehow . . . He sat back down.

He recognized now one of the things that bothered him. Besides captivity of course. Ever since he'd left the ting ground with Hans— No, ever since the *Phaeacia* had left for New Home, and he'd realized how isolated he really was, living with the Salmon Clan—ever since then he'd been comforted by the concealed pistol he'd carried in the holster pocket of his jumpsuit. His ace in the hole, his security.

Now it was gone.

Interesting, he told himself: I miss it, but somehow I don't feel as insecure as I used to with it, say a year and a half ago.

He touched his left side pocket and felt the palm-sized radio there. The emperor hadn't been overimpressed. He took it out, all ninety grams of it. He'd carried it for— how many kilometers? Nine thousand? Ten? Carried a radio that didn't work. Why? Certainly not for any comfort it gave him. Every time he remembered it, it reminded him of how cut off he was. More than once he'd thought about throwing it away. But how many spare radios were there aboard the *Alpha?* One or two? None? And if he did get back to the Northmen someday, Matt and Nikko would get word of it and come to debrief him on what had happened. Then Matt could fix it or replace the faulty power tap, or whatever.

Absently, Baver slid the power switch.

And the power light flashed on, a bright red spot in the dimness of his cell! He stared, the breath stopped in his throat. After a long several seconds, he moved the instrument close to his mouth and pressed the transmit button. A green light came on. It took an effort to control his excitement and speak quietly.

"*Alpha,*" he murmured, "this is Ted. *Alpha,* this is Ted. Over."

The answer came from more than 108 degrees of longitude west of him, in the not-quite-human voice of the *Alpha*'s computer. "This is pinnace *Alpha.* I am currently located on the Terran surface at coordinate XE: 09.585267, Yn: 56.471394." As it had begun to speak, Baver had thumbed the volume down so it was loud enough to hear, but no louder. The pinnace continued. "In local terms, I am in a sheep pasture 165 meters distant, at 151 degrees azimuth, from the main gate of the castle of Jørgen the First, Karlssen, Stennaeve, King of the Danes. The date is 2834, August 26, Earth Reckoning. The hour, local time, is 14:23:41."

To Baver there was a poignant homely beauty in the computer's voice, its sweet, ordinary, prosaic message, its textbook-proper speech. He melted hearing it.

"My primary security system is activated. Nikko Kumalo is inside the castle, interviewing Anders Henrikssen, Raadgiver, principle advisor to King Jørgen. Matthew Kumalo is with her, as her bodyguard. They have been away since hour 13:48:17, this date, and their sole open connection with myself is an input-only line, to record the interview. They predicted their return as before hour 20:00.

"If you have a message, you may state it at whatever length you please. Over."

Baver moved the switch to the pause position; for the moment he had no idea what to say. He could override the *input-only* instruction by declaring an *emergency-two*, but—what could they do right away, that would make a difference?

Was the emperor listening to his thoughts? Or perhaps some other telepath assigned by him? He'd simply have to hope not. He'd start by giving his situation, then his location, and go on from there until he was done or someone had intervened.

"This is Ted Baver," he murmured to his radio. "I'm in a prison cell in China, in the capital. Beijing isn't the capital anymore; I've passed through what I think was Beijing. There are some big old buildings still standing, but most of it's farm's and a big army camp. The new capital is in a valley, in a range of forested hills. It's a long day's horseback ride from there, north or maybe northeast; call it a day and a half. . . ."

He went on to describe the capital, the palace, and the ogre guards. Then dropped back to tell how he'd left the Balkans with Nils. He told briefly of Achikh and the Mongols. And that the emperor was a telepath, with, according to Kaidu, a dream of conquering the world.

When he was done, he felt surprisingly good, even hopeful. He did wish, though, that he had his recorder and cubes; he'd have copied the cubes to the computer, so they'd have them even if he never got back.

He wondered again what had been wrong with his radio. He recalled it getting wet, soaked actually, at least twice in his saddlebag, the first couple of days. But supposedly it was waterproof. Matthew could probably explain it to him, if he ever got out of there.

THIRTY-SEVEN

Farmer Wu had told his son to come home that night, and had said nothing about bringing the barbarian with him. But the boy wasn't willing to abandon the giant, even though he suspected the man had failed them. The moon had risen by the time he got back to Pine Point, and the overcast seemed to have thinned a bit; he'd had no real trouble finding his way to Nils's things. He'd raked up a pile of needles there as insulation from the ground, wrapped himself in his blanket, the one the barbarian had worn the day before, and gone to sleep. With the fixed intention of waking up well before dawn.

Actually, he expected his stomach to waken him. He'd had no supper, unless one counted the snack his mother had packed.

It was much lighter when he awoke, and he sprang to his feet. But it wasn't dawn breaking. Rather, the half moon was high, and the overcast had given way to clear sky. Stars glittered between the treetops, and he was cold, blanket or no.

The barbarian was there too, getting up from a needle pile of his own, as if Jik's wakening had wakened him.

He now wore the shirt he'd left behind, which with his breeches and boots was all he had against the chill. And seemed none the worse for it.

They didn't speak; there was neither point nor need. They simply gathered their things and left.

On the road, the night took on a special clarity for Jik, a rare beauty, the feel of a spiritual experience. His normal life consisted very largely of work and sleep. In summer he was usually in bed by dark, and it was getting light when his father wakened him to do his chores. His experience of night was very largely the occasional thirty-meter walk, sleepy-eyed and thick-headed to the odorous privy.

He wasn't sure how near it was to dawn, but decided they should jog. His father had emphasized the importance of getting home and out of sight before daylight. This would be doubly important with the barbarian along; it wouldn't do to be seen by some farmer walking early to his field, and there were the ravens to consider.

After a bit, Jik could see the wash of early dawn paling the sky. He speeded slightly; they still had perhaps three kilometers to go before leaving the last hamlet behind, and to detour through the forest would slow them. Also he was eager to reach home and breakfast. The reach and drive of his loping legs in the cool dawn air made him feel full-chested and strong, indomitable. He wondered if the barbarian felt the same. Perhaps the man often ran in the night; perhaps his strange eyes could see in the dark. That would explain some things. And it had been the barbarian's hand that kept him from falling in the irrigation ditch, earlier that night.

The dawn strengthened. Birds awoke in the trees, and with preparatory chirps warmed up for their dawn chorus. It would be awhile, though, before they were out and flying. He and the barbarian were almost beyond the clearing, and not far from home, when Jik's mood changed, suddenly and inexplicably. Fear struck him, fear without threat, followed as quickly by black despair. The ground began to tremble, or seemed to, and his vision blurred. He stumbled, stopped, uncomprehending. For a long minute the feeling persisted, intensifying, as if the world was dying, shuddering and twitching beneath his feet.

Then his vision cleared, the ground steadied, and the awfulness faded, leaving an ugly aftertaste. The chirping had stopped; there would be no bird chorus this dawn. Jik looked at the barbarian. The giant's expression was reassuring—neither frightened nor worried, only intent. Then he said something in some strange language that might or might not have been Mongol, and they trotted on down the cart road into the woods.

On the plain that had once been a residential area of Beijing, the general sat upright on his bed. His bed-girl of the night had begun to scream, but that wasn't what had wakened him. It seemed to him there was an earthquake, not massive, more a sort of trembling and twitching. Also something was wrong with his eyes, and he felt fear more powerful than he'd ever imagined.

The girl had stopped screaming and was crying loudly. He slapped her, and her wails softened to sobbing. Through his open window he heard shouts of fear, even terror.

With a curse he swung his legs from the bed, stood up and yelled for his valet. He'd have to go out there and enforce some discipline.

He still felt fear, ugly and black, but he wasn't paying much attention to it just now. He had things to do.

A two-storied longhouse stood in a small forest clearing. Its roof beam curved up at the ends, and it was shingled with gray-weathered, hand-split wooden shakes. The walls were sawn planks of Korean pine, dressed smooth and stained dark. Around it were flowerbeds, shrubs and fruit trees, inobtrusive outbuildings, and great shading spruces dark in the dawnlight. A brook flowed past, splashing over stone dams small and mossy, built for aesthetics of sound and vision.

In a small room, a man sat upright on a thick meditation mat, his bare legs folded beneath him in a lotus posture. He was on the far side of middle age, his hair dark stubble, his thin beard mostly white. In other rooms, other men also sat meditating. In one long room, more than a dozen novices sat in the lotus posture on a broad bench, facing a wall. Two adepts stood by with supple staffs to waken any who dozed.

All of them felt the malaise when it began. It was the old master, Jampa Lodro, who saw into it most deeply. This was no earthquake; it was something in the realm between the Tao and Maya. Something malevolent lay there, something of power and evil intent. Something interesting. He contemplated it.

Baver awoke in his cell, not remembering for the moment where he was or how he'd gotten there. His first thought was *earthquake,* and he feared the building would be shaken down on him. But it wasn't that strong; not at all. What was strong, what was truly powerful, was the fear, then the despair. At the moment he had no doubt that he would never leave this place alive, quake or not.

THIRTY-EIGHT

From the moment of his abrupt wakening, Songtsan Gampo had known what the cause was. Tenzin had said the demon was inside the fabric of the Tao, a position of great potential power. Clearly it was learning to function sooner than they'd expected, and he had not yet established himself as its god.

He waited till the phenomenon had passed. Then, without closing his eyes, he focused his mind on Tenzin Geshe and began to question him. After a minute he brought his attention back to his bedroom. The *geshe's* mind had been tired and shaken. Not a good sign. Not a favorable condition, considering what they had to do now.

Nonetheless— Stepping to a gong, the emperor struck it firmly. Time, it seemed, was one luxury he didn't have.

The demon in the Sigma Field hadn't known what to expect. It hadn't even known, really, what it was doing. It had expected power when, as a man, it stood beside the makeshift altar in the village and wielded the sacramental knife. Now, it seemed, it had that power. So it had flexed its muscles, in a sense, that was all. Thinking of the Great God, the mountain, it had flexed its muscles to see what would happen.

It thought of its condition much as Tenzin did: It was like an infant, in this instance a huge and mighty infant, poorly coordinated, its perceptions ill-defined, grasping its situation only vaguely and partially.

Also like an infant, it wanted what it wanted, without qualification.

Certain things it did know, automatically, as a function of its bodiless existence. Thus it had found in itself the ability to cover its thoughts—to "screen"—a development that disturbed the man who probed it. That man, the prober, would have been more disturbed if he'd known that the demon could recognize him. For Tenzin and the members of his Circle had ceased to be mere swirls in the Sigma Field. The demon not only recognized each mind, but now saw the faces and figures that accompanied the minds. Even though its new perceptics had nothing to do with electromagnetic radiation. Thus it perceived the *geshe* as a human would: a man of slender frame, small-boned and narrow-faced.

The demon had not yet learned, though, to find and connect with a mind whose owner was outside its field of focus. The owner must first come to it and enter that focus.

But once affixed to a consciousness within that field, the demon could follow it. Once it had followed a servant out of the *gomba,* and after a bit through the Great Gate and out of the Dzong to a market in Miyun. There it had lost the servant in a crowd, and for a few minutes of worry bordering on panic, had feared it couldn't find its way back to the people of power. Where it sensed that its opportunities lay. But after a time, Tenzin had reached to probe again, and at the touch, the demon had snapped back to the House of Power as if on some giant elastic band. Or more correctly to the Sigma Field location congruent with the House of Power.

Subsequently its field of focus had been a bit larger,

as if the adventure had broadened its range. And it had decided to bide its time—to wait and learn, growing in knowledge and power. Though by its impatient nature, that would be a hard decision to stay with.

Now Tenzin touched it lightly. But firmly, not tentatively; shaken though he was, the *geshe* knew better than to be tentative. The demon lay still, waiting, sensing that something unusual, perhaps pivotal, was about to happen. It coiled itself, so to speak, ready to withdraw further from the interface. Or to resist, or attack.

Tenzin too was wary. Adept though he was—superbly adept—he was not, in his soul, a master. In fact he was fearful. He valued and guarded his physical life more than any true master would.

The demon sensed this fear—it was not the sort of thing that screening hid—and briefly was tempted to strike and hurt. But it let be. The prober was its principal contact and teacher, and also he wasn't sure what revenge, if any was possible to the man's allies. None, he suspected, but lacked confidence in it.

Then there came another, unfamiliar touch! And a thought with it: *"My child, I am your god come to guide you, and to make you my right arm."*

The demon focused, looked, and what it saw was human. A tall strong man, still rather young, with a shaven head, long jaw, prominent cheekbones, rich brown skin with a pink undercolor, eyes slanted beneath black tufts of eyebrow. In its way a handsome man, by the demon's own past cultural concepts and many others. And clearly a compelling, potent man, a magician, a wielder of powers, Before the Great God had transformed him, he would have been strongly impressed by such a man. Now—Now *he* was the stronger! But the other ruled; he sensed that. He ruled outside, in the material world. Ruled with the help of those who sat in a circle. If he could possess such a man . . .

The demon coiled more tightly.

"Do not fear your god, my child," the thought went on. "Open yourself to me."

The demon opened itself just a little, setting its trap. It felt the man's psyche prod gently, seeking to enter his mind. To enter, and with the help of those others, to possess and rule him.

"Give yourself to me," the man whispered, "and I shall give you power and joy such that . . ."

For just a moment the demon felt itself lured, but not fooled. Instead it struck like a moray, grasped the reaching prodding mind and "heard" it "scream." *Subdue!* was the demon's thought, its purpose. *Hold, overcome, subdue! Subordinate and control!*

But the man did not collapse or submit. For a long minute they struggled, the others pouring power into the desperate man who had called himself God. Against their combined power, the demon could not hold him; not yet. For though its access to power was potentially greater, it knew too little how to use it.

Then the demon subsided, leaving its near-victim reeling, physically and psychically. And in the instant of letting go, saw the Sanctuary as if with 360 degree vision, saw people, furnishings—all of it. There was one in that room who, even in that brief flash, imprinted on the demon's mind, and for a minute afterward it examined the imprint. The being was an ogre, taller by far than any of the men there, manlike but not human, with close red fur. It wore a breast plate, and carried a sword that surely few men could even raise. Also the demon sensed far more than human strength there.

Beyond that—Beyond that there was something vulnerable about it.

The demon lay back now, his attention totally on the swirl that was the ogre. It left with the man he'd wrestled and nearly subdued, and in the Sigma Field, the demon followed them, staying as far from the interface, the boundary, as it could and yet follow.

How to gain access to the red-furred creature? At length and cautiously, the demon approached the interface again, closely enough to look. It saw a bedroom, large and luxurious; the man's. Clearly he was a great king. Just now, three attendants fussed over him, and by the door the red-furred ogre stood guard.

The demon subsided, and lay in wait until the ogre left, replaced by another.

Again he followed it. It showed no awareness that he was there, thus the demon stayed close enough to watch it visually. The ogre went to a barracks where others like it slept on thick, grass-filled tickings on the floor. There, after relieving itself in an adjacent latrine, and washing, it lay down to sleep.

Carefully the demon probed it in its sleep, it and some of its fellows. Before he subsided again, he knew considerable about it. It was called Maamo, and thought of itself that way. Maamo was more and different than his fellows, in a way the demon did not understand. There was no doubt that Maamo was dominant, not just because of size, strength, and intelligence, but for some deeper reason.

Throughout the night, as Maamo slept, the demon probed, exploring ever more deeply, absorbing a sense of the creature's mind and body in as much detail as it could.

He learned too that Maamo was like the emperor's dog: he had his trust. At times, to strengthen the bond between them, the emperor had even entered Maamo's mind to caress his pleasure center, as a man might pet his hound.

Also, Maamo—indeed all the Yeti Guard—had had a command of loyalty installed, loyalty to the emperor. The demon was familiar with posthypnotic commands; as a human he'd used them. His Christian tribe had never entirely given up shamanism and its knowledge. And he had no doubt that, given the power of his present position, he could remove or override that loyalty command.

Perhaps, the demon thought, it would not need to wait long. As a man, patience had been difficult for it. It still was. Action was its natural mode. Perhaps through Maamo it could still capture the great king's mind, *be-*

come his mind, and through him rule, until it had mastered its own, greater resources and mode.

Meanwhile it seemed there was danger in where he was, and that danger was the circle of wizards and the one who led them. Indeed, so far as he could see, the circle was the only threat he faced, the only hindrance. Without its help, the great king dare not wrestle him again. Therefore he'd have to destroy the Circle, and there too it seemed that Maamo could be his tool. Maamo and his furry brethren if necessary.

THIRTY-NINE

By the time that Jik and Nils got back to the farm, there was enough daylight to see that the giant had been splashed with blood from scalp to feet, apparently none of it his own. It seemed he hadn't failed them, at least not entirely.

Mrs. Wu still held little Kin, pale and tear-streaked in her arms, soothing him from the terror that had wakened him screaming in the dawn. She stared owl-eyed and pale at the man before he washed, or as nearly owl-eyed as her epicanthic eye folds allowed. And *while* he washed, for the display of muscles was unlike anything she'd seen before, though Wu himself was hard and muscular.

Wu poked the barbarian's wet shoulder. "Bailiff?" Wu said, then repeated. "Bailiff?"

The barbarian bared big square teeth in a grin that fascinated in an alarming way. He clutched with his hands in a pantomine of strangling. Bailiff was clearly a word he knew now, and he repeated it as he mimed. Then he walked fingers downward through the air, as if down stairs, and pantomined the killings and the fight in the barracks.

The blood was the only evidence for any of it, but it was enough. They did not disbelieve him.

While they ate breakfast—bread and butter, beans and curds and cabbage—Jik told his father what he wanted to do. He'd seldom been so forward before, but Wu nodded permission, even though it would lose him two more days of the boy's labor. He hadn't expected to see the barbarian again, and had no ideas of his own on how to be rid of this potentially very dangerous man.

After breakfast, the barbarian sat down on a bench, drew his sword, and with his knife scraped the dried blood from hilt and crossbar. Following which he borrowed a file and patiently, thoroughly, worked the nicks out of his sword before using a whetstone on both sword and knife. It took him more than an hour.

He knew all that passed between father and son. Jik would work that morning, then nap. At twilight, when the farmers along the road should be at home, the two of them would leave.

Meanwhile he himself could sleep all day, and would.

They moved briskly in the starlight, bypassed Lü-Gu through farm fields, then returned to the road on the far side of the village. Here even Jik had traveled only once before, but for several hours there was no chance of confusion, for there were no other roads.

At last they came to a crossroad. Jik pointed right and shook his head vehemently. "Emperor!" he said. "Soldiers!" Then pointed left and nodded. "Jampa Lodro!" he said. "Jampa Lodro!" He himself had never been that way, nor had his father, but the road to Jampa Lodro's was common knowledge.

Nils nodded. "Jampa Lodro," he said back, and they turned left.

Jik was young and lean and work-hardened, but not accustomed to hiking all night. He flagged near the end, and daylight arrived before they did. The morning was chill, and wet with dew, when they came to the forest clearing with its longhouse, landscaped grounds and out-lying fields. Jik knew its Sino-Tibetan name—*Gomba Dorje*—though not the meaning, Monastery of Enlightenment. Morning meditations were over, and breakfast, and a number of novices and monks were filing into the potato field, hoes in hand. Nils insisted on skirting the clearing to where the forest edge was very near the longhouse.

Despite the chill, Nil's shirt was in his small pack, and as they approached the longhouse, a novice sweeping a flagstone walk stared at him open-mouthed. It seemed to Jik that the boy hadn't even noticed the barbarian's eyes; he was too awed by his size and muscles.

The monk who answered the door gong wore an un-bleached linen robe. Clearly he was Chinese, not Tibetan, which made Jik less uncomfortable than he might otherwise have been at this holy and already fabled place. The monk noticed the barbarian's eyes, Jik had no doubt. Actually he'd noticed more than the eyes; he'd seen the aura. He bowed slightly and the barbarian bowed slightly in return. Jik bowed more deeply. He sensed that this monk was an adept, and he'd heard stories of what Jampa Lodro's adepts could do. Most of the stories would have set them laughing.

Jik didn't wait for the monk to ask what they wanted. "I have brought this barbarian here," he said, "because he is lost and has no home. Also, although he is very brave, he is afraid of being outside in daylight. My father says Jampa Lodro will know what to do with him." Actually the idea was his own, but ascribing it to his father would give it merit with the monks, it seemed to him. "He is obviously a good fighting man," he went on. "You might want to hire him as a guard. And do not worry about the eyes. He sees very well, even in the dark!"

The monk smiled. "Thank you. We will see what Jampa says." The man and Nils looked at each other again. Each seemed to listen to the other, too, although nothing was said, and Jik's scalp crawled. Then the monk turned and led them to the dining hall, where a novice was scrubbing tables with a stout brush and soapy water. He instructed the cook to feed the two visitors, then left. They were given two wooden bowls each. In one was barley porridge, in the other bean curd with a thick chunk of bread on top, and a small piece of cheese.

When Jik finished eating, he turned to see the monk standing just inside the door, waiting. "I have spoken with Jampa; I am to take the barbarian to him. You are to wait outdoors. I will be back shortly."

Nils got up as if he'd understood what was said, and after washing his bowls, left the dining room with the monk. Jik washed his also, and went outside to nap beneath a tree.

Though his name was Tibetan, Jampa Lodro did not have the Golok features so common among the Sino-Tibetan aristocracy. This was because he had two Chinese grandmothers. His build was compact, and he looked remarkably solid for someone not a soldier or peasant. In fact, he came from a family of army officers, and until age twenty had been trained to be one. Then, in defiance of his grandfather, he'd run away to the monastery of La Tso, above Chengdu in the mountains of Sichuan, and been accepted as a student by the most holy Phabong Rimpoche.

This was an honor, for the number of novices was severely restricted, a requirement instituted by Songtsan I for military, agricultural, and labor reasons. Applicants were closely examined as to their potential and their motivation.

Nonetheless his paternal grandfather had disowned him. Much to the distress of the family, for it was universally considered that to become a *drapa*, a religious student, was at least acceptable to any family. And to be accepted by a famous *rimpoche* was an honor.

Most especially acceptance by one with the rare reputation of Phabong Rimpoche. Phabong was a most exalted master, the most famous student of the venerable Tri Kunlek. Tri Kunlek was the great reformer, founder of the popularly termed "Bloodless Order," so called because it declined to sacrifice animals or divine from entrails. In fact, it rarely divined and did not sacrifice at all. It had also abandoned other practices of most older orders, practices with little or no spiritual virtue. It followed only a few practices which, if followed correctly and with perseverence, put one knowingly in touch with the Tao.

The Bloodless Order was most famous, though, for the spiritual skills of its leading adepts, who, it was popularly believed, could levitate, fast without losing even a kilo of weight, and consult with spirits who had won free of the physical plane. Its adepts were known for their modesty, and never talked about their abilities, but almost everyone knew someone who'd seen them do such things.

And Jampa Lodro was said to be as exalted a master as his mentor, Phabong, and Phabong's mentor, Tri.

Nils Järnhann knew none of this when he met Jampa Lodro. But he did know, at once, that the stocky, stubble-headed man with the wispy white beard was a wizard more powerful than Fong Jung Hing; and spiritually far more advanced than Nils's own mentor, Raadgiver, the Dane.

Jampa, in turn, recognized at once that the man before him had been born with more power, more potential, than anyone he'd known before. And that he'd already developed much of that potential. Jampa motioned Nils to be seated on a mat, then sat down facing him. Neither spoke a language that the other knew, but that was no obstacle. Within half an hour they knew each other as closely as twins.

FORTY

Fann dom då den stilla kjämpen,
hal av svett å omedveten,
där han låg ne'en döjda trollen.
Dröd ham fri och bar ham hemåt
till den danska kongens fäste.
Lämte hos en danske läk're,
Rådjiver han kalls i landen,
Rådjiver den mäkti sajkarl,
å sin dotter, sjöna Signe.
Vårde de den unga jälten.

[There they found the limp young warrior,
slick with sweat and lying senseless,
'neath the sea troll where he'd killed it.
Drew him free and bore him homeward
to the castle of King Jørgen.
Left him with a Danish healer,
Raadgiver the people called him,
Raadgiver, the mighty wizard,
and his lovely daughter, Signe.
Tended they the youthful hero.]

From—The Järnhann Saga,
Kumalo translation

* * *

Nikko Kumalo's interview of Anders Henrikssen, Raadgiver, hadn't taken long—little more than two hours. She had interviewed him before, more than once. This return was only to explore questions that had come up about the Psi Alliance in her interviews with others since then. When the interview was over, the Dane had taken them to see Ingrid, his granddaughter, a calm, mature-seeming, beautiful child of three years, her hair almost cotton white. Remembering them, the child put aside her doll and advanced with her hand extended, as if she were royalty and they were to kiss it. Which in fact Matthew did, inspiring giggles.

They'd met the mother before, too, and had thought her retiring and aloof. Signe Andersdatter was a handsome young woman, with long black hair that made her fair skin seem milk white by contrast, and her ice-blue eyes more striking. She'd be beautiful, Matthew decided, if it weren't for her coldness, and hauteur which, if not obtrusive, was nonetheless plain to see.

It seemed to Matthew that he could see passion there, too, a repressed passion generated by some resentment, some injustice. And it embarrassed him to notice, because Raadgiver was a telepath who would know his thoughts. He suspected that the daughter did too, for she colored slightly, and taking Ingrid by the hand, left the room with a thin goodbye.

Then Matthew suggested that he and Nikko should leave, if she had no further questions for their host. She didn't, and Raadgiver accompanied them from his apartment, down a stone staircase and into the flagstoned courtyard. Weeds grew between the flags, grasshoppers chewed on the weeds, and chickens preyed on the grasshoppers. Two red hens flapped out of the humans' way.

"Your daughter is a lovely woman," Nikko said, "and your granddaughter is charming."

Raadgiver smiled wryly. "I love them both. I only wish Signe had had a mother to bring her up, and Ingrid a father in the home." It seemed the older man needed to confide in someone, and Nikko was a professional listener. "I made no effort to remarry when my wife died bearing Signe," he went on. "I realized later that I should have. In fact the old duke—the king's father—urged me to. But it seemed to me then that it would complicate my life. Astrid had been just right for me, and I believed that I wouldn't be happy with anyone else.

"I was selfish."

They crossed the drawbridge, the moat beneath it late-summer thick with algae clouds and shingled with pond lilies. Frogs chirked and croaked.

"And Ingrid's father is away a lot?" Matthew asked.

"Ingrid's father is Nils Järnhann. Her blondness comes from him."

Raadgiver's answer shut up both Kumalos. The Dane continued; his unasked for comments had led to their embarrassment, and he would not leave them thus.

"Signe resented from childhood that I was a servant of the duke. She considered that with my intelligence, and even more with my psi, I should be ruler. But the Psi Alliance shuns authority, for good reasons. In a world like ours, or at least in our part of it, we must conceal, camouflage our abilities. And to rule in a violent world, let alone to gain a throne, takes talents quite different from mine. Later, when she recognized these things, it made it worse for her instead of better.

"When Nils showed up, she scorned him. She still scorns him, because the Svear are barbarians. She considers us far superior—refined, civilized, knowledgeable about history . . . And when we realized that his talents were greater than ours, that added to her resentment. Especially she resented his tranquility; when she insulted him, he took no offense.

"Yet I could read the desire he lit in her. She'd had nothing to do with men, and never intended to. She will never marry; if there's one thing I am sure of in this world, it's that.

"How they came to mate, I do not know. She screened it from me. But he did not violate her; that would be totally foreign to his nature. And if he had, it would show through her screen. I seriously doubt he even initiated the mating, which took place not long before he left. She'd have spurned him."

The Dane shrugged. Nikko remembered Nils's sexual magnetism.

"I was afraid she wouldn't love the child, but happily I was wrong. She resents deeply, though, that the father is a barbarian. Regardless of his accomplishments and objectivity."

They came to the pinnace. Matthew took the control pad from a pocket and keyed in the instruction. The shield flicked out of existence.

"Well," said Raadgiver, "you have listened with patience and understanding to the plaints of a man no longer young. They are small matters, compared to those of our peasants here. It is good to be gifted; I have lived comfortably, without hardship or the harshness of labor. I neither freeze nor greatly sweat, and do not know real hunger, only appetite. I have had the advantages of a long and rich tradition of scholarship, and communion with the richest culture on the planet, the Psi Alliance, dispersed though it may be.

"Yet our lives are not completely free of pain, though it might fairly be said that our pain is self-inflicted. We are simply humans with certain advantages."

He nodded as if agreeing with himself.

"Well." He put out his hand, and the Kumalos shook it. "If you wish to interview me again, I will gladly make myself available."

Then he turned and walked back toward the castle. Nikko and Matthew boarded the *Alpha*, and Matthew regenerated the shield. Nikko saw the green light flashing on the control panel, and acknowledged the signal orally.

"What have you got for us, Allie?" she asked.

"A message from Deodoro Baver," the pinnace replied.

They listened to it at once, amazed and dismayed. *In a prison in China! In the palace compound, guarded by soldiers and some sort of sentient predator, no doubt an ET left over from the pre-plague days. With telepaths around; one at least.*

"How the hell do we get him out of there?" Matthew asked.

The question was rhetorical, but Nikko answered. "I suppose we stock up on provisions and water, fly to China, locate the palace, and park over it at four or five kilometers—high enough to be sure no one notices, and far out of ordinary telepathic range."

Matthew nodded, taking it from there. "And see if we can identify the building he's in, from his description. Then set the viewer on the entrance at high gain, and watch. Hopefully they'll bring him out, maybe for exercise." He patted the rifle rack. "Maybe there'll be a chance to free him then."

Anything like that might well endanger Baver, of course. They agreed that it would certainly be dangerous to radio him that they were waiting. Better for him to be ignorant than for his captors to know.

FORTY-ONE

Hsu Min was a novice in Jampa Lodro's *gomba*, but he'd arrived as a telepath, and was full of himself. He had many opinions to outgrow.

Normally, the novice in meditation was beset by unwanted thoughts. These thoughts intruded from hidden depths. Some were enticing thoughts, some were ugly thoughts, and one undertook to contemplate them, observing them. One undertook to observe them until one perceived the pain or fear, or guilt or grief or false belief, that generated them. And until one perceived the false lessons one had learned from them. Thus one loosened the grip of maya.

When thoughts no longer intruded, one could begin to experience the Tao awarely. Ordinarily this took much meditation, the muchness varying with how evolved the soul was when it incarnated. Someone who had evolved to a relatively high spiritual level in their previous lives would progress more rapidly. And it seemed to Min that he knew how to recognize such a one: Usually he would be relatively delicate, physically, in order not to be tempted to violence. And normally he would be telepathic or otherwise psychic, at least sporadically, for it was maya that tended to cloud psychic abilities.

Being both delicate and telepathic, Min expected to progress quite rapidly.

Adepts commonly meditated with their eyes open, seeing nothing, but it was entirely acceptable to close them, to cut off the distractions of vision. Telepaths might also close their inner eye, so as not to be distracted by other people's thoughts, and in meditation this was customary among novices who were telepaths.

When the barbarian first came to the room of meditation, the sight of his gross physical nature disgusted Min, so that he closed all three eyes. Surely someone like the barbarian could never attain enlightenment. Such size and strength would come only to one born with the idea that reality was purely physical, and solutions violent.

Yet Master Jampa must have approved his being here. *Perhaps,* Min told himself, *he has brought him here to provide a challenge, an experience. Certainly he will be a distraction. Perhaps his presence will bring to the surface of our awareness things which are resistive, thus loosening elements of maya that might otherwise persist for a longer time.*

Snap!! Master Ho's slender staff rapped Min's shaven skull, causing him to recall that one does not dispose of a thought by elaborating it.

Nonetheless, Min had one more thought about the barbarian before he let the matter go; he decided to speak with him after supper, and examine the thoughts and images stirred up.

Jampa Lodro knew, of course whose knuckles knocked on his door post. "Come!" he said.

Hsu Min entered and bowed. Jampa Lodro had not lit a candle; it was dusk out, but not yet twilight.

"Master," Min said. His voice was quiet, but tight with urgency and upset.

"Speak."

"The barbarian giant is a murderer! A monster! He came here for refuge after killing many men!"

"Indeed? How did you learn this?"

"I questioned him."

"He speaks neither Chinese nor Tibetan."

"The man is a telepath!" Min said as if somehow the Tao had betrayed him by allowing this to happen. "I spoke to him in Chinese, and he read my question telepathically!"

Jampa said nothing, simply regarded the young man calmly, so Min continued. "He went about in a dark room somewhere, with a knife, and killed many men in their sleep!"

"Ah. And who were these men he killed?"

"Uh, I do not know." Min groped inward. There was that about Jampa Lodro that when he asked a question, you usually came up with the answer. "They—they seem to have been soldiers. Or—they were bailiff's men!"

"Indeed? Any others?"

"I—not that I know of. But he killed *dozens* of them, mostly in their sleep, though some—some in a fight."

"Hm-m. And why did he do this thing?"

Min stared blankly inward. If that had been part of what the barbarian showed him, he hadn't noticed. He'd been too shocked. After a moment, Jampa continued. "To enter a room full of bailiff's men must have been dangerous, unless he was one of them. Was he?"

Min shook his head. "I think not, master. No he wasn't."

"Well then," Jampa said affably, "let us ask him how all this came to be." The master got up from his mat, and after gesturing toward the door, left the room behind the novice.

Nils was not in the novices' room. One of the others said he'd gone outside. They found him sitting on a footbridge over the stream, his large bare feet dangling. He didn't even stand up to meet Jampa, let alone bow. *Truly a barbarian,* Min thought, and kept his third eye open to perceive whatever thoughts the two might exchange.

This student is Hsu Min, Jampa said mentally. *He is troubled over violence you have been part of. He believes it was with some bailiff's men.*

Most recently it was. I have been violent many times earlier, however.

Ah. Please relate to us the circumstances of this most recent violence.

The reply began largely with what Nils had learned from Wu and Chen, both verbally and from what lay beneath the words, and from the bailiff's wife: a montage of confiscatory taxes and insults, humiliation, and ruin. And by the bailiff's personal army—beatings, tortures, rapes and murders, perhaps mostly not ordered by the bailiff, but known and condoned by him. And of peasants preparing to rise against him, in a fight that might have killed his ruffian army and himself, but would surely have killed many peasants and townsmen as well.

The barbarian had never intended to murder them all in their sleep; it was necessary that some survive, to report that a single giant had done it, and not the people. Circumstances had wakened them sooner than the barbarian intended, but the bailiff's men had been less bold and skillful than he'd expected, and he'd had no difficulty escaping.

Between their reports and the grapple he'd left on the balcony railing, there seemed a reasonable chance that the emperor's investigator would accept the story of a single killer. Especially if the investigator was a telepath.

Jampa Lodro turned to Hsu Min and spoke aloud. "Are your questions answered?"

Min stood silent for a moment, still not satisfied. Finally he replied. "He bears the karma of many killings."

"Indeed? And you?"

"I have killed no one!"

"Ever? Can you say that with certainty? Have you examined your past lives so thoroughly?"

Min swallowed.

"We have all had the karma of murders to balance. All of us. It is usual that he who murders will himself be murdered, though often not in that same life. Also, usually he who takes lives in one existence must save lives in another.

"Yet there are other factors. Do we not make agreements between lives to do thus and so, that we may experience? And when soldiers fight, is there not a mutual understanding that one or both may die of it? Is there then karma there?"

Min said nothing; simply stood dumb. Jampa put a hand on the novice's shoulder. "Do not believe something because I or any other teacher says it. But if it seems correct, or if you need it as a tool, accept it as you will. And if later it seems incorrect, set it aside. In time, all shall be known by you, in the Tao."

Jampa turned back to Nils then, and bowed slightly. Nils bobbed his head in return, feet still dangling.

As the master and the novice walked away, Hsu Min spoke again. "Master, you bowed to him. First. And he scarcely bowed back."

Jampa answered drily. "Have you noticed his eyes?"

Min shivered. He'd tried to ignore them, forget them. "Yes, master," he said.

"They are blind, you know."

Min said nothing to that. He'd talked himself into believing otherwise. Jampa continued.

"They are pieces of glass, made to cover the nakedness of eyes punctured by the servants of another emperor, half a world from here." The master looked at the novice who walked glumly beside him. "He to whom I bowed," he went on, "is a *tulku* of much eminence. We shared our souls yesterday, when he first arrived. Thus I did not question him for myself this evening; I questioned him for you. You are a novice of more than usual promise. As for the depth of our bowing—to measure the depth of bows is to value the inconsequential."

As they walked on, Jampa said nothing more, either about the barbarian, or about the broader questions still troubling Min. The novice would have to sort them out for himself or not, as the case might be.

FORTY-TWO

Hans Gunnarsson, though no longer Skinny Hans, was not overfed. It was true that for the ten centimeters he'd grown since he'd left the ting, he'd gained more than twenty kilos, but the weight was sinew. He'd been living off the land, eating small birds, mainly, and an occasional hare. Which had sufficed, but mostly without satisfying.

Just now he watched something much larger moving through the treetops. He'd seen something like it a couple of days earlier, but hadn't had a clear look, and didn't know what it was. Now it seemed he might, for it had stopped moving, as if looking down at him through a thin screen of leaves. He stopped his horse, and without dismounting, carefully drew his bowstring, aimed and let go.

It thrummed, sending the arrow up and through the leaves. He heard a meaty "thunk," and watched whatever it was plummet; it landed with a "whump" on the forest floor. By that time he had another arrow nocked. When the animal didn't move, he slipped from the saddle and trotted toward it.

To stare dumbfounded. It looked like a—sort of cross

between man and dog, with coarse green-gray fur. It would, he thought, weigh about four tradestone—roughly twelve kilos. The arrow had entered its chest and thrust out its back.

It was, of course, a monkey, a macaque. They'd lived in those hills from ancient times, and increased with the return of extensive forest, despite a difficult climate. With the worsening winters of recent decades, they'd decreased again, the survivors tending to have the thickest fur and the greatest mass-to-surface ratio.

Kneeling, he examined it more closely. It had ears much like a man, and hands, and a gnome-like face, but its feet had thumbs. He wasn't sure if he'd killed some kind of person or not. It wore no garment though, or belt or anything else, so he decided it wasn't. He hobbled his horse, and within five or six minutes had gutted, skinned, and spitted the creature and constructed and lit a fire.

Even so, he didn't watch it roast. Without the fur, it looked more human than ever, though the proportions were wrong—the legs were as much like a dog's as a man's, and the forearms were too long for the upper arms. The genitals, on the other hand, were almost miniatures of his own.

At the first bite he nearly got sick, but controlled it. To find the meat tough and a little dry, but sweet withal. He thought wryly that now he knew what a cannibal knew—how the flesh of a man tasted.

As he ate, he thought about his situation. He had no idea where Nils might be, or how to find him. And summer wouldn't last forever. Nor did he care to winter alone in an unknown land, although if he had to ... Perhaps he should turn back westward to the land of the Buriat and winter there. He didn't doubt that Achikh would take him in. As for Baver—Hans shook his head. He'd seen the star man taken away, and there'd been nothing he could do for him.

He didn't stop eating till one thighbone was bare. The sun was only midmorning high, but his belly was stuffed, so he lay down in a gap, to nap where the sun had warmed the ground.

His dream was confused and ugly, even frightening. He seemed to waken from his nap to see a creature like the one he'd eaten, but it was as big as Nils, carried a sword, and wore armor. "You have eaten my child," it said. "Now you will have to live with my wife and me, be our son and tend our cattle."

"Where do you live?" Hans asked.

"Up there." The creature pointed into the treetops. Then, even bigger than it had been, it grasped Hans by the scruff as if he were a cat, and began to climb. He wanted to struggle, but it seemed hopeless. The creature's knife was within his reach, and he considered drawing and striking with it. But clearly it was a human of some hairy sort, and he had killed its child. It seemed to him he owed it something. If it wanted him to herd its cattle, he'd just have to do it.

When they reached the treetops, a skyboat awaited them, with steps. A hairy woman stood in the door. "Is this the one that did it?" she asked. Without waiting for an answer, she took Hans from the hairy man, and gripping him with both hands, began to roar, shaking him. She shook him hard and long, her roar seeming too great to come from any human throat. Terror swelled. Then she dropped him.

It seemed he fell and fell, so frightened that the scream stuck in his throat. When he landed, his eyes flew open, dispelling the dream. There had been no impact, and for a moment its absence changed terror to surprise, but he continued to shake, as if those great hairy hands still held him like a dice box. And the roaring continued, like the sound of an avalanche. The fist of fear gripped him hard again, for it seemed the world itself must break apart with such shaking. Yet when he looked upward, the treetops, which should have been lashing back and forth, stood quiet against the midday sky. With that, his terror faded to a large extent. Something like this had happened a few days earlier, he recalled, though not nearly so violently, and had stopped after a bit. This would no doubt stop, too.

He did not try to stand, though, until the sense of shaking died. Then gingerly he got up, testing his legs to see if they were broken, until he remembered that the fall had been a dream. He looked around. His horses had fled in panic. Belting on his shortsword and slinging bow and quiver, he found their hoof prints and set out tracking them. They hadn't gone far, perhaps a hundred and fifty meters. He found them trembling in a coppice of young oaks and old blowdowns, and stroked and patted them for a while before removing their hobbles and swinging into the saddle.

As he rode off, he wondered about the sanity of the world. The shaking had felt so real, yet seemingly it had not been. The fear had been real enough though! Much worse than the first time. If there was a third time that much worse than the second, what might happen to him?

And the hairy thing like a little man! Had that been real? It had tasted real, and his stomach still felt full. He shook his head, and wished Nils were there to ask questions of. Surely the Yngling would know the answers.

Half an hour later he found something new to puzzle and impress him: large bones, fresh enough that there still were fragments of shaggy brown hide which the ravens had left. The skeleton was far from intact, but the great broad skull and clawed feet were those of a bear. A large boar-bear, he decided, for surely no sow would have so large a skull.

He tethered his horses and examined the bones more closely. From the teeth marks, it had been killed by some other large animal; at least one had fed on it. Another bear, he told himself—what else could it have been?— but felt uneasy with the appraisal. His mind went to the giant hairy people he'd dreamed of.

He scouted around a bit, but found no useful tracks.

*   *   *

An hour and a half eastward, in a half-dry seep, he found tracks of an unshod horse, and thought at once of Nils. After they'd left the Mongol lands, more and more of the prints they'd seen along the road had been of horses shod, whereas the Mongol horses weren't. And the people of this land did not seem to travel the wilderness; these were the first horse tracks he'd seen since he'd fled the road.

The trail wasn't fresh, but he followed it. Nils had had three horses; this was only one. And it meandered somewhat, as if it had no rider guiding it. The young Northman clenched his jaw and continued; he would learn what there was to know from this, good or bad.

For another hour he picked his way along game trails, along and over ridges, skirting thickets, dropping to brooks which gurgled between moss-grown banks and around rocks. Once he paused to drink. Then, as he rode up into a saddle, he smelled carrion. His neck hairs bristled, and he paused. His horses fidgeted, and he spoke quietly to them, patting his mount's neck. Wetting a finger, he tested the air. The breeze was in his face.

He drew his bow from its saddle boot, nocked an arrow and rode on, staying with the tracks but giving much attention to the woods around him. The stench grew stronger. A little farther on he came to where the horse he tracked had begun to run, headlong, fleeing something. Ahead, ravens squabbled. Cautiously he went on until, near the top of the saddle, he saw the horse half eaten on the ground, forty meters distant. Several ravens were on it, feeding. They glanced at him, then ignored him. His horses almost danced with anxiety, but neither snorted nor nickered. It seemed to Hans that their silence was ominous.

Quietly he rode up to the carcass, the ravens staying till he was almost there, then flying to branches close at hand. Dirt and last year's moldered leaves had been scratched over it, partly covering it; the sort of thing bears did. He dismounted to examine it, keeping hold on the reins. Flies droned. Bees and hornets gathered juices from the hide, which was steel gray; one of Nils's animals had been steel gray. The head was obscured by leaves and dirt, and gingerly he brushed them away with a stick.

A cloud of flies rose up. The mouth and nostrils crawled with maggots, but the skin was white. Nils's gray had had white lips and nose.

Then his mount reared screaming, jerking the reins from his hand, and both horses fled wildly. Hans's head jerked up and around, to look in the opposite direction.

There, stalking toward him some fifty meters away, was an animal of a kind he'd never seen before, large and slab-sided. Its gaze was fixed on him, and he saw the face of death. Dropping his bow, he darted for the nearest tree, a pine with dead branches within leaping distance, and was there in an instant, leaping, scrambling, breaking branches in his haste, and didn't pause till he was eight meters up. He'd shed his quiver with his bow.

The animal was right below, looking up at him. It had made no attempt to climb, or even jump after him. Perhaps the dead branch stubs had daunted it. It was longer than a bear, long and rangy with a long tail. Its fur was pale orange-tan, with black stripes across shoulders and back. A cat, he thought, a giant cat. Their eyes met, the cat's golden and full of hate. Hans shivered. It seemed to him he knew what the cat's last previous kill had been: the bear.

After a minute it hissed at him, a throaty hiss, then turned and started toward its kill. It paused to sniff the bow, took it in its jaws and shook it. One end caught in the carcass, irritating the cat. It put a big paw on the bow, and twisting with its neck, snapped the weapon. Then it lowered its face to the carcass and began another meal.

It fed, rested briefly, and fed again. Twice it remembered Hans and snarled up at him, showing yellowed knife-like teeth. Finally it left, sauntering slowly up the slope above the saddle. To sleep, Hans thought, and digest its meal. Presumably it could watch its kill from where it bedded, if it was awake, but he couldn't see it. For half an hour he waited, giving it plenty of time to fall asleep.

Meanwhile he made certain decisions. The first and hardest was to salvage his quiver and arrows, which lay near the carcass. And his bowstring, while he was at it. He would need them to eat. He could make a bow of sorts from material at hand, but arrows and string were more difficult. He also plotted his course, down the saddle and away, the same direction his horses had fled, deciding in advance which trees to run to if the cat came charging down at him.

It didn't. He wasn't surprised. Even awake, it wouldn't be interested in him as prey just now; it had a kill. Its enmity was over his trespass. He remembered the story Achikh had told, of Nils in the arena, fighting a lion. And what Nils had said of it. Perhaps Nils could kill this cat too, with his sword, but Hans had no illusions as to what would happen if the cat attacked him.

The horses had run farther than he'd expected, but eventually their tracks were the tracks of a trot, and finally a walk. He found where they'd paused to browse on maple leaves, and not much farther on he saw them. They let him approach, and he patted them, talking to them for a bit, then swung into the saddle and rode off. He kept to the same general direction, for the sole reason that it put the cat farther behind him.

It was late afternoon when Hans came to a valley of farms. People wearing broad, somewhat bowl-shaped hats, bent at their work beneath the sun. Not far away was a sizeable village. He examined the situation for a minute, then rode out of the forest, keeping to a path between fields. As he approached, a nearby farmer looked up and called. Hans's lips thinned in disappointment; the language wasn't Mongol. Others within hearing looked up too. He ignored them and rode on. Perhaps someone in the village would be able to speak with him.

Some of the village buildings were of logs, others of baked mud. The street he rode on was dust like talcum powder; each hoof fall raised a puff of it. Somewhere, someone keened thinly, mindlessly, as if echoing the morning's terror. Few people were on the street: a man pushing an empty wheelbarrow; two women wearing shoulder yokes, carrying buckets in pairs from a public well. They stared as they passed him.

Ahead, a small boy ran into a house, his yells not of fear but excitement. A man stepped out, wearing an apron and holding a drawshave in one hand, as if interrupted at his work. He spoke emphatically to Hans as the youth rode by. The words had no meaning for the Neoviking youth, but he reined in his horse.

The man pointed at him, then held fingers to his mouth and wiggled them as if he wanted Hans to speak. Hans did, in Mongol. "I am here looking for my friend," he said.

The man nodded, quick bobs, and it seemed to Hans that he wanted him to continue. "He is very large and strong. And his eyes are strange; they have no darks to them."

The man nodded more vigorously, and turning, spoke rapidly to the small boy who stood beside him. Then he turned to Hans again and pointed up the street. It seemed that he was to follow the child, who had started past him, looking expectantly up. How could it be, Hans wondered, that they seemed to understand him, while their words were a mystery? But he nudged his horse with his heels, and followed the child.

A hundred meters on, they approached a shop from which came the clang of steel on steel. The child turned in through the open door. Hans stopped and waited in the saddle. He could hear the child inside, talking excitedly in his high-pitched voice. A minute later another aproned man, thick-shouldered, stepped into the doorway, a heavy hammer in one hand, and looked up at him.

"Who are you?" the man asked, In Mongol! "What have you come here for?"

"I am Hans Gunnarsson, of the Wolf Clan of the Svear. I am looking for my friend."

The man looked around quickly, then pointed. "Take your horses behind my shop, where they cannot be seen, and come in the back door."

Hans did, and found himself in a smithy. "I am called Chen," the man said. "I am the smith in this village, which is called Lü-Gu. This friend—what does he look like?"

"He is large." Hans gestured the height, the shoulder width. "And his eyes are strange."

"Ah-h!" The smith almost hissed it. "Nils of the Iron Hand!"

Hans nodded vigorously. "You know him! He has been here! I had almost given up looking for him."

The smith's grin was as much gaps as teeth. "He has been here. Indeed he has."

The child too was grinning, though it understood none of it. The smith looked at him and spoke in Chinese. The child ran out. "His father is a good friend of mine," the smith said. "He thought from your skin and height that you might be of Nils's people. And your hair: red! A color almost as outrageous as Nils's. Then he recognized your tongue as Mongol."

He paused. "I told the boy to say nothing of this. It's not safe for you here. Nils killed the bailiff and most of his hired murderers." Chen used the Chinese word for bailiff, but Hans understood the rest of it. "The emperor has sent an investigator with a troop of calvary, and he has questioned not only the bailiff's surviving men, but certain of his neighbors as well. The investigator has left, with part of the troop, but there still are soldiers at the bailiff's stronghold. It's the fort on the far side of town.

His words came more quietly now, almost secretively, although they were in Mongol. "I think I know where your friend is; at least I know where he was taken. His guide stopped on his way home, and told me. I cannot take you, though, till later. How did you come into the village?"

Hans described his route. Chen told him to leave the same way, to circle the village through the forest and hide in the woods below town. He'd come to him as soon as he could get away.

"It's too dangerous to be seen with you on the street. The investigator is one of the emperor's wizards who can look into someone's mind and see his thoughts and memories. He must know what Nils looks like, and have told the soldiers. And you—you are not as large, but still you are much taller than we are, and have the skin and other strangenesses."

The smith remembered something then, and his face took on a worried look. "Tell me. Where were you this morning?"

"Half a day's ride that way." Hans gestured.

"Did—did anything happen? Anything strange and terrible?"

Hans nodded. "It felt as if the world was trying to shake itself apart. I was greatly afraid."

The man's face relaxed. "Ah! I was afraid it might be something God had visited just on our village here.

"Well." He pursed his lips in thought. "People come in here from time to time. It's time for you to leave."

Before he left, Hans asked for a bow. Chen said he'd bring one when he went out to meet him.

FORTY-THREE

The emperor's face was grim, his mouth a slit; his fingers drummed the table. The situation having become dangerous, he'd given his orders to Tenzin telepathically to save time. But the *geshe* had been so shaken by the morning's disaster, it seemed best to receive his report face to face. The imperial presence might brace the man. Actually, it annoyed Songtsan Gampo to baby Tenzin, but the *geshe* was too valuable to see broken. And it wasn't as if he asked for pampering.

The gong outside his door was tapped lightly; Maamo stepped inside and bowed. His baritone was furry, distinctly nonhuman. "Your Magnificence," the ogre said, "Tenzin Geshe is here."

"Send him in."

The *geshe* entered and knelt, a sign, the emperor realized, of his mental state. Tenzin blamed himself for the demon's presence in what they thought of as the fabric of the Tao. "Come, Tenzin," the emperor said gruffly, and gestured at a chair. "Sit!" The *geshe* sat. "What were your results?"

Tenzin did not meet his gaze. "The demon withheld

itself," he answered. "It wasn't interested in what I might ask. I did get an impression, though: that its action this morning was not to coerce us, but simply a test of its abilities. For its own enlightenment."

"Oh?"

"I also believe it was dissatisfied with the results. Despite subjective appearances, and regardless of the overwhelming emotions it generated, it was unable to influence the physical universe directly. And I believe it does not fully appreciate how devastating its psychic effects were: It seems to have reached and terrified almost every psyche over a large area."

It's well it doesn't fully appreciate it, the emperor thought. The streets of Miyun had been the site of wild panic. People had died of terror; others had gone mad, some murderously so. Fires had been set. And among the Yeti Guards, all but Maamo had panicked.

Maamo! Starting with the concept and technique for creating elementals, Tenzin had created the transcendant yeti. Among its species, the creature was as superior mentally as physically, and had remarkable influence on the others.

"Did you learn how far afield his ravages extended?"

"We reached out to Lord Kang, who is in the desert, approaching the lands of the Buriat. He said he'd felt something and had wondered what it was. The others felt it as a depression too slight for most to be consciously aware of. At Beijing it was somewhat less than here, but even there it was severe."

And we don't know if it's found the limits of its reach, the emperor told himself. *But even if it has, suppose it puts us through the same thing daily. We couldn't govern from here; we'd have to move. And it may well have the ability, or the potential, to move about within the fabric. If so, we can't escape it!*

"What success did you have at placing anchor points in its field?" he asked.

For a moment the *geshe* hesitated, which in itself told Songtsan Gampo the answer. "Your Magnificence, I—I did not place any. It would destroy me if I tried. I would be vulnerable."

For just a moment the emperor scowled, facially and mentally. *He did not try!* But the man was no doubt right. Surely he was if he thought so, and such a tactic would be dangerous at best. What particularly vexed Songtsan Gampo was that Tenzin, a *geshe*, lacked the tranquility to face the danger without fear. The man had great talent—he'd created Maamo!—but in the face of danger, he lacked spiritual strength.

At that moment the emperor knew what he needed to do. "Well. I will bring Jampa Lodro here. By force if necessary, though I don't imagine it will be. I'll send guards, human and yeti. And Maamo, in case the demon should exercise his powers while they're enroute.

"Meanwhile I have something you *can* do. Return to the Circle; reach out and find Jampa. Presumably he's at his *gomba*, but find out. Let him know about the demon and find out how he was affected by it, how his people were. But don't let him know I'm sending for him. I am entirely unable to predict that man. I suspect he'll come willingly, but he might conceivably go into the mountains, if he knows, and leave us to cope as best we can without him."

He fixed the *geshe* with his gaze. "Can you do that?"

Tenzin colored not in anger but embarrassment. "Yes, Your Magnificence, I can do that."

"Very well then; you are excused. Return to the Circle and see to it at once."

Tenzin reported back within minutes: Jampa was at home. The demon's morning outrage had shaken the novices somewhat, but the adepts had been little affected.

The demon had spread itself as widely, and thus as thinly in the Sigma Field as it dared, constrained by the fear that it might lose its unity and disperse, a dispersal that might well prove irreversible. It felt good spread thin though, as if it was absorbing knowledge from the Field, receiving it subliminally, learning what it needed to know about it, and how it related to the physical world. It would yet learn to shake mountains and tumble buildings.

Days earlier the demon had affixed an attention unit, a part of itself, on Maamo, to serve as a homing unit. It was analogous to a transponder of ancient times, but simple and inconspicuous, without physical existence, and through it he became aware that Maamo had left his customary bounds.

The demon gathered itself to see what was going on. It approached the interface cautiously though, for often a telepath, the great king himself, was near the ogre. Not that the demon felt any threat to itself in that, but if a telepath was present, to probe or even closely monitor Maamo would expose the connection. Which might result in Maamo being killed, and the demon had plans for the ogre.

At its remove from the interface, the demon discerned a number of faint swirls in the Field; Maamo was traveling, transecting the field as part of a group of large life forms. Three were the sort of single swirls he was familiar with, and had the flavor of ogre. The others were unfamiliar, some of them doubled, like a figure eight. These made him curious, and slightly uneasy.

After a time, he approached the interface near enough to discern whether there was a telepath near. In this he was very careful. If there'd been even a trace of the psychic "flavor of telepaths," he'd have drawn back, hopefully before he was detected. But there wasn't. He moved in until the swirls became living beings, seen as if with eyes.

What he discovered were one splendidly uniformed officer—the emperor's adjutant—five soldiers from the emperor's human elite guard, and three ogres, including, of course, Maamo. The humans were on horseback, and had a string of remounts. The mounted men were what he'd perceived as double swirls. The horses were trotting, the ogres keeping pace with them effortlessly. The demon put its attention on Maamo's mind then, transferring his viewpoint to the ogre's eyes, or actually to its imaging center.

Being non-telepathic, Maamo did not discern the demon's thoughts as something foreign, at this or any earlier time, even though the demon had entered his mind. He felt impulses to remember and to think, but considered them part of himself and his own mental processes. They weren't at all like the emperor stroking his mind. That was something to luxuriate to, and he knew it was the emperor doing it.

Sometimes this newer feeling brought to mind things he'd forgotten; often things from when he was his old self, before he'd been—changed, before he'd become like someone new. Sometimes it had brought to mind things it seemed he'd never known before, things that others of his people had experienced in the past. And sometimes it had caused him to have a knowingness about his body, its parts and functions that, when it was over, had left him more aware of them, more in control of them than before.

This time it brought to mind the meeting between the emperor and the man who had changed him. Much of their talk Maamo hadn't understood, but unavoidably their words were recorded in his secondary memory.

There was more information than that: there was the meeting between the emperor and his adjutant, with Maamo present. From this the demon learned specifically what the adjutant's mission was: He was being sent to fetch a man named Jampa, a wizard more powerful than either the emperor or Tenzin.

A wizard who might conceivably be a threat.

Also, Maamo had learned, someone else was with this Jampa, someone the emperor hadn't expected to be there, someone who excited him. He'd referred to him as "the barbarian giant." Nothing was said of why this excited the emperor, but it seemed to be something apart from the wizard or anything else. The emperor seemed to value the barbarian highly. Therefore it seemed to the demon that, in a pinch, both Jampa and the barbarian might provide him with leverage.

Thus the demon decided to continue with the adjutant's company, even though they'd travel long hours from the palace. If nothing else, the trip might effect a further expansion of its readily accessible range, and provide a sense of the physical region. And it felt—somehow it felt that there was an opportunity there, though it couldn't quite see what it was.

It considered the risks, too: They were going to fetch a wizard, who might discern him if he got near enough to the interface to preceive physical reality in a useful way. But the wizard would not be intimately acquainted with the mind of Maamo. *Suppose I meld with Maamo, hide within him, suppressing my thoughts, simply watching the ogre's. Would the wizard detect me then?* The demon examined the idea. It would mean not using his own telepathy, or tapping power or information from the field in which he normally dwelt. It would mean perceiving little except what Maamo perceived, feeling little except what Maamo felt.

It was a challenge and a risk. Not a risk to himself; he considered himself safe from anything but the Great God, as long as he didn't open his mind to intrusion and control. And he had no intention of doing that. The principal risk was to Maamo. Of course there was also a risk that discovery would teach the emperor and his wizards more about his own abilities.

But he would take those risks.

With the decision came a glow. It was the right thing to do, he felt sure.

FORTY-FOUR

The adjutant's party traveled steadily, mostly at a trot, but slowing to a brisk walk at times to rest both horses and yetis. The demon mainly observed, and Maamo never knew it was there, resting in his mind. Some kilometers from their destination was a military post, to which a courier had been sent ahead of them. They stopped there for fresh horses—even with remounts, theirs were worn by then—and horses to bring their captives on. And a platoon of dragoons, to ensure that nothing went wrong.

The adjutant was determined to take Jampa Lodro and the barbarian into custody before dusk. Thus they didn't stop to eat at the post or along the road; they ate saddle rations.

It was little short of sundown when they arrived at Gomba Dorje. Jampa and the barbarian seemed almost to be waiting for them, and were taken into custody without incident. Actually Nils could have escaped into the forest; they'd become aware of the troops and their purpose half a kilometer away. But it was time, Nils decided, to go to the capital, so he simply removed his eyes and put them in a pocket.

The adjutant examined his prisoners. The barbarian supposedly was dangerous—he was said to have murdered a bailiff and a number of his men. Obviously that was either a rumor or an incorrect identification. The man was unquestionably blind, his sockets empty, his eyelids wrinkled and ugly. No doubt his hearing was acute, but it would hardly serve if he tried to use the sword he wore.

They took it from him, of course, as a matter of policy, but his hands were left unmanacled. Otherwise, at a trot he might lose his seat and fall from his horse, and the emperor had said explicitly that he was not to be injured. As a precaution, the adjutant even ordered a yeti to stay beside the man, in case he started to fall.

With the two in custody, the demon felt free to use his telepathy. Sensing it, Nils immediately closed his "third eye" so his own telepathy wouldn't be discovered. This, of course, made him in effect truly blind.

Jampa was aware of Nils's action, and also what he took to be Maamo's telepathy. But the ogre screened its thoughts so that Jampa didn't know the true nature of that telepathy. He was aware, though, that the ogre's aura, already larger than the others, had changed abruptly and substantially. And felt dangerous.

As the adjutant's column rode through the dusk toward the military post, the demon had a worrisome thought: suppose the Circle decided to check on their progress. They'd detect quickly that he was controlling Maamo. But if he closed his inner eye again, as he had on the outbound ride, and if he suppressed his own thoughts, contenting himself with listening to Maamo's ... would the Circle detect him? He didn't know, but it seemed wisest to try it.

And what if the Circle contacted Jampa Lodro telepathically? If they did, would the old man inform on him? Did he even know what it was he'd perceived? To kill the old wizard would cause a great furor, and he'd have to abort the whole action, no doubt losing Maamo as his tool, and gaining nothing.

No, he'd hide himself and trust them not to notice. He'd hypnoconditioned Maamo days earlier; to the ogre he'd never been there. Of course, they couldn't actually harm him anyway. Even if they had the soldiers kill Maamo, he himself would simply snap back into that strange but powerful place the Great God had given him.

The adjutant walked the horses more now, and trotted them less. Not so much to spare *them*; he didn't want to exhaust the yetis. The emperor would be dangerously angry if he felt they'd been abused. And the principal rush was over; they had their captives. Though they'd still have to move briskly; the emperor's order was to be back by morning. Otherwise he might have spent the night at the military post, where he'd drop off the dragoons.

The cart road from Lü-Gu ended at a junction with the road that passed Gomba Dorje, and which connected with the Imperial Highway northeast of Miyun. It was dusk by the time Hans and Chen reached the junction. The column had passed it on its way back, scant minutes earlier. The two turned left toward the monastery. It was full night when they arrived. There a master told Chen that Jampa and the barbarian were being taken to the emperor in military custody. And that three yeti guards had been with the soldiers.

"Yeti?" Hans said, when Chen had translated.

"Yetis are a kind of hairy ogre," Chan answered. "They are very big"—he waved his hand at arm's length overhead—"much bigger than Nils, and very very strong. No man is so strong! *No man!*"

Goosebumps flowed over Hans. He was remembering the small, hairy, manlike thing he'd eaten, and the dream he'd had afterward, and wondered if he'd eaten a yeti child. And the yetis were servants of the emperor!

At Chen's request, they were given a loaf each of bread. Then they started back the way they'd come.

"How far is it from here to the emperor's house?" Hans asked.

"One would have to ride all night to get there before noon. But surely you don't plan to follow them?"

"How else can I be of use to Nils? You needn't come though. He's not your clansman. Only give me instructions."

"Your horses are travel-worn, and clearly not well fed. And this"—he slapped the neck of his own spoiled village horse—"this fellow isn't used to travel. They can't keep up with the soldiers; not unless the soldiers take their time."

"Maybe they will take their time," Hans answered stubbornly.

"What will you do if you catch up to them?"

"I will follow at a little distance, and wait for an opportunity. I can't abandon him. He is more than my clansman; he is the Yngling of my people! Without him we'd be feuding clans fighting one another, or maybe dead in Poland."

Chen answered nothing, but his expression was troubled. It wasn't much later that they passed the cart road to Lü-Gu, but Chen did not turn off there. Neither of them said anything, but Hans was glad he wouldn't be traveling alone. There was too much he didn't know; he needed the blacksmith's advice at least.

With a possible long ride ahead of them, Hans instituted a regimen to make as much speed as possible without killing the horses. He was still not a grown man, but he was in charge, which was quite in contrast with the way of Chen's people. The smith didn't question it though, or resent it. It seemed to him that this youth, like Nils and like the Mongols, was different from others. Thus Hans had them ride in shifts of about a quarter hour each. Chen rode first his own horse, then rested it by riding one of Hans's. Because he had not run for many years, and did not walk a lot, he would ride every shift. Hans, on the other hand, would run every other shift, so that his own horse could travel unburdened at least one shift in three.

Where the forage was especially good on the roadside, they might pause for a few minutes, especially where there was a stream, or water in the ditch. They'd take the bits from the horses' mouths then, letting them graze and drink more easily. At such times the two men gnawed their loaves, and occasionally fed the horses a handful of oats from a small bag Chen had brought.

When they came to the junction with the Imperial Highway, and the military post located there, Chen turned them right. It never occurred to them that the column might have stopped there, might be there now, eating while the yetis rested and grooms prepared fresh horses for the adjutant and his men.

The highway to Miyun was much better than the other roads they'd ridden that day. It had been a highway of the ancients, and mostly followed near the edge of a rich valley extensively cleared for farming. Here and there a mountain torrent had washed it out, but the army had built it back with stone blocks from the Great Wall, re-bridging with heavy timbers.

For a while Hans continued to trot every other shift, but he'd run little for weeks, mostly riding, and began to tire. So he turned to riding two shifts out of three, and let the horses walk every other shift, an ambling gait. Finally he was so leg weary, he didn't trot at all, but rode the trotting shifts and walked only the walking shifts. And even that seemed almost beyond him. Grimly he vowed he'd never allow his legs to get so weak again. Even if he had two remounts, he'd run part of the time, as the elders said they should.

For hours they rode past the greatest concentration of farms Hans had ever imagined. He wondered how long it would be before dawn. Until the last two years, his people had been forest people, and he'd never learned to tell time by the stars. It would be best, he thought, if

they could get to the palace before daylight, and wondered if that was possible. He also wondered if the soldiers were there yet, with Nils.

And the yetis— He shivered at the thought of them.
By now he was sure it was one of their babies he'd eaten,
and wondered if somehow they'd know.

Behind him he heard a distant rumbling, and realized
it was hooves, many hooves, crossing a heavy plank
bridge. There was a hay field on his left, and speaking
sharply to Chen, he turned his horse off the road. They
crossed the field and sat their horses in the dark shadows
of the forest edge.

"What's the matter?" Chen asked. He was a strong old
man, and daughty, but his voice reflected weariness.

"Horses are coming. Many of them."

"From behind or ahead?"

"Behind."

Chen wagged his head, not in disbelief, but at the
youth having heard what he hadn't. He'd felt proud that
his hearing had remained sharp while that of many others
his age had not. Perhaps these Northmen had sharper
ears than others, or perhaps his own ears were tired like
the rest of him.

The night was crystal clear, and visibility good in the
open field, enhanced a bit by a newly risen sickle moon.
In a minute or so they saw horsemen approaching up the
road to their right, just now walking their horses. They
passed not a hundred and fifty meters in front of the
two, led by a very tall figure on foot, who was followed
by horsemen—fewer than ten, Hans thought—with two
other very tall figures on foot. Yetis and soldiers, he
guessed. He couldn't be sure, in the night, but one of
the horsemen seemed too large to be anyone but Nils.

Chen had interpreted it as Hans had. "That's them,"
he murmured. "The other soldiers must have stayed at
the army post. They were only along to help catch Nils
and Jampa."

Meanwhile they waited, their horses grazing as best
they could with bits in their mouths. Hans heard the

sound of grasses tearing. When the mounted party was out of sight, he nudged his horse with callused heels, and they returned to the road. They were hardly behind at all. But with the newly risen moon thin as it was, dawn wouldn't be far off.

FORTY-FIVE

Songtsan Gampo awoke with a start, not knowing what had wakened him. Vaguely he remembered troubled dreams, but nothing that seemed to account for his waking. Swinging his legs from the bed, he put his feet on the floor. Outside his balcony doors was black night.

He'd had trouble going to sleep in the first place. Finally, toward midnight, he'd had a serving girl sent to him, one he'd noticed and had had instructed. The cause of his wakefulness, he had no doubt, was his unsolved problem: the demon in the fabric of the Tao. Clearly he couldn't rely on Tenzin to handle it, but in the middle of the night, what could *he* do? So he'd had sex to satiation and soreness, and fell asleep before he could send the girl back to the maids' quarters.

He wondered how long he'd slept. Not long enough, he thought wryly, and getting out of bed, started toward his balcony. To better feel the night. *A strange-feeling night*, he told himself. *As if something is waiting to happen.*

Before he reached the balcony doors, the light of the oil lamp showed him the star man's weapon on his dressing table. The star man! He'd had him put in a cell beneath the guard building, and then forgot him. Not entirely—he'd thought of him a time or two—but always in passing, when he was busy with other matters.

He picked the weapon up and looked it over again, wondering how effective it could possibly be. It was so small, and hadn't even a blade!

What had the man said? *When the right button is pushed, and the right lever—touched? No, squeezed . . .* He examined it closely but cautiously. There seemed to be only one button and one lever.

Then a piece of metal was supposed to fly out of the little hole. It sounded like a fairy tale.

He pressed on the button, the safety. It didn't depress, so he pushed it forward. Ah! That must be it. Then if one lined the hole up with the target and squeezed the little lever . . . Looking down the top of the barrel, he pointed it at the girl asleep in his bed, then lowered it and called to her.

"Girl! Wake up!"

She didn't move, so he went to her and shook her roughly by a shoulder. Her eyelids fluttered and opened; she raised her head slightly from the pillow. "Get up! Now!" He slapped her. She blinked, became more fully conscious, then abruptly knew where she was and got quickly from the bed.

"Come with me," he said, and led her into his study. "Stand there." He pointed to the middle of a rug. She went there and stood, small and naked, her eyes frightened.

He raised the pistol and sighted down it. *With a bow,* he thought, *one usually wants to put the arrow through the heart.* He squeezed the trigger, and the gun fired with a bang that made him jump. The girl fell backward to the floor and lay there like a marionette with its strings cut.

Songtsan Gampo peered intently at her—clearly she was dead—and then at the seemingly harmless thing he held. Meanwhile the yeti door guard on duty had bounded in and stood staring, along with the emperor's night runner.

The emperor looked at the ogre. "She is dead," he said. "Leave her on the rug; pull it into the corridor and wrap her with it." He watched the yeti drag her out, then turned to the runner. "Send someone to take the body to the trash bin, and someone else to arrange a special pickup. Otherwise it will stink." He wrinkled his nose. "It does already. Also send to the guard barracks and have Corporal Nogai wakened. Have him select another guardsman and bring the star man to me at once."

As he'd spoken, he'd stepped to his desk chair and laid the pistol on an arm of it. On the desk itself he turned a sand glass over, one in a row of them. "Also have Nogai informed that I want the star man here in the time the third sand glass takes to empty. Run! You and Nogai both will be punished, you and the man you send to waken him, if the glass is empty before he arrives. Go!"

The runner turned and fled.

FORTY-SIX

The adjutant had called for another period of trotting. Maamo did it easily—he was, after all, the supreme, the epitomal ogre—but the others, tired as they were, found it difficult. With the exception of about two hours at the army post, they'd been trotting and walking almost continually since somewhat before noon the day before. Now the sickle moon stood well above the ridge to the east. The first light of dawn would soon show.

In the distance, Maamo could see a line of torchlights, motionless sparks on the wall of the Dzong. Just now, he judged, it was less than two kilometers to the edge of town, perhaps four to the Dzong's Great Gate. There would be food for them in the yeti messroom; then they could go to their beds and collapse.

Just behind him he heard the adjutant call a halt, and stopped.

"Everyone dismount."

That, of course, meant the humans. A yeti reached up and lifted the blind barbarian down; Jampa Lodro got down himself.

"We will rest here for ten minutes," the adjutant said.

"I do not want the yetis stumbling into the Dzong exhausted. It would be unseemly." He looked at Maamo. "I want you and your people to lie down and rest. When we arrive at the Great Gate, the three of you will go directly to your barracks. You'll have no further duty today."

Maamo nodded. It was what he'd wanted and expected to hear.

But it was not what the demon hidden inside him wanted to hear. As Maamo's hidden tenant, he'd intended to accompany the captives to the emperor and hopefully the Circle. There to take control of Maamo, and through him the other two ogres, to destroy first the Circle, then the emperor. To follow the adjutant's order would ruin that plan. Therefore—

He struck!

Maamo fell thrashing to the roadway, growling and gurgling, while the others, humans and ogres, stared thunderstruck. But in brief seconds he got slowly up again. "Excuse me, my lord," he said to the adjutant. I am all right now."

The man's mouth was a slack O, his brows high, his eyes as nearly round as they could get. "What happened to you?"

It was Demon-Maamo he faced, the ogre elemental possessed. He sensed a difference, but not what it was. "It is something that happens when I am greatly tired," said Demon-Maamo. "I'll have no further trouble when we've had our break."

The adjutant nodded dubiously and turned as if to speak to the soldiers. At that moment, Demon-Maamo spoke in the ogre speech—"Kill the soldiers, *now!*" and drew his huge sword. In a continuation of the movement, he struck the adjutant with it, halving him at the waist. It caught the man in the act of turning—he'd heard the hiss of the sword being drawn—and the torso continued a quarter turn before it fell to the road beside the tumbled legs. By that time Demon-Maamo was striking the human sergeant. The other yetis were slow to respond, even to the compelling personality of the elemental ogre, for the order was counter to their conditioning. By the time they acted, Demon-Maamo had killed a second and third soldier. The horses were stamping nervously, snorting, but they'd been trained to stand while cattle were killed around them, and did not panic. In less than five seconds, all the soldiers were dead.

"Do not harm the captives," said Demon-Maamo then. And knowing the loyalty conditioning the yetis had been given, added, "They belong to the emperor. We must get them to him safely. This one"—he gestured at the bisected adjutant—"was a traitor. He planned treachery."

He turned to Jampa. With a sword at his back, the old man could be no threat. And he could prove useful, if the emperor valued him so greatly. The same should be true of the blind man. "Do not move," said Demon-Maamo. "Tell your blind friend not to move." Then, to the other ogres: "Drive the horses into the hay field; all but theirs." He gestured toward the captives. "Take out their bits, and they will stay to graze."

While the other ogres moved the horses, Demon-Maamo threw the bodies into the ditch, ending bloody to the elbows and beyond. In the darkness the tall grass hid the bodies. By the time it was light, it wouldn't matter. There was water there, too, and he washed the blood off as best he could. It would do by torchlight, he told himself. It would have to.

Now the die was cast. He did not give his ogres the ten-minute break the adjutant had intended. For all he knew, the Circle might be checking them intermittently, and if they checked now . . . It seemed imperative that they get inside the Great Gate as quickly as possible, or it might be shut to them.

FORTY-SEVEN

Nogai and another guard arrived with Baver at the emperor's study. They entered and bowed deeply, the guards sweating. There might have been a minute's worth of sand left in the glass. In the meantime the emperor had dressed, and buckled on the imperial sword, a symbol of his family's warriorhood.

"You did well, corporal," he said. "I will remember your alacrity."

Nogai bowed low again. "Thank you, Your Magnificence."

"And you, star man. I have tried your weapon. It works admirably." He held it in his hand and casually pointed it at Baver. Baver only half noticed, for on the other broad arm of the emperor's chair lay his lost recorder! His heart lifted to see it. Obviously his captors had brought along his saddlebags. Probably the emperor wanted a demonstration.

"I'm glad you like it, Your Magnificence," he said. And was aware of mockery behind the emperor's smile. The man was playing with him.

"Indeed! Then you will be pleased to answer my questions. Among your people, are you a warrior? A soldier?"

"No, Your Magnificence, I'm not. As I said before, my job is to learn about other peoples."

"Ah yes," he mocked, "a spy. And you carried a small weapon, quite deadly, concealed in your clothing. What kind of weapons, then, do the soldiers among you carry?"

The emperor's dark eyes held Baver's. His tufted brows had risen slightly. The star man tried not to think, but at the question, information rose to near the surface of his subconscious, image-rich, concept-rich, and mostly very foreign. Seemingly the star people had no soldiers or warriors, but . . . There were weapons larger and more powerful than the one he'd tried, much more deadly, and useful at a much greater distance. Also there were stones which exploded, bursting, killing those around them. These they . . .

YOUR MAGNIFICENCE! It was Tenzin, interrupting telepathically with a great sense of urgency. *THE DEMON HAS CAPTURED MAAMO'S MIND, AND POSSESSES HIS BODY. HE HAS CAPTURED JAMPA AND THE BARBARIAN!*

The emperor's mind fired a question.

He has killed Xiaou and his soldiers, and has just entered the Dzong with the captives! He must have subverted the yetis.

An angry query.

He was inside the gate before I knew any of this. I believe he is coming to the Sanctuary to kill the Circle and myself!

Was it possible? Could the yetis be subverted? Perhaps against Xiaou or the Circle, if the demon was clever enough. *Then you must get out! Get to the barracks. The guards will protect you!*

No, Your Magnificence! We need protection here! THE DEMON IS OUTSIDE THE FABRIC OF THE TAO, AND WE WILL TRY TO CLOSE IT TO HIM! IF WE SUCCEED, WE HAVE DEFEATED HIM, REGARDLESS OF WHAT HE MAY DO OUTSIDE IT!

The realization thunderstruck the emperor. *Do it then! Right away!*

I have already examined the place in which he lay. The opening is not like an aperture, more like a depression. And it's hardened by his having occupied it these weeks. It will take time!

The emperor leaped to his feet, barking instructions, calling for the yeti guard, those on shift and ready. He watched his runner dart out, the orders indelible in the man's trained mind. The demon as Maamo might get other yetis to act against Xiaou or Tenzin, but if he himself were there . . . To him they were loyal, the emperor told himself, irrevocably loyal; they couldn't help themselves. He'd face the demon at the Sanctuary, with a squad of loyal yetis. But he needed to be quick!

The emperor's thoughts reached Tenzin in a tumult, but he received them clearly; he was used to human thought processes, excited as well as calm. He cut the thought connection and submerged into the deep and powerful channel of the Circle.

The entire exchange had taken only seconds, via a tight channel specifically between two telepaths who were very familiar with each other. But the intensity had been felt by everyone in the room. The emperor moved toward the door, then remembered the pistol, and his thoughts racing ahead to the *gomba*, stepped quickly to his chair. There he grabbed the recorder instead of the pistol, and thrusting it in a pocket, rushed out, followed by the yeti. Baver and the guards who'd brought him stared after them.

"What happened?" Baver asked in Mongol.

"An emergency," Nogai said. Knowing nothing of Tenzin's urgent message, he was as perplexed as the star man. Turning Baver by a shoulder, he shoved him toward the balcony doors. As they passed the emperor's chair, Baver stumbled, nearly fell.

From the balcony, Nogai saw faint dawnlight in the east. Then he looked toward the *gomba*, where everything seemed peaceful. *What does the emperor expect to find there?* he wondered.

Shrugging he turned away. "Come," he said to Baver. "We will take you to your cell."

When they left, the pistol was gone from the arm of the emperor's chair.

FORTY-EIGHT

Hans hissed Chen to a halt, and sat peering intently ahead into darkness. Chen strained to see, and thought perhaps he did see something, barely, uncertainly, at the edge of visibility. "What is it?" he murmured.

"The tall ones, the yetis. They seem to be driving the horses off the road."

"Off the road? What for?"

Hans didn't answer, just peered. After a long minute he said, "They are going on now. Yetis and some of the horses."

"Only some of the horses?"

Again silence. After another minute, Hans said "come on," and gigged his horse. "I couldn't see much, but I didn't want to go nearer. I don't know how well they see, those yetis, or how watchful they are to the rear. When we get to where they were, we'll know more."

Half a kilometer ahead, they had drawn nearly even with the horses, who grazed in the pasture now. "Look!" Chen said, "they still wear their saddles! Strange!"

Hans had already noticed. Now he was looking at the tall grass in the ditch. The horses had trampled it in crossing. But—he moved his horse to the edge and stood in his stirrups.

A body! In an instant he was out of the saddle and waist deep in grass, bending, pulling. He dragged it out where he could see it, dropped it, and wiped slimy blood from his hands on the grass. Then while Chen watched benumbed, he waded about, swearing aloud and counting silently. Once he stumbled over a leg, one of two without a torso, and fell to his knees. He found six dead men before he came out onto the road again.

"None of them is Nils," he said.

"Jampa Lodro?"

"I don't know him." He gestured. "These all wear soldier clothes. You can look."

Chen shook his head. "Jampa would not be wearing a uniform."

Hans grunted. He was looking across the ditch at the horses grazing there. "We should take some of the soldier horses," he said.

"No," Chen answered, "they will wear army brands. People will recognize them at once."

The young Northman stood vexed for a moment, then grunted and climbed reluctantly into the saddle. He thumped his weary horse's ribs with his heels, twice before it moved, and they rode on again toward the town. Shortly they were among buildings, mostly of sun-baked bricks. The road had become a street, stone-paved and wide for its time.

Anxiety began to grip the youth now. He'd hoped for some opportunity, some inspiration, but didn't feel even the beginning of one.

The road turned and began to climb gently toward the Dzong; another kilometer found it steepening somewhat. Vaguely in the distance, the dark bulk of the wall stood across the street. Nearer, rolling ahead of them toward the wall, was a cart, its horses' hooves clopping, its iron tires grating on the stones. As they drew up on it, they saw it held melons, and Chen's strong hand reached to take Hans's sleeve, slowing him.

The blacksmith muttered rapid Mongol. Hans listened intently, then nodded, and urged his mount past the cart, scarcely glancing at it as he passed.

Chen pulled past more slowly. When he was still a hundred meters from the Great Gate, he stopped and accosted the cart's driver. "I admired your melons when I passed. Are they for sale?"

The farmer looked at him appraisingly. "One or two perhaps. The rest are for the palace," he said importantly. "The emperor himself has stated a preference for my melons over any others." Half turning, he gestured. "They were selected last evening for the exact ripeness, and packed in straw as you can see." He straightened on his seat and gestured upward. "I bring them to the gate at daybreak." The first tinge of dawn showed in the sky behind them. "The gate guards know me. They let me right in."

"Really! I'm not surprised. They *are* superior melons; I can tell by looking at them. It would be a shame if they sat in the sun, to soften or sunburn."

"Not only that!" the farmer said. "The emperor likes them for breakfast! They will be cool for him and his officials!"

"Um-m! Chen reached in his tunic and drew out a small leather bag. "What do you charge?"

Hans lay in the darkness beneath the cart, listening, gripping the tongue braces. The sides of his feet were braced against the side rims of the cargo box, while his soles pressed the rear bunk. His quiver was on his chest, atop his cross-slung bow; all in all his position was both precarious and uncomfortable, even with his tailbone resting on the ground. He didn't wonder what he was doing, though, or how he'd gotten himself into this situation, or what he'd do when he got inside the Dzong. He was a Northman out to rescue the Yngling. And Chen had told him the palace was on the hilltop. Therefore he needed only to go uphill.

Chen made his deal and moved aside. The farmer clucked to his horses, and Hans raised his buttocks till his belly was as close to the cart box as quiver and bow allowed. The cart rolled slowly toward the gate while the apprentice poet groaned inwardly and ground his teeth. Holding himself spreadeagled below the cart was even harder than he'd expected.

FORTY-NINE

Nils had not kept his "third eye" closed. Early on, mind still, he'd peeked. And found the ogre—the "troll" as he thought of it—with its own third eye closed. Smoothly, like a stealthy tendril, he'd slipped an awareness unit into its mind and discovered what kind of entity he had to deal with. For hours the awareness unit had laid quietly, absorbing what there was to learn. He'd come to know the child, the jungle cult leader, and the demon of the Sigma Field, as well as the beingness of the elemental ogre, Maamo.

He also sensed the power the demon would command with its third eye open, far more than he himself could overcome in any simple duel. For even outside the Sigma Field, the demon—the master and his merged acolytes— had the skills it had gained there, and the power of its own composite nature.

Thus as his horse carried him up the hill, Nils had no plan at all.

Demon-Maamo peered uphill. In darkness his eyesight was more penetrating than a human's, though in daylight its resolution was no better, if as good. The hint of dawn in the sky had scarcely influenced visibility, but he could see the *gomba* plainly enough, up the moderate slope across night-shadowed gardens. The broad graveled path he walked curved, and would come little nearer to it than it was then.

He spoke, and the other ogres stopped the two horses. Demon-Maamo stepped to one of them. With his great ogre hands, he grasped the blind man and lifted him from the saddle, then hoisted him across one shoulder and left the gravel path, uphill toward the temple.

He was more tired than he'd realized, and the blind man was heavy. It might have been better after all, he thought, to have stayed with the horses and approached from above. The older human was soon puffing, and Demon-Maamo growled an order. With a slight grunt, one of the other ogres picked Jampa up and carried him too. Three times they encountered low stone walls, built for aesthetics, not defense. They lifted their long legs over them without setting down their burdens.

At the *gomba,* the yeti guards on the encircling porch watched them come. When Demon-Maamo was thirty meters away, their sergeant called firmly to him to halt. Demon-Maamo looked at the half-drawn bows, then at the sword in the sergeant's fist. Then, especially, he looked the sergeant in the eye. But he did not stop till he was two strides from the steps.

"The emperor is threatened by the monks!" he said quietly. "I have come to save him from them."

"The emperor says you are not allowed to enter this place," the sergeant countered. His voice was not as firm now. The warrior he faced, he'd grown up with, and even as a cub had recognized him as the pack leader, so to speak. Not long since, there'd been a change in Maamo; his dominance then had grown beyond challenge. Now it seemed he'd changed again; his dominance intensified, grown threatening.

Demon-Maamo swung the blind man off his shoulder and flopped him roughly to the ground, then drew his sword. The ogre carrying Jampa put the older master down on his feet. Then both of Demon-Maamo's ogres drew their swords; though less decisively than Maamo had. All of this felt uncanny to them, this uncertainty of duty and counter-duty, this threatening other yeti guards with weapons.

"Would you prevent me from saving our emperor?" Demon-Maamo demanded, then started up the steps.

The sergeant gave way. The contradictions troubled him, but he was reluctant to disbelieve Maamo; Yunnan ogres do not easily lie.

Also, his orders had been to avoid fighting Maamo, to delay him only. The emperor's strategy, unstated, was to keep the demon in the body and occupied until the Circle of Power had closed to him the fabric of the Tao.

Then he'd want him killed.

In two strides, Demon-Maamo was on the porch. Behind him came the other two, one pushing the blind man ahead of him. The other brought Jampa Lodro. Demon-Maamo thrust open the door to the hallway, and entered. Six ogres of the night watch followed, and his own two with the humans. Others, he sensed, were in the Sanctuary with the Circle and the emperor. Oil lamps lit the hall. He strode down it to the far end and pushed the door open.

Two ogres stood just inside. They made no move to stop him. The emperor stood beside the Circle, between it and the door, with four more yeti guards arrayed beside him. The demon sensed more than the emperor's lack of fear; he sensed his readiness, his confidence. And while he, as Maamo, was physically stronger, the emperor, he thought, had the Circle to help him. He, on the other hand, was not in the place of power given him by the Great God. And to go to it would lose him the great ogre, the physical tool he needed to destroy the Circle.

Tenzin and the Circle sat as if alone, as if none of this was taking place. For them there was no *gomba,* no sanctuary, no danger. There was only the Field. They hadn't yet gotten it closed to the demon, nor could the work be hurried. They worked with total attention, total intention, divorced from all else. If they died now, the demon could not be stopped.

As motionless as they were, as vulnerable, it seemed to the demon that they somehow endangered him; at any rate it was time. He gathered himself to leap, to attack.

The emperor sensed it, and moved to distract him. "You are a reasonable demon," he said. "Let us bargain. Tell me what you most would like."

Demon-Maamo gestured at the Circle. "These, dead."

"I understand. But let us look at alternatives."

Demon-Maamo brandished his sword, and instantly the ogres by the emperor stepped between them. He growled. "Out of my way!" he said.

They faltered. It was Nils who broke the situation. He had opened his third eye fully when they'd entered the Sanctuary and the demon-troll's attention had become fully occupied. As was the emperor's. Psychically, commandingly, the Yngling spoke.

"Arnoldo Kkechuwa!"

Demon-Maamo stopped, spun around. "Who calls me that?"

"Your father."

"*What!?*" The word burst from him.

"And your mother. She who suckled you, who defended you from your father and the others. *She* came to call you Kkechuwa."

Demon-Maamo stared at the Northman. "Who are you?"

"I am he who knows." He paused, using time. "I am he who dwelt within you. I know your soul. I am he—" Another pause. "I am he who saw you steal from your mother. Who saw you rape your little sister, then strangle her so she could not tell. I am he— I am he who saw you weep miserably in a corner of the church, unable to confess to the priest, unable to find solace in solitary confession to the Virgin. I am . . ."

Demon-Maamo howled his pain, drowning out the Yngling, drowning out the patient droning of the Circle and its leader, who sat oblivious. The ogres stared. None were telepathic, but it was clear to them that something powerful was happening, something uncanny between Maamo and the blind man. The fur stood stiffly along their spines, and the one who's held Nils's arm had let go and backed away half a step, staring not at his emperor or his leader now, but at the captive.

"I am he who saw you sacrifice to a god who was not God, saw him devour you all and give you nothing. Saw this would-be ruler of the world, this emperor and his *geshe*, save you unwittingly. I am he. . . ."

Hans watched through a window. Clearly Nils was in danger. He'd nocked an arrow and half drawn his bow-string, surprised at how stiff the blacksmith's bow was. The largest troll, the one who was clearly chief, was the one who threatened Nils, but others were in the way. Hans had no decent shot at him, and didn't dare move to some other window; that might be when the attack came.

This time the troll chief didn't howl; he roared! Raising his sword, he took a first step toward Nils, and Hans shot. Shot the troll who'd held Nils's arm, for he still had no clear shot at the troll chief. The arrow struck deeply, for the yeti guards wore no mail, only a breastplate. It severed the spine, slashed through the heart, penetrated the cartilaginous sternum and stopped against the breast-plate. The troll collapsed while its chief paused to stare. At the same time Hans shouted, "Run, Nils, run!"

The ogre nearest Hans's window turned and leaped toward it as if catapulted. Despite himself the boy jumped back. The railing behind him was buttocks high to his long frame; he toppled backward over it and fell to the ground, a meter and a half below the porch. The first ogre through didn't see him at first, then did, and hopped over the railing, sword in hand.

There was the sharp "blam!" of a pistol from a corner of the porch, and another. The ogre jerked, turned, and came back over the railing like a leopard. The pistol fired again, once, twice. The ogre faltered, slapping at its chest. Another came through behind it, and others through other windows, windows with both glass and shutters closed. The pistol banged again, then again, and was silent, empty.

Inside, Demon-Maamo had turned to the window and the shout, the source of the arrow. Then realized that the ogres were moving toward the windows as if in relief at having something they could attack unquestioningly. Ignoring the blind man now, he spun and pounced to the Circle, striking with his sword. As he killed the first monk, the shared trance was broken, but before the others could react and scatter, he'd killed three more. Tenzin fled toward a window and the ogre rushed after him, cleaving the *geshe* diagonally from shoulder to waist.

Outside, gunfire snarled, the racketing noise of an automatic rifle. He didn't notice. He turned toward Songtsan Gampo, who'd drawn his own sword. The only ogres who'd stood firm through the confusion were the four beside the ruler. The emperor was pointing, shouting: "Kill him! Kill him! Kill the traitor!"

Through the windows came roars of pain, screams of terror, confusing them further. One ogre who'd gone out a window climbed back in, yammering loudly in the ogre speech, then ran across the Sanctuary, jumping corpses, slipped in a pool of blood and nearly fell, catching himself with one hand, before bounding headfirst through a window on the other side, bursting out its glass.

The four beside the emperor neither left nor obeyed him. Now the giant ogre turned to him and attacked. Only one of the guards stepped to meet him, and Demon-Maamo overwhelmed him, cut him down. The other three stepped back. Demon-Maamo struck, smashing down the emperor's futile parry, splitting him from crown to pelvis, snapping bones like twigs.

Then he turned to Nils, snarling, big fangs bared, and took one step. Gunfire hammered from a window, and the great ogre body went down. In the interface dimension between reality as we know it and the Sigma Field, there was a terrible psychic scream of frustration and anger that seemed to go on for a long time, though objectively it lasted for perhaps five seconds. Then it cut off abruptly. Before it died, the Circle had done enough, accomplished its work.

FIFTY

Most of the automatic rifle fire had been from Matthew Kumalo, standing in the door of the low-hovering *Alpha*. He'd shot not specifically to kill ogres, but to protect Deodoro Baver and Hans Gunnarsson. First at those ogres in the process of attacking them, then at those which failed to flee, and still posed a threat. He'd killed or otherwise downed perhaps half a dozen.

Inside the Sanctuary, with both the emperor and Maamo dead, the remaining ogres had no leader. But they knew that death and destruction lay in one direction, and they, like the survivors outside, fled in the other, out the windows, without harming Nils or Jampa or the remaining members of the Circle.

The hair still prickled on Nils's bare arms from the demon's psychic scream, when Hans looked in through a window. "Nils! Come quickly!" he called. "Matt has come in the sky boat to take us out of here!"

Nils first picked up the emperor's sword, then helped Jampa through a window and left, while the monks fled into the hallway. Baver had a rifle by then, and stood on the porch at a corner, in case any further threats developed. It was he who'd shot Maamo. When they were all out, he called to Nils: "Is it safe in there?"

"Yes."

Baver went to the window, peered in, then handed the rifle to Nils—he knew the Northman had learned to shoot one in the Orc War—and climbed through. The place was a slaughter house, and it took him a moment to identify the emperor. Physically he was unrecognizable, but he was obviously human and wore a robe, a blood-soaked robe. Baver felt gingerly in its right-side pocket and found his recorder slimy with blood. In the stress of the moment, the emperor had forgotten it and gone to his sword, never to learn that he hadn't picked up the pistol.

After Nils had helped Jampa aboard, Baver and Hans boarded too. Then Nikko lifted. Dawn had progressed, and with the hull on one-way transparent, the Dzong was visible to them in some detail.

She took the craft straight up, like a bubble in a pool, to five kilometers. Both Hans and Jampa Lodro looked out fearlessly; the old master in particular was delighted. When Nikko stopped their climb, they could see across the entire district.

Matt looked at Nils. "What now?" he asked.

Nils, in turn, looked at Jampa. *Do you wish to stay here and lend your leadership?*

Jampa shook his head. *They'll be happier without me. I'll go back to my students. But first I'd like to know more about this.* He gestured about him at the pinnace. Psychically he'd already gathered the basics of what lay behind the bloodbath he'd witnessed.

It was Hans who said then that he was hungry. Matthew got food from cold storage—Danish cheese and bread, potatoes and leftover roast pork—heating the leftovers in the two microwaves. He'd seen Nils eat before, Hans was a teenager who'd said he was hungry, and Baver looked leaner than he'd ever seen him. So he served a lot of it. Meanwhile Baver had checked the handgrip of his recorder, and inside found his cubes, the empty and the full. He copied the full cubes into *Alpha's* computer.

Nikko had locked the pinnace on a coordinate at five kilometers, and joined them at breakfast. While they ate, they talked—all but Jampa, who had no mutual language with any of them but could understand them all. Nils asked questions for the old master, who seemed content with what he learned.

Mostly though, Matt and Nikko debriefed Baver, Nils, Hans, and each other, to the computer. Not singly in isolation, it wasn't that critical, but together, sharing their experiences.

Matt had seen Baver being taken to the palace, but his guards had carried their swords unsheathed. He hadn't dared a rescue under the circumstances, and didn't see him when he came back out. He saw and recognized Nils a little later, being carried to the *gomba,* and had followed his progress on the viewer. It was while watching the *gomba* that he'd seen first Hans and then Baver again. He'd moved to make a pickup, and Nikko had lowered to fifty meters, but both Baver and Hans had seemed so intent, so purposeful, it seemed best to let them continue whatever they were separately doing.

Hans had found Nils's and Jampa's horses browsing a flowerbed approximately where they'd been left. The gravel path had been raked that evening, and it was plain to see where the ogres' tracks had left it.

Baver had left the emperor's apartment with his guards, and in a lower corridor shot them both. It was, he said, the most difficult thing he'd ever done, despite having already killed men in the fight with the Kalmuls; these men weren't trying to kill him. Next most difficult was the minute immediately afterward, wondering if the emperor or any guards had heard. But they seemed all to have left, including the one at the nearby side entrance where Nogai had been taking him. Presumably the emperor had used the front entrance and never heard the shots.

He'd explored the inner garden then, looking for a

place to hide through the day, and had found nothing suitable. The portal to the inner garden proved unguarded, however, and from outside it he saw a grove of shaggy evergreens that looked like a possibility. He'd planned to use his radio there, and see if he could call in a rescue. As he'd approached the grove, he'd seen the building behind it. From close up he'd heard a sort of roar or howl, and froze where he was. Then he'd seen someone on the porch, and in the dawnlight thought he recognized Hans.

According to Matthew, his worst moment—worse than Kazi's dungeon—was when the ogres came boiling out of the Sanctuary to attack Baver and Hans. He'd had to spray slugs around freely, with a fair chance of hitting the people he was trying to protect.

The sun was high—the local time was 0847 by the computer—when they finished. Hans had fallen asleep in his seat. Nikko took the controls again and started up the fertile valley toward the army post. Slowly, with Matthew operating the viewer on high mag, Nils watching for some sign of Chen. Close outside of town they saw three horses, two of them Mongol ponies, grazing in a ditch by the road. Nearby, Chen slept in the shade of a mulberry tree. Nils had Nikko land him in a forest glade on a bordering ridge, from where he trotted down to tell Chen that Hans was all right. And that all three horses were his to take home with him.

When Nils got back to the glade, the pinnace landed again, picked him up, and took off for Jampa's House of Enlightenment. The Kumalos offered to wait till nightfall to land there, if landing by daylight would cause a disturbance. Through Nils, Jampa said it undoubtedly would, among the novices, but that would be good for them. And in fact, several of those working in the field fled headlong to the forest when they saw the *Alpha* settling toward the longhouse. Matthew and Nils got out with Jampa and shook his hand where the monks could see.

Then the old master sauntered to the longhouse, and the *Alpha* lifted again.

"Well, Nils," said Matthew, "it's back to the Balkans now, I hope."

The Northman shook his head. "Not at once," he said. I want to see Achikh, at Urga. He is my *anda*, my soul brother. I should see him again before I go so far away."

Nikko called up a map on the computer screen, found Urga and its coordinates, and they lifted.

APPENDIX

THE PSYCHOME AND THE PSYCHE

In telling a story, some concepts may be unfamiliar to readers, while an in-story explanation may be inappropriate. And invariably some readers will be troubled because of its absence. Here, story considerations dictated that I avoid discussing the *psychome* or even mentioning it, though it helps greatly in understanding Yunnan ogres. This short section clarifies *psychome*.

In writing it, I have drawn heavily on the discussion by Alexei Park in his "Psyche and Humanity." (In *Toward a Science of Humanity*, edited by Mei-Ti Lomasetewa. Star Press, Deep Harbor, New Home. A.C. 906).

The ogre "psyche" is not a true psyche. It is a pseudo-psyche. On many planets there is what might be called a common *psychome*,* or mind/spirit pool, for all of that planet's life. This is the equivalent, in the Sigma Field,

---

*Instead of *psychome,* I could have used the more descriptive term "spirit pool," specifying that the animal mind is a function of it. I've coined and use the term *psychome* (*psyche* = spirit or mind; *ome* = mass, body or group), analogous to *biome,* because the term *spirit* carries too much semantic luggage for many people.

of the sum of planetary genomes in the field of physical-biological phenomena. A useful but very limited analogy for the psychome and the planetary genetic sum is the head and tail of a coin. A somewhat closer analogy is the individual psyche of a person, and the person's physical body.

For most purposes, the planetary psychome is subdivided into lesser psychomes that are more or less separate and distinct. These are the Sigma Field analogs of those gene pools which are capable of mixing. There is a gene pool for all the species and breeds of cattle that are able to hybridize with each other to produce viable offspring; also there is a gene pool for Yunnan ogres. Each has its corresponding psychome.

When an animal dies, its body, including its genes, loses its integrity, and through a sequence of decomposition processes reverts to ions and relatively simple molecules. Much of this goes on in the alimentary tracts of scavengers, from vultures to maggots. The animal's pseudo-psyche, including its life experiences, also ceases to exist as a separate unit, and is reabsorbed into the species psychome, but the process is far tidier.

In understanding the psychome, it helps to contrast it to the human psyche.

Like all other species, *Homo sapiens*—humankind—has a psychome, and each person has a pseudo-psyche. It was the collective species memories of the human psychome which, misinterpreted, gave rise to the 20th century concept of "the collective unconscious," as defined by the psychiatrist, Karl Jung. The human pseudo-psyche, however, is subordinate to the actual human *psyche*.

The human psyche is a non-biological unit. Its integrity, which is to say its individual identity, survives body death and customarily recycles, reincarnates, to play again. This recycling may be prompt or delayed; it may be here or elsewhere. In an entirely real sense, therefore, the terrestrial biological phenomenon known as a human being *is possessed by a non-terrestrial phenomenon*, the psyche (or soul). The psyche, through this act of possession, often loses its awareness of being a psyche, and ordinarily loses all memory of existence before the act of possession. It becomes and controls the person it is born to be. The purpose of this strange arrangement seems to be to play (often involved) games, to have physical experiences, and in general to make existence interesting.

Homo sapiens has been a possessed species for a very long time, as have suitable species on many other worlds. By contrast, most biological species are not possessed.

THE OGRE AS A
HYPNOCONDITIONED SOLDIER

From—"Behavioral Modification on Post-Plague Earth," by Shigeru Ruiz. Pages 47–64, in *Modern Perspectives on the Psyche and the Mind*, Viljo Tabayoyon, ed. University Press, A.C. 816.

. . . With regard to ogres as hypnoconditoned warriors, Songtsan Gampo seems to have seen more potentials and fewer limitations than were actually there, at least given the state of the art.

First, he had hypnoconditioned his ogres as if they were simply hairy people. That was not the case. If you condition a man to absolute loyalty, he will often be loyal regardless of risk to life. This is because the true psyche is innately a game-playing unit, and many will stay with the game despite extreme danger. On the other hand, an intelligence based on the psychome—that is, one without a true psyche—will rarely do so, with the exception of the long-domesticated *Canis familiaris*, the domestic dog. The Yunnan ogre operates on the basic imperative **SURVIVE!** It will fight ferociously, to a point—to the death if cornered—but when death appears imminent, and if there is an avenue of flight, it will flee. Otherwise it stands to the death only to protect its cubs, and not often then. Among animals ruled by the psychome, death in defense of young seems to be more a matter of miscalculation than intentional self sacrifice.

Also, while many humans will panic in the face of a bizarre and unfamiliar danger, many will not panic if they are well trained and disciplined. Even well-trained and disciplined ogres will panic and try to flee, in the face of a sufficient threat. . . .

LINGUSTIC CONSERVATISM IN 29th CENTURY SCANDINAVIA

In this paper, "Scandinavia" refers to the Scandinavian Peninsula comprising the pre-plague nations of Norway and Sweden. The Danish peninsula and islands, whose people are equally Scandinavian, genetically and historically, has developed a very different culture, and its language is no longer intelligible to the people of the Scandinavian Peninsula.

The dialects of 29th century Scandinavia are mutually readily intelligible. In fact, they differ less than the dialects of 21th century Scandinavia, and far less than those, say, of the 19th century. Furthermore, the language changes there, over a period of more than seven centuries, have been remarkably modest. Thus Dr. Kumalo, having hypno-learned 21st century Swedish before departing on the First Expedition, was soon able to converse with 29th century Swedes.

Since the plague, the Scandinavian people have dropped the neuter gender. Further, the conjugation of most verbs has changed, becoming more regular but also somewhat flexible, quite possibly for reasons of poesy. (The most common pre-plague conjugation has been almost totally abandoned, perhaps also for reasons of poesy.) And in writing, the usual 29th century spellings are more closely phonetic. Here again, poesy seems to have been a factor, as most post-plague Scandinavian writing has been the recording of oral poetry.

Many words have changed, but most such changes are not great. Existing parchments show that the major vocabulary changes took place during the first two post-plague centuries. Many changes amounted simply to the dropping of sounds which already tended to be elided in the pre-plague languages. (Of course, almost the total pre-plague technical and commercial vocabularies were lost, but they were no longer relevant.)

Several cultural factors seem to account for this remarkable linguistic conservatism. The first two seem to be responsible for the modesty of changes over the first two post-plague centuries. (1) The Scandinavians in general retained a knowledge of writing and reading, even if they didn't do much of it, and tended to follow old spellings. (2) The old spellings tended to follow standard pronunciations, which in turn tended, somewhat, to stabilize pronunciations and usages.

After the first two centuries, another factor came to play the major role. As fighting and heroes became increasingly prominent culturally, poetry became much used to celebrate champions and events, and poets became the models and arbiters of language. There is clear evidence that the changes in the conjugation of verbs grew out of poets modifying words to make them more graceful and more amenable to popular meters. The same is true of words which have lost syllables. It has even been suggested that the neuter gender was dropped because neuter grammatical endings sounded less pleasing. Further, many words have more than one form, providing poets with choices to fit whatever meter they may have selected.

Every clan in every generation has its principal skald, who not only composes but teaches poems, and who knows the works of poets outside the clan. Besides these clan skalds, every village has its principal reciter of poetry, often a man or woman with a debilitating physical handicap. These village skalds may or may not compose poetry of their own, though usually they do. They function not only to entertain but to learn as many poems as possible. Commonly they are provided with partial or complete subsistence for their efforts.

Beyond these are wandering skalds who travel not only from village to village, but from clan to clan, and tribe to tribe. These wanderers, almost invariably treated with respect, recite publicly, and also teach the local skalds favorite poems from other clans and tribes. Thus, in their old homeland, a poem composed by a skald of the Ice-Bear Clan of the Norskar, far up the Norwegian coast— a poem celebrating a famous polar bear hunt—could be heard and learned verbatim by skalds of the Eel Clan of the Jötar, at the southern tip of Sweden, and the Reindeer Clan of the Svear, near the head of the Gulf of Bothnia.

During the long winter nights, many persons other than skalds learn to recite their favorite poems, or at least their favorite cantos, verbatim. And while they tend to favor tales of their own heroes, more than a few of those tales are from far away.

I said *verbatim*. That is very important. Those who recite verbatim, copy not only the words but the pronunciations of the composer, as far as they're aware of it.

The principal skalds usually own and pass down to their successors, written copies of numerous poems, especially the more popular. And additional copies may be made by persons who can afford the parchment and ink. (The ink has to retain its visibility well, of course, and ink-making is an art among the Scandinavians.)

Spellings, like pronunciations, in general tend to follow those of the skalds, and through poetry, those of different tribes and clans influence each other. Poets among the

Svear and Jötar in particular spell very much alike, and their considerable written volume has influenced considerably the orthography of Norse poets as well. (Yet there is flexibility in spelling. A poet may spell a word differently in the same poem, to accommodate cadence.)

Moreover, the common people tend to follow the usages of their poets not only in poetry, but in general diction, pronunciation, tonality, and spelling.

It is therefore not surprising that Scandinavian speech and writing remain readily intelligible between clans and tribes. Linguistically they are tied together by poetry, the stories of heroes and occasionally of scoundrels, recited dramatically around fires in longhouses and log huts throughout the Neoviking culture.

PRONUNCIATION GUIDE FOR NEOVIKING NAMES AND WORDS

For those who are interested, here are descriptions of how Neoviking words and names are pronounced. There are dialectal irregularities, particularly between tribes, but taking the Scandinavian peninsula as a whole, those irregularities are modest.

Consonants—Most of the consonants are pronounced more or less as in Anglic, with the following exceptions: The letter *g* is almost always pronounced hard, as in *go*; the exceptions to this can be ignored here. *J* is pronounced like the *y* in *yes*. If you wish to go a step further in refinement, *R* is trilled in stressed syllables, but not in unstressed.

In most dialects, the two-letter consonant *kj* is pronounced like the *ch* in "chair," and we recommend this. In other dialects it is pronounced as *sh*, or intermediate between *ch* and *sh*. The sound of another two-letter consonant, *sj*, is more difficult to describe. For simplicity, we recommend that you pronounce it like *sh*. Actually, in some jytska dialects it is pronounced somewhat like *wh*, but with the lips more or less compressed, giving the *wh* somewhat the sound of *fwh*. The other dialects vary somewhat, pronouncing *sj* more or less like the familiar Anglic *sh*, but mostly with the lips more rounded and the tongue-tip raised.

Vowels—The following are approximations: *A* is pronounced *aw* or *ah*, depending on the letters which follow, and varying with the dialect, but *aw* more often than *ah*. The pronunciation of *e* resembles *ay* in "pay," or the *e* in "yet," but *ay* more often than not. *I* is pronounced *ee* or *ih*, but *ee* more often than not. *O* is pronounced like *oo* in "boot," or (more or less) as short *oh*, but *oo* more often than not. *U* is pronounced rather like "yew," or as similar to the *u* in "put," but "yew" more often than not. *Y* is always a vowel, and can be approximated by saying *ee* with the lips rounded. *Å* is pronounced as "oh." *Ä* is rather like the *ai* in "air," or sometimes as *eh*. The doubled vowel *ää* is simply a longer *ä*, rather like *ai* in a drawled "air," the second *ä* marking the dropping of a soft *r* in older Scandinavian, and is found before a *v* and sometimes before an *n*. *Ö* and *Ø* are pronounced rather like the *ur* in "fur," but with the *r* only suggested, not fully sounded.

There are no diphthongs in the Neoviking dialects, except for *ei* (pronounced "eye") and *au* (pronounced "ow") in some proper nouns.

Thus "lagman" is pronounced "**lawg**-mahn"; "Isbjørn" is "**ees**-byurn"; and "Järnhann" is "**Yairn**-hahn."

If one wishes, of course, one can go further than the above in approaching actual Neoviking pronunciations. For example, the sounds tend to be articulated with lips and tongue-tip, rather than farther back in the mouth, and usually the stress is on the first syllable.

In 29th century Neoviking, all the dialects are tonal. In some the tonality is moderate. In others it is as extreme as in the dialects—the so-called *sjungande sven-ska*, "singing Swedish"—spoken on the Ostrobothnian coast during the technological era. Unfortunately, tonality can only be learned by listening.

LUNAR CALENDAR OF THE WOLF CLAN (& OTHERS)

	Jan	Feb	Mar	Apr	May	Jun	Jul	Aug	Sep	Oct	Nov	Dec
Iron Cold	—											
Hunters'		—										
Starving			—									
Sun Back				—								
Snow Melts					—							
Greening						—						
No Night							—					
Warm								—				
Harvest									—			
Rutting*										—		
Butchers'											—	
Rivers Frz												—
Sun Hides												—

The reconciliation of the Neoviking lunar calendar and the solar calendar is described briefly in the text, page 70.

*In some clans, the Rutting Moon is termed "the Spawning Moon."

Niven • Pournelle • Flynn
FALLEN ANGELS

In 1995 Earth finally had its act together. There were two manned space stations orbiting, one from the former Soviet Union, one from the United States. Even better, the human race had finally agreed that something had to be done about the environment—and was doing it, one green law after another. By the year 2020 the Greenhouse Effect was just a bad memory, and the air was a clean green dream.

There was only one problem. All that pollution, all that CO_2—the Greenhouse Effect itself—was the only thing holding off the next, regularly scheduled ice age! With the carbon dioxide gone the glaciers came, and came down fast. In the mid-21st century, the icebergs had reached North Dakota and weren't slowing down.

But by then an alliance of the most extreme "deep ecology" Greens and the zaniest of religious fundamentalists had taken over in the winter-bound U.S.—and they weren't about to give up their power merely because they were destroying civilization. And they needed a scapegoat. So they decided that it was the "air thievery" of the folks they left stranded in the orbiting space stations that was causing the New Ice Age.

FALLEN ANGELS is the story of two spacemen. Shot down and stranded on a hostile Earth, they think there is no hope for them. But they're wrong. Help is on the way. Help from the one nationally organized pro-technology group left on Earth; the only ones who would dare fly in the face of their unforgiving authoritarian government; the only ones foolish enough to risk everything to help two strangers from space. Science fiction fandom. *Angels* down. *Fans to the rescue*!

72052-X • 400 pp. • $5.95